He saw a charging stallion, armored in purest platinum and snorting fire as it raced the winds. He saw the rider then, a knight bold and ready, the great lance poised to strike. The knight also was clad in platinum, and the crest on his helmet was that of a majestic dragon. On his chest he wore a breastplate with the symbol of the Triumvirate: the Crown, the Sword, and the Rose.

Within the visor that covered the face was light, brilliant and life-giving, and Huma knew that here was Paladine.

The great charger suddenly leaped into the air, and massive wings sprouted from its sides. Its head elongated, and its neck twisted and grew, but it lost none of its majesty or beauty. From a platinum-clad steed it became a platinum dragon, and together knight and companion drove the darkness before them with the aid of the lance—the Dragonlance. It shone with a life, a purpose of its own, and the darkness fell before it. Born of the world and the heavens, it was the true power, the true good.

HEROES

Volume One

THE LEGEND OF HUMA

Richard A. Knaak

Cover Art by
JEFF EASLEY

Interior Art by
JEFF BUTLER
VALERIE VALUSEK
LARRY ELMORE
GEORGE BARR

DRAGONLANCE® HEROES

Volume One

THE LEGEND OF HUMA

©Copyright 1988 TSR, Inc.
All Rights Reserved.

First Printing: March 1988
Printed in the United States of America.
Library of Congress Catalog Card Number: 87-51254

9 8 7 6 5 4 3 2 1

ISBN: 0-88038-548-0

TSR, Inc.
P.O. Box 756
Lake Geneva, WI
53147 U.S.A.

TSR UK Ltd.
The Mill, Rathmore Road
Cambridge CB1 4AD
United Kingdom

TSR, Inc.
PRODUCTS OF YOUR IMAGINATION™

This book, my first, is dedicated to my family, both near and far, for putting up with me for all these years.

It is also dedicated to the Department of Chemistry at the University of Illinois in Champaign-Urbana, whose peristent efforts finally convinced me that I was destined for some other career.

① Mountain of Changes, Prison of Wyrmfather
   (later known as Dragon Mountain).
② Ruins
③ Solamnic outpost of Buoron
④ Citadel of Galan Dracos

SANCRIST

HYLO

SOLAMNIA

Palanthas

Vingaard
Keep

Citadel of
Magius

Solanthus

Thelgaard

Kyre

ERGOTH

Caergoth

QUALINESTI

THORBARDIN

KHAROLIS

PROLOGUE

It is very rare that I, Astinus, Master Historian of Krynn, find myself penning a personal note for inclusion in my chronicles. I have done so only once in recent memory, that being after the mage Raistlin came within a breath of becoming an all-powerful deity, mightier even than Paladine and Takhisis. He failed, else I probably would not be writing this, but it was a failure deserving of note.

While commenting on that incident, I came to realize that a vicious error had been discovered in my older volumes. By the handwriting, I suspect that one Paulus Warius, an assistant of mine some three centuries before and notable more for his clumsiness than his ability to keep records, must have accidentally destroyed part of some three or four older volumes and then replaced the damaged pages with what he assumed were correct copies. They were not.

The error concerns the transitory period between what are now called the Age of Light and the Age of Might. Ergoth, for instance, was a much older empire than is noted in the false history. Vinas Solamnus in fact commanded Ergoth's armies by 2692 P.C., not fourteen centuries later as the false history claims. The Second Dragon War, noted incorrectly as a Second and *Third* war by Warius because it lasted more than forty-five years, ended in 2645 P.C. It was here I first learned of the grave mistakes, for I had opened the pages concerning those last few years in order to make reference to Huma, Knight of Solamnia, a man of very mortal flesh who faced and defeated Takhisis, goddess of evil, the Dragonqueen. I had intended, after the end of the Second Dragon War, to note Huma's exploits but, as it always happens, my mind was on my work.

I have spent more time with this than I had originally allotted myself. Perhaps it is because I, too, felt some relief after that struggle, for I had been ready to close the final volume of this world's history at one point. It would have been a shame, as my collection at that time consisted of only a few hundred thousand volumes. For this alone I remember Huma.

His story, fortunately, is still intact in this volume, and I will let that speak for him.

Astinus of Palanthas
360 A.C.

Chapter 1

*The army passed through a village on its way north-*west to Kyre. The village, called Seridan, had been set upon by plague, starvation, and madness, each seeming to take turns and each killing many of the inhabitants. In a lifetime long ago, the village had been prosperous. Now, shacks and makeshift shelters stood where clay brick buildings had fallen to the raids of bold goblins and marauding dark dragons. For some reason, the village had never been destroyed. It just continued to waste away—much like the people who tried to exist there.

The appearance of a column of knights did little to cheer the village. In fact, the inhabitants seemed to feel more than a little resentment at the way the riders and footsoldiers paraded through the mud track that was all the village could call a road. The strife-worn residents felt resentment for the way of life they assumed the Knights of Solamnia led, a way of life that they believed must be better than what each of them faced daily.

At the head of the column, resplendent in his chain and plate armor, rode Lord Oswal of Baxtrey. The intricate pattern of roses displayed on his breastplate revealed him to be a member of the Solamnic order that took that same flower for its symbol. The purple cloak that flowed behind him was attached by a clasp bearing the likeness of a kingfisher with its wings partly spread and a crown above its head. Below the bird, grasped tight in its claws, was a sword with a rose atop it.

Most of the knights were clad as Lord Oswal, although their armor was much more worn and their cloaks tended to be plain in comparison with their commander's. Lord Oswal's cloak was a sign of his rank—High Warrior, master of the Order of the Rose, and currently second in command to the Grand Master, he who ruled the knighthood itself.

As they rode, the High Warrior glanced quickly at the rider to his side. They might have been from the same mold, with their hawklike features and the long flowing mustaches that were popular among the knights. Oswal's features, though, were tempered by age and a truer understanding of the world he lived in, whereas the other, younger by some twenty-odd years, still held steady to the belief that his was the hand that would change the world. They were, in fact, related. Bennett was his nephew and son of Trake, the Grand Master himself. The arrogance so set in Bennett's face indicated that he already saw himself as his father's successor.

Lord Oswal hoped Bennett would learn temperance by then. The young knight was of the mind that the knights followed the will of Paladine and, therefore, that they would triumph because their cause was just. Lord Oswal knew that that was not always the case.

The expressions of the younger knights in procession were carefully prepared, emotionless masks. Soon enough they would learn the cruel facts of the world. Lord Oswal knew that the younger knights—and many older ones—still saw themselves as heroes—heroes for a world already lost.

One, in particular, Lord Oswal thought, and opened his mouth to shout.

"Rennard! Up front!"

Huma watched the tall, almost gaunt knight ride forward. If Lord Oswal wished to speak to Rennard, then something was afoot. That something might involve Huma himself, for Rennard seemed to watch him keenly—although Huma was already blooded. Perhaps, like Huma himself, Rennard still believed that here was one who never should have been accepted into the ranks.

Huma bounced as his warhorse stumbled in the mud. The visor of his helmet slammed down in front of his face, startling him. He reached up and raised it, allowing the cool wind to bite at his handsome, if somewhat weathered, features. Though his mustache was not as grand as that of Bennett or the High Warrior, there was some dignity in the slight gray that prematurely touched it and the rest of the hair on his head. His visage was surprisingly soft—so much so that the others occasionally commented on his youth, although not when he was nearby.

Huma could not help staring at the grimy, torn clothing of Seridan's women and children. Even his own armor, worn as it was and much less intricately decorated than that of Lord Oswal, seemed made of gold when compared to what they had. Their rags hung loosely, and Huma wondered how often these people ate and how much—and what they ate, for that matter. The rebellious part of his nature wanted to take his pack from the saddle and throw it to the villagers. Let them have the rations stored in there. It probably would be the best meal they had eaten in weeks.

"Keep up, you!" the knight behind him growled—and Huma realized how close he had actually come to giving away his rations. He knew it was wrong, as the knighthood rules proclaimed, but it was still a strong desire. Another sign of his inadequacies, he thought with a sigh, and wondered why his petition to join the knighthood ever had been granted.

His thoughts were interrupted by Rennard. Like Huma, the older knight carried a shield whose markings proclaimed his place in the Order of the Crown. Rennard, though, had many years of practical experience and therefore was a commander in his own right. His visor hid all but the two piercing, ice-blue eyes and only hinted at the face. Rennard had few friends even among the Order of the Crown.

Rennard returned Huma's stare, then looked at the section as a whole. "Gaynor. Huma. Trilane. . . ." He barked eight names in all. "Break from the column for patrol duty."

The words betrayed no emotion. Rennard was methodical, a strategist of high caliber. One could not ask for a better leader in time of combat. Nevertheless, his presence always seemed to chill some part of Huma's soul.

"Lord Oswal wants the dead woods to the south searched over. Possibly goblins, maybe the ogres. We have to return to the column before sunset." Briefly, Rennard looked up at the perpetually overcast sky. Always, it seemed about to rain, but it never did. "Before total darkness. We do not want to be in the woods at night. Not this close to the western border. Understood?" When the knights assented, he turned his horse, a tall, pale animal much like its rider, and signaled the others to follow.

In minutes, thankfully, they were far away from Seridan. The ground was hard and easier for the mounts to trod upon. That was not surprising—the fire, which had killed much of the forest they rode toward, had baked the nearest fields. No food would grow here for years to come.

It was all so useless sometimes, Huma thought. Where was Paladine? Huma wondered that the god could allow this to happen, and he glanced at the ashy stubs of trees as the patrol rode along. Krynn might as well be in the claws of Takhisis already, the way things were going.

He clamped his mouth tight. That he dared call himself a knight after thoughts such as that!

As they reached the first patch of gnarled, twisted trees, the knights lowered their visors. From a distance, they might have looked like demons, for the horns or wings that decorated the sides of each knight's helmet were now more evident. The more elaborate, the higher the rank, save in Rennard's case. Typical of his ways, he had only a crest that rode from the front all the way down the back.

The woods were but one more sorry victim of the seemingly endless war that had razed the continent of Ansalon. Huma wondered what this land had looked like before the Dragonqueen's creatures had ravaged it. The dead trees gave the woods an evil look. The patrol was unusually tense. Eyes darted here and there, as each knight sought a foe behind the blackened trunks.

Huma clutched at the hilt of his sword. For a brief moment, a motion seemed to catch his eye. A wolf? In this barren land? As the knights moved on, he noted no new movement. Nerves. There was no life in these woods. There was nothing but sorrow.

Rennard called for a halt with the raising of one hand. Even he did not seem to wish to speak, as if the sound would release an unwanted presence.

"Spread out. You four to my right," he said, gesturing at Huma and three others. "The rest to my left." He drew his sword.

The others followed suit and moved into position, with one man between Huma and the patrol leader. Rennard gave the signal to advance. The knights kept a slow but steady pace.

The woods curved over a hill, one of the few in this area. If goblins or ogres lurked anywhere nearby, they would be here. Rennard pointed at the knight to Huma's left and sent the man forward. The rest of the patrol stopped and waited. The scout climbed off his horse and made his way to the top of the rise. The others watched anxiously as he peered over the top, and as quietly and quickly as he could, returned to the knights and horses. Huma, who had taken the reins of the other's horse, handed them back.

"Well?" Rennard asked quietly.

"Goblins. The ugly creatures are eating. A marauder patrol, I think. Must be at least twenty. No more than several dozen, I think."

Rennard nodded in satisfaction. "Nothing we cannot handle." Huma thanked Paladine that his visor hid his own worried face. Rennard pointed at the scout, Huma, and the two knights to Huma's right. "Ride around the right side. We'll

13

take the left. When you hear an owl, ride in. Huma, you will take charge of your group."

Some of the other knights shifted uneasily, but no one would argue. Huma gazed at the visors of his three companions and had no trouble reading the eyes of each man. He almost asked that someone replace him as leader, but Rennard was already turning his band away.

Huma chose to say nothing, and he turned his own mount. Whatever their personal feelings, the three were Knights of Solamnia. They had been given an order, and they would obey. To his relief, they followed him without murmur.

The ride was not long, but it was slow and cautious. The goblins were sloppy in every aspect of their lives, including military procedure, but there might be an enterprising leader among them who might have thought to post guards. Goblins in general were of little strategic use in the plans of the Dragonqueen's warlord—save as marauders. Knowing this and knowing that most goblins fought with little, if any, true skill, did not ease Huma's mind, however.

Huma could see no guards, and he dared to climb from his horse and survey the goblin camp from a small rise. That the creatures were ugly was an understatement. Their skins were a sickly green, teeth protruded from every inch of their mouths, and their eyes reminded the knight of frogs' eyes. The goblins were squat and misshapen, but they were also very strong. Many carried axes, and a couple even hefted crude bows. Their armor appeared to be compilations of everything they could rummage from the battlefields.

As Huma watched, a goblin came rushing over to the apparent leader, who was twice as big and ugly as any of his subordinates. The smaller goblin whispered something to the patrol leader, who stiffened and barked out orders.

Huma knew what had happened. Either the newcomer had been a guard or he had wandered away from the camp for some reason. Whatever the case, the goblins apparently realized that Rennard and the others were approaching from the other direction, and they were now preparing for a fight. Within seconds, the normally disorganized goblins had formed themselves into an attack formation that, with the element of surprise, meant that Rennard and his companions would almost certainly be struck down. There was no time to send someone to warn them.

"Get ready!" Huma whispered as he climbed back onto his horse. Sword in hand, he turned back to the others. "We go now!"

"Now?" one of the others asked. The trio looked from one another and back to Huma.

Huma had no time for their hesitation. Sword and shield ready, he kicked his mount in the sides. The horse charged, and Huma, waving his blade above his head, shouted the charge.

"Paladine!"

His courage shocked him, but no more than it shocked the goblins. As one, the creatures turned to face this unexpected menace. The horse charged into the midst of the camp, the knight's sword already coming down on the nearest goblin. The goblin raised his rusty broadsword in some semblance of defense, but Huma's swing shattered the weapon and then the owner himself.

Huma's only desire was to cut down as many of the enemy as possible and give Rennard and his men the chance they needed. Another goblin fell to his sword, and then the rest rushed toward the lone attacker, readying bows and raising pikes. The goblins would not be content to take him prisoner, he knew.

Then Huma heard the shouts behind him and knew that the other three had joined the fray. He fought with greater enthusiasm now, knowing that a chance for life still existed. Some of the goblins broke away from the four horsemen. The others tried to regroup under the hurried commands of the patrol leader.

More battle cries filled the air and Huma glanced up to see Rennard and the others coming from the goblins' rear. Those of the enemy patrol who had tried to flee fell under the powerful hooves of the warhorses. Rennard methodically cut down two who tried to stand against him, then he urged his mount onward. His movements hinted of a near-eagerness.

One of the knights in Huma's group was dragged from his

horse and a heavy ax finished him before Huma could react. Seconds later, Huma rode down the goblin standing over its kill. The ugly creature had only time to look up before the warhorse's front hooves caught it in the head, cracking the skull open.

The goblins, knowing they were lost, fought with a rare determination. Only three horsemen blocked their path to freedom. Huma barely blocked a savage swing. An arrow flew past his head.

Suddenly, a howl shivered through the air.

Something leaped at Huma's steed. The knight caught a brief vision of something akin to a wolf in form—but the resemblance ended with the thing's corpse-white pallor, as though it had been skinned. The yellow, dripping fangs seemed as long as his fingers and as sharp as needles. Then Huma's warhorse screamed and turned, despite the knight's protests. Straining every muscle, the animal raced from the skirmish, mindless of the frantic rider clinging to it. Somewhere close behind, the thing howled again. Huma could only clutch the reins and hang on for the wild ride. The sounds of fighting faded as the maddened horse rushed deeper and deeper into the charred forest.

What could so terrorize a trained warhorse? Certainly no earthly beast.

Then, even that thought vanished from Huma's mind as his mount broke through the blackened limbs of a knot of trees and found the earth was suddenly far, far below.

Chapter 2

It was dark when Huma returned to consciousness.
Lunitari, in wane, glittered weakly, casting a slight crimson
tinge. Like blood, Huma thought, and then he forced that
thought quickly away. If Lunitari were in wane, which of
the other moons would be waxing? Solinari was nowhere to
be seen. If it was indeed Nuitari that waxed, Huma would
never know it. No one saw the dark moon—no one save the
Black Robes, those mages who worshipped the dark god of
magic. The dark moon was invisible to common folk and
perhaps even to those who followed the paths of white and
red magic as well.

As his senses cleared, he became more aware of his surroundings. The horse lay beneath him, its neck broken by
the fall. The heavy padding in Huma's armor, combined

with the mass of the horse, had prevented the knight's death.

He tried to rise and nearly blacked out. All that padding had not been enough to prevent a concussion. While he waited for his head to clear again, Huma looked around.

This might once have been a river in a time when the rains had fallen more often. Its depth, at least four times Huma's height, was more than enough to kill a crazed steed, even one as strong as the warhorse.

The other side of the river bed lay some distance away. Judging by the sickly growths that barely could be called plants, he suspected this river had dried up many, many years before, possibly in the early days of the war, when the Dragonqueen had sought a quick, decisive victory over the followers of Paladine.

Huma dared once more to attempt to stand. He found that the pounding in his head subsided to mere annoyance if he did not bend his neck abruptly or look down too swiftly. With this in mind, he succeeded in staying on his feet.

"Gods." The word came unbidden, for Huma was only just now realizing that he was alone in hostile territory. The others must think him dead. Dead—or perhaps a coward who had run.

A mist was developing, sending cold, feathery fingers wisping through the ravine. He could wait out the night and begin his trek at first light—which might mean walking into another goblin patrol—or he could travel by night and pray that whatever lurked out there would be just as blind in the dark mist as he. Neither prospect pleased him, but he could think of no other choice.

He found that the pain in his head had lessened a bit so that now he was able to search the ground for his sword. It lay near, undamaged. His pack was another problem. Part of it was buried beneath his mount and, while Huma was strong, the animal's position made it virtually impossible for him either to lift the horse or roll it over. He had to satisfy himself with a few rations, a tinderbox and flint, and a few personal items, pried from the unhindered portion of the pack.

Huma did not like the thought of traveling by night, but

he liked the idea of traveling alone in plain sight by daylight even less. He picked up his things and, sword in hand, started up the sides of the river bed. The mist would be thinner above, and the high ground was always more advantageous, strategically. At least, Huma hoped so.

* * *

The mist never got worse, but neither did it get any better. Huma could make out most of the stars, but his ground-level vision extended only ten feet or so, and he was hard-pressed to make out details in the red moon's weak attempt at illuminating the shroud-covered land. The sword stayed at the ready in Huma's left hand. He had no shield; it must have been lost in the horse's mad flight.

Thinking of that, Huma could not help remembering the demonic visage he had glimpsed. If that thing were out there somewhere . . . His grip on the hilt tightened.

He had traveled an hour when he heard the harsh, mocking voices. Goblins! Huma ducked behind a rotting tree trunk. No more than ten yards separated him from them. Only the mist had saved him. At least three, maybe four, goblins seemed to be joking over the fate of someone. A prisoner, perhaps. Although one part of Huma urged him to slip away safely, another demanded that he lend whatever aid he could. Carefully, he slipped closer and listened.

A rusty, grating voice jarred his aching head. "I thinks the warlord himself will reward us fer this one."

A deeper voice joined the first, "Maybe he'll give us the bull. I'd like to be the one to skin him fer a rug. He killed Guiver."

"You never liked Guiver!"

"He owed me money! Now I'll never get it!"

A third voice cut in. "How do ya think the ogres will kill 'im?"

Huma strained his ears and caught the sound of a knife being sharpened on stone. "Real slow. They got sneaky minds fer that kinda stuff."

Something rattled chains, and Huma tried to place the location. Somewhere far to the right, he thought.

"He's awake."

"Let's have some fun."

Chains rattled again, and a voice, resonant and spanning the distance with no trouble, responded. "Give me a weapon and let me fight."

"Ha!" The goblins snickered. "You'd like that, wouldn't you, Cowface? We ain't fools, ya know."

"You'll do until some come along." Suddenly the voice grunted, as if exerting great effort. The goblin voices—four, Huma estimated—quieted until the grunting became a gasp for breath. The chains rattled.

"I thought he was gonna do it for a minute!"

"Two coppers'll get ya that he can!"

"What? You fool! You'd bet on something like that?"

"Guiver would've."

Huma, so engrossed in the goblins, almost missed the soft tread behind him. When he did, he was sure that he had been seen. The newcomer, though, continued walking and Huma soon realized that the creature, a goblin guard, could not see well in the mist. Still, a few steps more would bring the goblin close enough that not even a dense fog would save the knight.

Summoning his courage, Huma quietly circled behind the guard. He matched the goblin step for step, save that his own stride was half again as long. Each step brought him that much closer. Only a few more . . .

A roar bellowed angrily from the camp. Knight and goblin turned without thinking, then stared at one another as realization sank in. Huma was the first to react, leaping at the goblin in a desperate attempt to silence him. Sword and body caught the creature and it fell to the ground—but not before the goblin let out a muffled shout.

* * *

"Pigsticker?"

Huma cursed his luck and scrambled away from the body. The goblins had abandoned tormenting their captive—who was evidently the source of the bellowing—and were now cautiously making their way in the direction they believed their companion had called out from.

"Pigsticker!"

"He's probably tripped on a rock again."

"Well, what's he gone and done, then––cracked open his head? Pigsticker!"

"I think I should stay back here. Just in case."

"Snee's back there. Ya come with us or I'll give ya a piece of what the bull's gettin'."

"Okay, okay!"

The goblins were making more than enough noise to cover Huma's movements, and the mist hid him even though one of the creatures, amazingly, had thought to carry a torch. They soon would come across the body of their dead comrade, though, and that would bring Huma's advantage to an end.

His maneuvers brought him close to the perimeter of the camp. He thought he saw a large shape huddled on the ground, with perhaps a horned helmet atop its head, but the mists gave it odd proportions for a human—or even an elf or dwarf. A campfire burned low. A shadowy, lumpy figure moved near it, and Huma knew this must be the goblin, Snee, who had been left to guard the prisoner.

Despite the low illumination from the fire, Huma had no delusions about his chances of sneaking up on this goblin. The ground ahead gave no cover, and the jittery goblin was turning this way and that. Huma made out what appeared to be a wicked, two-handed ax in its paws.

Huma's free hand flattened across some small rocks, and the glimmerings of a plan flickered in his concussion-wracked head. Taking a handful of the rocks, he dared to get up on his knees. With a quick prayer to Paladine, he threw them to the far side of the camp, away from the prisoner.

The guard reacted predictably, much to Huma's relief. As the goblin scurried to investigate, Huma scooped up another handful of pebbles, stood up, and quietly made his way toward the back of the prisoner. Midway there, he threw the other handful, this time assuring that they would go even farther. His heart pounding, he covered the remaining ground.

Whoever the prisoner was, he was huge. Huge and smelly. The helmet actually seemed to be some sort of head-dress, although Huma did not examine it closely enough to make sure.

"Be very still," Huma whispered.

Huma felt the body stiffen, but no reply came. From his angle, Huma could see that, unlike the arms which were chained, the legs were bound with rope. He reached down to his belt and pulled out a dagger, even as the other goblins suddenly let out a collective shout. They had discovered their comrade.

"Cut your bonds and run! I'll do my best to give you time!" Even as he said it, Huma wondered at his own daring—or foolishness, it was hard to say which. He only knew that, as a knight, it was his duty to risk his life for others.

Huma straightened even as Snee hurried back to find out the reason for the shouting. At first, the goblin mistook Huma for one of its companions, but recognition followed almost instantly and the goblin brought its ax around for a wild swing at the young knight. Huma dodged easily and nicked the goblin in one arm. At that, some sense returned to Snee, and the goblin called out for help.

There was no skill in the goblin's attacks, only brute force. Huma easily dodged each swing of the ax, but he knew that each moment of delay cost him greatly. Already, he could hear the other goblins stomping back to camp.

Then, the goblin who was the apparent leader gave a shout of surprise and yelled, "The bull's loose!"

Indeed, something was loose, and Huma wondered who or what exactly he had released. With a wild, primitive cry, the shadowy form went tearing past Huma. The startled goblin dropped its ax with a clatter and followed it to the ground immediately afterward.

Unarmed and with his hands chained, the other surely could not survive against three opponents. Yet, when Huma turned to offer aid, his first view was of a giant, hulking form that overwhelmed the goblins as if they were small children. One had gotten too close and now squirmed helplessly in the air above the former prisoner's head. The other two were backing away fearfully. Huma paused, suddenly unsure if moving closer was a wise move.

The freed prisoner tossed the hapless goblin at the nearest of its two comrades, who, dodging the living projectile, squeaked and turned to flee. The two goblins collided with a bone-breaking crunch. They fell into a heap and lay still.

The lone survivor did not have time to react. The tall, muscular figure reached forward with both arms and wrapped its metal chain around the panic-stricken goblin's neck. With a single jerk that gave evidence of strength in those massive arms, the chains snapped the goblin's head back. The lifeless form dropped to the ground like a sack of oats.

Huma came to a halt some twenty feet from the prisoner he had released. Whatever it was, it was at least a foot taller than Huma—no small man, himself—and almost twice as wide. The arms looked to be as thick as Huma's legs, and the legs looked as if they could bear their owner through a twenty-mile run without any sign of strain.

The other had been satisfied to contemplate his revenge, but now as he straightened, he seemed to be studying the knight.

Again, the voice was deep and resounding. "You have my gratitude, Knight of Solamnia. I owe you my life, a debt I can never repay but one that I shall endeavor to compensate you for if it takes the rest of my days."

Huma stayed poised, but some of his unease vanished. "You owe me nothing. Anyone would have done the same."

The tall figure chuckled ominously. "Would they?" He turned to face the knight and, even in the dim light, it was obvious that the one he had freed was no man or elf. The horns were *part* of the creature, as was the thick, dark fur that covered the top and much of the back. As the goblins had so crudely put it, the other resembled nothing less than a bull with a body of a man.

A minotaur.

The minotaur took a few slow steps toward Huma, as if to prove he meant no harm. Although Huma's training cried out that this was an enemy—and one of the most fierce—his natural curiosity was fascinated by this creature. Few in the region ever saw a minotaur. The creature's homeland was far away on the eastern cost of Ansalon. Still, Huma's curiosity did not prevent him from raising his sword to a more defensive position.

The creature's head seemed overly large, even for a body as massive as the minotaur's. Dark, thick fur covered the top and the back half, and a thin fuzz covered the rest. The minotaur's eyes were much like those of a real bull, save that an intelligence lurked within those orbs. The snout was short and broad, and the teeth that the creature's grin revealed looked more adapted to tearing flesh than green grass. Huma remembered some of the stories about this race, and he took an involuntary step backward.

The minotaur held up his long, wide hands and displayed the chains that bound them together. The fingers were thicker and more blunt than a man's and they ended in sharp nails—no, claws. Huma's own hands were like those of a year-old child in comparison.

"Unlike the goblins, who always need six times the number of their adversaries before they even dream of attack, I think you have the advantage over me. I'm sure you know how to use that fine weapon."

"I do," Huma finally managed to blurt out. "What were you doing here? Why were you a prisoner of these goblins? I've always heard the minotaurs were allies of the ogres."

The crimson illumination of the moon gave the former captive's eyes a fearsome look. "*Slave soldiers* would be a better term, Knight of Solamnia. We are no more than slaves to our cousins. They hold our lands and our families as hostages, though the word they use is *protection*. That is why we do what they cannot. One day, though, it will be the minotaurs who will rule. We await that day."

"Which does not explain why you were a prisoner here." Huma presented as confident a face as he could muster. It would not take much of the minotaur's strength to snap the young knight's neck. He had already seen proof of that.

The beast-man dropped his shackled arms and snorted. "I killed my ogre captain, human. I struck him down with my bare hands. A good blow. Cracked his skull with one shot."

The thought of striking, much less actually murdering, a superior appalled the knight. He raised his visor and dared to step close to the minotaur.

"You murdered him?"

"You like ogres? Thanks to me, no lives will be lost against his ax—and he was good, I'll give him that. Many died on that ax, human, even the weak, the helpless. I found him over the bodies of an aged male and two children, perhaps the old human's grandchildren. I did what I thought right. There is no honor in slaughtering the old, the feeble, or the young—at least, not among my kind. Not that they would have tolerated my betrayal. I had thought it was so among the Knights of Solamnia, too. I see that I may have misunderstood." The minotaur held up the chained wrists once more, causing Huma to take several quick steps back. "Either kill me or free me from these chains. I do not care to discuss this. The goblins have drugged what little food they gave me. This exertion has almost done me in."

Indeed, the minotaur was slumping. Huma came to a decision, overturned it, came to another, and finally settled again on the first. Even then, he did not act. Could he truly believe the words of the strange figure before him? The minotaurs were supposedly an honorable race, but they served the gods of evil. That was the way it was always taught.

Huma's sword arm shivered, as much from his thoughts as from the long, awkward position he held it in. The man-beast waited patiently, as ready to die as to be freed. The calm and faith with which the former captive faced his rescuer finally made Huma's decision for him. He slowly and carefully sheathed his blade.

"Which of these had the keys?"

The minotaur fell to his knees. His breath came in huge huffs, like a bull about to charge. "The one I threw. He will have them if any do. I never saw the keys. They had no reason for them. After—after all, why would they want to release me?"

While the exhausted defector rested, Huma went over to the goblin and checked the numerous pouches wrapped around the creature's waist. Each held a large number of items, many of them disgusting trophies of war—knowing goblins, more likely looted from the dead—and a few unrecognizable. In one of the pouches, he found the keys.

The minotaur's eyes were closed, and Huma suddenly worried that one of the goblins had, after all, inflicted some mortal wound. At the clinking of the keys near his face, though, the burly figure opened his eyes.

"My thanks," he said, after Huma had freed both wrists. "By my ancestors twenty generations back, I will not rest until I have balanced the scale. You have my oath on that."

"There is no need. It—it was my duty."

Somehow, the minotaur managed a very human expression of skepticism. "Nevertheless, I will honor my oath as I see fit. Let it not be said that Kaz is less than his ancestors."

Huma stood. "Can you walk?"

"Give me a moment." Kaz looked around quickly. "Besides, I have no desire to be out in the open tonight. I would prefer some sort of shelter."

"From what?" Huma could not imagine what would worry such a powerful fighter unless it was a dragon or some creature of similar proportions.

Kaz rose slowly. "The captain was a current favorite of the warlord. I fear he might have unleashed some of the renegade's pets."

"I don't understand."

The minotaur suddenly turned his attention to acquiring a decent weapon. He spotted the ax dropped by Huma's first opponent, picked it up, and tested it. "Good. Probably dwarven." To Huma, he replied, "Let us hope there is no need. I do not think either of us would live through it."

In the hands of the goblin, the ax had looked large. Kaz, however, wielded it with the ease of one who was used to weapons of even greater size. The ax was meant for two-handed use; the minotaur needed only one massive paw to grasp it.

"In which direction did you plan to go?"

"North."

"To Kyre?"

Huma hesitated. He knew that many knights, even Bennett, would never have released such a creature from its bonds. They would have marched it at sword point through the wasteland. Most certainly, they would never tell the minotaur the final destination. If the so-called prisoner was in actuality a spy, such a slip of the tongue might prove fatal for more than just Huma. Yet, Kaz seemed a person of honor.

Huma held back only a moment more, then finally nodded. "Yes, Kyre. I hope to rejoin my comrades."

The minotaur swung the ax over his own shoulder and attached it to what Huma realized was a harness designed for just such a purpose. It was one of only two pieces of clothing Kaz wore, the other being a sort of kilt, or perhaps a large loin cloth.

"I fear that Kyre is an unwise choice for now, but I will not argue you out of it."

"Why unwise?"

Kaz gave his imitation of a human smile, a smile filled with anticipation. "Kyre is now the front. My cousins, the ogres, must be there even as we speak." He chuckled, sounding again like a snorting bull. "It will be a glorious struggle. I wish I could be there."

Huma grimaced at the obvious pleasure in killing that his new companion expressed. Some of the tales concerning the strange minotaurs were evidently too true.

Steeling himself, Huma wiped the drying blood from his weapon. He glanced only briefly at his newfound companion, who seemed to recognize some of the revulsion in Huma's face.

"You may come with me or go back to your own, Kaz," Huma said. "Whatever you desire. You may find the knighthood leery of accepting you as a deserter."

Kaz did not hesitate. "I know some of what you feel, Knight of Solamnia. I understand all too well our many differences. Still, I owe you a debt and I would rather face your comrades than return to my own ranks and to a slow torture before I am executed. I have no desire to face ogres' tender mercies."

Something howled in the night, far away. It was a wolf, Huma decided, yet not a wolf. It was too cold, too—evil.

"We had best be off," Kaz quickly decided. "This is no place to be at night. The scent of death is sure to draw visitors here and I, Knight, would prefer to move on."

Huma's eyes were still staring back at the direction of the

cry. He nodded sharply, suddenly much more pleased with the minotaur's companionship. "Agreed." He reached out his right hand in friendship. "My name, friend Kaz, is Huma."

"Huma." The pressure exerted by the hand that covered Huma's was not enough to crush every bone, but it came close. "A strong name, that. A warrior's name."

Huma turned quickly away and picked up his bags. How wrong the minotaur could be! A warrior, indeed! Within his armor, Huma could feel every portion of his body shiver. He tried to imagine Bennett in his place, acting in the proper manner of a knight born to command. The thought only frustrated Huma more, for he knew that Bennett would never have ended up in a situation such as this.

They left the camp, with its dying fire and scattered refuse, and headed in the direction Huma had chosen. Neither spoke now, for varying reasons. Behind them—thankfully, sounding no closer than before—the cry rose again.

Chapter 3

The two wanderers found it impossible to travel too far before being forced to rest. Huma's head still bothered him, and Kaz was not fully over the effects of the drugged food he had been fed following his capture by the goblins.

"I was a fool! They caught me napping like a newborn and trussed me up good! I am many things, but not crazy enough to try rising to face two pikes that had me pinned to the ground. Even goblins can't miss at that range." The last made Kaz laugh, though Huma found little humor in the statement.

They finally agreed to stop at a small rise that would provide some protection. It was uncomfortably too much like the position that the first goblin patrol had chosen. Still, it was better than wide-open terrain. Huma only prayed he would keep his eyes open long enough to wake the minotaur when it was Kaz's turn to watch.

They talked a little while, perhaps because neither felt safe about sleep. Huma spoke of the knighthood and its basic beliefs and organization. Kaz found the Knights of Solamnia interesting. Many aspects about it appealed to the easterner, especially the great respect for honor.

Kaz went into very little detail about his own people. They were great mariners, it was true, but their lives were now controlled by the ogres. They still had their tournaments of honor, where one rose in rank by defeating his opponent, but the ogres cared little for this method and chose new measures more appealing to their ways. Because of that, Kaz had already built up a great hatred of his so-called masters before his deadly clash with his captain. Anything was better than servitude to their kind, he felt.

That Huma trusted Kaz with his life disturbed the Solamnian a little. He had already seen how savage the minotaur could become. Huma never could have snapped an opponent's neck with the efficiency and—eagerness—that Kaz had shown. Yet he felt that the minotaur could be trusted where his word was concerned. The debate in Huma's mind raged on until he fell prey to weariness. Then it became a moot point.

The night passed without incident, as did the first hours of day. They ate what little rations Huma had left. A brief look in the goblins' bags had made the knight lose all desire for any food the creatures might have been carrying, and besides, the goblins' food might have been tampered with.

The day was bleak. A chill wind was picking up, and Huma was thankful that he wore good, strong padding beneath his armor. Kaz, however, seemed unbothered by the cool weather. His race was one of explorers and mariners, as well as warriors, and the lands of his birth could get exceptionally cold in the dark months. The barechested footsoldier did not even wear boots. Had Huma walked as far in his bare feet, they would have been scarred, bleeding, and mangled. The lands here had been baked hard and rough by the past.

About midday, Huma noticed the riders in the distance.

The riders did not come in Huma and Kaz's direction, and soon the group was lost from sight. But Huma believed the Knights of Solamnia, and that meant odds were good that the column—or at least a portion of it—waited nearby.

Kaz, on the other hand, was not so confident about the identities of the riders. Here, so close to the front, they could be anyone.

"True, they appeared to be humans—or perhaps elves—but they may have been among those who serve Takhisis. You have never seen the Black Guard, the Warlord's elite troops. Nor the renegades for that matter."

The minotaur had used that puzzling word before. "Who are the renegades?" Huma asked.

"Sorcerers unschooled. Mad mages. All of them, somehow or another, have escaped the notice of the orders of magic. Not all are evil. It is said, though, that one with tremendous power has made a pact with the Dark Queen herself, and that she is so desperate for victory now that she has shunned her own Black Robes."

Magic. Huma knew more about it than most of his comrades. He had grown up with it. His best—his only—friend had turned to sorcery. From the first, Magius had told Huma that some day he would be a great and powerful sorcerer, even as Huma leaned toward the knighthood that his mother had claimed was his birthright.

Thinking of Magius made Huma think too much of his early years, times that, while cherished in some ways, had left him bitter and unsure. He had not seen Magius in years, not since the day his friend had completed his studies and entered the tower for some sort of test that would decide his fate. On that very same day, Huma had made a decision of his own and had set out to confront the Knights of Solamnia and petition for a place among them.

Huma shook away the thoughts.

They continued walking. Kaz continually scanned the horizon, but he seemed a stranger to the terrain. At one point, he turned and asked, "Are all of the human lands like this?"

"You've never seen any of them?"

"Only the worst areas. Where else would the ogres put us

but in the worst positions? In our own way, we are more expendable to them than the goblins. They trust neither of our races, but they know they can control the goblins."

Huma nodded his understanding. "There are still lands untouched by the war, but they grow fewer each year. Where my home was, is now a wasteland akin to this." With that came a rush of bitter memories. He forced himself to concentrate on the path ahead. The past was behind him.

The minotaur's head snapped forward. "We have company of some sort."

The knight squinted. More than three dozen figures, all human, headed in their general direction. Survivors of some village, he realized. Lost survivors, evidently, with two broken-down wagons hauled by animals half-dead and led by men who looked no better. There were women, too, and even a couple of children. As they drew closer, he suddenly realized that most of them were gazing at his companion. What he could read in those gazes, he did not care for at all.

"We must be careful, Kaz."

"Against this pathetic rabble? You needn't bother. I can take these all by myself." Kaz started to reach for the ax strapped to his back, but Huma caught his arm.

"No!" he hissed. "That's murder!"

The usually quick-reacting warrior hesitated. The mind of a minotaur worked much differently from that of a man. Kaz saw a threat; there were more than enough men to take him down if he failed to react. His world did not accept compromise. One triumphed or died. Huma stood dumbfounded; he did not want to fight Kaz, but he could not very well allow the minotaur to go tearing into the refugees.

Though Kaz lowered his hand, the damage was already done. The villagers saw only a monster who had threatened them. They already had seen their homes destroyed, and friends and relatives killed. Frustration at their helplessness had built higher and higher, with no outlet. Now, a lone minotaur who represented all that was evil, all their suffering, stood in their path.

Several men and women shuffled forward, a ragged mob. They were pale and frightened, a suicidal fright. All they wanted was one chance to strike back before they died.

Huma was appalled at the sight. The group moved like living dead. Farm tools, knives, rope, even various household items were clutched as weapons. Kaz stood his ground, but he gave Huma a quick glance.

"If they come a few steps closer, I will strike no matter what you say. I will not stand and die at their hands." The minotaur's eyes glared blood red. Before long, he would act. Huma jumped in front of the mob, sword raised in the air. "Stop! He means no harm!"

It was a pathetic attempt, and the results were as he had feared. The murderous mob came to a halt, but only to decide what to do about the young knight barring their path.

"Step aside!" one grizzled elder yelled. A cloth was tied over one eye, and the red stain on it indicated a recent wound. His skin was cracked, and his sparse hair clung to his head. "We want him! He's got to pay for what he's done!"

"He's done nothing to you!"

A woman a little older than Huma, and apparently once pretty, spat at him. "He's one of them! What does it matter whether he was the one who killed my children! If he's not done it here, he's done it elsewhere!"

It would have been futile to try to explain. They would not have listened to Huma, and, even if they did, it would not excuse the horrors they had suffered. Kaz was their only focus.

In desperation, Huma brandished his sword. There was some murmuring and a few less hardy souls stepped back, but the apparent betrayal by a Knight of Solamnia against his own race was more than some could stand. The mob moved forward again, but this time it was obvious that Huma was also their target.

Behind him, he could hear his massive companion pulling out the ax. "Have no fear, Huma. We will crush them."

There was anticipation in those words, even more than the first time Huma had noticed it.

Not even the sight of an angered minotaur clutching a huge battle ax in one great hand was enough to deter villagers. Thin, bony arms, from which hung the rags of clothes, rose. Some were empty-handed, some were willing to strike with whatever was in them. Huma stepped back.

Would he really kill these people to protect one who had been an enemy only a few days before? No knight would do so. Huma knew that. Yet he could not leave Kaz to them.

"Kaz, you'd better run!"

"They'll kill you now, Huma. Kill you for aiding me. Better we stand and fight."

That was the last thing Huma desired, but there appeared to be no other choice. Either he moved aside and betrayed the minotaur or he stood and betrayed those he had sworn to defend. The sword wavered.

A strong wind rushed up from behind him.

The mob froze and all eyes stared upward. Behind him, Huma heard Kaz whirl and curse.

"Dragon!"

A cloud of dust kicked up, obscuring Huma's vision as he turned. He could hear the flapping of great wings as the dragon evidently prepared to land. In his mind, he saw one of the deadly black dragons or perhaps a huge red one, come to strike them all down. His sword would be less than useless.

Even before the dust had settled, Kaz was charging. Dragon of darkness or light, it mattered little to him. He had no future, whichever the case. He only hoped to do some damage before the leviathan crushed him. The minotaur shouted a battle cry as he ran, and the ax whirled about his head. Huma got his first glance of the dragon as Kaz struck.

The knight raised a hand and shouted, although he knew it was much too late already. "No!"

The might of a minotaur was truly impressive. It was said that an ax in a minotaur's hands could split boulders in two. Had Kaz struck, it was quite possible that he might have conquered. Instead, he suddenly froze in midswing and his momentum, great as it was, threw him headfirst to the ground beneath the dragon's great maw.

The dragon glanced only briefly at the fallen berserker and then looked up to study the human. Huma stared back. As a knight, he was accustomed to the comings and goings of the Dragons of Light. They served as guardians and messengers, but he had never seen one this close.

It was tall and sleek. The entire body was silver, save the two eyes that glowed like sunshine. He knew instinctively that the dragon was female, although he would have been hard-pressed to explain his reasoning. The jaws were longer than his arm and the teeth were so long that the dragon easily could have bitten off Huma's head with one snap. The snout was long and tapered.

The dragon's voice, contrary to the beast's appearance, was deep but melodious. "A Knight of Solamnia. What do you do out here? You are far from your comrades. Are you seeking this garbage here? Rest assured, the minotaur will go nowhere. Not while the power of my will holds him."

Huma lowered his weapon. The villagers had melted into the background, although they were in no real danger.

"Are you well?" The question appeared legitimate. The silvery dragon was actually concerned.

"Please," Huma choked out. "Don't harm him! It's not what you think!"

The glimmering orbs of the dragon seemed to appraise him. The leviathan was curious. "Why do you wish to spare the life of this creature? Is there information you desire? I can wrench information from him with little trouble."

The dragon waited with the patience of one who measures time in centuries, not minutes.

"He is my companion. He has turned from the evil of the Dark Queen."

Had someone informed Huma that the face of a dragon was capable of revealing very human surprise, he would have scoffed. This, though, was the case. He remained silent as the dragon digested this unusual piece of information.

"The minotaur would have struck me. It is obvious that he meant me great physical harm. How, then, can I justify your claims?"

Huma stiffened. "You must take my word. I have no proof."

She actually smiled at that. On a dragon, even a smile was fearsome. Lord Oswal had once said that a dragon's smile was like that of the fox who was preparing to eat the hen.

"I beg your pardon, Knight of Solamnia. I did not mean that I had no faith in your words. You must admit, it is not every day that one finds a minotaur fighting side by side with one of your kind."

"No offense was taken."

"What of them?"

Huma did not turn. He still remembered his indecision and what might have resulted. "Their fear and anger is understandable. They've suffered much. I hold nothing against them."

She acknowledged his answer with a sinuous twist of her narrow, lengthy neck. To the villagers she said, "You travel off-course. Turn to the southwest. There are clerics of Mishakal who will care for your injured and give you food. Tell any others you meet on your way."

She received no argument from them, something that Huma was quite thankful for. The dragon watched the refugees set out in the proper direction. Then she looked down at Kaz with near-distaste.

"If I release this one, his well-being is your affair. I have as little love for his kind as those unfortunates do."

Huma was hesitant. "I cannot promise his reaction when you release him. He is quick to anger."

"A trait of the minotaurs. If they were not constantly killing one another in their contests of strength and rank, I think they would have overrun Ansalon long before this." She sighed, an action that forced Huma to close his eyes as hot air warmed his face. "Very well."

With those words said, the minotaur suddenly leaped to life. He did not renew his attack, but rather paused some distance from dragon and knight, the ax ready in his hands. He eyed the dragon warily.

She returned the gaze with something akin to disdain. "You heard everything."

It was no question, and the massive warrior's expression indicated to Huma that Kaz had heard all too well. He still did not trust either of them, though.

"I heard. I am not sure what to believe."

"I easily could have crushed you, minotaur." The silver dragon lifted one massive claw as proof. Had either one of them felt the force behind it, there would have been little left to mourn.

Kaz turned his gaze to Huma. "You saved my life once, Knight Huma. It appears you have done so again, only this time with words." The minotaur shook his head. "I shall never be able to sufficiently repay the debt."

Huma frowned. Debts, again! "I want nothing from you, save peace. Will you put away the ax?"

The minotaur straightened, took one last look at the hulking figure before him, and hesitantly returned the ax to its resting place. "As I have said, I cannot go back. What is to become of me?"

The dragon snorted, sending small puffs of smoke floating. "I have no interest in you. Huma is the one who should decide."

"Me?"

"You've shown excellent judgment so far. Would that more of the earthbound races showed such common sense." There was no mockery in the dragon's tone.

Huma felt oddly pleased by the compliment, coming as it did from a creature as regal as the silver dragon. He thought carefully for several moments, tossing about ideas that had half-formed during the trek, and then turned to the minotaur. "We must join the column. If you truly wish to prove yourself to others than myself, you'll have to tell them what you know about the ogres' movements and make them believe you." Huma paused. "You *do* know something of use to them, don't you?"

Kaz gave it long thought and then grunted. "I know more than I should know. If you can convince them not to slay me out of hand, I will do as you say. Perhaps what help I can give you will hasten the day when my people are free once more."

"You'll have to give me the ax."

The minotaur let loose with a bellow of rage. "I cannot go among them unarmed! It would be a loss of face! This is not our way!"

Huma's temper flared. "You're not among your people! You're among mine! If you step among them armed with that well-worn ax, there will be no hope for compromise. At the very least, you will become a prisoner. At the worst, you will be dead."

The dragon leveled a glittery stare at the minotaur. "The knight's assessment is quite accurate. You would do best to listen to him."

Kaz snorted and snarled and called upon the names of some six or seven prominent ancestors, but in the end, he agreed to surrender his weapon to Huma when the time came.

The silver dragon spread her great wings. She was a magnificent creature, the very aspect of power and beauty joined into one. Huma had seen tapestries, wood carvings, and sculptures in Vingaard Keep that had sought to capture the essence of the dragons. They were all pale specters when compared to the actual being.

"I was flying to rejoin my kin in northern Ergoth when I caught sight of you. The situation was unique. It interested me, so I decided to land," she said. "I should move on, but it will not take me far out of my way if I transport the two of you to your destination."

The thought of soaring through the sky on the back of one of the legendary dragons nearly overwhelmed Huma. He knew that there were knights who fought astride the huge beasts and even talked with them, but Huma had never been so privileged.

"How do we hold on?"

"If I fly slowly, you should have no trouble hanging on with your arms and legs. Many have done it before, although you are the first to fly with me. It will save you much time and hardship." She lowered her head so that it was level with his own.

Huma would fly! Magius had once said that this was one of his greatest reasons for joining the orders of sorcery—to float among the clouds.

Huma straddled the long, sinewy neck just above the shoulders and could not help but smile at the dragon, who had turned to watch. He knew she understood his enthusiasm all too well. Reddening slightly, Huma reached down a hand to Kaz. The minotaur stared at the offered hand and at the back of the dragon.

He shook his head vehemently. "My people are creatures of the land, sailors of the seas. We are not birds."

"It is perfectly safe." The dragon appeared slighted. "A babe could ride with no fear."

"A babe would be foolish enough. I am not."

"There's nothing to fear, Kaz."

Huma's remarks stung well, as the knight had hoped they would. If a mere human could face this challenge, then so could he, a minotaur. Snorting furiously, he took hold of Huma's hand and climbed up. He sat directly behind the knight and did not speak, although every muscle in his body tensed. He gripped the dragon's neck with his hands and legs.

"Are both of you prepared?"

Huma looked back at Kaz, who stared ahead without seeing. The knight turned back. "As best we can be, I guess." His heart was pounding, and he felt more like a small child than a Knight of Solamnia. "Will we fly high?"

The silver dragon actually laughed, a deep, throaty chuckle. "Not as high as you might like, but I do not think you will be disappointed."

She gave the minotaur one last amused glance, then began to flap her wings. Huma watched in fascination as the ground fell away beneath them. Within seconds, the silver dragon was spiraling high in the sky. Huma lowered his visor to keep some of the wind out of his face. Kaz merely held on for dear life and changed neither method nor mind even when the silvery leviathan ceased climbing and finally maintained a slow and steady flight.

Huma raised his visor and leaned as close to the dragon's head as was possible. "This—this is fantastic!"

"Perhaps you should have been a dragon yourself!" she shouted back. "If you could see the world as I see it!"

She did not try to explain, and Huma did not ask her to. For a brief time, the war, the knighthood, all his problems vanished.

Huma settled back and absorbed the splendor.

Chapter 4

The war was meant to be swift and final. Takhisis, Queen of Darkness, Dragonqueen, had sent forth her children, her slaves, her warriors, her mages, and mystics in one great collective force. The focus of her attack was the Knights of Solamnia, for she saw in them the power and danger that the elves once had represented. The elves were now a shadow of their once-mighty strength; their self-exile from the outside world had sapped them of vigor. They could wait for her attention until the knighthood had been ground under.

Yet the knights had their own allies and, most important, the discipline and the organization that were sorely lacking from the Queen's followers. The knights also had dedicated their lives to her eternal foe, Paladine.

It was said that Paladine himself had created the knighthood. Certainly it was true that Vinas Solamnus, the Ergothian commander who had turned against the tyranny of his emperor, introduced the Oath and Measure by which his soldiers would abide, but it was always his claim that he had stumbled across a grove on far-off Sancrist Isle—a place beyond the western shores of Ansalon itself—in which Paladine himself awaited. With his twin sons, the gods Kiri-Jolith and Habbakuk, Paladine had introduced Vinas Solamnus to the creation of a powerful force for good.

From Habbakuk came the Order of the Crown, which looked to loyalty as its greatest aspect. All new knights became members of this order, the better to learn to act in concert, to aid one's comrades, and to follow faithfully the Oath and the Measure.

From Kiri-Jolith, god of just battle, came the Order of the Sword. Those who wished to, could choose to enter this order once they had proved themselves as members of the Crown. Honor was first and foremost to a Knight of the Sword. No hand was to be raised in unjust anger, no sword drawn because of personal jealousies.

Last, from Paladine himself, came the Order of the Rose. These were to be the elite, those knights who had so come to embrace the workings of Paladine that nothing mattered more. Wisdom and justice ruled their lives. From their ranks most often would be chosen the Grand Master, he who would command the knighthood overall.

Although it had never been so during the life of Vinas Solamnus, the Order of the Rose became the order of royalty. Whereas all knights laid claim to royal blood, the Order of the Rose was open only to those of the "purest" blood. No one ever defied this rule, although it went against all the teachings of Paladine.

The war had settled down to the most horrible stalemate. Men, dragons, ogres, goblins—the casualties mounted, the carrion creatures fed, the plagues began.

"I had not believed . . ." The silver dragon's voice trailed off. Huma had not realized how quickly the destruction would spread across yet another once-unspoiled region.

Below them, frighteningly real, lay the evidence.

Whole groves of ancient, proud trees had been thrown free of the earth, either by dragons or magic-users. Fields were no more than great mounds of upturned soil with the tracks of many feet trampled into them. The dead reposed in great numbers, knights and ogres both, although there did seem to be more of the latter—or was it merely blind hope on the part of the Solamnic knight?

Huma's face paled. He looked at the dead scattered about, then covered his eyes while he regained his composure.

"A futile struggle here," Kaz was shouting in his ear. The minotaur had lost his fear of flight in his great interest in the battle. "Crynus picks and picks, and the knighthood's commanders return the favor with little bites of their own. Neither will gain from this."

The words made Huma stiffen. Kaz could not help his nature. A battle was a study in skill and position to him. Even personally involved, he would ponder strategy and tactics. Even as his ax screamed through the air.

The silver dragon turned her head toward them. "Obviously, we cannot land here. Kyre is certainly lost, to both sides, it would seem. These fields of wheat will feed no one."

Huma blinked. "There is hope, then. The supply lines of the ogres must be strained. The knighthood sits more securely with its."

"But their strength is not as great as that of the ogres," interjected the minotaur.

So intent were they on the desolation below that none of them had noticed the large, dark forms riding toward their general position. It was Kaz who spotted them. He suddenly gripped Huma's shoulder tightly. Huma turned his head and followed the minotaur's gaze.

"Dragon!" he shouted to the silver leviathan bearing them. "Six at least."

As they neared, Huma began to make out more definite shapes and colors. Reds—led by a black dragon? Squinting, Huma realized it was true. An enormous black dragon—bearing a rider. As they all were!

"I cannot fight them all," said the silver dragon. "Jump when the earth is close. I will attempt to lead them astray."

The silver dragon skimmed down near the trees, trying to locate some place suitable to land before her deadly counterparts reached them.

"You must jump when I say so! Are you ready?"

"It galls me to flee from any battle, even among the clouds. Is there no way we can help, Huma?"

Huma kept his face turned away from the minotaur. "No, we'd best jump."

"As you wish."

They passed over what had once been a farmhouse; it was now little more than a low, crumbling wall of bricks forming a crude rectangle. Beyond that, though, was clear field.

"I'm slowing! Ready yourselves!"

They poised.

"Now!"

Kaz moved first. He toppled over as if struck in the chest by an arrow. The silver dragon's talons fairly touched the earth as she glided into another turn.

Huma leaned to jump—and hesitated.

"What are you doing?" the silver dragon screamed at Huma as the six dragons drew nearer.

"You cannot fight them alone!"

"Don't be a fool!"

"Too late!" he shouted quickly.

Each of the dragons carried a tall, sinister figure clad in unadorned ebony armor. Their faces were hidden by visored helmets. Whether they were human or ogre or something else was beyond Huma's ken.

The rider of the tremendous black dragon, a hulking figure who dwarfed Huma, motioned to the others. The reds pulled back to await the outcome. The black dragon shrieked eagerly as the rider prodded it.

The two dragons closed with much bellowing. Claws slashed and one talon dug into a forearm of the silver dragon. She, in turn, raked the open chest of the black, leaving great gash marks across it.

The armored rider swung a wicked two-headed ax, and Huma automatically dodged the attack. As the two dragons grappled, Huma was able to angle close enough to strike back.

The other riders hung back in nervous anticipation, their dragons shrieking angrily at being unable to participate.

Then the silver dragon caught the black across one wing with her claws, and the other shrieked in pain. The black rider was thrown to one side, and left open to Huma's thrust. Without thinking, the knight struck at the opening below his opponent's shoulder. The point easily cut through the thin mail, and momentum carried it deeper. The rider grunted and slumped backward.

A chorus of cries from riders and dragons alerted the black to the injury of its charge. With frenzied movements, the black tore away from the silver dragon.

Huma readied himself for the mass attack that would surely follow, but, oddly enough, the enemy did not press its advantage. The remaining dragons formed a protective circle around the black dragon and its badly wounded rider, and then all six great beasts turned in the direction from which they had come. While knight and silver dragon watched in stupefaction, the enemy flew away.

Huma found himself breathing calmly again.

Below him, the silver dragon also had regained her poise. Her wounds still bled, and Huma wondered just how severe were the injuries.

As if in response, she turned to look at him, concern obvious in her every movement.

"Are you injured?"

"No. What of you? Do you require aid?" How did one treat a dragon? "I don't know if I can help, but I can try."

She shook her glittering head. "I can heal myself. I merely require rest. What concerns me more is the odd circumstances of this battle. This was more than merely a patrol. I cannot put my mind to the answer, but I believe this is a sign."

Huma nodded. "We must pick up Kaz and hurry to Lord Oswal. He will want to know all."

The silver dragon edged downward and saw something that made her smile cynically. She said, "It appears we have more visitors. Ones who, I believe, will not be pleased to discover a minotaur in their midst."

Following her gaze, Huma saw them. Knights of Solamnia. More than twenty, he estimated. A patrol of his own colors. The silver dragon was right. The knights would be likely to run Kaz down, at the cost of a few of their own lives, no doubt.

Kaz, hidden in the wreckage of a farmer's wagon and oblivious to the riders coming from behind, rose to wave at Huma and the silver dragon. Even if the knights had failed to see the minotaur, they could not miss the landing of the dragon. One knight spotted the bull-headed creature and yelled out a warning to the others. Immediately, the patrol went into a full charge. The minotaur whirled at the thundering sound and stood momentarily poised. Then the battle ax, which Huma had allowed Kaz to keep, was suddenly out and swinging expectantly. Swords were raised and lances aimed.

Huma could think of only one thing to do. He shouted out his plan to the silver dragon. The oncoming warriors looked up in astonishment, and their orderly riding became haphazard as they momentarily forgot all else at sight of the magnificent denizen of the air. The silver dragon came down behind Kaz and was able to grab the minotaur by his shoulders. Kaz let out a startled cry and dropped his ax as the great talons applied pressure to both shoulders and hauled him off the ground. The knights tugged hard on the reins, desperately trying to halt their steeds while cheering for what they thought was the end of a marauding minotaur.

Kaz continued a stream of curses that would have made the worst brigand blanch, but he was powerless in the grip of the silver dragon. When they were some distance away, the silver dragon dropped the minotaur gently to the ground and then landed nearby.

Huma leaped off her back and immediately confronted Kaz. If not for the minotaur's oath to serve him, Huma suspected he would have been slaughtered then and there. Fire glowed in the minotaur's deep-set eyes, and he snorted continuously with anger.

"No fighting!" Huma ordered.

"They will kill me! At least let me fight to the death, not stand there like some ineffectual gully dwarf!"

Very quietly and with a cold anger that surprised him, Huma repeated himself. "I said no fighting."

The minotaur exhaled sharply and seemed to slump. He stared at Huma. "As you wish. I will put my faith in you who have saved my life twice."

That again! Huma let out an exasperated breath and turned as the reorganized patrol rode hesitantly up to the odd trio. The patrol leader, the only one seemingly unaffected by the sight of the great dragon, called a halt and then leaned forward to study the young knight.

"It seems Bennett is not rid of you after all, Huma."

Belated recognition dawned on Huma. "Rennard!"

Rennard raised his visor. Some of the other knights shifted uncomfortably. Rennard's face was deathly pale, and when he spoke it was almost as if his features did not move. He might have been a handsome man, but that handsomeness had been ruined by near-death in his youth, from plague. His face was gaunt and lined, and some of his detractors liked to joke that Rennard had, in fact, died of the disease and just never realized it. Such colorful comments never were spoken in his presence, though. Few knights were his match.

Huma was pleased to see Rennard. The older knight had taken Huma under his wing from the first, when he came to Vingaard to present his petition for entry into the knighthood. Rennard had supported him when others had urged that he be rejected—a boy who could only claim his father was a knight and whose mother could give no evidence to support him.

The knights had gotten over their awe of the dragon by this time, and now all eyed Kaz. There was a great amount of muttering, much of it concerning what so strange a being as a minotaur was doing here. Rennard beckoned to one of the other riders. "Bind the minotaur. I'm sure that Lord Oswal will be most interested in him and what he is doing this far from the action."

Kaz stepped back, fists raised. "Try! The first who lays a hand on me will never do so again!"

One of the knights drew a sword. "Insolent beast! You won't live long enough!"

"No!" Huma stepped up to Rennard. "He's no enemy. He was running from the ogres. I found him a prisoner of goblins and rescued him. He killed an ogre in order to save human lives!"

Several of the men made snide comments on the gullibility of the young knight, and Huma knew his face had glared crimson.

Kaz snorted. The slur on Huma's honor was as much a slur on his own, since he owed his life to the human. "This is the honor of the Knights of Solamnia? This is how they treat one of their own? Perhaps I was mistaken to believe the knighthood might be as honorable as my own race!"

The knight who had drawn his sword began urging his horse forward. "I'll have your head, minotaur!"

"You will do nothing of the sort, Knight Conrad." The angered knight tried to face Rennard down, but, as had happened countless times before, it was the pale knight who was victorious. No one could face the ice-blue eyes.

"In truth, there is nothing any of you could say against Huma's ability to judge," continued Rennard. "And you know it. Act like knights, not petty Ergothians or high, mighty elves."

The other warriors quieted, although it was clear they were not pleased with being scolded like children. Rennard did not care, Huma knew. Rennard was concerned only with Rennard.

To Huma, he said, "The minotaur is placed in your custody, Huma. I know more about their kind than these others apparently do. If he will pledge to come among us in peace, that will be all the assurance I need."

Huma looked at Kaz, who stared at the patrol in general and at the gaunt knight in particular. After some consideration, the minotaur finally agreed. "I pledge to you that I will come in peace and that I will accept Huma's judgment in all matters."

The last was a criticism of the knights' lack of faith in one of their own. The knights shifted uneasily. They did not like the idea of so powerful a prisoner riding loose among them. The silver dragon looked on with an expression of mild amusement. Rennard's face was devoid of reaction, but

Huma felt he was amused by the remark.

The patrol leader jabbed a thumb behind him. "We have a few extra horses, which we recovered about a mile from here. One of them is tall and strong enough to carry the minotaur, I believe. When you are satisfied, I want the two of you up front. We have much to discuss, and you, Knight Huma, must have a rather interesting report."

The other knights made room as Huma and Kaz stepped into their midst. There were five extra horses—four war-horses and one drafthorse that apparently had been abandoned by its owner. The drafthorse and two of the warhorses proved to be unfit for riding and had been taken along mainly for the meat on their bones. The tallest of the horses, and the only one capable of supporting the massive form of the minotaur, was skittish, but not so much that Kaz could not control him. Huma found a greyish silver steed and took an immediately liking to it. When they were mounted, they rejoined Rennard.

Huma scanned the desolation. "What happened here?"

The lack of emotion only made Rennard's words the more frightening. "What usually happens, Huma? Mages fight their own private wars and tear up the lands, leaving nothing but rock and craters for those bound to the earth. Dragons burn or freeze or tear up the remaining fertile, green regions. By the time the armies clash, there is little if anything worth fighting for."

Mages were a sore subject with Rennard. No one knew why. Huma had never mentioned Magius to him for fear of alienating him, and losing one of Huma's rare champions.

"Did we lose?"

"Stalemate. The fighting just moved north, although we were sent to assure that their northerly retreat was no feint. We were just about to turn back when we saw you."

The silver dragon, who had stayed patiently silent all this time, finally interjected. "You did not see the dragonriders, then?"

Rennard's head snapped up and the other knights stiffened. "Dragonriders, did you say?"

"Six of them. All clad in black and all riding red dragons, save the leader, who rode a huge black dragon. They seemed to be searching until they noticed us. I tried to buy some time, but your fellow knight refused to leave me. He insisted on joining in the battle."

With most of the faces hidden by visors, Huma could not properly gauge the reactions of his comrades. Some few seemed to indicate approval with slight nods, while one was heard to mutter something about unnecessary foolhardiness. Rennard, meanwhile, seemed preoccupied.

"A huge black, you say?"

"The largest. Young, though. The rider chose to fight us one to one. We did, and then a strange thing occurred. Huma wounded him severely and the black was forced to retreat from the battle. Rather than seeking revenge, the others joined the black to seek help for their crippled leader. They would have slaughtered us had they all come at once. I still do not understand."

Rennard's face remained typically blank. How much this disturbed him was impossible to say. When he spoke next, it was as if the tale of the attack had already slipped his mind. "I can only thank you for the service you have given one of our own. Will you be joining us? I am unfamiliar with the healing of dragon wounds, but if the powers of a cleric of Mishakal will help, there are a few with the main force."

The great beast flexed her wings—which unnerved more than one knight and many of the horses—and declined his offer. "My own talents will suffice. I merely need rest. I will rejoin my kin. You might possibly see me afterward." The last comment was directed more at Huma than Rennard.

"It has been fascinating to know you even this brief time, Knight Huma," the dragon continued. "Good tidings to you. May Paladine watch over you."

Without further ado, the silver dragon lifted herself high into the air. Huma and the others were forced to look away as the dust rose. When it had settled at last, the astonishing creature was already far away. The group watched her vanish into the clouds, still awed by her presence. Rennard turned and took stock of those under his command—including Huma and Kaz—and turned his horse. He gave no command, and none was expected. The others simply followed, the two newcomers riding just behind the patrol leader.

It was not until they were well on their way that Rennard motioned the two to ride beside him. He continued to watch the path ahead as he spoke. "These riders. Have you ever seen or heard of them before, Huma?"

"Should I have?"

"Perhaps. Minotaur—"

"My name is Kaz." He appeared tired of being addressed as if he were not quite there.

"Kaz, then. Surely, you must know them?"

"They are the Black Guard. One of many of their names. They serve the renegade mage Galan Dracos and the Queen's warlord, Crynus."

"What of the warlord himself?"

Kaz shrugged. "He is a giant, although whether an ogre or human or something else, only a special few seem to know. He is a master strategist who is willing to take chances, even with himself. His favorite mount—mount . . ." The minotaur stopped speaking, and his eyes widened.

A thin, deadly smile spread across Rennard's face, a frightening sight on that deathlike visage. Rennard turned to Huma. "What I believe he was going to add was that the favored mount of Crynus is a huge black dragon called Charr. Both man and beast are obsessive risk-takers and one-to-one combat is something they relish greatly."

"And . . . and I fought against him." The realization shook Huma. He had faced Crynus himself and lived.

Then, he suddenly thought, so had the warlord. He had been badly wounded, true, but Huma was sure he lived—and somehow Huma knew that the warlord would seek him out. To regain face. To regain honor. To more than balance the score.

To kill him.

"I understand the warlord takes his battles very personally," Rennard added, almost casually. He suddenly urged his horse to a quicker pace and the others followed suit as quickly as they were able. Even then, they did not move fast enough to suit Huma, who suddenly watched the sky nervously.

Chapter 5

If the devastation had looked terrible from above, a close view proved it to be even worse than that. Now, Huma could see with what thoroughness death had swept through this region. Kyre, a once-teeming city near the border with Ergoth, was no more. The fields were scorched. The dead lay scattered like broken toys. Most of the buildings were mere shells, if that much. As the patrol swept around the city's east walls—or what was left of them—the stench of grisly decay rose. Huma prayed he would not lose control, and it gave him no satisfaction that several of the other knights looked sick. Rennard rode on in seeming indifference.

By the end of the day, their horses and their armor were covered with mud. Realizing that they would not reach the main force for hours and knowing of the treacherous paths ahead, Rennard called for a halt at a dry location in the vicinity, along hard-packed earth that had once served as a country road. Behind them, they could make out curls of smoke rising from Kyre. The fires had long gone out, but the smoke refused to die, as if a reminder of the knighthood's failure.

The night passed without incident. Kaz, true to his oath, attempted to stand guard over the young knight all night long, until both Rennard and Huma insisted that the exhausted minotaur take his turn sleeping.

They continued on at first light, Huma and Kaz again riding beside the patrol leader. Huma attempted to draw Rennard into conversation, but the other knight was as taciturn as ever. He would speak when he deemed it necessary, not otherwise.

By noon, they neared the outer fringe of the southern flank. The battle had become nothing more than one great series of skirmishes, as each side tested for weaknesses. The patrol had been fortunate. Had they arrived at another time of day, they might have ridden directly into such a battle.

Some of the knights gave a ragged cheer at the sight of the riders, mistaking them for reinforcements. Morale appeared low, and when the knights recognized Rennard and Huma, the cheers died on their lips.

The camp of the southern flank lay southeast of the ruins of the city. Rennard pulled his mount to a stop. Before the patrol lay a great tent surrounded by Knights of the Sword. The pale knight did not dismount. Instead he summoned the captain of the guard. At the sight of Rennard, the knight in question blanched and quickly saluted.

The deathly face stared down at him. "Who is in charge here?"

"Lord Killian. You will not find him here, though. He has gone out among the men in an attempt to boost spirits." The guard sounded as if he had very little faith in the attempt.

Rennard nodded. "Perhaps you might assist us, then. Where will we find Lord Oswal's command headquarters? When our patrol set out, it was located near here."

Under Rennard's cold gaze, the guard informed them that

command had moved another full day's journey, this time to the northeast. The ever sardonic Kaz muttered something about chasing one's own tail, but a stern look from Huma quieted him. The group was on the move again within seconds.

The lands to the northeast proved to be in much fairer shape. The first living trees came into sight only an hour after the knights had resumed riding. As the minutes passed, more and more trees dotted the landscape. They were short and stubby, for the most part, but they were trees! The mood of the party lightened a little.

Not once during their trek did they lose sight of the two vast armies maneuvering for position among the hills and trees. To the north lay the mountain ranges that marked the boundaries between Solamnia and old Ergoth. The ranges included several heaven-shattering peaks, home to a large colony of fearsome ogres. Those who dared travel through the mountain regions risked their lives and limbs.

Huma's mind wandered as the ride dragged on. What would Lord Oswal say when Huma confronted him? There had always been bad blood between the High Warrior and the Grand Master, and Lord Trake had been none too pleased with his brother's decision to back young Huma. Such a decision could, in the long run, prove disastrous for Lord Oswal. In his position, he stood to lose much influence and power if Huma failed as a knight. The knighthood, for all its vaunted good, was a political organization. Not that this was Huma's true concern. Rather, he wondered what would become of the army if someone other than the High Warrior commanded it. Lord Oswal was the knighthood's most brilliant general.

Rennard called out and pointed to the west. All eyes turned. The already overcast skies were becoming pitch black in the space of moments. The watchers saw the darkness advance like a plague of locusts in a field of grain, and they knew what they viewed—sorcery of the vilest kind. The Queen's minions were once more at work in their attempt to shatter the lines of defense.

Rennard slowed, looked at the others from behind his visor. He stared at Huma and Kaz. "Will the minotaur fight for us if you ask him, Huma?"

Kaz snorted loudly. "Ask me yourself, ghoul!"

The pale knight ignored the jibe as he might ignore the wind in his face. "Will you fight for us?"

Huma felt Rennard's eyes burn into his. "The decision is yours, Kaz."

The bovine face broke out into a savage, toothy grin. "Then I will fight, and gladly, as it will give me a chance to stretch my muscles. Besides, I was outcast from my kind the moment I chose to smite the ogre and run. They would kill me the moment they captured me. With you, I still have a chance to prove that my honor is not dead."

"Then let us add our strength to our brethren." With those words, Rennard spurred his horse. Someone shouted a battle cry. Huma gritted his teeth, hoping that someone would take his grimace as raw determination and not an attempt to quell some of the feelings tearing his body apart.

The creeping darkness came forth to greet them.

* * *

They might as well have been fighting at midnight without a moon. There were screams from the wounded and dying and lusty cries from warriors of both sides. Murky, huge shapes soared through the air. Sometimes they struck at the figures on the ground, but rarely with full strength. The dragonfear had not yet been unleashed. There was too much chaos on the ground; the dragons might very well consume their own allies.

Brilliant flashes of pure power revealed some of the carnage wrought on the field. Mages of white and red contested with the black. Concern for sage limits held the Red and White Robes from victory. Carelessness prevented the Black Robes from the same. Still, there was some effect; the vast inkiness that had come so swiftly now halted its deadly progress and even reversed a little. The Black Robes could not maintain the attacks against their colleagues, and the strength of the dark cloud, for more than a short time.

The sky suddenly was filled with dragons, more than any person possibly could have imagined. They had been gathered, slowly and quietly, just for this moment. As the darkness retreated, they boiled out of the cloud cover. There were far more than those who fought alongside the knights. Red, black, green, blue—the sky was filled with colors of death.

Although outnumbered, the dragons of light rose to face them. They were not enough. The Dragonqueen's children quickly began to penetrate the ranks of the knights. Their ultimate goal lay beyond. They were flooding the hilly regions with their numbers, protecting the ogres and other landbound allies who even now flowed forth in greater numbers from within the hills themselves. Already beset by far too many foes, the sorely beleaguered knights looked to the party of newcomers for respite.

Swords high and lances straight, Rennard's patrol regrouped into charge formation. The dragons racing above them did not faze them. The line would hold.

Huma was among those without a lance, but he knew that his sword would find an opponent soon enough. Eager to break the stalemate, the ogres already were pushing forward. The first wave had chosen to strike even as Huma and his companions had reached the fighting. The hilly ground slowed the warhorses. Huma saw one man go down as his horse lost its footing, and several more stumbled. Then they were striking at the fore of the ogre assault.

Metal flashed all about him, and everyone seemed to be screaming at full pitch. Huma desperately fought off each weapon hurtled at him and struck down several of the ogres while barely realizing it. An ogre face peered into his; it was hairy and savage with long sharp teeth like the minotaur's, and a broad, flat visage with red-rimmed eyes. The ogre's breath was fetid. Huma kicked the attacker away.

Laughter, oddly appropriate because of its ferocity, assailed Huma's ears. Among the combatants, his ax swinging to and fro, the mammoth Kaz was an avenging force of chaos and death. Each swing took its count. Bloodlust glittered in the hulking creature's eyes and then Kaz was lost from sight as more ogres sought the young knight's life.

An ax nicked Huma's leg. The only thing that saved him from losing a limb was that his strike had been first and true. The creature had been dead even as it retaliated. Shock, though, caused Huma to briefly lose control. He nearly dropped his sword and would have been cut down then and there if not for Rennard. The tall knight was cutting through the enemy at a methodical rate. The ogres attempted to flee this killing machine, but Rennard sought them out. Huma stared. At that moment, there seemed little difference between knight and minotaur.

Even so, the charge was insufficient, and it looked as if the knights would be routed. Then more huge forms joined the battle—this time from the Solamnic side. Reinforcements had arrived. The ecstasy was brief. Another ogre hurled itself at Huma.

As abruptly as it had been created, the stygian blackness vanished. Resistance from the Queen's magic-users lessened. The knights pushed forward with renewed hope. Huma saw the ground erupt, and he shivered inwardly as countless enemy warriors were thrown high into the air, only to come crashing down seconds later.

"Huma!"

The voice was Rennard's, and it seemed to be warning him. Huma turned toward the voice as shadow resurged abruptly. Someone grappled with him. Huma succeeded in manuevering his blade between them and thrust it through his adversary's throat.

Huma turned his horse in the murk, seeking out his companions by hearing alone. It proved his undoing, for something heavy flew through the night and struck him soundly on the back of his helm.

He crumpled forward and slipped from his steed.

* * *

Huma had not known death would be so beautiful or kind. She reached forward and mopped his brow, then lifted his head slightly so as to allow him to drink a little water.

The water cleared his head slightly, and he knew that he was not dead. The face above him was not death, but that of a young, beautiful woman with white—no, silver hair. The hair fascinated him so much that he attempted to reach out and touch it. To his surprise, the agony that this simple motion produced was enough to whirl him back into unconsciousness.

* * *

"Are you ever planning to wake up?"

The gruff but concerned voice broke through the haze in Huma's mind. His eyes fluttered open, then shut tightly against the light.

"A little light shouldn't kill you, not after ogres and dragons failed to."

Huma dared to try again, more slowly this time. A tiny amount of light filtered through his eyelashes.

He opened his eyes a little further, and forms began to take shape around him. Chief among those was the ugly, inhuman face of a minotaur.

"Kaz?" His voice frightened him; it was little more than a croak.

"A good guess."

Huma stared at his surroundings. He was in a tent used by the knights for their wounded. Most of the other cots were empty, and the few that were not contained figures deep in sleep—or perhaps deeper than sleep. He shuddered. It brought the pain back.

"What happened to me?"

The bestial face broke into a near-human grin, and Kaz let out a deep chuckle. "What didn't? First, you nearly looked right into the flat of an ax—don't worry, it only creased one side of your head. You slipped and fell and nearly got trampled to death. The good news is that you were unconscious all of the time. It's a wonder you didn't break any bones, friend Huma. You certainly are bruised enough."

"Everything hurts."

"It should. Tell me, are you usually this careless?"

Huma smiled, but the smile, like everything else, proved to be painful.

"He is awake?"

He turned his head quickly toward the melodious voice, forgetting the pain, and gazed on the vision from his dreams. The silverish hair swept around her head. She wore a gown akin to that worn by healers of Mishakal, save that no medallion graced her smooth, ivory-colored neck. The gown did not hide her feminine attributes, and Huma forced himself to look away before embarrassment ruined all.

"Awake, alive, and in less pain than he thought, apparently." The minotaur rose. "I shall leave you in the hands of this healer, Huma. While you have been resting, I have been put to work identifying what I can of my former masters' battleplans."

"They allow you freedom of the camp?" It was an astonishing gesture on the knighthood's part, if true.

Kaz snorted in contempt. "Only as long as I am accompanied by two armed guards. They deigned to allow me to visit you privately."

"You wrong us, Kaz."

The man-beast shook his fearsome head. "No, I may wrong you and a few others, but I do not wrong the knighthood."

Kaz stalked off without another word. Huma watched him leave. The inflammatory words had taken their toll on him. Did the knighthood deserve such scorn? It could not be.

"You have interesting companions."

Huma turned his attention back to the woman. "What?"

She smiled, and there seemed to be only perfection in that smile. Her lips were full and red, and above them, perfectly positioned, was a pert nose and two almond-shaped eyes. The eyes were like sunlight in color, a direct contrast to her glistening mane. Overall, she did not look quite human, and Huma suspected she drew much of her beauty from elven ancestors.

"Are you quite through?" she asked in apparent amusement.

He realized that he had been staring at her in abject fascination. His face reddened, and Huma began to study the ceiling.

"I apologize. I didn't mean to annoy you, milady," he said, reddening more deeply as he stammered slightly.

The smile broadened and became—impossibly—more perfect. "I never said I was annoyed." She took a moist cloth from a bowl near him and began to mop his head. "I am also no 'milady.' Gwyneth will do nicely. It is my name, after all."

He dared to smile back to her. "My name is Huma."

She nodded. "Yes, I know. Both the minotaur and knight who brought you in used your name several times. I'd never seen a minotaur before this one."

"Kaz is a friend." Huma decided to leave it at that. He lacked the energy to explain further. A thought occurred to him. "You said a knight. Do you know which one?"

"I could not forget." A shudder ran through Gwyneth. "He was much like a dead man in form and voice. I felt, though, a certain sadness within him."

Huma had never heard Rennard described quite like that, but he knew that somehow the pale knight had delivered him from the field of death.

"Are you better?"

The pain seemed less now. "Yes. Do I have you to thank for this miracle?"

She blushed. "No, I am only assisting the healers."

Huma attempted to rise and discovered he was still too weak for such a maneuver. He grimaced in pain. Gwyneth eyed him as one might eye a bad child.

"Do not try that again."

"I do not think I could. Did not one of the clerics heal me?"

"There are only a very few of them in camp. You will have to accept what little aid they could give you. Even healers have their limits." Although she still smiled, Gwyneth's tone indicated that she thought the clerics overtaxed.

"Where are we?"

"In part of the westernmost woods of Solamnia. You were unconscious for a day's ride. We are about that far from the front."

"We won?" Huma could not believe that the lines had held.

"No one won. It was the same as always. If not for your group, the ogres might have broken through. Fortunately, they have failed again." She paused, deep in thought, and then resumed in a new vein. "Enough of this war talk. Do you feel like eating something? You've not had food for the last two days."

Huma agreed readily to some nourishment. He was dismayed, though, when Gwyneth began stirring a chalk-colored paste. She looked up, saw his expression, and smiled pleasantly. The spoon came out of the bowl. Gwyneth leaned down to feed some to Huma. He glared at the substance.

"It is not as bad as it looks, Huma. Taste some." Feeling like a child, he gingerly opened his mouth. It was true, he discovered; the paste tasted better than he'd imagined. He forced himself to continue eating, more because he did not want to look foolish in her eyes than because of any desire for such food. Huma was quite pleased when the last of the stuff was gone.

Gwyneth also seemed pleased as she put the bowl away. "I'm sorry to leave you, but I do have other tasks. I'll look in on you from time to time, I promise that."

He reached out a hand to her. "Thank you again."

She hesitated, and Huma dropped the hand out of embarrassment. They were saved any further awkwardness by Rennard's appearance at the tent opening. Gwyneth gathered her things and whisked out of the tent. Huma's eyes watched her leave, then focused on the knight.

"The minotaur said you were awake and recuperating. I was pleased to hear that." The flat level of Rennard's voice made it sound as if he were reading off a supply list, but Huma believed his words. Like Gwyneth, he knew that there was something behind Rennard's perpetual mask of indifference.

Rennard's visor was up. Huma had no trouble now staring into the face that so many turned away from. Rennard's presence here was important. Few other knights cared enough about Huma to visit him.

Rennard kneeled next to him. "Keep your guard up at *all* times, Huma. It is your one failing."

"That and being struck on the head."

The thin lips pursed into a slight smile for only a moment. "Yes. You must put a stop to that as well. It could prove detrimental."

Had he not know better, Huma would have taken the statement as serious. "What goes on? Gwyneth—?"

"The young woman?"

Huma reddened. "Yes—she said that we were back at a

stalemate once more."

Rennard sighed and reached up to remove his helmet. The act revealed frost-colored hair plastered to his head. Rennard was one of the few knights who chose not to sport the long, thick mustaches but rather to go clean-shaven; he was also one of the few who kept his hair cut short well above his collar. No one questioned these decisions; Rennard was Rennard.

"For the moment, that appears to be where things are. Bennett claims this is a sign that victory is ours. He repeats over and over that the big push by Crynus has crumbled. No one has seen or heard of Crynus since your brief battle with him. Bennett has even gone so far as to praise you in his own fashion."

"Praise me?"

"I quote: 'Thanks in part to that one's astounding luck, the warlord Crynus may be dead or at least incapacitated.' "

Huma turned away. Bennett was right, though. He had been lucky. A true knight would have made better use of the opportunity and assured himself of the warlord's destruction.

"I know what you're thinking, Huma. Stop it. You are every part the knight that Bennett and his lapdogs are. More so. You've not lost sight of the true world." Rennard lapsed into an uneasy silence as Huma turned back to him.

"How long before they release me?"

"When you're ready, no sooner. There'll be more than enough waiting for you when you're fit."

"Lord Oswal—does he have anything to say?" Huma felt a tremor of fear. The elder knight was like the father Huma had never known.

Rennard stood up and replaced the helmet on his head. He nodded. "The High Warrior wishes you the best and speediest of recoveries. He says he still has the utmost faith in your abilities."

Which was the High Warrior's way of stating how proud he still was of Huma. It was a rare boost for the young knight's confidence.

"Rest well, Huma. I will attempt to see you when next I'm free."

Rennard departed, leaving Huma to his own thoughts. He wondered whether he would ever truly be a knight such as Bennett, Lord Oswal, or Rennard. He thought of the evil warlord Crynus and wondered if that dark figure would bother to seek personal vengeance on an insignificant person such as Huma.

Something padded softly by the tent where Huma lay. Not a horse, more like a hound. A slight stench wafted to his nostrils. He heard something scrape against the wall, as if to test its strength. The light of the gray day allowed Huma only the vaguest glimpse of something.

A cleric of Mishakel entered the tent to check on the conditions of the wounded. The form on the other side of the wall scurried away, nearly silent despite its sudden movements. The odor quickly dissipated.

"Cleric?"

The mere presence of the elderly cleric soothed Huma. The cleric was short and slightly rounded. There could have been no more than two dozen hairs on his entire head.

"I am Broderin. May I be of assistance to you?"

Huma thought carefully before speaking. "Are—are there any wolves near the camp? Wolves or large dogs?"

Broderin stiffened as if he expected some great beast to come lunging through the tent flaps. Then he regained his composure. "Wolves? Dogs? There may be a few of the latter, but not anywhere near here. As for wolves . . ." The cleric chuckled nervously. "A wolf among the ranks of Paladine's knights? I think not. There are no wolves save those on the other side of the field, my son. Regrettably, most of them are of the intelligent kind. Why do you ask?"

"I thought I saw one."

This sent the old man into another fit of anxiety. Though this voice was more or less steady, his eyes darted hither and yon, as if seeing wolves everywhere. "You must be mistaken, my son, or perhaps you are suffering delusions due to your wounds. Yes, that must be it."

"Are you positive?" It had seemed very real.

"I will have someone take a look around. Perhaps a stray hound escaped from somewhere. It is always possible." The cleric turned to one of the other wounded, indicating that the conversation was at an end as far as he was concerned. Huma watched him momentarily and then closed his eyes.

His sleep was, thankfully, restful and uninterrupted save for one brief dream in which something pale stalked him through an endless forest. The stalker was always just out of sight and just behind him.

As with most dreams and nightmares, he did not remember it upon waking.

Chapter 6

Huma stepped outside the tent to view the camp for the first time. He did not know his exact location, but he could see that command had moved once again, nearer the border, apparently. This close to Ergoth, the land was dotted more regularly with trees—healthy ones. For reasons that could only be guessed at, the ogres had been more careful about avoiding the destruction of the landscape nearer the mountains. It could hardly have been due to the beauty of the land; as far as anyone knew, the ogres were not the most appreciative of races when it came to beauty. In some areas there was actual forest—tall, ageless trees that perhaps remembered quieter times, perhaps had even seen the first elves.

Huma estimated that two to three hundred knights were

encamped in the general area. The men stationed here were a mixture, consisting of the personal guard of Lord Oswal, wounded knights in various stages of recovery, a few outriders who were assisting the knighthood with their knowledge of the region, and even a few mages to add to the clerics. The mages and clerics remained as far apart as possible. Mages distrusted most clerics as religious zealots, while the clerics, albeit more tolerant, still did not trust the independent ways of the magic-users, who concentrated more on power than on belief in the gods.

No one really trusted the mages. That was why they were not allowed to carry arms. That left them vulnerable in at least one way.

"How are you feeling today?"

Huma's face lit up briefly, but he quickly masked it with an expression of brave seriousness. Gwyneth, a bucket in one hand, came over to him. Despite his best attempts, Huma could not help smiling.

"I am sick and tired of that tent and more than happy to see the world, even if it is just the camp."

She laughed gaily, then suddenly became serious. "Will you be going soon?"

He nodded gravely. Rennard had been to see him several times. Huma knew he was checking up on the young knight for Lord Oswal. If Huma hoped to keep his self-respect before the High Warrior, he would have to assure his readiness as soon as possible.

The wind picked up and blew some of the long, thick locks into Gwyneth's face. She brushed back the hair and appeared to be about to say something when a familiar, hulking figure came into view, escorted by two Knights of the Sword.

"Huma!"

Kaz came up and attempted to greet his one true human friend with a hug that would have sent Huma back to the tent with three or four broken ribs. Huma succeeded in sidestepping the minotaur and, therefore, ended up with only a bruised shoulder where Kaz slapped him in pleasure. It had been four days since Huma had laid eyes on Kaz. As Lord Oswal's trust in the minotaur increased, the latter's counsel was becoming more and more important. The knighthood had been battling the ogres for years but knew very little about them. Kaz, raised under the oppression of his cousins, knew all too well.

"Gwyneth," Huma said, remembering the woman, but turned toward her too late. She had vanished.

The minotaur was more perceptive than his appearance would indicate. "Have I come at an inopportune time? You have my apologies, if I have intruded."

Huma waved off the apology. "I should apologize to you. It is good to see you, Kaz."

"I had no idea that your kind could ask so many questions—and over and over! I have been drained of all knowledge, yet still they press for more."

"They're desperate, Kaz. We want to break—" Huma cut off as a tall figure, clad in crimson robes and cowl, made his way past them with no acknowledgment whatsoever. The face was narrow and bony, and the man reminded Huma of a fearsome instructor he had once had during his early days as a squire.

The minotaur's eyes followed the red-robed figure. "The mages are extremely nervous. I can smell their fear. It sickens me on occasion."

Huma found he had to favor his left side a little. He was not yet fully recovered. "What frightens them?"

"The unknown. They are quite accustomed to dealing with their black-robed counterparts, but it is rumored that Galan Dracos has unleashed his fellow renegades. You saw part of the magical battle?"

"Who could not? It fairly covered the heavens."

"There were a dozen powerful mages on our side when we entered. Four of those died, and another may never regain full use of his mind and body. Do you know how many opposed them?"

"How many?"

"Three."

"Three?" The knight shook his head. "They must have been powerful, but how do the mages know they were not black-robed sorcerers?"

Kaz smile knowingly. "Two were Black Robes, so they

say. The survivor, who escaped, was not. His powers were too wild and unpredictable for one brought up under the tutelage of the three orders. A renegade. More than that, they would not say."

Huma could not help but think of Magius, whose tall body and handsome features would have been more at home in a royal court then in the dank, secluded towers of the spellcasters. Even up to the time of his Test of Sorcery, Huma's childhood companion had been a maverick. His skills were such that he had long before surpassed his instructors. Magius always had been one to experiment, even when his life was put into danger. But at times, he had talked of abandoning his schooling.

Kaz was summoned once again and, with a groan, he bid his farewell. Huma returned to the tent and slept for the better part of the day. Rennard stopped by to inform Huma that fully recovered or not, the younger knight was to be ready for guard duty within the next day or so. Huma might have complained, but he was more than happy to be given another chance to prove himself.

Gwyneth also stopped by, but the conversation was short and served little purpose. She seemed to want to say something, but whatever it was, was unspoken. He did not see her again during his recovery.

* * *

On the day that Huma was to receive his first duties since being nearly trampled to death, the camp became a flurry of activity. Columns of knights rode past the command center, a massive tent topped by a banner bearing the kingfisher symbol and guarded continuously by a contingent of Knights of the Rose. Here was where Lord Oswal and his officers planned their strategy. Huma could only guess at the reason for all the movement. Rumors abounded that the mountainous eastern border had fallen to the ogres and that the creatures were making their way toward Vingaard Keep. Another rumor warned that plague had struck one of the towns which the knights had been using as a waystation. Huma took the rumors for what they were—fearful wondering.

When Rennard approached, Huma was assisting the clerics, carrying hot and cold water for them and bringing them food. It was not much, but it helped. It also kept Huma's mind from straying to more unpleasant matters.

Huma stood erect when the other knight appeared. The act almost drenched Rennard with freshly boiled water as the buckets went swinging to and fro. The blank features twitched, but whatever emotion that indicated was lost on Huma.

"I see that you are more than fit enough to resume your duties as a knight," Rennard said gravely.

The hard work had made Huma sweat profusely, and moisture had accumulated around his brow. His face was grimy, and his clothing was stained. He did not dare speak, not knowing what he might say, so he merely nodded.

Rennard folded his arms. "You are captain of the guard tonight. Lord Oswal thinks you're ready for such responsibility." He looked up and down Huma's form without a change in expression.

It was already near dark. Huma swallowed. "May I be permitted to clean up and suit myself?"

"By all means. I've already assigned the watches. When you're ready, come see me." Rennard unfolded his arms and walked off. Salutes had always been unnecessary with him. Besides, saluting was difficult with a bucket in each hand.

* * *

Huma had feared that some knights would resist his appointment as captain of the guard. Such was not the case. The guard consisted of knights who either were unfamiliar with their captain or were too new to have been influenced by Bennett and his associates. This was not to say they were green, untried knights; no squire who passed into the ranks of knighthood was untried.

A few veterans were mixed in for safety's sake, but these men were loyal to Lord Oswal and would judge men on merit, not on birth.

One such veteran snapped to attention as Huma passed. Huma felt uncomfortable at commanding men twice his age and ten times his experience, but he knew that every knight, save the commanding officers, was required to stand guard duty now and then. Nevertheless, Huma felt a tremor of nervousness as he took the report from the older sentry and breathed easily only when he was on his way to the next. It did not matter whether that man would be less experienced than the first; commanding was what frightened Huma. If something should go wrong, he would be to blame.

The perimeter of the camp took him to the edge of the forest region, and Huma eyed this area with some trepidation. Anything could be hiding out there, and it was not hard to imagine eyes and flitting, shadowy figures everywhere he looked.

It was not until after midnight that he came across the vacant position.

The slope of the land kept the position from view until he was almost on top of it. Huma stood there a moment, transfixed by the realization. He could have assigned someone else the task of checking on the sentries, but as his first command, he had wanted to do it himself. He should call out for assistance or run back to warn Lord Oswal and the others, but he knew that either option would take too much time and would alert whoever—or whatever—was out there.

Sword drawn, Huma stepped into the dark woods. By rights, he knew he might be bringing trouble down upon himself, but some mesmerizing presence within the forest seemed to draw him in. He could not see it, but he felt its power. Helpless, he plunged deeper into the woods, the urge a part of him now. He had forgotten his real reasons for daring to enter, save that someone or something that he was determined to locate lurked within.

A shadow padded alongside Huma, red but sightless eyes locked on his presence. Another shadow stalked the knight from his other side. Huma saw neither, heard neither—and would not have, even if all his faculties had been intact. It took great willpower to see the night beasts when they stalked the forests.

A flickering pattern of glittering lights danced before the entranced knight. Most of the gleams fluttered away at his approach, but two remained fixed, staring at him. Huma stumbled toward them, mindless of the still, armored form he had nearly tripped over. The gleaming orbs beckoned, and a dark shade seemed to materialize about them.

For the first time, a voice broke the silence. It was little more than a hiss, but it demanded all of Huma's attention.

"Brave knight. So secure with your little toys."

The form shifted to the side a little. Huma's eyes followed obediently. The shadowy figure seemed to examine its catch. "Could you be the one, I wonder?"

A leathery hand reached up to take hold of Huma's chin. His head was turned left and right, although the knight's eyes never left those of his captor. "Yesssss. Dracos will be pleased—even the warlord will be pleased. It cannot be coincidence. He has had his hand in this to save his own neck." The eyes and hand traced a downward path to Huma's sword. "There will be no need of this anymore."

A gleam far behind the shadowy figure suddenly pulled Huma's gaze away. His captor, caught up in the capture, failed to notice the odd light. Others, though, marked the action. There were gutteral growls, and the stench of death became strong.

The gaze of the creature returned quickly to the face of its captive.

Two pairs of eyes met. Huma's were no longer entranced.

The knight reacted instinctively. The sword was driven with a strength born of shock and fear. The physical form of the dark figure proved to give little resistance. Claws scratched wildly at Huma's face, but he ignored them, attempting to thrust his weapon as far as it would go. Suddenly, he met resistance, although the shadowy foe did not fall. The clawing finally stopped, however. The figure shuddered twice and was still.

Huma slumped to his knees, exhausted by the effort.

Things of the dark padded toward him for a moment, then hesitated, as if sensing something unexpected. Huma raised his head and caught a glimpse of something pale and vaguely wolflike in form. Then it was gone.

How long Huma stayed there, he did not know. Gradually, he came to notice the soft footfalls of someone walking in his direction. They were coming from the wrong direction—from deeper within the forest. Huma rose, albeit a little unsteadily. He had not recovered completely, he realized.

"Here, let me help you." The voice was strong, and the hands that held Huma were powerful. While the knight took a deep breath, the newcomer looked over the remains of the attacker, chuckled, and said, "Well done. You've pinned him to the tree trunk. An impressive display of strength and quite deserving where that one was concerned."

"Who—?"

"Save your breath for walking. You've gone deeper into the forest than you think."

As they walked, Huma dared to cast a wary eye toward the newcomer. He was tall, this stranger, and clad in extravagant, well-made clothing. Elegant gold locks of hair gave him the look of a regal lion. The stranger's countenance was less visible, but Huma received the impression of a handsome, almost pretty face, one well at home in the royal courts, perhaps flirting with young, well-to-do maidens. There was a familiarity to it, too. Someone he had not seen in years. . . .

"Magius!" Huma blurted out the name in shock.

They stopped. The newcomer released him. They stared at one another, and the knight noticed that the other seemed to glow from within.

"Huma. It's good to see you, even under the circumstances. I wondered how long I might—if you'll pardon the expression—keep you in the dark."

"You're alive!" Huma had never been sure what happened after that test in the tower. "You're alive!" he repeated in wonder.

The face of Magius was visible, even in the dark. His mouth twisted into a rueful smile. "Yes. I apologize."

The smile on Huma's face crumbled, and he asked, "Apologize? Why should you apologize?"

"Do you think I was out here by pure coincidence, Huma? I hope not. It was because of me that your life was placed in jeopardy."

"I don't understand." The thought of danger made Huma reach for his sword. As his hand touched empty air, he remembered what had become of his weapon. He turned. "My sword! I have to go—"

"No!" The mage's voice was loud and commanding. "We should not stay out here alone any longer than we need to. Go back when you have men at your back. The dreadwolves may have fled, but I could be wrong. It would not be the first time. The gods know, it would not be the first time."

Magius urged him back toward the camp, and Huma saw the wisdom. He would, however, get some answers.

"What was that back there? What did you mean earlier?"

Some of the magnificence of his old friend seemed to evaporate. Magius was suddenly an older man than Huma, although both were the same age. The mage did not look directly at the knight. "I think you had better ask one of the Red Robes back at camp. He should be able to give you the official version."

"Are you in some kind of trouble?"

"Trouble of the sort which I will be sure to lead away from you now. I was a fool to even think of coming to you."

The glow of dim fires was the first evidence that the camp was near. Huma heard the sounds of men in action. Someone had noticed the absence of the two knights—one the captain of the guard, no less.

Magius also heard the activity. He stopped abruptly. "Whatever you hear, I have not changed, Huma." The mage grabbed his dearest friend by the shoulders. "Believe me! If the test did anything, it proved that!"

The glow that had surrounded the magic-user so pompously suddenly vanished, but not before Huma caught sight of the fear in his friend's face. Not just fear for himself, but fear for Huma as well.

"Listen." The shadows covered the mage's face now, giving him an unearthly aspect. "The creatures won't bother you any longer. It's me their masters are after. They sent them after me once they learned I was gone."

With a chill, Huma said, "You're running from the Dragonqueen's creatures."

Something snapped a dried branch. Both men froze. Huma studied what he could of the forest but saw nothing.

Magius leaned close and whispered. "I must leave. You know me, Huma. You know what I am capable of. Believe in that. If things take a turn, either good or bad, I will contact you."

Tall, dark shapes became visible between the trees. Magius glared at them and whirled away. Huma opened his mouth to speak but realized that would be dangerous folly. He prayed Magius had been right in leaving Huma's sword at the tree, pinning the abomination to the trunk.

Summoning up his courage, Huma resumed the trek back to camp, praying as he walked that the first thing he met would be a fellow knight and not something out of a mage's nightmare.

* * *

As it happened, he met the searchers only minutes from the site where the sentry had disappeared. Huma felt guilty about forgetting the hapless sentry, one who had been even less experienced than he. There was nothing Huma could do for the man, though, and he knew he should be more concerned with what might very well still be lurking outside the camp, and what that might mean. If the enemy had infiltrated this far past the line . . .

Rennard took his report, none too surprised, it seemed, that it was Huma who had stumbled upon trouble. News of the attacker, who could have been only a mage, did trouble him, although no emotions were evident in his mien. A party that included Huma and Rennard returned to the spot where Huma had been led. The lifeless form of the sentry showed no marks, as if the unfortunate man had merely fallen to the ground, dead. Rennard spat, and in an unprecedented display of emotion, cursed all mages in general. Huma cringed. He had left out all mention of Magius, though it went against the Measure and the Oath. How honorable was a knight who lied?

Magius, though, was his friend.

Seen with clear eyes, the shadowy attacker proved to be all too solid. Rennard removed the sword from the tree and let the mage's body fall. Much to his own surprise, Huma reached down and pushed the cowl back from the face.

Even in the dark, the face repelled. Only Rennard seemed untouched by the evil stamped on it.

Human the mage might have been, but he looked more like a reptile. His skin was dark and scaly, and it glittered in the light of the torches. The eyes were narrow slits, and the nose was nearly nonexistent. Huma noted teeth that would have put the minotaur's to shame. More than one knight called on Paladine.

The corpse was muffled within a thick, coarse robe of brown cloth. Rennard fingered it, then released it as he would a viper. "He does not wear the black of the Dragonqueen." He pointed to a pair of knights. "Take this thing back to the camp. I want to see what the spellcasters have to say. The rest of you, fan out. Make sure he left no surprises behind. Huma, you stay with me."

They watched the others depart, and then Rennard swung around and glared at Huma with such anger that its very appearance on the otherwise bland face made the younger knight step back.

"Who was the other?"

"There was no one."

"There was another." A chill followed his words. "I know. I see no reason why you would seek to hide the presence of a mage, unless . . ." He stared intently into Huma's eyes. Huma met the gaze and battled with it. Surprisingly, it was Rennard who was forced to turn away.

It was a hollow triumph. "Obvious. For such effort, I can think of only one you would protect—but why would Magius be out here?"

"I didn't—" Huma could think of nothing to say. How did Rennard even know about his childhood friend?

"You are a fool, Huma. A brave, competent knight, but you have too much humanity in you, too much trust in others. A mage, especially. You cannot trust mages. They will always turn on you. They are treacherous."

Despite his respect for Rennard, Huma stiffened at this insult. "Magius is none of those things. We grew up together. He would not betray what he believed in."

Rennard shook his head sadly. "You will not understand until it is too late." Then, as if all had been said that could be said, Rennard dropped the subject. "Come. We'd best return to camp. I think this is something Lord Oswal should hear about."

The pale warrior returned the sword to Huma. Without waiting to see if Huma followed, Rennard began walking. Huma hurried after him, wondering what the other knight would report and what Huma himself would say, knowing all too well that one of those who listened would already know he had lied.

What would the Oath and Measure demand?

Chapter 7

ONCE THERE HAD BEEN AN INSTRUCTOR, GARIG, WHO WAS determined that the young squire Huma would fail the preparations for knighthood. Garig was a beast of a man who more resembled a bear in face and form. Some wondered that he was a knight at all, brutal as he could be. As a matter of fact, Garig intended to wear Huma down inside of a month.

Huma had stayed, though. Stayed, learned, and excelled, though Garig frightened him immensely. Lord Oswal, the High Warrior, had encouraged him. Like Rennard, Lord Oswal had seen something in Huma that he was determined to cultivate, despite the boy's dubious bloodline. At last, the squire stood up to the overwhelming instructor and defeated him soundly in what could only loosely be called a mock combat. That was a victory as much over fear as over Garig.

Now, Huma was afraid again as he stepped into the presence of the man who had helped him overcome that earlier hurdle.

The High Warrior was dressed and fully awake. Huma marveled—as did many others—that the elder knight never seemed to rest. The commander of the military expedition sat on a plain wooden stool that contrasted sharply with his elaborate uniform. His helmet lay on the table beside him, and more than a dozen charts lay scattered on the same table. Huma felt as if the helmet, too, were inspecting him, somehow.

Only two other knights were in the room. One was a shorter, round man whose very appearance belied the strength and intelligence within. Very little hair graced his head, save for a small goatee and a few wisps in the back. Arak Hawkeye was not a man of much humor. His latter name had come from his precision as a bowman. Even the nomadic tribes of the southern regions knew of Hawkeye. He could outride and outshoot any of them. It was his personal goal to teach a band of knights to ride and shoot much in the manner of the plainsmen. He wore crests representing the Order of the Crown, of which he was ranking commander for this campaign.

Between them, and only barely noticing the young knight, stood Bennett, son of the Grand Master, nephew of the High Warrior, and the representative of the Order of the Sword. Bennett's presence here unnerved Huma the most. The personification of knighthood, Bennett could recite every line of every volume of the bylaws put down by Vinas Solamnus so long ago. He lived by them, which was why Huma had been able to remain in the order so far. Despite his influence, Bennett would do nothing that went strictly against the Oath or the Measure. When charges concerning Huma's parentage had failed to oust the new knight, Bennett did not turn to more unsavory methods, as some, even in the knighthood, would have done. Instead, the Grand Master's son treated him as a necessary evil, to be ignored whenever possible. Influential as Bennett was, Huma found it difficult to make any friends as time went on.

Bennett was much like his father and his uncle in appearance, though he was definitely more like the former. Those who had known Lord Trake in his younger days swore that there was no difference between sire and offspring. Both had the same hawkish features, the look of a bird of prey. The House of Baxtrey was of the oldest royal blood. The same features could be found on many of the nobles of the Empire of Ergoth. As Bennett turned away, his mind supposedly on the business at hand, Huma's eyes briefly met his. The glance was cold.

"You may leave or stay as is your desire, Rennard."

Rennard stiffened. "I will stay, if it pleases the High Warrior."

It did not please Bennett, that was obvious. Trake's son hated Rennard almost as much as he hated Huma, but for different reasons. Only one person other than Lord Oswal could defeat the Grand Master's offspring in mock combat. Soundly, too. For someone like Bennett, who prided himself on perfection, it was almost intolerable. These two rivals stared openly at one another now, Rennard with as much regard as he would give a blade of grass.

Lord Oswal turned to Huma. "Normally, Lord Arak would take your report, but seeing as we are dealing with situations that change from one minute to the next, I would like us all to hear it immediately. Both Arak and Bennett have agreed to this." Bennett glanced at his uncle and then away again. "If you would begin, then?"

"Milord." Huma cleared the lump from his throat. After the first few words, his uneasiness fell away and he poured out the details of the attack in crisp, precise sentences. The three commanders listened carefully. Huma did not omit the presence of Magius, though he did leave out most of their conversation.

When he was done, he stood there silently, his eyes staring straight ahead at nothing, his body at full attention. The Lord Knights turned to one another and discussed some of the points. They whispered, preventing Huma from knowing what had caught their attention.

Lord Hawkeye stepped away from the other two and

turned to Rennard. "Knight Rennard, have you anything to add?"

"Only that I have men searching the woods for any sign of infestation and that I appointed a new captain of the guard in Huma's absence."

The urge to react was nearly overwhelming, but Huma's training enabled him to resist. Rennard had stood by him.

"I see," said Lord Oswal. "That will be all, then. Knight Huma, it is my recommendation to Lord Arak Hawkeye that you be allowed a second chance. It is obvious that you were pitted against magic of exceptional magnitude and that your leaving the camp without giving warning was due to this."

Bennett's stare was deathly, but Huma was too relieved to care.

"Thank you, milord—milords."

The High Warrior waved a hand. "You two are dismissed."

Lord Hawkeye added, "Knights Huma and Rennard, you are both relieved from duty for the night. Get some rest."

Rennard merely nodded as if he had known all along how the meeting would turn out. They left as the three commanders turned to one another. Bennett's voice was rising in anger. He apparently felt that the Measure demanded far greater punishment for what was to him an obvious act of deadly thoughtlessness. Both Huma and Rennard, however, were out of hearing range before any reply was made.

"That went well," Rennard added casually.

Huma could not look at him. "Thank you, Rennard."

"For what? That? Someone must save you from yourself. Besides, I would not give Bennett the satisfaction. Not even for the Oath. Or the Measure."

His words left Huma hanging. Rennard lived by a code of his own, it seemed.

They walked in silence the rest of the way.

A great bronze tower loomed before Huma. It hung on the edge of nothingness, and that nothingness was known as the Abyss. The tower, though metal, was crumbling from great age.

Huma felt himself drawn unwillingly toward the single gate of that tower. Things that should have been dead offered to lead the way. Lepers gave lipless smiles. A plague victim, once a woman, reached out to take his hand. With a convulsion of horror, he saw that it was his mother. Huma cringed, and she vanished.

The mold-enshrouded gate descended for him. From within, a hand beckoned him forward. A tall figure awaited, dressed in tattered clothes with a rusting crown upon—its head? There was no face beneath that crown, only two red orbs in a sea of infinity.

Behind him, the gate closed silently.

Huma awoke sweating. The camp had not risen yet, although the knights would be stirring soon. Huma was thankful for that. After the dream, he had no great desire to return to his slumbers.

Such vivid dreams had never plagued him before. There were those who said such dreams held significance, although what this one meant was beyond Huma. Not that he did not recognize the bronze tower and the evil that dwelled within it. It was a vivid page from his education, when a cleric of Paladine had introduced him to the gods who would throw down light. The name by which this particular evil went was Morgion, and he thrived on decay of the world.

If ever a god had profited by this endless war, it was Morgion. Decay was everywhere, even in those cities untouched by the war itself—and if not physical decay, moral decay, as in the jaded city of the Ergothian emperor himself, a man who, it was rumored, was so pampered he did not even know there was a war on.

If decay was rampant, disease had become a natural way of life. Huma hugged himself at the memory of his mother. Her death by plague had changed everything. Alone, he heard the calling of his father, the man he had never known but who controlled his very existence. The price, though . . .

Shaking off the dream, he rose and readied himself for the day ahead. Rennard had promised to speak with Lord Hawkeye about increased command for Huma. The incident concerning Magius was forgotten as far as the gaunt knight was concerned. There were more important things to attend to.

A muffled groan made him look down. Kaz, waking from the noise, blinked and revealed two blurry eyes. The expression was so much like that of a farm animal awakening that Huma could not suppress a brief smile.

The minotaur settled back down to sleep. As of yet, Kaz knew nothing of the night's events. Satisfied that they had finally drained him of all information possible, the commanding knights had finally allowed the minotaur a decent night's sleep.

Yawning, Huma gazed out beyond the fringe of the camp to where the first glint of dawn was revealing itself between the trees.

His eyes locked in gaze with the sightless orbs of what could only be the creature Magius had called a dreadwolf.

In some past time, it might have been a true wolf. The general body structure conformed, but it was as if some perverse necromancer had raised it from the dead and only partially succeeded. Not one hair graced its bone-white body. There did not even seem to be skin. It was like the ghost of some animal killed and skinned by a hunter. Although it was a good twenty feet away, Huma could smell the odor of the night before. The stench of decay. Of death.

It knew he was there. Despite the obvious sightlessness of its eyes, it sensed him, knew him. Behind the dead eyes was a cold, evil intelligence that seemed to mock the knight.

Without taking his eyes from it, Huma leaned toward the minotaur. "Kaz."

He felt Kaz stiffen. A husky whisper came back to him. "Huma?"

"Roll over. Look beyond me."

The minotaur did so. The eyes opened—barely—and at first Kaz did not see it, as blurry-eyed with sleep as he was. Only when he dared to open them farther did Kaz notice the horrid creature. The stench filled the minotaur's nose.

"By my ancestors," Kaz hissed. "A dreadwolf, Huma!"

"I know." The minotaur knew of them, then. What was the wolf creature doing here? the knight wondered. Magius had said they would leave when they discovered him gone. Why was the foul creature still here, and daring the dawn as well? How had it made its way past the sentries?

The dreadwolf continued to stare at Huma with its dead eyes. It was here for him, there was no doubt about it. It was, he realized, a messenger of some sort.

"I must go closer."

Kaz rose quickly, ax in hand. The creature, though, scarcely glanced at Huma's unusual companion. It seemed to grow more eager as Huma took a couple of tentative steps toward it.

"Huma, no!" Kaz was speaking loudly now. That no sentry came running disturbed Huma. Was the beast's master so powerful that he could lock an entire camp into slumber?

Huma shrugged off the minotaur's hand and moved even closer to the dreadwolf. The tail of the abomination wagged back and forth in a lazy motion. It opened its jaws and Huma now could make out the rotting, yellow teeth still sharp enough to tear the flesh from his arm. The dreadwolf licked its jaws, and the mouth settled into what Huma feared was a knowing grin.

When the knight had dared to step within ten feet of it, the creature opened its maw again. What came out startled Huma so much, he was almost ready to turn and run.

"Huuuuumaaaaa . . ."

Behind him, Kaz swore an oath. Huma steadied himself. His sword was out, but he did not know how much good it would do against an unliving thing like this.

"Huma." His name came more clearly now, and it was followed by dark laughter.

"Who are you? What do you want?"

The dreadwolf seemed to contemplate him before it spoke again. When it did, the amusement was more than obvious. "You gave us a merry chase, Knight of Solamnia. Cost us a valuable servant, too. We think you be as great a danger as your treacherous friend, Magius."

"Magius." Huma showed no reaction to the foul creature. Did they have Magius?

"We know where he is now. He will learn what it is to betray Galan Dracos."

Galan Dracos. Leader of the renegades, Servant of the Dark Queen. Huma knew the name and knew the evil behind it.

As if in contempt, the dreadwolf sat on its haunches. Huma wondered briefly whether it had any reasoning of its own or whether it was merely a puppet of a controlling force.

"Crynus was very taken with you after that brief clash. He was very near to capturing your friend when you happened along. No surprise when we realized who you were. Your good friend Magius used you as a decoy, young knight. Did you realize that?"

Heavy footsteps beside Huma told him that Kaz had moved closer. The dreadwolf turned its sightless eyes toward the minotaur briefly and then ignored him, resuming its speech.

"It was the desire of Crynus to pluck you from the camp personally and remove you to his citadel, there to battle with you at his leisure."

Huma's throat felt dry. "I was lucky."

"Luck is a skill. Were you to live much longer, you might learn that."

Both knight and minotaur tensed. Each expected the forest to overflow suddenly with the ghoulish forms of countless dreadwolves. Nothing materialized, and the single creature mocked them again with its nearly human smile.

"You have nothing to fear from me. No, if anything, you should fear yourself, Knight of the Crown. At the moment, you are your own worst enemy."

With another laugh, the dreadwolf sprang to its feet. Kaz swung at it, but the creature merely spun around and sprinted off into the woods. Both knew there was no following.

"What was that all about?" the minotaur wondered.

"He came to mock me, it seems." Huma sheathed his sword. "But why would Crynus even bother with someone like me?"

"Perhaps he is more interested in this friend of yours. Perhaps this friend is not so close to capture, and this is merely some ploy. Who is this Magius?"

Huma briefly related the details of the night's incident.

The minotaur's face darkened as he realized all this had happened while he slept. As Huma finished, some of the other knights began to stir.

"What should I do?"

Kaz shook his head. "I know what I might do, but your ways are not mine, Knight of Solamnia. I suggest you try the walking corpse. He seems to be your ally."

Kaz was right, Huma decided. Maybe Rennard could explain the words of Galan Dracos.

Suddenly a great wind picked up and several huge shapes seemed to materialize out of the sky itself. All around the camp, knights were looking up into the sky at a sight that could only inspire them. Majestic, winged creatures circled the camp several times; gold, silver, bronze, copper, the dragons were magnificent in their glory. A few brass dragons flew alongside, but only a few. They much preferred the heat of the deserts.

Huma estimated some thirty to forty of the creatures, quite a massive force, especially if organized. That was the one advantage they had over their dark cousins; the dragons of Takhisis were apt to fight among themselves, sometimes even in battle. The dragons of light were always quick to take advantage of such incidents.

With the coming of the dragons, Huma momentarily forgot his fears. The presence of dragons always filled him with an almost childlike delight. He began to hurry to where they were landing, ignoring the shouts of Kaz, who had no desire to confront dragons so soon again.

Huma was not the only one running. Even the veterans came rushing, for a visit by the dragons often meant news of great importance.

When Huma arrived at the place of landing, he saw that the three commanders of the army were already engaged in conversation with an immense dragon of gold. Despite its massiveness, the dragon spoke in quiet, almost scholarly tones. The creature's news must have proved troubling, though, for Huma noted the dark look on Lord Oswal's face.

Huma spotted Rennard. The knight seemed even more pale than usual and looked surprised when Huma called to him.

"What news, Rennard?"

"The eastern forces are in retreat."

The tonelessness of Rennard's voice caused Huma to miss the magnitude of the gaunt knight's statement. When realization did hit, Huma could only stand and gape before finally drawing enough breath to spit out the same words he had just heard. He repeated them once more, then shook his head.

"It's not possible! The knighthood has never suffered such a defeat!"

"It has now."

They were forced to wait while the commanders and the gold dragon continued their discussion. Kaz stepped up next to Huma, the look on the minotaur's face indicating that he had heard the news. The young knight wondered how the mammoth easterner felt. Still, the minotaur could not return to the enemy after killing one of his commanders.

As if reading his thoughts, Kaz looked down. "I have not regretted my act, Huma. I chose to strike down the ogre, and I would do so again. Besides, there is no true home for me among my people now. To them, I would be a coward and a weakling for showing pity to the helpless."

Most of the other dragons had landed by this time. Huma noticed one silver dragon that, if possible, seemed familiar. He was about to discard that as a ridiculous notion when the dragon turned in his direction and nodded. It was the same creature that had carried them to safety, the same dragon that had confronted the deadly black beast upon which had sat the warlord, Crynus, himself.

A horn sounded from the direction of the front, a single mournful wail that died a slow death, as if he who blew the horn had lost all hope. As well he might have.

The blackness once more was spreading across the heavens. Within minutes, it would overwhelm the first lines of the knights. Only the gods knew what would happen within its range.

Bennett and Arak Hawkeye cursed loudly, while Lord Oswal now truly looked like an old man. His shoulders sagged, and he was forced to turn away from the dragon.

The leviathan said nothing, but sympathy was evident.

"Milord!" Bennett was now shouting. A wind was picking up rather quickly. Some of the dragons beat their wings nervously, sensing, perhaps, the sinister powers summoned to conjure this new threat.

Lord Oswal seemed to recover at the sound of his nephew's voice. Wasting no more time, he ordered the men to prepare for battle and lie in the nearest hollow. The camp would be left at the mercies of the wind. Now was not a time for tidiness. Now was life or death.

Lowering his visor, Rennard shouted, "It was a ploy, our defeat of that other darkness. I'll wager that the mages will find themselves up against even greater odds when they attempt to push it back, and I'll wager they lose."

The wind forcing his breath back into his lungs, Huma followed the other knight's example and lowered his visor. He gasped for air. Kaz, beside him, was forced to tolerate everything. Huma knew that the minotaurs sailed the roughest seas with relative ease, but still, Kaz had his hands over his face and he had fallen to one knee.

Even so, the wind continued to grow.

Loose equipment was beginning to blow away. The horses snorted wildly as a tent was torn from its stakes and tossed among them. Huma rushed over and pulled it free of the beasts. Unable to maintain his hold on the tent, Huma watched it go whirling away into the woods.

The entire area became a deathtrap of a hundred assorted forms. The campfires were blown high and wild by the wind, and some tents burst into flames.

Kaz was forced to cover his eyes lest he be blinded by the dust rising from the earth. "Sargas forgive me! It's the king of all hurricanes, but on land!"

Indeed, the minotaur's words seemed to ring true. No tornado or storm that Huma had ever witnessed contained the power to cause such destruction. Trees were bending perilously close to the ground. A little more pressure and they would be torn from the earth and flung skyward, and there appeared to be no letup in the raging darkness. It was only a matter of time.

Huma battled to maintain some sort of balance. How

much more terrible was it out there at the front? Only the single horn blast had given them any warning. Crynus had planned well. Galan Dracos had planned well.

Suddenly, calm reigned. The wind died to near-nothing and refuse rained upon the ground. Kaz stood, and Huma opened his visor to get a better view.

"The spellcasters! They've done it." They were there, far to his left.

There were twelve in all, six of the Red Robes, six of the White. Even from his position, Huma could see the strain they were under. This was not the storm of the other day. That had been only a pale illusion, perhaps a test, or even a trick. Whatever the case, these mages were now dealing with a power far, far stronger than they had anticipated.

One of the Red Robes fell, exhausted.

A breeze developed.

A horseman cut off Huma's view. Huma looked up to see Bennett, fully in charge of himself and the situation, despite all the confusion. At the moment, with his hawkish, regal face and his intricately decorated armor, he might have been one of those who had ridden with Vinas Solamnus.

Bennett scanned the area, then turned his gaze to the younger knight. "Get the horses. If we don't release them, they'll be killed when the magic-users fall."

As he spoke, another Red Robe wavered and then stumbled. The breeze increased to a squall.

"We're pulling back!" The wind forced Bennett to yell. We must not rout, though! If we do, nothing stands between the Queen's jackals and Vingaard Keep! Nothing!"

The ten remaining mages could no longer keep a unified effort. Several collapsed, and the few left standing were insufficient for the task. What kind of power were they up against?

The sudden earth-shaking gale nearly threw Huma and Kaz to the ground. Bennett was only barely able to keep his horse under control. The warhorse was used to blood and steel, not wind so strong that it nearly swept the rider from the animal's back. The steed's natural instincts were to run for cover.

Bennett shouted something unintelligible and then raced

off. Huma, remembering his earlier instructions, half-crawled toward where the horses screamed their protests. Kaz followed. His balance restored, he now moved more easily than the knight, thanks to his bulk.

Releasing the warhorses proved to be difficult. They had been worked up to a frenzy and regarded any moving object as a threat. The nearest kicked at Huma, and others snapped at his arm. Despite the danger, Huma had to get closer if he was to release them.

As he drew near, iron-shod hooves came down on him, and only because a heavy form bowled him over did he escape crippling punishment. One hoof struck his right arm, a glancing blow but still sufficient to numb it.

Huma struggled up and undid the reins. He had hoped to calm a few of the animals and possibly ride one to safety, but they were too far gone. He was half-dragged for a couple of yards before common sense got the better of him and he released his grip.

"Kaz!" Huma did not see the minotaur and then suddenly remembered how the latter had blocked the attack by the maddened warhorse. Huma turned and saw the motionless form. Kaz had deflected the blows with his own body. The knight remembered the minotaur's oath and let out an uncharacteristic curse. He would not have the minotaur's death on his hands.

"Kaz!" He kneeled next to his savior and turned him over. To his relief, the minotaur opened his eyes.

"You are uninjured?" the bull-headed creature asked.

"I should ask you that!" Huma almost laughed. If Kaz had the strength to be concerned about him, then the minotaur had the strength to live. He helped the huge creature to his feet.

"Can you run?"

The minotaur leaned forward. "Give me a moment. I fear the horse has pushed all the air from my lungs."

While Kaz recovered, Huma looked around. The camp was nearly deserted. A few knights struggled with equipment off to the south, and Huma thought he saw riders to the east. The tent where the clerics of Mishakal had treated the wounded was no longer there. There were no bodies that Huma could see; the mages had bought them enough time to escape, at least. He could only hope that Gwyneth had escaped safely, as well.

Meanwhile, where were the dragons?

Huma had not seen them since the eruption of the storm. The vast wall of chilling darkness was nearly upon the camp now, bringing along the visibility of a moonless night. Huma did not want to know what lurked within that darkness, but he forced himself to look up at it. When he did, he finally noticed the dragons of light.

They were organized into what Huma recognized as one of their fighting formations, a sort of double "V."

Against the coming fury, they looked pitifully tiny.

The wind was now joined by pouring rain. Kaz snorted angrily and commented on the smell of wet humans. He was now well enough to move, slowly but steadily. The torrent made movement tricky. Better slow and steady than risk having one or both of them lose their balance.

It might as well have been night. No trace of sunlight remained. Ahead of him, Huma could make out dim shapes. At their present rate, even those would disappear as the power of the Dragonqueen overwhelmed the light.

Overwhelmed the light . . .

Had the knights lost at last? Huma shuddered at the thought of a world with only darkness. A world that the Queen ruled.

Now, the only light was the bolts of fire that burst through the skies. They did not seem part of the storm and Huma glanced upward, wondering perhaps if it was the work of the dragons. Had they met the enemy at last? He wished—a mad wish, an afterthought—that he could help them in some way.

"Huma!" The hiss startled him until he realized it was Kaz. The minotaur's voice was hoarse. He was weaker with injury than he had led the knight to believe. "Huma! A light ahead!"

It was true. Only a dim glow, like one of the insects of night, but a glow nonetheless. They had already started toward it when Huma recalled the dark sorcerer who had sought to ensnare him. Still, this light did not demand his obedience as that one had. Rather, it seemed to offer badly needed help. To be on the safe side, Huma drew his sword.

They stumbled through mud, nearly falling once. Slipping and sliding, they continued toward the light.

For a time, the glow seemed no closer than before. The distance gradually lessened, though, and Huma soon realized that the light was also coming toward them. He tightened his grip on the sword. At his side, Kaz was tensed.

"I've been looking for you."

Before them, seeming to glow himself and quite untouched by the torrential winds and rain, stood Magius.

Chapter 8

Magius's spell of light surrounded them like a tent.
Beyond it loomed total darkness. They could hear the raging of the magical storm, although now they could not feel it; the spell that protected Magius protected Huma and Kaz as well. Only their footing was questionable, as the minotaur discovered. Huma helped him to his feet. The bottom half of the man-beast's body was slick with mud.

Magius smiled amiably at the sight, raising Kaz's anger. Matters were not helped any by the spellcaster's commentary on the slow pace of his companions, or the way in which not one speck of mud had dared to mar the magnificence of the mage's clothing. Another spell, Huma knew, because Kaz had already attempted to kick some of the muck toward the backside of their savior. The mud had halted just inches from the unsuspecting target, seemed to hesitate, and then fallen to earth.

Neither the knight nor the minotaur had any idea where Magius was leading them. They only knew that they were at last safe from the violent sorceries unleashed by the Dragonqueen's magic-users. That such power was at the evil ones' beck and call had thrown Huma into a deep depression. Now more than ever, all seemed to be lost.

Magius abruptly raised his free hand. The glow from his person dwindled away. Only the light from his simple staff, the light which Huma and Kaz had first noticed, continued to keep them from total darkness.

They could see nothing ahead of them, but they could hear that the storm had ceased. They also could hear something else: the padding of many animal paws and the heavy breathing of large creatures. Huma's hand whitened from strain as he tightened his grip on his sword. The creatures, night dwellers if they were able to travel with such ease, continued past. When they had been gone for several minutes and nothing followed, Magius lowered his hand.

He turned momentarily back to the others. "Outrunners. Things bred and misbred by Galan Dracos. Small wonder some began to call him the Queen's mortal consort. His twisted imagination is truly worthy of her."

Huma wondered who the "some" were whom Magius talked about. He longed to ask many questions about the mage's last few years. Before going off for the Test, Magius had been a sarcastic, vain trickster who poked fun at his best friend and who constantly ridiculed the knighthood for its closed ways. Only Huma really understood that Magius was terribly insecure—one of the reasons he had sought to learn magic—and that the taunts thrown at Huma served another purpose. The very same knights who despised young Huma were his champions. The honor of the knighthood always came first.

This Magius, while he still had that streak of mischievousness, had gained a serious, brooding side that could overwhelm his personality.

"Huma," the minotaur whispered. "Where are we going?"

Both of them had assumed that Magius was leading them

to wherever the Solamnic forces were regrouping, or rather, where Huma hoped they were reforming. The young knight was becoming more and more certain that they were, in fact, heading in the opposite direction.

"Magius?"

"Hmmm?" The spellcaster did not even turn around.

Hesitantly, Huma asked, "Are we heading back deeper into Solamnia?"

"No."

"Where are we going?"

Despite his carefree appearance, the magic-user's voice carried uncertainty, perhaps even some fear. "We are going to my citadel, my domain."

Huma finally made clear his true concern. "Ergoth?"

"Yes." Magius continued walking, but the other two came to a halt. Small wonder the storm had abated so soon! They were walking through the enemy lines!

"He has betrayed us!" Kaz reached out with his bare hands. Magius's neck would be a fragile thing in the grip of the minotaur's powerful claws.

"No, Kaz!" Huma struggled briefly with the minotaur, but Kaz would not listen. The latter fully expected to be turned over to his less-than-forgiving brethren and executed.

The massive hands formed a circle around the mage's neck—and could go no further. The same spell that protected Magius from the mud also protected him from personal harm by physical means. The former benefit was, no doubt, just a fortunate side-effect, although with the vanity of Magius, it was difficult to say.

Magius turned around, still in the near-grip of Kaz. Without warning, the minotaur swung one hand at the spellcaster's head. If he had expected to succeed by sheer force, the minotaur was mistaken. Not only was the mage unmoved, but his attacker's hand was flung back.

The magic-user was wearing the irritating smile that Huma had watched him cultivate over the years. Suddenly, even in the midst of the overwhelming darkness, it was the past once more.

"I have not betrayed you, either of you. True, we are

moving into Ergoth, but much of that land is still essentially untouched by the ogres and their foul mistress. We are, in fact, more likely to be safe here than if we had followed the mad rush by the oh-so-stalwart knighthood."

Huma grimaced at the description and felt embarrassment, though he knew the knighthood had done all it could. Magius failed to mention that the magic-users had fled, also.

The minotaur refused to be convinced. "By Sargas and my ancestors for twenty generations—"

Magius held the light of the staff in front of Kaz, who backed away for fear a spell was being unleashed. "If anyone draws attention to us, it will be you, minotaur! Call on your dusty kin if you must, but do not call upon that dark god unless you desire his personal attention now!"

Sargas. It was several seconds before Huma identified the name. Sargas—Sargonnas, consort of Takhisis, the Dragonqueen. A power unto himself. The minotaurs worshipped him. A reflex action on the part of Kaz, to be sure, but one that could carry a deadly price at a time when gods and goddesses watched and listened with much interest.

Sargas would not be pleased with a minotaur who had fled to the safety of Paladine's appointed mortal guardians. Sargas was the god of vengeance and plots of great evil. Kaz had no choice but to be calm himself and to bow to the human's common sense—at least, in this respect.

"Now," Magius said, straightening his cloak, "may we continue? I will tire eventually, and I have no desire to be within the range of the Queen's sentinels."

For what seemed like days, they followed the mage through the darkness. Huma began to wonder if all of Ergoth lay under shadow and whether that shadow was now extending over Solamnia as well. He felt a twinge of guilt that he was not assisting in the regrouping of the forces, but he consoled himself with the fact that he might do some good here, where the warlord would least suspect his presence.

At last, the trio began to notice a failing in the darkness, as if it were either weakening or they had at last reached its boundaries.

"The power level used to create and maintain this monstrosity must be monumental," said Magius. "The renegades of Galan Dracos are talented, but even they have their limits. Yet it appears to have served its purpose. The stalemate is broken." Magius did not seem visibly concerned.

Dark, spectral shapes formed, reaching for them. The demonic shapes coalesced into towering trees and thick bushes.

"Magius, what happened in the east?"

The spellcaster slowed, though his eyes were still on the path ahead. "Something happened in the east?"

"The dragons came." What, Huma wondered, had become of them? Had they all perished, including the silver one to whom Huma had become so strangely attached? "They said that the east had collapsed."

Magius stopped, turned, and studied his friend's face. "Indeed?" The mage wore a thoughtful expression.

Kaz crossed his massive arms. "You know a lot, magic-user. Much more than you are telling us."

The cynical smile returned. "I will do my best to enlighten you when we have reached our destination."

"And how long will that be? I could swear we have been walking for days."

The resplendent figure shook his golden hair. "Patience! This may be the most dangerous part of the journey."

As Magius turned forward, Kaz muttered, "More damned riddles!"

The dim forest soon lightened into near-dawn and then, quite suddenly, it was day. Overcast, as seemed perpetual on Ansalon with the Queen's coming, but day, at least. The trio paused to drink it in. Even Magius seemed pleased.

"We should be fairly safe now. I chose the shortest, safest route possible under the circumstances, but we still have a day's journey ahead of us. I will not have Dracos or even the Black Robes know the whereabouts of my grove."

Kaz merely shook his head and looked at Huma, who could only shake his head in return. He, too, was unfamiliar with the grove Magius was speaking of.

An unexpected inconvenience popped up.

"I am starved," said the minotaur.

No sooner had he spoken than Huma felt the ache in his stomach as well.

Magius sighed. He tapped his staff, and a pouch materialized. It was plain leather, nearly as big as a knight's saddlebag, and tied shut. "It is not much, but we will have to make do under the circumstances."

Not much, as far as the mage was concerned, was more than enough for three healthy appetites, even when one belonged to a minotaur. Huma eyed the bag as Magius pulled out fruits, bread, and even a small flask of wine. The contents were more than double the volume of the pouch, and there still appeared to be more inside. What other tricks did his childhood friend have that the mage took for granted? How powerful was Magius, and to whom did he dedicate that power?

Biting into an apple, Huma studied the rich garments of the other. By rights, Magius should have been wearing either the White robes of Good or—and much more likely—the Red Robes of Neutrality. Instead, Magius wore a blue and gold ensemble that would have been more at home on a courtier in Ergoth. The gold, Huma suspected, was real gold laced into the cloth. The cape was white, but so soft and well-woven that it was either magically created or the work of a fine artisan. Magius also wore hip boots of fine, polished leather—and not any ordinary leather, either. The knight was at a loss to identify it, but he had seen similar boots before. The Grand Master had a pair much like these.

This was not the clothing of a mage. Not any mage that Huma had ever heard of.

Kaz spoke, breaking Huma's train of thought.

"God of the Sea! I have never savored a wine such as this!"

The look on the minotaur's face appeared to amuse Magius. "My compliments on your taste. It is a rare treat given to me by the Qualinesti elves. I find it has become my personal favorite."

"You've been among the Qualinesti?" Huma had heard of the elves—and of their cousins, the Silvanesti—but he had never seen any but half-elves, as Gwyneth seemed to be.

The thought of Gwyneth opened up memories and

dreams that Huma did not wish to dwell on. He forced the past into a dark recess of his mind.

"I've been among them," Magius was saying. "I went to feel them out. They remain as stubborn as their kin. Each thinks that they can save the world single-handedly. Their pride is at the expense of mankind."

The mood grew rather somber after that. Huma found himself gazing in the direction from which they had come. Not one sign of the oppressive darkness remained.

Night came and, at Magius's suggestion, they camped until morning. When Huma suggested setting up a watch, Magius only scoffed. He assured them that his powers would be sufficient to the task. Despite that, both Huma and the minotaur were adamant. The mage, disgruntled, finally agreed, providing that he was given the last watch.

Knights who sleep deeply do not live long. This rule was one of the first squires learned. There were far too many foes who moved in silence. Thus knights quickly developed a sense that warned them when someone, or something, was near.

Thus it was that Huma knew.

It was the last watch, the one Magius had requested. Huma, lying on his side, carefully opened his eyes a crack. His narrow view gave him a glimpse of the minotaur's feet and the still form of Magius himself—most definitely asleep.

Whoever it was, it was standing behind him, he knew that now. Slowly and cautiously, he turned, as if still sleeping, until he was lying on his back. His hand drifted to the hilt of his sword, and he had confidence enough in his ability to think he might yet have a chance.

He opened his eyes just enough to let the day in.

It was with great difficulty that he held back from shouting. Through pure reflex he rolled away and came up on one knee, sword drawn. Behind him, Kaz rose with a mad snort, more than ready for combat.

It loomed higher than even the minotaur—a tall, massive overhang of rock and vegetation. Had it been there the night before, Huma might not have noticed anything unusual about it. He might not have noticed the massive appendages of stone that could loosely be called arms. He might not have noticed the way the outer shell of dirt and vegetation was constantly changing. Huma might even have missed, somehow, the two blue-gray crystals that seemed to stare down at him from what could only be some sort of face.

He took in all of this in a few brief seconds. The living mound shifted slightly forward, pulling up earth, insect, and plant life with it. It seemed not to have one true body, but to borrow from wherever it stood. Huma readied himself. Kaz had the huge battle ax poised. Then laughter filled the woods. Laughter from Magius.

"Cease your posturing, brave warriors. The elemental has no intention of doing battle with you. He is mine—a gatekeeper, you might say."

Kaz whirled on the mage, and the ax tore deeply into the tree where Magius had been sitting. The ax missed his head by inches. Magius turned as pale as Rennard, and his mouth hung open in mid-laugh.

The angry warrior was not allowed to savor his revenge, for his footing suddenly became nonexistent. A very selective tremor shook the hapless minotaur. Huma lanced down at his own footing, which was as solid as ever, and then back at Kaz. With a roar, the minotaur lost his grip on the ax and fell backward.

Meanwhile, Magius had recovered from his own shock. He was careful, though, to keep his laughter quiet and less mocking. He shook his head as Kaz tried unsuccessfully to rise.

"You will never stand on two legs unless I say so, my hot-headed friend. Have I your word that you will cease your attempts to do away with me?"

As the minotaur's chin bounced against hard-packed earth, he grunted agreement. Magius looked at the elemental. It seemed as if the two crystals turned to meet that gaze, though Huma knew he might be imagining it. Without warning, the ground beneath Kaz returned to its normal consistency. Kaz hesitated, expecting another trick.

"Oh, do get up!" the spellcaster muttered. "You're perfectly safe."

Huma relaxed, but he did not return his sword to its sheath. The earthen creature disturbed him.

Rising, Magius stepped between Huma and the creature. Like a man training a hound, Magius raised one hand and said, "Speak to me."

The voice was deep and echoing, but also like listening to a pile of rocks and pebbles being shaken violently in a bucket. The first words were practically unintelligible. It repeated itself.

"All well. No one enters grove. Citadel welcomes mage's return." The mound fell silent.

Magius nodded his satisfaction. To the others he said, "Beyond that dense clump of trees, perhaps three to four hours' journey, is our destination."

Kaz clenched his fists, then thought better of it. He had already seen a little of what the magic-user's servant could do. "That close and you made us sleep here?"

"I believe you heard the earth elemental mention the grove, did you not?" The mage's face was quite sober.

"What of it?"

"Only I would dare enter the grove during darkness, and that is because I have spent time mastering it. To have led you two through it would have surely have meant your doom."

Huma looked off in the direction his friend had pointed. "What is the danger? Can a blade or ax put an end to it?"

The laughter of the mage held little humor. "There are far more deadlier threats than mere physical ones. Let us say, it would take a strong mind to come out of there in one piece. A strong mind or a simple one, take your pick."

Riddles, as Kaz would have said—so Huma thought then. He did not trust challenges that could not be met face-to-face. In many ways, it was another sign of the changes Magius had gone through since their last meeting before the Test.

"The elemental will guide us and do what it can to protect any of us who might fall off the path. May the gods have mercy on he who does, because the grove will not."

It took them only half an hour to reach the edge of the

grove. In all his days, Huma could not recall seeing such a thick growth of foliage. Trees, grass, bushes, and even vines grew within and around one another, creating a veritable wall of defense around the domain of Magius. Try as he might, Huma could not fathom the depths.

Open paths dotted the grove at various points, but tended to twist aside soon after, making it impossible to guess which was the best to take. The earth elemental passed several of these, including a couple which seemed far more inviting than the one the creature finally chose. Kaz eyed the chosen path critically and shook his massive hand.

"Look at this." He pointed a clawed hand at the sharp, thorny vines at the entranceway. "Why, the path we just passed was clear and well worn! Surely, this is the wrong path!"

Magius looked at him with open contempt. "The most attractive lure catches the most flies, my friend. You are welcome to try the other path, if you like. Here, we face a little prick from a plant. There . . . it could be anything."

Shifting uncertainly, Kaz looked from one path to the other. In desperation, he looked to Huma for support.

Huma, in turn, looked at Magius. The mage was noncommital. Huma stared at the vine-covered path.

"I believe him, Kaz."

"Then I will go where you go."

"I'm glad that's settled." Magius shook his head in amazement. He lifted his staff and tapped the backside—it looked like a backside, anyway—of the elemental. The living mound shifted forward, the earth before it becoming its form as it moved into the grove. Magius followed without any hesitation. The minotaur glanced at Huma, then followed the mage.

Huma, alone, took a deep breath, kept his sword ready—for what, he could not say—and stepped onto the path.

Chapter 9

The path twisted and turned with amazing regularity.
Had not Magius reassured them more than once, Huma
would have thought that they were wandering in a circle.

He did not like the grove, which, even by day, was
gloomy and full of shadow. Without the light from the staff,
they surely would have strayed from the path.

Huma ducked away from a thorny vine crisscrossing the
trail. After the first sharp sting from one of the countless
barbs, he had closed his visor. Still, each thorn scraped at
the metal on his body, and in irritation, Huma slashed stalk
after stalk. Yet whenever he chanced to turn back, there
would be no trace of his handiwork.

Ahead of him, Kaz cursed and brought his battle ax down
upon a prickly bush. The injured minotaur chopped at the

plant until only shreds remained. Almost immediately he walked face first into a hanging vine. The sharp blades of the ax came out and cut that vine to ribbons, too.

The abrupt drop at the next turn caught all of them by surprise. The shifting of the soil as the elemental made its way fooled Magius. His staff came down and the mage, expecting some sort of resistance, toppled forward. Kaz, next, stumbled forward onto the spellcaster. Huma twisted to avoid adding to the ungainly pile, lost his footing in a different place, and fell off the path.

Huma came to an abrupt halt, thanks to the huge shell of a once-mighty tree. He rubbed the back of his head, which had absorbed part of the shock, and looked up—at nothing.

There was no path. The trees of the grove dotted the area. Bushes, tall and many years old, filled most of the spaces between the trees. Shadows filled the rest. Deep, dark shadows.

Huma closed his eyes and opened them again, this time assuring that his gaze was not directed at the shadows. A chill ran through him. What he had seen—he froze. What had he seen? It defied any description he could have given it. He only knew that it was somewhere out there, waiting for him to carelessly turn toward it.

"Magius! Kaz!" The names echoed back to him. A quiet, mocking laugh seemed to come from everywhere.

"Huuuumaaa."

At the sound of the voice, Huma reached for his broadsword—only to find his weapon gone. He remembered then that he had been carrying the sword in his hand. Yet he could see no sign of the blade when he searched the ground in the dim light.

Something tall and misshapen broke away from the other shadows and briefly passed through his vision. His nerves tightened as the mocker laughed once more. Huma pulled out a dagger, hoping that iron would make an impression.

His view vanished as something literally popped into existence right before him. He thrust hard with the dagger and encountered—mud and dirt. His hand sank into the mire, and he lost his grip on the small blade.

With wide eyes, he stared up into the ice-blue, crystalline

eyes of the elemental.

Huma fought off a desire to hug the strange creature. The elemental stared down at him and spoke in the same gravel-filled voice it had used when responding to Magius.

"Follow." A single, wonderful word to the knight, at that moment. Suddenly, blessedly, his sword was back in his hand.

The two crystals were sinking swiftly into the depths of the mound. At first, the living mound did not move and the knight thought the creature must be frozen in place. Huma sheathed his sword and leaned against the backside of the elemental's earthen shell. He decided to dig the elemental out of its quandary. As his hands touched the mound, though, the earth beneath his fingers began to heat up incredibly and Huma quickly pulled them away. Two gleaming objects emerged from the mound.

Its crystalline eyes in place, the elemental repeated its previous message. "Follow."

Huma jumped out of the way as the thing churned forward. Rather than turn as a man might, the elemental merely shifted its face to whichever direction it wished to travel. It was disconcerting, to say the least, and Huma, still staring in wonder, completely ignored the earthen servant's command again. The mound did not repeat itself. It abruptly shambled up a small rise and promptly vanished.

Huma's first instinct was to unsheath his sword. Then, he gritted his teeth and, with four long strides, he found himself standing before a loudly cursing minotaur and an anxious mage.

"Huma!" Kaz fairly crushed him in a bear—or rather, a bull—hug.

Magius smiled with relief. "When you fell off the path, your bovine companion was all for rushing after you. It was all I could do to explain to him that having two of you lost out there would be quite foolish."

The minotaur dropped Huma and spun on the mage. "You wouldn't go after him! Someone had to!"

"Someone did." Magius pushed back his aristocratic locks. "While I can make my way through the grove, I would much prefer to send the elemental, who has nothing to fear, than risk myself purely for the sake of appearances."

"You are a coward!"

"I'm practical." Magius turned to his old friend. "If the elemental had not been here or had failed to find you, I would have followed you, that I promise."

Huma's acceptance of the mage's explanation was met with a derisive snort by Kaz. Magius ignored the latter and, after a quick tap of the staff on the elemental's present backside, the group was off again.

Though they did not encounter any more difficulties, Huma kept his eyes warily on the path at all times. Finally, they emerged into light. Brilliant light. It was as if the eternal cloudcover had finally given way to the golden rays of the sun. Even Kaz broke into a big, genuine smile. When Magius turned to speak to them, he, too, was grinning from ear to ear. He raised his staff high.

"Welcome to my home."

They stared out into a wild, golden field. It would have been quite easy to believe that somewhere within the field elves danced and played. Butterflies and small birds flew hither and yonder while the bright, ripe wheat waved lazily after them. Small, furred creatures hopped among the occasional trees that dotted the forest perimeter. If there were truly a paradise on all of Krynn, this seemed to be it.

In the center of this wondrous field stood the citadel of Magius, a tower that, like the field surrounding it, might have been made of gold. A single gigantic wooden gate acted as a door. Windows dotted the top half of the tower, and there was even a small walking area up at the top. The tip gave the citadel the appearance of a spearhead, well-crafted and needle-sharp. The sides gleamed metallically, and Huma's one regret was that it briefly reminded him of the sinister bronze tower perched precariously on the edge of the infernal Abyss.

Magius bowed and indicated they should go before him. The elemental had vanished, perhaps to patrol the outer limits of the grove once more.

"You are safe here, my friends. As safe as anywhere on all of Ansalon."

The knight and the minotaur stepped out into the field

like two children. Gone was anxiety concerning the war. Gone were the hatred, the fear. There was only the breathtaking beauty of the open land before them.

The mage watched them pass, the smile briefly vanishing from his face.

As they walked, a strange thing seemed to happen. The citadel grew. With each step it grew taller and taller. By the time they reached its gate, Huma and Kaz were forced to stare up into what seemed the ceiling of the sky itself.

"How can the dragons not see something of such scale?" There was no suspicion in the words of Kaz this time, only wonder.

"Like this field," Magius replied. "Things are not always what they appear to be—or are seen to be. Someone created this place long before men ever set foot on Krynn. I have spent much time trying to discover their secrets, but the fragments hint at the handiwork of ogres. I cannot believe that ogres could ever build a place of such beauty. Perhaps, this was made as a garden paradise for the gods themselves. I think that would be more appropriate."

Huma chose to spoil the serenity of the scene by coughing just then.

The mage grimaced. "Forgive me. You must be tired and thirsty. We shall go inside and be refreshed. After that, we shall speak."

Magius raised his staff again and muttered a long string of seemingly nonsensical words. The staff, whose earlier glow had diminished, suddenly blazed with a new life. Both Huma and Kaz were forced to momentarily shield their eyes.

The gate opened, perhaps moved by some great, invisible hand. Magius was continually amazing Huma, although it might very well be that the castle, too, was a product of these ancients.

They passed through the gate and into a hallway which, while smaller than that of any noble's estate home, outshone most by pure extravagance. Sculptures of elves, animals, tall manlike beings, humans, and what could only be the gods themselves lined the walls. Like an oversized serpent, a single stairway curled its way up to the floors above. A gold and red tapestry displaying the constellations draped one side while another one depicted a mountain that virtually towered over the landscape. It was so real that it drew Huma's attention. At the back of his mind nagged the feeling that he knew this place from somewhere, although, in fact, Huma knew he had never seen the mountain before. He continued to stare at it until Magius's voice broke the tapestry's spell.

"Not all of it is original, but one cannot have everything. Be careful!"

The last was aimed at Kaz, who was busily inspecting an ageless sculpture of an odd-looking dragon. It was long and narrow, almost like a snake with legs and wings. What little remained of the coloring indicated it had once been green and blue, intermingled, an odd hodgepodge of colors for any dragon.

"This sculpture was made by one of my people."

"Impossible. It must be elven. Look at it."

Kaz snorted. "Do you think we have no artisans? I recognize the telltale patterns in the clay, even if your 'well-versed' mind cannot make anything out of them."

"Why would anyone want to mold a dragon like that? I've never seen one so long and narrow. Did such exist?" Huma asked, turning to Magius.

The mage shrugged. "I have never uncovered evidence of such a beast. It is my belief that this is purely an artistic representation, the product of someone's imagination. Another reason why it cannot be the work of minotaurs, not to mention the fact that it is far too old."

"We were the first civilized race."

"Civilized or domesticated?"

Kaz moved swiftly, but the statuette froze in midair some three feet before Magius's face. The mage's look of contempt was matched only by the intense disappointment draped across Kaz's visage. "Make your next throw a good one, cow, because it will be your last. And next time use something a little less valuable."

With a wave of his free hand, Magius returned the dragon sculpture to its resting place. Kaz snorted continuously, and his eyes were crimson. Suddenly Huma stepped between them, brandishing his sword.

"Stop it!"

The outburst was so savage that both mage and minotaur stared at him as if he had lost his mind. Huma looked from one to another with what he hoped was a ferocious expression.

"Ansalon, perhaps all of Krynn, may be lying helpless beneath the Dragonqueen, and you two are acting like schoolchildren!"

Kaz was the only one of the two to look ashamed. Magius took the reprimand as he did all else. He merely shrugged and pretended as if the incident had never happened.

"There's much more to see, but I imagine you two might wish to get some rest. Am I correct?"

"On that point, at least," Kaz muttered.

Huma sheathed his sword, but his temper was still aroused. "What happens after that? Can you contact your order? We cannot stay here forever. You came looking for us. Don't you have a plan?"

"Of course." The answer came quickly, but there was something in the spellcaster's eyes that Huma thought belied his response. Here, again, was a Magius with whom he was unfamiliar. Here was a Magius who held back secrets from the one person he should have been able to trust. How he had changed.

Or is it I who am changing? thought Huma. In the old days, he would have never truly questioned Magius or probed at his friend's answers. The knighthood had opened his eyes to the veiled half-truths that played so large a part in most people's lives.

Deliberately, Huma said, "I should like to hear your plan."

"In good time. There are far too many matters here that I must attend to immediately. While I do so, you two may relax and perhaps enjoy some food."

Magius tapped his staff on the ground. Huma felt a shiver cut through him. Then he saw the mist.

It fluttered about Magius as a pet bird might around its master. Huma could not feel any sort of breeze, nor was there any seeming source of the mist. It moved as if with a life of its own.

"Guests. Guide." Magius spoke the words, not to Huma or Kaz, but to the cloud—and it responded:

"Guesssstssss. Guiiiiiiidde." The mist's voice sounded like steam escaping from a doused campfire.

"Rooms for the night."

"Rooommmmss."

Magius grimaced. "Air elementals are so slow." He waved his hand at the floating mist. "Now, if you please." To Huma, the spellcaster said, "When you are fed and rested, things will be clearer."

Kaz let out a deep "hmmmph," which Magius ignored. The air elemental, given the command to begin its duties, floated impatiently around the two "guests."

"Commme. Rooommmmmss. Guessssstsss."

Their host watched as they followed the mist creature up the spiral stairs. When they were out of earshot, Kaz leaned toward Huma, who had taken the lead, and whispered, "This mage is your friend?"

"Yes." Huma found it difficult to answer with assurance.

"Pray that he still considers you in the same way. I think that this tower and its secrets would make for a very secure, very permanent prison."

The knight did not argue the statement, having already considered that possibility.

If this were indeed a prison, it was one to which many a villain would have begged entry and incarceration. After becoming at least partially used to the misty servants, Kaz and Huma had no difficulty enjoying the meats and fruits, not to mention the wines, which would have been fit bill of fare at any royal court.

The rooms, too, were resplendent, albeit much too large for a normal-size person like Huma. Kaz, on the other hand, found the furnishings perfect for his bulk and pointed this out as more clues that the tower was some remnant of his own race. Huma knew that no one had ever recorded minotaurs this far west until the wars had begun, but he kept his doubts to himself.

They had been given separate rooms, something which

Kaz had at first protested as an obvious ploy to divide and conquer.

"Had he desired to, Magius could have struck us both down any one of a hundred times," Huma countered. "You saw the way he handled you in the corridor."

"Luck. Let me take him on, one to one."

"And he will leave nothing but ashes. Magic is as much a part of him as breathing is to us."

The minotaur smashed one massive fist into the wall. To his satisfaction, it yielded quite nicely. "In my homeland—"

Huma stopped him before he could go any further. "This is Ergoth. These are human lands. Human ways."

"Are they? Have you forgotten the battle already?"

"I have not. I only think that you should trust me. I know Magius far better than you."

Kaz quieted, but not before replying, "I hope you do. For both our sakes."

It was those words that Huma contemplated as he sat against the bedboard. Despite the drain of energy from their walk through the grove, he had found himself unable to sleep. Kaz, on the other hand, might have been dead, save for the fact that his snores resounded through the walls and into Huma's room.

The candles, lit before he had entered, had melted to the point where many were of little or no use at all. The flickering made odd shadows around the room, and Huma eventually found his eyes returning to one particularly high and deep shadow in the far corner. It was so dark, he almost believed that, if he chose to, he could have walked right into it and through the wall.

"Huma."

A hand, open, thrust out from the shadow. It was followed by another. The knight edged away from that side of the bed and toward his sword, which hung next to the bed.

"Huma, I must speak to you."

"Magius?"

"Who else?" Arms followed the hands, and then the rest of the mage appeared as well. "Forgive me the dramatic entrance," Magius whispered, "but I wish to avoid speaking with the minotaur, who might be displeased with some of what I am about to say."

"And I won't be?" Huma was feeling irritable. The mage's tricks were beginning to wear even on his boyhood friend.

Their eyes met, and Magius quickly turned away. "You might be. But at least you also see reason. My powers need only slip once for that two-legged bull to do me in."

"I could not entirely fault him, Magius."

"I know." The spellcaster put his face in his hands. "How dearly I know."

Huma stood up, walked over to his childhood friend, and rested a gentle hand on the other's shoulder. "Tell me, and I will promise to listen with an open mind."

Magius looked up, and they were briefly back in their early days, when neither had cared about anything more lofty than fun. The look vanished almost as soon as it appeared. The elegant Magius held out one hand. Instantly, the staff was there, awaiting his commands.

"You see before you a magic-user of great power—and even greater potential. I was not the first to say that. Fat, cheerful Belgardin said that the day he sponsored me."

Belgardin. Huma remembered the old mage. He had been the first to see the power welling within the young Magius. Power such as he had never seen before. Belgardin was a high adept of the Red Robes, and this enabled him to realize the help the boy needed while still calculating the prestige that accompanied the training of a possible Master of the Order—any order.

"He was right. You remember. I excelled at all things. I was the brightest candidate they had ever seen. I mastered spells even some established adepts had difficulty with. I was a prodigy." The hint of conceit in the voice of Magius was quite reasonable; everything he had said was true.

The mage's face fell serious. "You ordinary people hear of the Test and all the rumors about what goes on." Magius made a cutting motion with his free hand. "The rumors pale in comparison to the truth."

The Test was the final proof of a mage's ability to cope with the power. It did not matter which of the orders he or she belonged to. All magic-users took the Test.

Magius dropped the tip of his staff to the floor and leaned heavily upon it. "I cannot say what others have gone through, just that some did not survive. I went into the Test with every possible scenario plotted out in my mind. I thought they would send dark elves after me, force me to kill an elderly or ill person. Perhaps, I believed, they would have me stand at the edge of the Abyss and face the Queen herself. I knew some of it would be illusion, but much of it would be very real. Real enough to kill me."

Huma nodded understanding. Word naturally leaked out. Some of the rumors, it seemed, carried elements of truth.

The handsome face broke into a smile, one that seemed mad under the circumstances. Magius laughed lightly, although Huma could not guess what he found so funny. "They fooled me completely. Or perhaps even they do not truly know all that goes on during the Test. I suspect that sometimes the power itself takes a hand. Whatever the case, I was confronted with the one thing I found I could not accept.

"My death. My death in the future."

There was nothing Huma could say to that. He might deny that it was real, try to convince Magius that it had to be all illusion, but what could he say that he himself believed?

"Somehow, I succeeded in surviving. I think that madness was what waited for me if I failed. I fooled them by entering into another type of madness then. A madness created by the realization that what I saw would indeed come to pass. I left the tower, left the Test, knowing my fate and determined to do something about it.

"And I found I could not. Not by the strict bylaws of the Orders. Despite their supposed freedom from restrictions, neither the Red nor the Black Robes offered anything that could assist me. They were still too limited, and I certainly was not cut out to wear the robes of white, as you well know."

Magius chuckled at the last, then sighed. The candles had burned down to nearly nothing.

"With a realization of the restrictions placed upon me by

the Three Orders, I decided that I would be forced to step beyond the lines they had drawn in order to—if you'll pardon me for saying so—change the future."

Huma stepped back involuntarily. The wild spells, the outlandish clothing, so different from the austere robes of other mages. He shook his head, not believing that it were possible to do what Magius had done.

"Then and there," Magius was saying, his attention focused inward, "I turned from the formalized, stifling training of the Conclave and became a renegade."

Chapter 10

"Does it shock you so, Huma? I was young, unbridled. I probably would have left for other reasons. Disgust for the Test, perhaps, which I still find a barbaric way of trimming the dead leaves."

Huma slumped back on the bed. To one brought up under the strict beliefs of the knighthood, all magic-users were untrustworthy. A renegade was considered blacker than even the Black Robes, for he would meddle with spells even they would balk at using.

Magius read the look and smiled ruefully. "A renegade is only what he makes of himself, Huma. There are very few, since it is hard to escape the notice of the Conclave, but some of those few are very good people. Not powerful enough, sometimes. Had they taken the Test, most of them would have perished. While they live, they do what little they can to help others. Of course, there is always the other side."

"Galan Dracos."

"Yes." Magius had gone pale. "Even the Queen's dark clerics fear him. She needs him, though."

The knight stiffened. "You know a lot."

"I—I heard much of him as I traveled. I thought he might be the one to aid me, to give me protection. He has no fear of the Three Orders."

There was motion in the next room. Magius stepped back into the shadows. "I do not think we can continue our discussion for now. Try to understand that everything I've done is for good reasons. We'll talk later."

Magius melted into the darkness. Leaping up, the knight put a hand into the shadowy corner. Only walls, as he suspected. Whatever portal Magius had opened had just been closed.

With a snarl, Kaz burst into the room. "I heard him! Where is he?"

Startled by the ferocity of the minotaur, Huma stepped back. "What is it, Kaz?"

"This is a trap, as I suspected! My ax is gone! My daggers are missing!"

"What are you talking about?" Huma reached for his own sword, which hung near the bed. Only—

The sheath hung as before, but it was empty now. Hurriedly, Huma went through his belongings. Like Kaz, he was missing all his weapons. They had disappeared even while the two old friends had talked.

Huma put a hand to his head. The room was becoming terribly hot. He felt flushed. Kaz was suddenly by his side, supporting him.

"What has he done to you? Are you ill?"

"I'm fine." He waved his sympathetic companion away. "It's nothing."

Huma had been a fool. He had believed that the past still counted, when now it was all too obvious that the mage had been lying. The inconsistencies, the overlengthy explanations, left more questions than they answered.

Huma reached for his armor. "We're leaving—somehow."

Kaz helped him suit up.

The hallway was apparently unguarded, although the knight was sure that unseen servants watched their every move. He wondered how far Magius would allow them to go.

"I don't like this," Kaz muttered. He, far more than the human, distrusted the workings of any magic-user.

They reached the long, spiral staircase without incident—which only served to make them that much more cautious. Huma reached out and touched the bannister with one finger. When he felt nothing, he dared to grip it. He took a step downward. Another. A third. Kaz followed as closely behind as his huge bulk permitted. Their pace quickened unconsciously.

On the sixth step down, Huma blinked. He was no longer on the step, but back at the top of the staircase. Five steps below, Kaz whirled about, searching for him. Before Huma could warn him, the burly easterner set one foot down on the sixth step. Huma had only a quick glimpse of Kaz before the latter vanished, to reappear beside him a moment later.

"More tricks," muttered Kaz.

They tried again, achieving the same result. Each time, the one who put a foot down on the step never noticed the shift. It was magic of the most complex and subtle nature.

They were trapped in some loop. Huma quit first, realizing the folly. Kaz continued for some time after, hoping there might be a way out. In the end, though, the minotaur joined Huma in the corridor.

"What now?"

Huma dropped the pack he had been carrying and undid the empty sheath. "Nothing. We won't be going anywhere, it seems."

"We cannot stay here!" The red glare was returning to the giant's eyes.

"Have you any ideas? There are no windows, and the walls are solid. At least for us."

"We could climb down to the corridor."

Huma picked up the empty sheath and walked over to the stairway. He lifted the object over the rail and dropped it.

The sheath disappeared.

While Kaz looked on, Huma turned and pointed to the floor. The empty sheath lay behind them.

"We wait. We have no choice."

The minotaur's shoulders slumped in defeat.

There came a time when sleep forced itself upon them, despite their attempts to stay alert. Thus it was that Huma dreamed. Dreamed of Gwyneth and a mountain. Dreamed of a silver dragon in flight. Dreamed of evil spellcasters and gods battling. They all mixed together so randomly that he was never really sure what the dream was about or how it even began.

It ended abruptly, he knew, for it ended when the voice broke through his sleep.

"Wwaaaakkee."

It took Huma several moments to realize that the sibilant whisper was not part of his dreams. Rather, it was a misty servant with a summons.

"Maaassteerr. Wiiissshhheess. Sssspeeaakk."

Huma rose and Kaz, hearing the elemental, did likewise.

"Hhuuumaaaa. Ooonnnly."

"I will go with him whether your master likes it or not! Now lead on, or I'll inhale you!"

Whether or not the air elemental actually understood the minotaur's words, it drifted toward the stairway. Huma followed, with Kaz close behind. The elemental led them downward. There was some hesitation on Huma's part when they neared the level that had repulsed them earlier. He took a single step. This time, much to his surprise, he found his progress unimpeded. The aerial servant hovered near him, as if impatient to move on. Huma continued down, slowly at first, then more quickly as it became obvious that Magius had set no traps.

A loud shout of anger caused him to quickly look up at the level above. While Huma's back had been turned, Kaz had attempted to follow the knight. Much to the minotaur's annoyance, the spell still held him in thrall.

Wordlessly, Huma turned and followed the servant down the twisting stairway and through corridors unseen the day before. These halls were much more like the grove, darker than it seemed possible, in some places. Now and then, things flitted in the flickering light of the few torches. Only when they passed these torches could Huma be sure that he was still following the servant.

"Maaassteerr."

Huma did not understand at first, for the room he entered was as dark and gloomy as all the corridors had been, and he could see no evidence that it was inhabited. Then he noted the sound of something moving.

A single word was uttered, and the room was lit by the staff of Magius. The sounds Huma had heard were those of the mage rising from a chair. As the other turned around, Huma's mouth opened in complete shock. To his eyes, Magius seemed nearly twice as old as he had appeared earlier. One would have never believed that the two men were of the same age.

"Huma." The magic-user's tone almost begged for friendship. All the anger that Huma had contained within him began to melt away as he studied the sudden deprivation of vitality.

"Magius, what—?"

"I know. I leave you with more questions and fears each time we meet. I'm afraid I can't change that even now, although I will attempt to clear up a few difficulties. First, I want you to see this."

The mage led him into an adjoining room, where Huma found himself facing the earth elemental that had led them through the grove. Something lay before the living mound, something unnervingly familiar.

Huma recognized it. "A dreadwolf."

It was bent at awkward angles, and Huma realized that one limb was torn away. Odder still, it was petrified. Reaching down, he verified the thought. It was like touching a rock.

The sightless eyes still seemed to watch him. Huma turned to Magius for explanation.

"There were three more, but they perished in the grove. Somehow, battered and torn as it was, this one made it to the field, where he," Magius indicated the earth elemental, "finished it. The damage is done. Galan Dracos knows where I am and probably knows that you are here as well. I have no choice."

Huma listened, unsure what Magius was leading to.

"Come with me." They returned to the other room, and Magius walked over to a wall on which hung a high, gold-trimmed mirror. It was oval, decorated in elaborate scroll-work. Magius tapped the staff on the floor and said, "Show me."

"There. The peak in the center." A huge mountain loomed in the foreground. Recognition came swiftly. It was the same mountain so prominently displayed on one of the two great tapestries. "When I was tested in the tower, I saw that—the mountain. I remembered it well, for it was the final site conjured. I did not know it was real until I found this place, and the tapestry in the hall. When I saw it hanging on the wall, I knew there was more truth to the scenes in my Test than even my instructors knew. This mountain means something to the war. It conceals something. It is the one puzzle I cannot fathom. I don't even know its exact location, but it is west of here—southwest possibly."

He turned to Huma and held out the knight's weapons, though his hand had been empty moments before. "The minotaur also has his weapons back. The elemental will lead you to the underground passages and to horses that I have kept for emergencies."

The tower suddenly shook.

Magius whirled around and stared at the mirror. "Show me!"

The mountain scene vanished, to be replaced by a visual of the citadel, surrounded. A huge, black dragon with a rider. Other dragons, red, nearby.

"Moons of Krynn!" Magius smiled bitterly. "Am I worthy of the attention of Crynus himself?"

"Crynus!"

The mage looked at Huma and the bitter smile deepened. "Oh, yes, you two have met. Had I the time, I would tell you much of importance concerning him and the Black Guardsmen. As it is . . ." The tower shook again and the ceiling began to crumble.

"Arion!" In summons to the spellcaster's urgent call, the misty servant formed before them. "Take them to the stables! Hurry!"

"Maaasssteerr."

"Magius, let me help."

"Help me?" The mage smiled. "I once stood at the side of Galan Dracos. I was second only to him among his gathering of mages. It will take more than dragons to stop me."

A powerful gust of wind thrust Huma through the doorway even as he pondered how truthful Magius was being. Not just about his abilities, but his reasons. Would Huma ever know for sure?

"Huma!"

"Kaz!"

The minotaur came bursting down the dark corridor, heedless of any threats. True to his word, Magius had returned the minotaur's weapons, including the huge battle ax.

The massive warrior's first words were quite predictable. "What madness has he brought upon us now?"

"Only the warlord, six dragons, and Paladine knows what else."

More masonry crashed down.

Kaz raised the ax high over his head. "By my ancestors for thirty generations, I will not die crushed under rock!"

"Fooollss! Fooolooowww!"

"That *thing*—"

"—is our guide out of here! No more words!"

They hurried after the air elemental, which now seemed to possess startling speed. It was glowing slightly silver now, so there was no chance of losing it in the dark corridors.

The stable proved to be more like a cave with ventilation. There were half a dozen horses, ranging in all sizes, but all well-muscled and sleek. While the two chose their mounts, the air elemental vanished.

"Where are we?" asked Kaz.

Huma leaped on his chosen horse, a tall, silver mare, and glanced toward the cave entrance. "West of the grove, I think. The hall tunneled underneath it."

"Good. One small difficulty out of the way." The minotaur climbed aboard his own animal, a beast at least as tall as himself.

Another jolt shook the cave. Huma freed the other animals; he would not leave the horses to die if the cave collapsed.

"Yaaah!" The horses were swift, and for ten minutes Huma and Kaz rode without looking back.

Behind them, the two could hear the cries of the dragons as they tore at the defenses of the citadel and its master.

What use was there in fighting a battle that could not be won? Still, Huma knew that the next battle would be his.

They broke through a clearing, and Huma dared to look back then. "Riders!"

There were at least eight of them, ebony-armored figures on coal-black steeds like creations of the Abyss. Black Guard. Huma's hand strayed to his sword to assure himself that it was still there.

Something else broke through after the riders. Pale, canine things with sightless red eyes. Six or seven, perhaps. Dreadwolves.

Suddenly, the earth before the dark riders burst up with tremendous fury. One rider succeeded in keeping his balance and two managed to evade the explosion, but the rest vanished momentarily behind the huge mound, which Huma recognized as the earth elemental. A point in the favor of Magius, thought Huma. The mage had sent one of his most trusted servants to assist his old friend.

The dreadwolves had enough warning to dodge the milling confusion, though one fell victim to a horse that lost its balance. The others continued the chase.

A tree limb struck Huma in the arm, and he turned around just in time to avoid a low branch. Kaz rode a few yards to his right, his larger form causing him some grief. The horns on his head snagged branches with worrisome regularity. Kaz hung on grimly, though.

Huma glanced back whenever terrain permitted him, but the same sight always greeted him. The dreadwolves, at least, moved with a constant pace and did not seem to tire. Only six of the ebony riders had regrouped and managed to keep pace.

"We can't . . ." A branch struck Kaz in the face as he tried to speak. "We can't keep on like this. The horses will perish."

Huma agreed. They were pushing the animals at a killing pace. Huma came to a difficult decision.

"Split up! Ride to the north!" He had to point to get his idea across. Kaz frowned but accepted. Huma indicated he would ride to the south. Lacking a plan of his own, the minotaur obeyed.

When Huma gave the signal, Kaz pulled his horse sharply to the right, nearly taking off his own right arm as the animal was forced to twist around a tree. Huma watched him vanish and then pulled tight on the reins of his own mount.

The animal was near to collapse. It slowed as quickly as possible, stumbling several times in the brush. Huma did not wait for it to come to a stop before leaping from the saddle. He landed feetfirst and scurried for the shelter of the trees.

The dreadwolves were fast closing, and Huma barely had time to ready himself. Among the items in the stable-cave, he had found a small, wooden shield, and this he had strapped to his free arm. The broadsword was out in one smooth, silent motion. He prayed that the dreadwolves would run after the horse first. It was the only way he would have a chance.

He was determined to stall them long enough for Kaz to flee. Huma knew it likely would cost him his life, but he could foresee no escape for either of them unless one remained behind. He could not ask that of even Kaz.

The first of the dreadwolves came running past. Single-minded to the point of obsession, the ghoulish creature followed after the abandoned horse, which had now realized its plight and was racing off again. It would not get far, and Huma was disgusted that he had to sacrifice any animal for this.

Two more dreadwolves raced by. Another followed. There were at least two more. Huma steadied himself and tried to maintain his patience.

Another. Another. When no more appeared, Huma risked a peek around the tree trunk. It proved to be a mistake, for the first of the riders appeared at that point and he spotted Huma all too easily.

Huma had chosen this particular tree because of the massive root system that partially extended above-ground. It was a fortunate choice, for the rider, intent on being the first to claim the prize, forced his horse just too close. The left forehoof of the dark steed caught on one of the roots. With a sharp cry, the animal fell forward and the rider was thrown far into the air, finally landing in a contorted heap. Huma assured himself that the rider was dead, and he turned to face the others.

The rest of the riders materialized in a group. The gaps between the trees were so small that the riders were forced to slow down and navigate through the forest one at a time, breaking their loose formation. Huma gave a cry of challenge and charged.

He caught the first of the Black Guard as the rider attempted to bring up an ax for a strike, only to find it had snagged in the branches of the tree. Huma made his attack count, and the man toppled off his mount.

Inspiration came then, and the knight leaped onto the abandoned horse. The animal fought him. Struck by a skull-crushing hoof, one opponent went down as Huma mastered the steed. Fending off the other attacker, Huma urged the animal forward, this time heading south. As he had hoped, the four riders followed.

Something lunged at him. A white blur. Only luck enabled him to catch it on his sword, although the dreadwolf did succeed in tearing apart some of the chain mail on his leg. The knight found himself riding with a still-squirming dreadwolf impaled on his sword. The creature's weight forced him to virtually drag it along in order to keep his sword. Huma's arm felt as if it were about to be wrenched off.

The horrific jaws snapped at him, and the sightless eyes rolled in the skull until the dreadwolf finally slid off the sword and tumbled behind Huma. Huma glanced back and saw with horror that the creature was rising as if unharmed. The dreadwolf turned its head just in time to see the front hooves of the first horse of the pursuers come down on it.

The ghoulish creature was trampled without notice and destroyed.

Both his own animal and those of his remaining pursuers were near their limits. Froth spewed from the horse's mouth. The steed began to stumble as it ran. The knight heard a crash behind him and dared a quick glance. One of the other horses had collapsed, causing another to spill.

Huma brought his mount to a halt, then turned it. The two guardsmen still riding charged him from two sides, their intent to cross him up. The rider to Huma's right swung a mean blow with his sword, and the rider to the left followed with another an eyeblink later. Huma's timing was perfect. He blocked the first with his shield and deflected the second with such accuracy that he provided himself with an opening. The tip of his blade caught the rider on the left between the breastplate and helmet. The rider collapsed backward and was dragged on by his unknowing horse.

Unwilling to fight one-to-one, the remaining rider turned back toward his two other comrades, who were extricating themselves from their injured horses. Huma struck wildly and missed a killing blow, but the Guardsman fell off his horse and did not rise from the ground.

By now, the other dreadwolves had returned. Huma's horse wobbled and fell to its knees; the knight jumped off and away before the beast collapsed on him. He then stood, shield and sword in hand, and faced the five creatures and the two riders who had regrouped. A stark realization that he would die clouded his mind. When the first of the dreadwolves lunged for his throat, he met it with the overwhelming thrust of one whose sole remaining goal is to take as many of the enemy with him as possible. Thus, he cut, chopped, and thrust almost blindly, seeing little clearly any more. Even the shield became a weapon as he brought it down on at least one white form, hard enough to crush a skull.

Yellowed fangs dripping ichor flashed by his face. Steel threatened to divide his throat in two. Huma met each attack and then counterattacked.

He eventually realized that he was striking at air. The knowledge brought his senses back. He blinked the film from his eyes and stared at the tableau before him.

The last two guardsmen were dead, their weapons scattered far away. Blood oozed on the ground. The five dreadwolves lay strewn in pieces around the area.

Exhaustion took him suddenly. He went to his knees and, for a long time afterward, simply stared at what he had done.

Chapter 11

HOW LONG IT WAS BEFORE HE FELT THE PAIN, HUMA COULD only guess. He had eventually wandered away from the terrible scene, as much to ease his growing distaste with himself as to escape from any other pursuers. Vaguely, he knew that there would be others, for, if nothing else, both Dracos and the warlord Crynus were determined to the point of fanaticism. And Huma calculated that Crynus, at least, would be interested in his whereabouts.

The pain increased. Huma numbly stared down at the multiple wounds he had received from his opponents. His armor was battered and torn; the mail was almost useless. A part of his mind wondered when this damage had been done. He could remember nothing of the fight save the thrusting of his sword at whatever moved.

Huma found a stream and washed his wounds as best he could. The cool water soothed not only his body but his mind.

After finishing at the stream, he decided to follow its path. It ran southwest, more or less, and he recalled that Magius had recommended that route. That thought brought Kaz to mind, and the knight felt guilty that he had abandoned his one true friend. Was the minotaur safe somewhere?

A huge shape sent tree limbs swaying as it raised a tremendous wind. Huma instinctively flattened against a tree and stared upward. He caught a glimpse of a wide, leathery wing, but it was gone almost immediately and he could not even be sure of its color. Whatever type of dragon it was, it did not return.

The day passed before Huma even realized it. Hunger demanded his attention, and he burrowed through the saddle bag he had taken from one of the horses. The Black Guard, it seemed, had little in the way of personal effects. At the bottom, he found what he had been looking for—three days' worth of rations.

A moment later, he was spitting them out, despite his hunger. Another lesson about his adversaries—their taste in food, even the generally bland iron rations, was abysmal. Huma knew he would cause himself more damage than good by eating these things; in its present condition, his stomach would never be able to hold them.

Eventually, he was able to secure food in the form of birds' eggs and berries. It was not very filling, but it eased the hunger. His search for food told him something else as well; most of the bushes had been stripped of edible berries. Recently, too. It was too thorough to have been the work of animals. Besides, Huma had spotted no forest life other than birds. If he stayed too long in this area, he could starve. The stream, too, seemed depleted.

For three days, he wandered along the stream. The face he saw staring back at him from the water on that third day made him smile in self-mockery. The reflected knight was unkempt, his mustache spreading in a hundred different directions, his armor dented or torn and covered with blood and dirt. Self-consciously, he tried to wipe some of the grime from the symbol of the Order of the Crown. He saw his own face vanish and one like Bennett's appear. Trake's son was, of course, immaculate. The breastplate ever gleamed. His proud mustache was thick and neatly trimmed. He was a true knight.

Another face joined Bennett's. This one was no Knight of Solamnia, but a foreign-armored, heavily bearded bear of a face. It was sneering.

Had he not seen it there and then, the bearlike man would never have believed that a man could move so swiftly. Somehow, the battleworn figure leaning over the stream produced a broadsword seemingly out of nowhere, and the hapless stranger barely managed to avoid the swing—and that because of the other's awkward angle more than anything else.

Huma could not immediately identify the man who had attempted to sneak up on him. He was wearing a motley collection of armor, some of it ogre make, some of it bits and pieces of Solamnic armor. Huma would have let the man go, but now he wondered whether he faced a brigand, a man who might even steal from the dead.

His erstwhile opponent suddenly yelped, turned, and ran off at an astounding pace for one with such an ungainly form. Huma gave pursuit.

His exhaustion slowed him. As it was, Huma was just closing on the man when the other scurried around a small hill. Huma followed suit . . .

. . . and immediately backtracked as more than a dozen horsemen and many, many more footsoldiers turned to stare in surprise at the two newcomers.

A tall man with silver-black hair and a neatly clipped black beard barked out an order. Huma did not hear the exact words, but he knew they had to do with him.

His luck ran out at this point, for the woods here were thinner and the riders quite familiar with the terrain, judging by their confident maneuvers. When he realized he could not escape them, the knight turned and steadied himself. These were not the human forces of the Dragonqueen, that much he knew, but whether they were allies or enemies was uncertain.

The first men rode at him. They were good horsemen, but he was able to ward them off at a distance with his sword. He was hard-pressed when a third man rode in and more footsoldiers after that, so that Huma found himself trapped in a rapidly shrinking circle. Still, none of the soldiers attacked. None had the desire to face that flashing blade.

"Stay your weapons! That is an order!"

The other riders arrived. The man who shouted the command urged his mount up to the circle, where the soldiers made way for him. He rode up to Huma and studied him. The commander was a man of strong features, though his face was lined from the responsibilities of leadership. Like many of the Knights of Solamnia, he had the rather hawkish features that spoke of old Ergothian blood—royal blood. His visage, though, was not as severe as those of the Grand Master or Bennett. The slight smile that played across his face would have been out of place on either of the two great knights.

"A Knight of Solamnia? A little far from Vingaard Keep, are you not, Knight of the Crown?"

Huma flushed at what the man must have thought of him. He did not offer a very competent picture of the knighthood. Huma tried to summon up some dignity, and replied, "I have been on my own for days. I have fought off monsters and warriors. My path has not been entirely by choice."

He did not yet trust them enough to speak of the other things.

"I see." The commander shifted in his saddle. "I am Lord Guy Avondale out of Durendi, a bit too far to the south for my tastes at present. Who are you, and what are you doing in the middle of Ergoth? Have the Solamnics broken through at last?"

"I am Huma, Knight of Solamnia, defender of the Order of the Crown. I was forced this direction by the Black Guard when the Dragonqueen's dark minions crushed our lines." He might have lied, built up their hopes, but he chose not to.

Avondale's face turned white. The soldiers with him began muttering nervously to themselves.

"Do I understand you correctly? The knighthood has been crushed?"

"No, Lord Avondale. Our lines were crushed, but we were to regroup farther back. I, unfortunately, was pressed in the wrong direction. Vingaard Keep still stands as it always has and always will."

The other gave him a sarcastic smile. "We in Ergoth are only too familiar with the strength of the knighthood, although it seems to have availed little. Glad I am to hear that the knights have not been totally vanquished, though."

One of the other riders moved closer, and Huma whirled, his blade daring the man to try something. Avondale held up a hand to calm both of them.

"There is much I wish to ask of you, but you appear to be all in. You," the commander pointed at the horseman who had moved closer, "give him your horse for now."

"Yes, milord."

Huma looked from the proffered horse to Guy Avondale and back to the horse. The noble frowned when he realized the young knight's thoughts.

"This is no trap, Huma. We are as much the foes of the Dragonqueen as you are. Let past differences remain where they are—in the past."

"I wish only the same, Lord Avondale." Huma grunted and climbed thankfully onto the steed.

"Fine. When we get back to camp, I'll see that you are fed. Then you can either rest or come straight to me."

A thought came to Huma. "Milord, have there been any rumors of a lone minotaur wandering this region?"

"A minotaur?" Avondale looked at his seconds in puzzlement. They shook their heads. "It seems not. If there is one, we shall deal with it, never fear."

Huma's voice grew urgent. "Milord, that is what I do not want! The minotaur—I realize this will be difficult to accept—is an ally and must not be harmed. His name is Kaz."

"Indeed." Avondale studied Huma once again. Longer, this time. "I have never heard of such a thing and most definitely never thought I would hear it from a Knight of Solamnia. But I will do as you request. Is that sufficient?"

"Yes, milord."

"Fine." Avondale turned to his aide. "Return this column to some semblance of order. Have that one locked up when we return." The noble found himself looking into the eyes of the young knight. "The man you were chasing was a deserter. You have my gratitude. I look forward to our talk."

The horsemen and footsoldiers realigned themselves and, on Lord Avondale's order, began to move south. Although Huma would have preferred to continue on toward the southwest, he trusted Lord Avondale.

Suddenly, a wave of nausea struck Huma, and he nearly slid off the side of the saddle.

"Gods!" The commander's jaws worked, but, at first, he did not know what to say. "Derek, help keep him up! We do not want him to fall beneath the hooves of his horse." Avondale took a closer look at Huma. "Gods!" he repeated. "He's covered with wounds!"

There were no healers of Mishakal with the army. A new wave of plague had struck near Caergoth, and the clerics there had been among its first victims. Avondale muttered something about the plague being very particular, for it most often struck where it hurt the most. Caergoth had been previously untouched and was to have been the main source of supplies for Avondale's forces. Huma slept for a full day, which worried the noble, for overwhelming fatigue was one of the first signs of the plague. Only when Huma woke, full of energy and gratitude, did Lord Guy relax. When he was satisfied that the young knight was completely well again, Avondale requested his presence for a private conversation.

The commander was a decent man, despite all Huma had heard about Ergoth from the higher-ranking members of the knighthood. Avondale was a brilliant strategist as well, although he would have much preferred utilizing his abilities to better his lands. The Emperor of Ergoth, a faceless entity known as Bestell III, had decreed that Lord Avondale should command the armies in his name. The noble, while a very loyal servant to his country, wished that his lord and master could have at least spared some of his highly trained and highly experienced royal guard to replace part of the already vastly depleted forces. Like his predecessors, though, Bestell III was concerned with his own well-being. There was always some reason that prevented him from deploying his personal guard anywhere farther than the capital's gates.

The news of the knighthood's disaster only added to Lord Avondale's growing list of woes. "I still find it hard to reconcile, but I know you tell me the truth, Huma. As of now, I do not see how I can return you to your comrades. We are riding to Daltigoth, on orders of the emperor, and then will most likely turn back up north. I feel like a puppet whose master pulls the strings up and down."

Huma sat alone with him in the commander's tent, the first time the knight had been permitted to leave his tent. The young knight had been provided with sturdy Ergothian armor that Avondale admitted had been intended for his son before the latter's death in his first battle. The strong mail went well with the surviving pieces of Huma's armor. The damage to the helmet and breastplate had proved repairable after all. Huma was thankful for that. As much as he admired the craftsmanship of the Ergothian armor, much of it was too showy even for the most aristocratic of the Knights of Solamnia. Avondale had confided that he wore his ceremonial armor only if he was presenting himself to the emperor. For lesser dignitaries, his battle armor would have to do, even if it disturbed their sensitivities.

Huma had told him everything, except the ill-fated quest he was on. "Is there any way I might be granted free travel in your country?"

"We are in the midst of war, Huma. How could I permit you to travel freely?"

Huma took a sip of the wine that Avondale had offered him. It struck him as amusing that a noble would treat a minor Solamnic knight with such respect. But the Ergothian was no fool; he knew that few other men could have survived Huma's experience. Thus, he was treating Huma accordingly.

"If I may speak candidly . . ." Huma glanced at the guards

outside.

The knight sighed and continued. "It has been rumored that somewhere to the southwest there is a key to ending this eternal war. Somewhere in a range of mountains."

Avondale pondered this. "There is a range of mountains in that general direction. Few ever travel there. It is said to be a haven for the dragons of darkness and, perhaps, other things as well. There may indeed be something of importance in that vicinity."

For a moment, Huma's spirits soared. "Can you accompany me?"

The commander laughed. "I'm afraid the emperor would have my head for that. Besides, it is unfit terrain for troops on horseback. Patrols have gone to those mountains and vanished. Mages refuse to go there, and clerics warn everyone away. Does that give you any idea of what you are asking?"

"Yes, milord." Huma slumped down on the stool and held his head. The tent was suddenly very warm.

"Are you all right?"

"Yes. A moment, please." Huma wiped sweat form his forehead. The fever subsided.

Lord Avondale looked worried. "Perhaps we had better continue our talk tomorrow."

"That would be better, milord."

"So I see." The noble rubbed his chin. "Come with me to Caergoth, and I will see to it that you are able to go on to the mountains on your own, if you still desire to."

"Caergoth?" The heat had left Huma blurry-eyed. He found it difficult to focus on the commander.

"Yes, Caergoth. The clerics will steer us from the plague areas. What do you say?"

"Thank you." Huma rose swiftly, and his head began to swim. He desired nothing more than to lie down. He still had not regained much of his vigor. "If you would excuse me?"

"By all means." Guy Avondale watched the Solamnic knight hurry off. His brow wrinkled in worry. He took a sip of wine and then stared into the glass.

Before being pressed into the service of their emperor, most of Lord Avondale's soldiers had been simple tradesmen and farmers. Thus it was that they knew of the Knights of Solamnia as little more than legend. Now, they had one such legend traveling in their midst, and the tales of his adventures, real and imagined, were already making the rounds through the camp. Huma was almost as awestruck as the Ergothians, for he did not consider himself a legend, and the open stares he received embarrassed him greatly.

Most of the stories revolved loosely about the chase and his berserker's stand against the ebony-armored servants of the warlord. He had slain a legion of them, it appeared, including a massive pack of the demonic dreadwolves, much feared by men who knew their families lived virtually unprotected while they were away at war. Huma found it puzzling that men of Ergoth, the land from which his own knighthood had forcibly sprung, could look up to him as a champion.

Avondale seemed amused. When Huma protested that the stories were getting out of hand, he only smiled and replied that such was the true trial of every great legend, living up to his own reputation. "They need their heroes. It gives them hope—hope that somehow the darkness that is Takhisis will be defeated and they will be able to return to their loved ones."

Occasionally, dragons would sweep in with some word of the war. Northern Ergoth and Hylo had been overrun. Huma grew anxious. He wondered if Kaz had continued north or if he had turned south to seek Huma. Even if the latter were the case, a minotaur would not be welcome in any town in this land. It was not just Kaz that Huma worried about; the battle-scarred easterner would do his utmost to assure he did not die alone.

Huma asked for news of Solamnia, but the dragons who arrived knew nothing of what had occurred there. There were rumors that the knights had been pushed back nearly half the distance to Vingaard Keep. Of the east, nothing could be ascertained.

They made camp near the ruins of a once-prosperous town, two days from Caergoth. The town had perished from plague in the early days of the war, and some people believed the newest wave had originated in its ruins. Avondale was of another mind.

"You will recall," he said to Huma that same evening, "that I mentioned how particular I believed the plague was."

"I remember."

The noble tapped his fingers on the table in his tent. "I believe it is so particular because it is purposefully being directed by human agents."

Huma did not want to believe that anyone would deliberately spread disease, but he knew something of the cult of Morgion. They were rumored to have agents in all societies, all organization, all countries, waiting for the command to unleash the deadly gifts of their god.

"Could you not be mistaken?" Huma would have preferred it that way.

"Perhaps."

Huma was no longer confined to the camp itself. Avondale had applied that restriction on the first day, but had relaxed it once he was assured that Huma would not do something foolish, such as ride off without assistance. Thus it was that Huma wandered from the campsite, eventually picking his way toward the nearest ruins. The ruins disturbed him, as did anything associated with plague, but Huma knew that there would be no traces of disease after all this time.

Huma had had no intention of entering the remains of the ill-fated town—until he caught a glimpse of the four-legged shadow that quickly melted into the maze of decrepit buildings. It might have been merely a wolf, or perhaps a wild dog.

Drawing his sword, he stalked after the shadow-thing. He did not notice how deep into the ruins he had gone until he heard the scurrying of something among the desolate buildings. It was not the sound he would have expected of a four-legged creature. Training and experience told him that this new intruder walked on two legs.

Huma tried to make out shapes in the darkness. He saw the faint glow of two crimson eyes before they vanished into one of the buildings. The knight took a step toward the site.

He heard something skitter within the house to his left. Turning in that direction, Huma could make out nothing but more darkness.

A tall, formless mass bumped him as it moved swiftly past his backside. He whirled and was rewarded with a yelp of pain from the figure before it literally melted into the night. Huma rushed after it, sword before him.

There was no place the figure could have gone but through the battered doorway before the knight. Huma kicked away the remainder of the door and dove in.

The room was empty. He checked the other rooms of the small house. They, too, were inhabited only by the usual vermin. His quarry had vanished. He took a few angry steps toward the back of the building, kicking up dust as he moved. Behind the back of the building, he saw nothing but more rubble. Unless something were lying flat on the ground beneath those particular ruins, he suspected it must be elsewhere. There just was nowhere to hide out there.

The floating dust caused Huma to cough badly. He suddenly felt weak and nauseated, and it was a strain just to walk, much less hold his sword. In irritation, he threw the blade to the floor, raising even more aggravating dust. His armor was caked with the stuff, but he did not care. He was staggering now. The dust seemed everywhere, filling his eyes, nose, ears, and throat. He made it to the doorway and, with a sigh, slumped down and sat staring at the lifeless street. This, too, became much too tiring, and he decided that a nap would do much, much more good. The knight closed his eyes, and snores quickly followed.

Dark figures clad in long, enveloping cloaks and hoods seemed to form shadows around him. Their faces could not be seen beneath the deep hoods, and only one of them revealed hands. That one removed a small vial from his belt and uncorked it. With gentle care, he poured the contents on the floor. The contents, a reddish powder, reacted immediately with that which Huma had believed to be the dust of ages. The two hissed and steamed, canceling one another until nothing remained save the natural layer of gray powder that had accumulated through the years. The hooded figure resealed the bottle and turned toward the fallen knight. He snapped his fingers, and four of his companions scurried over to take hold of Huma.

Within a minute, the room was empty. Had anyone looked inside, they would have seen no indication of recent entry. There was no sign of the knight and no sign of his shadowy captors.

A mocking howl cut through the bleak air of the ghost town.

Chapter 12

Voices hissed incomprehensibly, seemingly in some sort of debate. It took the groggy knight several seconds before he came to realize that it was he the voices were arguing over. He wished his eyes would work so that he could see who was so concerned with his welfare.

Another voice, somehow familiar, cut in, full of anger. "Why do you delay?"

"He is marked."

"Of what concern is that, Skularis?"

The one called Skularis hissed at some offense in the question. "There is something amiss when a Knight of Solamnia bears such a mark."

A second voice, more like the croak of some great bullfrog, snapped, "He would not understand, Nightmaster!

This one on the ground is more one of us than him."

The first speaker, the Nightmaster, tried again to explain. "We have agents among them. Powerful ones, indeed." The other speaker croaked his agreement. Huma stirred a little. They seemed to think he bore some kind of important mark. All he had right now was a burning forehead.

"I am aware of what the mark means," the familiar voice—where had he heard it?—said. "I am also aware that it is not going to kill him as I had originally thought. Excellent. He bears information I need. His very existence is important to me."

"What would you have us do, then? We cannot do him harm, not if one of ours has marked him for protection."

The evident outsider snarled, and Huma's senses came alive as he recognized the sound. Only the dreadwolves made a sound like that.

Someone must have noticed the shifting of his body, for a gloved hand reached down and turned Huma's head from left to right. The glove was quite rotten; it stank so badly that Huma instinctively pulled away from it. The one identified as Nightmaster chuckled obscenely.

"He is not one of us, but one of us has sought to protect him. This grows more and more interesting."

"What shall we do?" the croaker asked.

"You must hide him, you wretched cadavers!" the outsider snarled. "Hide him until my servants can contact you! Has the plague taken your minds as well as your bodies?"

Huma's eyes seemed willing to open at that point, just a crack.

Two figures resembling high mounds of moldy, stinking cloth stood conversing with—a dreadwolf. No one else. It took Huma's fog-enshrouded mind several moments to realize that Galan Dracos—from his citadel far away somewhere—was using his unliving servant as his eyes, ears, and mouth in Ergoth.

That they were still somewhere in the ruins was only a guess. What little he could make out lent credence to that guess, for the room was filled with rubble and part of the ceiling was gone. Huma did not know how long he had been unconscious or how far they had dragged him.

Then the more menacing of the two ragged assailants lifted an arm, revealing a bony, scarred hand with the index finger pointed at the renegade's messenger. "Have a care, mage. You have her blessing for now, but she is a fickle queen to those who fail her. You would do well to speak more civilly with those you need."

The pale form of the dreadwolf bristled with barely contained fury as Dracos allowed his emotions to be transmitted through his servant. The smaller of the two hooded figures shuffled back, two blotchy hands held up in obvious fear.

The other, the Nightmaster, must have smiled, for his tone was full of mockery. "Your powers are fearsome to the fear-filled, but not to one who enjoys the protection of Morgion."

Morgion! Huma was barely able to stifle the shock that leaped through his taut body. He was a prisoner of the cultists of Morgion, god of disease and decay!

"This is a foolish waste of time," Dracos finally muttered.

"Agreed. Very well, *mage*. My brethren will keep this one for your lackeys, but only because it serves the Master's goals to do so. Not because I fear your power."

"Of course not."

"But the mark—" said the croaker.

"There are times, brother, when we all must make sacrifices for the greater glory of Morgion."

"And the Queen, of course," added Dracos purposefully.

"And the Queen. Pity. I am still curious as to the reason for the mark." Skularis put a hand to Huma's forehead.

Huma reeled from the shock, feeling as if his very soul were being invaded. He cringed, but he had no room to maneuver away from the clawlike hand.

Quite suddenly, he was no longer in the ruins. A kaleidoscope of sights and sounds enveloped him. Huma felt no fright. A part of him knew this state was only in his mind, though he could not explain how this should calm him. Huma thought he could hear the sounds of horses riding into battle, the clank of armor, the cries of battle, and steel against steel. He saw a vision of three knights. Each wore a symbol of the knighthood: the crown, the sword, and the rose. They all wore visors, but Huma knew somehow the two in back could only be the twin gods Habbakuk and Kiri-Jolith. Two of the Solamnic Triumvirate—which meant that he who stood before them . . .

With a horrible abruptness, Huma was wrenched from that vision and returned to the real world once more. Had he not been gagged, he would have screamed, for the bony, disease-ridden hand pulled sharply away from him, seeming to take strips of his flesh as it did. Through blurred eyes, Huma could see the two cloth-enveloped figures staring down at him.

"I could not penetrate his mind. He is shielded through sheer willpower alone. Fascinating."

"And the mark?" croaked the second.

"No longer there. It was too weak. He is too much a pawn of the prolonger of pain, that which fools call Life. He is not one of us—could *never* be one of us."

From behind them, the voice of Dracos issued forth once more from the maw of the dreadwolf. "Then there can be no more hesitation."

"None. He is yours when your servants come." The cleric snapped his fingers. Huma's eyes chose that moment to clear. Hooded figures emerged from the darkness, disease-wracked ghouls like the dead of a battlefield come back to some semblance of life.

"Take him to the catacombs. Bind him to the altar."

"No sacrifices!"

Even Huma could not miss the curling of the cleric's lip. "Have no fear, cur. He will be alive and well. It shall be interesting to see if you have better luck than I did."

Dracos had no reply for that, or at least the dreadwolf repeated no message. Huma struggled, but his bonds held together. Four of the cloaked figures grabbed him roughly and lifted. Their combined odor was nearly overwhelming.

He had hoped to get some idea where they were and where they were going, but his view was obscured by the moth-eaten sleeve of one of his bearers. He suspected that they still were quite close to the building where he had foolishly fallen victim to one of the cult's traps. Huma knew something of the followers of Morgion. They were expert at keeping their plots and membership secret. That they were taking him to the catacombs meant that they lived beneath Caergoth itself, a frightening revelation. Small wonder no trace of the origins of the plague could be found. It was not from something within or near the city, but beneath it.

A breeze wafted some of the stench from his nostrils. Huma assumed that they must have stepped from one of the ruined buildings back into the night. He sought desperately for some plan of escape, suspecting that the catacombs would be virtually impossible to traverse. But he was tightly bound and gagged, and his situation seemed hopeless now.

The group had traveled a short distance from the building when Huma heard what appeared to be the hoot of a night bird. The ragged figures came to an abrupt halt as they belatedly realized what Huma had recognized instantly.

There was a hiss as something hurtled through the air and then one of Huma's bearers went down, an arrow in his chest. The knight had time to brace himself as the others lost their grip on him and he fell to the ground face up.

Then it was pandemonium as brilliant light left the hooded figures with nowhere to hide. Well-placed arrows took down two more before the cultists could get their bearings. The one called Skularis ran past Huma's field of vision. He was foregoing the honors of command for the safety of fleeing. It was a short-lived flight, however; not one, but three arrows caught him in the back. The Nightmaster wobbled like a mad puppet and collapsed in a heap.

Armored figures were now rushing out even as the light dimmed. Of the cloaked villains—there had been more than a dozen, Huma was shocked to realize—only four were still standing. They lacked any substantial weapons, and the first soldiers to wade into the combat made the mistake of believing themselves safe from harm. That mistake was made evident when one of the dark clerics pulled forth a small pouch and threw it at the nearest armored figure. Huma could hear the man's scream and the shocked cries of other soldiers as all the ravages of the plague seemed to occur within the space of seconds.

A familiar figure stepped before him and leaned down to test the bonds. "What a fool I was! I should have known . . ."

The archers were taking over. By the time Avondale had finished cutting Huma's bonds, the last of the cloaked menaces lay dead.

"The dreadwolf? Did you get it?"

"Dreadwolf?" Avondale scanned the area worriedly. "I have not seen it!"

"My sword!" Huma's weapon lay half-buried under one of the cultists. He tugged at it mindlessly, his only concern that the four-legged horror must be stopped. Somehow, impossibly, the creature had evaded the fighting and was escaping. Huma did not want the dreadwolf tracking him down again and transmitting to its master the knight's location and activities.

He heard Lord Avondale call after him, but he ignored him. He had to see the thing destroyed.

A scrabbling of running feet alerted him. He followed the sound at full speed, only barely missing numerous holes and mounds that threatened to send him flying if he made a misstep. He did not think of the dangers.

Huma leaped over the remains of a stone wall. The plague had not directly caused all the damage around him; the crazed riots and torching of plagued homes had done that.

He landed on rubble. Suddenly, his foot slipped from beneath him and he was falling backward. By the strongest of efforts, he succeeded in keeping his grip on the sword. The errant foot twisted beneath him, and he gritted his teeth in pain.

As he lay there, stunned, the fearsome visage thrust itself into his face. The long, yellowed fangs hovered near his throat, and the blood-red tongue flickered in and out of the massive jaws. The sightless eyes revealed only death to the trapped knight. The dreadwolf's front claws pressed sharply into Huma's chest.

"Rather would I deprive the mage of his puppet friend!" The jaws closed in on the knight's throat.

Huma swung the blade hard against the dreadwolf. It was an awkward angle, and the cut he inflicted was negligible. But it did throw the beast off his chest.

The dreadwolf rolled over once and landed on its feet. The crimson eyes glowed fiercely, and the thing's lips curled back in hatred. Huma raised his sword high.

Suddenly, the creature burst into flames. One second it had stood there, preparing to strike, the next it was a fireball. Huma looked on in amazement, and then noticed a new figure stepping out from behind the ruins of what had once been a fairly large inn.

"Magius!"

The mage quickly raised a finger to his lips and indicated the need for silence. He was thinner, and much of the vanity was gone from his manner. The once-brilliant gold sheen of his hair was now a miserable brown, and it was cut much shorter. Had it been burned away? Magius was also wearing something else Huma had not seen him dressed in since the early days of training—a crimson robe.

"Come! I have laid a confusion spell on Lord Avondale's men, but it will not be long before they realize which way you really ran!"

"But—" Huma knew it was madness to follow his old friend again, but the bonds forged strong yesterday were just as powerful today.

"Come!" Magius repeated urgently.

Huma followed.

They moved with astonishing speed through the town, eventually coming to the far southern end. Two horses awaited them there. Magius indicated that the more massive of the beasts was for the knight. Only when they were well on their way did Magius speak.

"We must ride hard for some time. There is a Solamnic outpost to bypass."

"Outpost?" Somewhat unfamiliar with regions south of Solamnia, the news came as a great shock to Huma. Knights of Solamnia! In Ergoth!

"Was that you who unleashed the light?"

"Yes," Magius replied. "I'll explain in the morning, after I am sure we have lost whatever pursuit the Ergothian no doubt has organized already!"

Huma slowed the horse. "Why are we running from Lord Avondale?"

The mage's eyes flashed. "Are you blind? Do you think the Ergothian was aiding you out of the goodness of his soul?"

Huma refrained from snapping back that, yes, he had come to trust the noble. Where was the crime in that?

"You told him that there was something in the mountains, didn't you? You told him about the path!"

"You're babbling, Magius. I don't even know about any path."

Magius grimaced, and Huma realized that the mage had let something slip. The spellcaster recovered quickly, though, and said, "You told him there is something in the mountains to the southwest that could bring victory against Takhisis. He is first and foremost an Ergothian noble, Huma. Ergothian nobles are noted for their willingness to do whatever they must in order to increase their own prestige and power. Think what you have told him. What a great prize it would be for him to deliver to his emperor. Think about how the emperor would reward the man who succeeded in bringing peace to Ansalon at long last. An Ergothian noble would kill for something as valuable as what we seek."

The words—or perhaps it was the tone—almost seemed hypnotic. Huma kept telling himself that Lord Avondale was a good man. Yet would his loyalty not be first to his emperor rather than to a wandering knight? He had offered Huma safe passage, but only if the knight first traveled with him. Huma shook the madness from his head. He was not sure anymore what was right or wrong, except that he wanted to find that mountain. He was now headed that direction, and it seemed pointless to turn back now.

He did not notice the bitter smile that crept onto the worn face of the mage as the latter turned forward once more.

With Magius guiding them, they rode a twisted path through the plains and wooded lands southwest of Caergoth.

It was near dawn before the two finally came to a halt. Magius revealed a small, nearly hidden lake. They tied the horses near good grazing. The mage went to sleep shortly after—again without explaining things. Huma propped himself against a tree and sat staring out at the calm lake. He pondered the renegade mage who now wanted Huma as badly as he wanted Magius. Dracos.

The dreadwolf had been reduced to ash, leaving Galan Dracos without his spy and blind to the doings of Huma and Magius, at least for the time being. With the war taking so much of his personal effort, the renegade magic-user had been forced to rely on his spies for too much. Huma suspected that Dracos knew at least as much as Huma did about what Magius sought, and perhaps more. Somewhere, sometime, there would be more spies—and Huma had no doubt that sooner or later Galan Dracos would temporarily turn from his many other tasks and personally endeavor to put an end to both his enemies and their quest.

He picked up a small pebble and tossed it into the center of the lake—only to watch it come flying back out at him. Huma tried to stand, but his legs buckled. What had he walked into this time? he wondered angrily.

Abruptly, a woman's head popped up from the edge of the lake. Though slightly green, it was very lovely. The eyes were narrow slits, as if the woman had just awakened. She had a tiny, pert nose and long, full lips. When she rose from the water, Huma saw that she was slim and long-legged, although she would not stand even as high as his shoulders. Her sole garment, a thin gown, was soaked and clung to every curve. A nymph. He had heard stories of them. They were said to be of the Age of Dreams, when there was no recorded history. Whether they were a race was debatable. They were very rarely seen.

"Hello, manling." Her voice was melodious, like a small forest bird's. She smiled, and Huma's face reddened. Still, attractive though she was, another female form, Gwyneth's, superimposed itself on his imagination. He managed to get to his feet.

"Hello." It took him some time to build up the nerve to reply. The nymph disturbed him even as she attracted him. Such creatures, legend said, were not only playful, but deadly. More than one man had been lured to his demise, if there was any truth in the ancient tales. Huma's hand stroked the pommel of his sword. Her kind was magical, and, despite his friendship with Magius, Huma still shared some of the knighthood's distrust of sorcery.

Huma looked down by his side and was surprised to find that Magius still slept. Huma suspected the sleep was no longer natural, and he shuddered.

The nymph gave a surprised laugh. "I thought you were someone else," she said. "I like you, too, though."

"Oh?" He tried his best to be casual, though his heart and mind were racing. "Why did you think I was someone else?" If others visited the lake, Huma did not wish to remain here long. Should they be anything like the nymph, Huma suspected he would stand no chance if it came to conflict. His hand involuntarily gripped the handle of his weapon.

"You look like Buoron. All that silly metal. He comes to visit me. Would you like to see my home?"

Huma stepped back anxiously. Her home, according to what little he knew, was probably at the bottom of the lake. If she decided to compel him . . . "No, thank you," he hurriedly answered. "I would not wish to impose."

She pouted. "You even sound like Buoron."

"Were you expecting him?" Huma glanced quickly around the edge of the lake, half-expecting to see a heavily armored figure come crashing through the trees at any moment.

The nymph walked onto the shore. Huma turned to Magius, but the mage still slept.

"He won't wake until I let him. I don't like him."

The knight's brow wrinkled. "You know him, too?"

She waved off the spellcaster as inconsequential. "Not him. His image."

"Where?" Huma did not know what to make of this creature. She seemed fragile, but her power was strong enough to have trapped Magius with ease. Perhaps that would not have been possible if Magius had not been so exhausted, but it still bespoke great ability.

"I see it in my mirror. It shows me what others are dreaming. It gets so boring out here. I miss the cavern builders."

"Cavern builders?"

"The ones that dig in the ground, silly. You know, short funny men."

Dwarves. It was maddening to try to make sense of some of the things the nymph said.

She was standing close to him now, innocently leaning just close enough to unnerve him. "Are you sure you would not like to come see my home? I won't let you drown as long as you do not get boring."

There was the real trap. How many males had succumbed to that beauty and followed her down, only to find themselves trapped in a sea cave? Instinctively, he uttered a prayer to Paladine.

The nymph stepped away. "I wish you would not do that!"

Although not technically evil, she was not a creature of Paladine, nor Gilean, either. Therefore, true prayers to either, could annoy her or even drive her away.

Huma was about to apologize when he heard the sound of a heavy horse coming through the brush not far away. He tried to rise and grip his sword.

"Why, here comes Buoron. I hope you two will fight. I have not watched a good fight in centuries."

The horse and rider broke through the foliage and onto the narrow strip of plain surrounding the tiny lake. The man wore a cloak over most of his body, but Huma could see the glint of armor underneath. The newcomer did not notice them at first. When he did, he merely gaped at Huma. The cloak slid open, and Huma was given his first good view of the armor beneath. Huma looked from armor to face, and back to armor again. He recalled Magius's hurried mention of an outpost somewhere in southern Ergoth. A Solamnic outpost.

The nymph smiled sweetly. "See why I mistook you for Buoron? You even wear the same armor."

It was true. Buoron was a Knight of the Crown.

Chapter 13

BUORON TURNED TO GAZE AT THE NYMPH. HE WAS A
rough-featured man, neither handsome nor ugly, but weathered. A deep sadness was in his eyes. Oddly, he was also
minus the impressive mustache that most knights sported.
Instead, he wore a black beard clipped in the same style as
Lord Avondale. Huma wondered how long the other
Solamnic knight had lived in this region.

"Leave us now," Buoron said to the nymph.

"Will you not fight?"

Buoron seemed disgusted by the question. "He is one of
my comrades. I will not fight him."

"Oh." She frowned, then brightened. "Will you fight the
mage?"

"Mage?" The other knight brushed an errant lock of hair

from his face and looked at the slumbering bundle. "He must be sorely tired to sleep through all this."

"She's put him under," Huma explained.

A sigh. The knight seemed to expect this. "Why?"

The nymph pouted. "I do not like him. He is one of the dreamers I showed you."

"Is he now?" Buoron straightened, his interest keenly awakened. "Which one?"

"The one who keeps dying."

Huma's eyes narrowed. At one point in their travels, Magius had revealed that his death scene now repeated itself constantly in his dreams. The nymph could not have known that. Or could she? Did she really see others' dreams?

"Release him," the rider ordered.

"Do you not want to sit with me?" She shifted all too purposefully. Buoron's face reddened again.

"No. Leave us. This is important."

The water creature put two delicate hands on her hips and gave an angry look. "I do not like you anymore. I no longer want you to come visit me."

She ran off into the water and, when it proved deep enough, dove beneath the surface. There was nothing to indicate that she was anything but human, save for the slight greenish cast to her skin and the amazing fluidity of her movements. Huma wondered how she breathed.

Buoron muttered, "She does not mean what she said. She's been angry with me more than a dozen times before, and each time she forgets before I've drawn another breath. I believe it's the nature of her kind, though I've never seen another."

Huma looked down at the still-slumbering Magius. "Will she remember to release her victim?"

"Give her a few moments. She can hold onto the spell for only a brief time longer. You know my name, brother of the Order. What might yours be?"

Huma straightened. "I am Huma, Knight of the Crown, out of Vingaard Keep."

"Vingaard!" The name was spoken as if the name of Paladine himself. "Have they broken through at last? Is the war finally coming to a close?"

Huma shook his head and then stared at the ground. Quickly, he described what had happened. Buoron was not pleased.

"One of her games," Buoron said with a gesture toward the water, "is to take the dreamer's mirror, an ancient artifact, shake it, and see whose dreams she gets." The bearded knight shivered. "The dreams of the Dragonqueen's servants are darker than you could ever imagine."

"Has she always lived here?"

Buoron shrugged. He did not like speaking about the nymph. His relationship, no matter what it was, was something the knighthood would not condone. "She was here when I joined the outpost. Her treasures are incredibly ancient." He paused. "I came upon her by accident. The other knights never come this far. I was chasing a stag, and I had no desire to lose it. It is not often we eat such splendid fare at the outpost. For one reason or another, the stag rushed through here. I fell when my steed came to an abrupt halt, and when I finally had cleared the pain from my head, I found myself looking into her eyes."

Huma could read the embarrassment in the other knight's features. "You need have no fear, brother of the Order. I will tell no one of this lake."

Buoron shrugged. "They know, more or less. I have made no secret of my comings and goings, and I have done little more than sit with her. A nymph is not real. I would want something more." Magius began to stir. The other knight pointed at him. "Your sorcerous friend wakes. I doubt he will take kindly to having been kept under a glamour spell all this time."

Huma glanced down. Magius was not yet truly awake, but any decision on Huma's part would have to be swift. "He need not know."

The bearded knight said nothing, but gratitude flared in his eyes. It was obvious to Huma that he cared more about the water nymph than he had indicated.

Magius leaped up as some sense told him that he and Huma were no longer alone. He turned to stare at the newcomer.

"Greetings, Red Robe." Buoron's salutation was crisp and

functional. Magius received only the respect due one who traveled with a fellow knight.

The mage had recovered. He bowed low in the manner so typical of him and returned the greeting. "My greetings to you, Knight of Solamnia. I had no idea another of the noble knighthood was so far south."

Huma's expression did not change, but he was disturbed by yet another lie from his friend. When they had fled from the ruins, Magius had commented on his desire to bypass the outpost.

"We have an outpost down here," Buoron replied. "A small one and often forgotten. I do not doubt it will be abandoned as the years pass."

"Yes." The magic-user was visibly uninterested. Instead, he was staring down at the spot where he had been sleeping and then at the lake. "My apologies for not rising sooner. It is unlike me. I did not mean to be impolite."

Buoron fidgeted and his horse, a cream-colored charger, stepped nervously about as it felt the shifting of its rider. "Not at all. It happens often here. I, myself, have fallen into the very same sort of sleep."

"It is still no excuse."

"How far is it to the outpost?" Huma finally asked, causing Magius to glare at him.

"Not far. An hour's ride. You must come, of course. Despite the terrible news you bring, your presence would be appreciated."

Magius chuckled enigmatically.

The other knight was taking a distinct dislike to the spellcaster. Pretending not to have heard the mage's laugh, Buoron indicated the duo's mounts.

"These beasts appear to have been ridden all night. They need some proper care if you plan to move on." He was careful not to ask the purpose of their journey, assuming that Huma would inform him if and when it was proper.

The mage gave in. "Very well. It shall have to be a short stop, though. We have far to travel."

"Um." That was all that Buoron would say in reply, but he watched both men with interest, Huma noted, as they untied their animals and mounted them. When they were ready, he pointed to the west. "That way. Ride on ahead. I'll be only a moment."

Huma and Magius urged their steeds through the trees and brush. The former glanced back and saw Buoron dismount and remove a small wooden carving from one of his saddlebags. The water nearby began to bubble, and the head of the nymph broke the surface. Then Huma's view was cut off by the trees. When his companion turned to him, the knight reacted as if his thoughts had been on the trail ahead.

It was not more than a minute or two before Buoron came riding up behind them. He nodded to Huma and immediately took the lead.

As they rode, Huma plied him with questions about the outpost. "Are there many outposts here?"

"We are one of only two. The other lies on the western side of that stretch of mountains." Buoron pointed to a chain of peaks that became visible only when the trio of riders emerged onto the top of a hill. "Essentially, we oversee the eastern half and they the west. There is little down here to interest the Dragonqueen, though. We have been reduced to chasing would-be brigands when we should be charging into the lines of the foul ogres."

"Are you a large outpost? I'd not known there was anyone here."

Buoron laughed, bitterly, it seemed. "Neither did I, until I was ordered down here some five years ago. No, we're not a large outpost. Eighty knights trying to keep watch on a countryside rivaling the size of Solamnia. We had more once."

Huma did not need elaboration. Now, with the war going so badly, they truly were cut off from all others save their counterparts on the western side of the mountains. They could not abandon the outposts and go riding north to join the struggle. They had been ordered down here, and they would stay until that order was changed. Duty was something ingrained into every knight. Rennard had expressed the importance of that, time and time again.

"Have you ever been to the mountains?" Magius asked abruptly.

"No." Buoron had no desire to converse with the spellcaster.

"Has anyone?"

"Only to the outer peaks. We stay away from the inner range."

Magius appeared quite interested. "Why is that?"

"The paths are unsafe. That's all."

Huma watched his companion's face fall. Magius was probing for something more out of the ordinary.

This deep into southern Ergoth, it was difficult to believe a war raged in the land. To be sure, the skies were as overcast as they had been in the north, but there was more of a peace in the woods and fields. It was a false peace, Huma realized, for it would vanish the instant the Dragonqueen's hordes were finished with Solamnia. With Solamnia gone, the Queen of Darkness would sweep over the rest of the continent in less than a year.

"We are almost there."

Huma took his first look at the Solamnic outpost. It was not a towering edifice like Vingaard Keep. The entire structure was made of wood, treated so that flames could not turn it into a deathtrap. The walls surrounding the complex appeared to be more than four times Huma's height. The top edge was consistently punctuated by gaps set aside for archers. Only one building was visible over the wall, a watchtower upon which even now a sentry was standing, his attention fixed on the approaching trio. The man raised a shout and pointed toward them. Buoron did not call out, but he gave the sentry a weary wave.

Huma glanced at Magius; the mage was staring longingly at the distant mountains.

There were renewed cries when the sentry noticed that one of the two strangers was a fellow knight. The wooden gates swung open as the three neared them, and it appeared that nearly all of the outpost's inhabitants were coming out to welcome the newcomers.

"Buoron! Back so soon? What have you brought with you?"

The tall, elderly speaker must have been a knight even when Lord Oswal was a child. He was deeply wrinkled and his voice shook slightly, but his moves were graceful and Huma suspected he could still handle a sword. Unlike the majority of the knights, who seemed to favor Ergothian beards, the aged knight still sported a traditional, if somewhat silver, mustache. He was a Knight of the Rose, the only one Huma could see upon first inspection.

"Hail, Lord Taggin. Two travelers in need of rest, one of them a brother to our ranks. He has news of the utmost importance."

Taggin nodded grimly. "I'd thought as much." To the rest of the assembled knights, he said, "Return to your duties! Remember that you are Knights of Solamnia, not a gaggle of hungry geese!"

Some disappointment showed in the faces of the knights, many of whom, Buoron explained, had been assigned to the outpost for nearly ten years. Taggin had been there twice as long. In fact, he had manned the outpost by himself for many years.

Huma could not help smiling. Somehow, he felt that he was among a different breed of knights than those back at Vingaard Keep. They were less strict with the rules, more willing to bend to circumstances.

As it turned out, the outpost included only three buildings. One was the tower, which also served as armory and stable. The second was a type of longhouse, which Huma recognized as the living quarters of the company. The third and, surprisingly enough, the most insignificant-looking of the three was Taggin's command center and quarters. All were made of wood. To Huma, raised in a village, it was more like home than the proud Keep had ever been.

The outpost's builders had planned as well as they could. Huma noted that the structure was close enough to the woods to allow the knights easy access to hunting and to gathering fuel for fires, yet was far enough into the plains so that any attempted assault would force the enemy to rush across long stretches of flat, open field. Water was provided by a small stream and a deep well. Later, Huma would discover that the knights even grew their own crops in a fortified extension behind the rest of the outpost. Again, Huma could not help marvel at the differences between the knighthood here and back in Solamnia.

Taggin ordered Buoron to deliver the two over to him as soon as they were clean and fed. Magius quite bluntly stated that he would talk to no one until he was finally allowed some rest. The commander frowned at the mage's arrogant manner but conceded the necessity.

Huma awoke to the sound of men preparing to ride out. He glanced briefly toward Magius, who stirred restlessly and then turned to the nearest window. The mage peered out. The sun was going down. A number of fully armored knights were riding out of the gate, more than one armed with weighted nets in addition to their normal weaponry. For a patrol, it contained a large number of horsemen.

He saw Buoron walking past the doorway and signaled to him. The knight waved to him and turned back. Huma began to dress. Buoron entered.

"Are you better now?" The other knight was talking low.

"Much. I've not slept this long in weeks." Huma was silent until he was fully clad. Then he and Buoron stepped outside. By this time, the last of the riders had left and the gates were closed.

Huma indicated the gates. "Why the heavy patrol? Is there activity by the ogres?"

Buoron shook his head. "I am beginning to doubt if there will ever be. No, this problem is more local. We do a little trade with the Qualinesti elves, though they generally tend to stay to themselves, like most of their kind."

"One of the few who meet with us regularly told us a beast has been lurking about this general region." The bearded knight smiled. "We wanted to ask them what they were doing so far away from their own lands, but our relationship would not stand the strain. Instead, we thanked them and began to investigate."

"Did you see this creature?"

"We simply call him the Beast. He's crafty, perhaps an ogre scout, even. Three times he's given us the slip. Tonight, though, they think they can hunt him down to his lair. With any luck, the patrol will take him alive."

"For what purpose?"

"If he's a spy, he might have information. If he's some sort of animal, Taggin still wants to see him. The Qualinesti are concerned about his presence; the commander wants to see why."

Lord Taggin was finishing up his daily routine when Buoron brought Huma to speak to him. The elderly knight greeted his visitor amicably—protocol was unimportant out here—but he seemed nervous.

"You have no idea how it stands at present?"

Huma shook his head. "None. The hope was to regroup. That is all I know."

"I see." Taggin stared at him with penetrating eyes. After several moments, the elder knight said, "Nothing we can do. It will be best to break the news to the men first thing in the morning, Buoron."

Buoron, who had been standing quietly through the entire talk, did not hesitate. "I'll do it, Lord Taggin."

"Fine." The commander cleared off everything from the table he used for his work. "You are excused, lad."

Huma turned as Buoron did, but Taggin immediately stopped him. "Not you, Knight Huma. I still have a few things to ask you. Be seated, please."

Nothing was said until Buoron had departed. Huma felt uncomfortable alone in the presence of Taggin but was disciplined enough not to show it. Taggin tapped his fingers on the table. After evidently gathering his thoughts, he spoke.

"What is the purpose of your travels?"

"Milord?"

The nervousness of the senior knight had vanished. His voice and stare were both steady. "Don't hedge, Huma. This is not Vingaard. I will not hold you to anything you say. This is between us. I like to think that I'm a good enough judge of character, and I trust you despite the company you keep."

"Thank you, milord."

Taggin smiled ruefully at the politeness. "I'm already well aware of my status and especially of my age. Please, call me Taggin. Now then, what is your purpose for coming here? I can think of a hundred different routes that would have taken you back to Vingaard long before now. Why head south?

Is it the mage? Despite his less-than-savory attitude, I gather the two of you are close."

"We grew up together." Huma was hesitant about expanding on his friendship with Magius any more than necessary.

"Did you? Unusual combination. Still, a man is more than symbols or robes, be they white, red, or even black."

"He is not evil, Lo—Taggin."

The outpost commander smiled slightly. "I did not say he was."

Huma began to break down in the presence of understanding. "He fears for his life, but he also thinks to end this war."

"Which was his first priority?"

"I—" Huma tensed. "I would have to say his life is more important to him."

"Understandable. Providing, of course, it is not to the detriment of the world."

Huma had no answer for that.

Lord Taggin stood up and paced around the room. "Why have you decided to join him on this—shall we say 'quest' for want of a better word? Is it merely out of friendship?"

"Yes. No. Both."

The elder knight raised an eyebrow. "Both?"

To explain his answer, Huma first had to tell Taggin of the Test and how it had affected Magius. The Knight of the Rose listened patiently as Huma told him about Magius's premonition of his own death. Taggin's expression changed little.

"You've been quite honest with me," the commander said when Huma had finished. "I'd like to digest it and then speak to you again come the morrow."

Now that it was over, Huma was sweating. "Yes, milord. Thank you."

Taggin sat down in his chair. "I've lived a long life, Huma. I've seen more than you think. I want you to consider that tonight. Dismissed."

Huma saluted and left. Once outside, he exhaled sharply. He found Buoron waiting for him.

"You've not eaten for some time," the bearded knight finally said. "Would you like some nourishment?"

Huma smiled thankfully. "I could use some food. Magius

might as well."

"He can fend for himself. He's a magic-user."

The comment cut deep. Huma glanced back at the knights' quarters. At last, he replied, "He's probably still asleep. When he's hungry, he'll awaken."

"Fine." Buoron led him away, and Huma did not resist.

Night grew, aged, and finally passed away. Magius remained asleep. Huma decided that the mage must be purposely building his strength. Magius might have been dead, judging by the way he appeared, all pale and nearly as stiff as a corpse. Huma had checked his pulse, though, and discovered nothing wrong.

As the first hour of day passed, the sentry gave a shout that the patrol was home at last. Men rushed to open the gates, speculation on the success of the hunt rampant. Huma found Buoron and joined the rest. Taggin stepped out of his quarters and merely watched.

The first man at the gate peered through a spyhole and turned back in excitement. "They've got something!"

Immediately, Taggin walked toward them. "Everyone on duty return to his post! By the Triumvirate, this is a military establishment, not a circus! You'll see the thing soon enough, if it's truly a beast!"

The gates were opened, and the weary but triumphant party rode in. A number of them appeared wounded, but Buoron whispered that all had returned.

The Beast was not visible, having been wrapped up in weighted nets. Some patches of brown fur were evident, but the nature of the Beast was hidden; the creature had been forced into a ball. It snorted and growled.

Taggin had the Beast dragged to a pen, which had been built days before just for this event. While Huma looked on, several knights took hold of the bound mass and pulled it into the pen. The Beast squirmed and some of its wrapping came loose. The knights hurried out of the pen while the creature continued to try to free itself.

The patrol leader came up to Lord Taggin and saluted. "Found it in the gully. Killed a stag recently and was eating it. Sensed us but by then we had surrounded it. First men tried to net it, and it pulled them in. Got more men wounded trying to rescue the others. For a moment, I thought we were going to have to kill it. Fortunately, we did not have to. It tripped in the tangle of nets, and we had it."

The elder knight nodded. "Paladine watched over you, that is obvious. I'm glad no one was killed. The cage should hold it now."

"Best not to call it a cage. A prison would be a more proper term, milord."

"Prison?" Beside him, Huma and Buoron exchanged glances. "What have we got here?"

The Beast was still unrecognizable, having succeeded in freeing its limbs but not in uncovering itself. It was obvious now, though, that some of its growls were actually muffled words.

The patrol leader looked overly proud. "A spy from the Dragonqueen! One of her ugly creatures from the north. The war has finally come to us."

There was a gleam in the knight's eye that Huma, at least, found disturbing.

Taggin stepped closer to the prison cage. The Beast had finally begun to tear away the nets still covering it.

"Sargas be damned! I'll tear all of you apart!"

Huma froze. Buoron looked at him, possibly wondering why the sight of the Beast so astonished Huma. Having recently come from the north, Huma should have been familiar with such creatures.

The Beast pulled the last net from its horned head. It turned on its captors, breathing heavily. With blood-chilling fury, it shook the bars of its new prison.

"Fools! Cowards! Let me fight one of you! Give me a fair chance! Where is your vaunted honor?"

From its present angle, the Beast could not see Huma. Huma, though, could see the Beast quite well. He stared wide-eyed at the furious man-beast and wondered just how he was going to save Kaz from execution.

Chapter 14

It was to Buoron he first confided his secret.

"You were fortunate that no one else noticed," said the bearded knight. "Your mouth fairly hung open when he was brought in."

Huma shook his head. "I was stunned. The last I had seen of Kaz, he was riding north and I was riding south. We had a great number of pursuers following us. I was apparently the main prize, for they followed me."

"And paid the price," Buoron remarked quietly. Huma had told him of that incident, without any embellishment. It had not failed to impress the other knight.

"I am amazed that Kaz is here, and has been for at least a couple of days more than I have. He must have turned south almost immediately and just missed me. After we separated,

I was forced to let loose my horse in the hope I might lead my pursuers farther astray. I was on foot for some time after that. Still, he must have been riding hard to have gotten all the way here. He must have lost his horse soon after."

"Did he know where you were heading?"

Huma thought long. It seemed ages ago. "In general. Enough, at least, to bear southwest."

Buoron stared out a window in the direction of the cage. Kaz was slumped in sullen anger. "There are many paths that an expert warrior could use to travel safely. He must have discovered our existence down here as well and assumed that you would stop here. Perhaps he even assumed this was your destination."

That made some sense to Huma. "I did mention wanting to return to the knighthood. He may have assumed that I would go here if I could not make it back to Solamnia."

"Or—" Buoron hesitated. "Or he really is a spy, and this was his intention all along."

"No." Huma was unsure about much lately, but the minotaur's loyalty was not an issue.

"You may have trouble convincing the others of that. A minotaur is a minotaur. They will question him and, whether or not he speaks, will probably execute him."

"For what? He's done nothing but defend himself."

Buoron grimaced. "Haven't you heard what I was saying? He's a minotaur. They do not need any other reason."

Huma paced. "I must speak with Taggin."

"Do it soon, then. They will start the questioning today, likely after morning vigils."

"Will I find Taggin in his quarters now?"

"I think not. Being a Knight of the Rose, he will be at his daily prayers by now. It was only because of the hunt that he delayed at all this morning. Speaking of which, have you eased your mind of late?"

Huma stopped his pacing and whitened. "No. I've not. It would serve me right if Paladine turned his eye from me forever."

Buoron shook his head. "I think Paladine is a little more forgiving than that. Come."

Taggin was unable to see Huma after prayers. The commanding knight was conferring with his seconds and with the patrol leader. Huma knew better than to demand entrance; it would only hurt his chances of convincing them to free Kaz.

With the leadership busy, Huma decided to face the minotaur. It was not right that he pretend not to know the massive easterner. Kaz had always treated him honestly.

The minotaur's place of confinement was a cage like those used by traveling shows to contain their exotic animals: a metal cage with bars, a single gate, and grass and straw piled on the floor. Kaz did not pace to and fro. Instead, he was sitting, staring sullenly at the meat and grain mixture his jailers had left him. It was hardly an appetizing dish, and Huma wondered if it tasted as horrible as it looked.

Two knights guarded the cage, and they quickly blocked Huma's way.

"May I question the prisoner?"

"That is for the Lord Commander to do. Any who wish to watch may do so."

"May I at least speak to him?"

The two knights looked at one another. They were no doubt wondering why one of their number would wish to speak with a minotaur prisoner. At last, the one who had spoken the first time replied, "Not without the Lord Commander's permission."

By this time, Kaz had heard the voices. He was slow in reacting, possibly because he was not sure whose voice he was hearing. Then, he suddenly turned and leaped up against the bars.

"Huma!"

The two sentries started, and the one apparently in charge turned and banged a mailed fist against the bars—far enough away that the minotaur could not grab it. "Be silent, Beast! You'll have your chance to talk when the inquisition meets."

Kaz snorted angrily. "I had thought the knights an honorable band, but I see that honor is something very few of them possess!" He raised a long, muscular arm through the bars, his hand open as if in supplication. "Huma! Free me from this cage!"

The knights stared at Huma with narrowed eyes. "He seems to know you well. How is that?"

"We have met and traveled together. He is not the Dragonqueen's slave. He is his own creature. He is a friend."

"A friend?" The guards looked at Huma in amazement—and much disbelief. Other knights were beginning to gather, curious as to what the shouting was all about.

The other guard finally spoke. "Perhaps, Caleb, we should notify Taggin."

"I will not interrupt him now." Caleb, a tall, plump man with a carnivorous look, pointed at Huma. "If I did not know better, I might think you a spy for consorting with mages and minotaurs. As it is, I think you are just a fool. If you want to speak to this creature, ask Taggin. I would lock you up until the inquisition, if I had my way."

There were murmurs of agreement, and Huma was startled. He had gone from favored visitor to seeming outcast in the space of a few seconds.

"What is going on here?"

Everyone, even Kaz, froze at the sound of that voice. It was Lord Taggin, clad in his formal dress armor. At least twenty years had slipped from his face. He was now the very image of authority.

"You men have become rabble of late. I can see that I am going to have to make some changes." Taggin turned to Huma. "I'm told you have some knowledge of this minotaur." Behind the commander, Buoron looked down. "We will begin the questioning in half an hour. I expect you to be present and to have your facts prepared. Understood?"

"Yes, milord."

Taggin turned to the sentries. "As for you, there are tenets of the knighthood that you seem to be failing. I expect both of you to learn from this incident."

The Knight of the Rose did not wait for them to answer. Instead, he walked past them and up to the cage. Kaz glared down at him. Taggin seemed unimpressed.

"Know this, minotaur. The basics of the knighthood stay the same. Your hearing will be impartial. You will be given every chance to prove yourself and to prove what this knight says of you. I will promise that."

Kaz did not reply, save for the mere ghost of a nod.

Taggin spun around and headed toward his quarters.

* * *

"You never cease to amaze me with your ability to become the center of attention, Huma."

Huma and Buoron looked up as they entered the knights' living quarters. Magius, in full splendor in his robes of red, stared at them from across the room. Again, Huma wondered at the change. Had Magius really returned to the Order of Lunitari, or was this merely another of his whims?

"The mage returns to the land of the living," Buoron remarked dryly.

The mage stirred. "Really, Huma, the only thing more foolish than you parading around in sheets of metal is the company you tend to keep. Myself excluded, of course."

"If you have nothing worthwhile to say, Magius, then don't say anything." Huma surprised himself by his comment.

Magius ignored the barb. "I see the minotaur has succeeded in getting into trouble. We really do not have time for this. Had I not required the rest, we could have been gone by last night."

Buoron smiled nastily. "You go nowhere without Lord Taggin's permission."

"Won't I?"

"Not with me, Magius. Not unless Kaz is freed." Huma added.

The mage sighed. "Very well. I do hope it won't take long. I know how long and boring inquisitions can be."

"Huma, is this filth really your friend?" Buoron interjected.

"If you can believe it. I still hope to find the old Magius underneath there."

For once, the magic-user had no retort. He merely looked at Huma and then studied something interesting on his staff.

"Are you coming with me, Magius?"

His childhood friend looked up. "To an inquisition? Hardly. They might decide to put me on trial. I shall await the outcome here."

Huma let out a sigh, although whether it was from relief or worry he could not say.

Unlike the formal inquisitions of Vingaard Keep, the sessions at the outpost were quick, straightforward, and to the point. Kaz was questioned about his whereabouts for the last half-year. His crime against his former masters and his subsequent meeting with Huma were gone over in minute detail as Lord Taggin looked for some slip that might prove the minotaur untrustworthy.

In the course of the questioning, many facets of the minotaur's past came out. He had been one in a long line of champions in his clan. He had even been given the name of one of his more remote ancestors, a powerful fighter who had been ruler of the race for twenty-three years before finally falling to defeat.

Kaz, though, had grown up in a time in which no true ruler commanded the minotaurs. As Huma had learned, those who controlled the race now were, in turn, puppets of the Dragonqueen's commanders. Each minotaur, male or female, was conscripted into the swelling ranks of the Dark Queen's armies upon reaching fighting age. There were never enough of the race in any one unit to create an atmosphere of rebellion. Kaz's people were severely punished for even the smallest infractions.

The tall warrior admitted he had done his share of fighting. It was part of his nature. Yet he had slowly become sickened by the senseless slaughter around him. There was no honor in much of what he was forced to do. The ogres cared not whether they faced an army or village. All who stood in their path were to be destroyed.

Kaz then went into detail about that final incident, when he had come across the butchering ogre captain. For a brief time, the knights in attendance were solely on his side.

The news of the collapse of the Solamnic lines and the chaos that followed brought renewed anger from those knights. From there, Kaz described the attack on the citadel of Magius and the flight that had resulted in the separation of Huma and Kaz.

Perhaps the highlight of the questioning occurred when Kaz described Huma's brief but bloody encounter with the warlord. The tide of feeling again flowed toward Huma. Those who had frowned on his odd friendship began to look at him with renewed respect.

After Kaz, Huma spoke. He did not plead with the knights, only spoke to them of the minotaur's acts of bravery and justice. He also pointed out that honor was just as important to Kaz as it was to the knighthood.

Lord Taggin looked extremely tired when all was said and done. Standing and facing the minotaur, who was bound and under guard, Lord Taggin took a deep breath and said, "The minotaur Kaz has cooperated in all ways. He has given us a good look at the workings of the Dragonqueen's forces, and his words are confirmed by Huma, Knight of the Crown. By rights, he has earned an honorable death."

Kaz snorted angrily and began to struggle with his bonds. Huma started to rise, but Buoron pushed him back down. Taggin continued.

"There is, however, another possibility. Paladine is the god of justice and wisdom. To execute the minotaur would be as great a travesty as we could commit. Therefore, I am placing him in the capable custody of Knight Huma, whom I believe we can trust to keep him under control."

A cheer arose. Opinions of Huma had swayed so much again that he was now nearly as great a hero to his fellows as he had been to the Ergothians.

"Remove the minotaur's bonds."

Knight Caleb reluctantly obeyed. Kaz gave him a toothy grin as the knight removed the last of the bonds; an instant later, the minotaur was bursting through the crowd. Kaz took hold of his former companion and lifted him high with a cry of pleasure.

"I thought never to see you again, friend Huma! You should know that out of respect to you I held my temper while I searched! Glad I am that I chose to turn south immediately. It did occur to me that you might have gone north in search of me."

Huma flushed. "I could only hope you were safe. My path led me southward even when I did not wish it to. Magius—"

Kaz misunderstood. "Yes, I saw that dragon-spawned mage friend of yours peering at me. He seemed quite willing to sacrifice me for the sake of expediency. I was so enraged by his satisfied expression that I began contemplating a suicidal escape attempt." The minotaur bellowed in laughter, although Huma could not see why.

Taggin cleared his throat. Huma quickly steered the minotaur over to him. "Lord Taggin, Knight of the Rose. I present to you Kaz, minotaur."

"Of a lineage that has produced more than a dozen champions of my race." Blood did not count as much in the land of the minotaurs as it did among the aristocratically minded Knights of Solamnia, but a lineage that produced champions was highly admired by other minotaurs. To the knights, it was as if Kaz called himself a noble of his people.

Taggin greeted the minotaur and then turned serious. "When the others are gone, we will speak. I've summoned the mage, too."

It did not take long for the room to empty. One look from the commander sent Buoron out the doorway. Kaz looked puzzled, but Lord Taggin refused to talk until Magius had arrived.

With obvious reluctance, the mage entered. Kaz stiffened, and his eyes reddened in anger. Huma feared an attack, but Kaz stood his ground. Magius pretended the massive figure was not even there.

"I have decided to come as you requested, Lord Taggin."

"How very decent of you." The elder knight was no more willing to hide his animosity toward the mage than Buoron had been. "I've decided to allow you to continue your journey and will even provide an escort."

Magius sniffed. "How very decent of you, Lord Taggin, but we do not need an escort. Huma and I can make it on our own."

"But you won't be alone, wolf-spawn," Kaz hissed. "I will be going with you whether an escort does or not."

Taggin held up a hand for silence. "You have no choice. I will send an escort, anyway. It is not a politeness; it is a requirement if you intend going on with this—quest."

Magius glared openly at Huma. "Would that you had taken an oath of silence. Your tongue flaps well, it seems."

Huma bristled but would not satisfy his companion with a childish retort.

The outpost commander stepped up to Magius until less than a hand's span separated their faces. "You will be leaving tomorrow morning at dawn. No sooner, no later. If you think to sneak away, do not bother. We will find you, and then I will lock you up. We can hold a magic-user. Trust me on that."

It was quite satisfying to Huma when Magius was the first to back down. "Very well. Since we apparently have no choice."

"You do not."

Turning to Huma, Magius pointed to the minotaur and asked, "That must go with us as well?"

"Absolutely." Kaz added to Huma's answer with a menacing snarl that revealed his teeth.

"The morning, then." Magius turned back to Lord Taggin. "Is that all?"

"No. Do I understand that this is all based on a dream?"

The mage smiled, sadly it seemed. "The Test was no dream. A nightmare is appropriate. A nightmare I hope to change."

Taggin stared into his eyes. "You have not told him everything, have you, Magius?"

Huma's eyes widened, then grew wider still, as the magic-user continued to delay his response.

Magius glanced at the others, then abruptly turned toward the door. "No. When the time is right, I will."

They watched him depart.

"Watch him, Huma," Taggin finally whispered. "Not just for your sakes, but for his."

The younger knight could only nod. Again, he wondered how he could ever still believe in Magius.

A knight stood waiting on the top of the tallest peak. His visor was down, so it was impossible to identify him. He wore the sign of the Knights of the Rose, and in his left hand he held a magnificent sword. He appeared to offer the weapon to Huma.

Huma crawled over crag and ravine. He lost his grip more than a dozen times, but each time he regained it before he had a chance to fall. Although Huma was near the top, the other knight did not help him. Instead, the strange figure continued to hold out the sword.

Huma stumbled over and accepted the proffered weapon. It was a beautiful sword—an antique. Huma sliced the air three times. The other knight looked on.

The young knight thanked him for the weapon and asked him his name. The visored knight did not speak. Suddenly growing angry, Huma reached forward and lifted the visor.

He was never sure what he saw, for something howled and Huma bolted upright in his cot, the dream shattered.

Taggin was there to see that nothing went awry. He paid particular attention to the activities of Magius, but the spell-caster was behaving himself this morning.

The escort arrived. Ten men had volunteered. Huma was relieved that Buoron was one of them.

When the entire troop was ready and mounted, Buoron signaled for the gates to be opened. As they rode out, each man, with the exception of Magius and Kaz, saluted the out-post commander. Lord Taggin had said nothing to Huma that morning, but he returned the salute with a slight wave of assurance.

Their route was to take them through open field for the entire journey, giving them an ever-expanding view of the chain of mountains. They were at least several days' journey from their goal. Huma wondered which peak Magius was seeking and what he expected to find. The mage was being very quiet. As a matter of fact, his eyes had been fixed on the mountain peaks from the moment they had left the outpost. Magius stared at the great rocky leviathans as if his life depended on them—which it quite possibly did.

Had Huma looked back at that moment, he might have noticed the swift form that darted into and out of whatever shelter it could find. It did not care for the day, which was harmful to its kind—not that it really thought of itself as other than an extension of its master. Nevertheless, it had made the long journey to act as the eyes and ears of the one who held its existence in his hands. For him, it would suffer the burning pain of daylight, daylight that seared it even through the ever-present cloud cover.

Wherever the knight and the mage traveled, the dreadwolf would follow.

Chapter 15

The great giants loomed over them, oblivious to the tiny, uneasy creatures at the outermost edge. The mountains had been magnificent from a distance; they were overwhelming up close. Not even Magius spoke. As one, they could only stare.

The mountains here were old, much older than many of their counterparts to the east and even to the north. More than one peak vanished into the cloud cover, testimony to unbelievable heights. Time had weathered all the mountains, some so much that they resembled the shells of gigantic sea creatures. The wind, ever-present and ten times wilder than on the plains, filled the air with almost human shrieks as it danced through the chain.

"Sargas," whispered Kaz. Nobody reprimanded him for

the quiet exclamation.

It was, of course, Magius who broke their concentration. He shifted uneasily on his mount, his gaze fixed, for the most part, on the peaks within the heart of the chain. "We will accomplish nothing sitting here gaping. Are you prepared to go on, Huma?"

Huma blinked. "Yes. I guess we might as well. Kaz?"

The minotaur gazed up at the peaks—and finally smiled. "I am quite familiar with such landscape, my friend. I have no qualms."

"We will wait here for you for three days, just as a precaution," Buoron said.

Magius sniffed and looked disdainfully away. "It is not necessary."

"Nevertheless, we will. What you say matters not."

"Let us go, then," Huma quickly put in. He had a great desire to get this over and done with—if that were possible.

"Agreed." Magius urged his horse forward.

"Huma," Buoron said somberly, and held out a hand. His face was much like the mountains before them—hardfeatured, but still admirable in its own way. "May Paladine watch over you."

"And you as well."

The other knights nodded their farewells as Huma passed. Huma did not look back as he rode, afraid that the desire to turn back from what might well be a foolish quest would ensnare him. Yet he showed no sign of fear to Magius or Kaz. A knight such as Bennett would have ridden into the mountains prepared to face the Dragonqueen herself, if need be. Huma knew he could never do that, but he would do his best to ride with dignity.

All too soon they entered the mountain range. The peaks stood all around them, fantastic walls and barriers that seemed ready—waiting?—to close in and wipe out all trace of the tiny creatures who had dared to infest them.

"Mountains such as these have always made me realize how an insect must feel," Kaz commented.

Ahead of them, Magius laughed scornfully. "These are mere lumps of rock. Impressive at first, but no more deserving of such reverence than the tiniest pebble on the beach."

"You have never truly known the mountains, then. Be careful, lest they bury you beneath their insignificance."

A cry rose from somewhere within the range of mountains. It was a harsh, predatory cry, and all three riders glanced around quickly.

As the seconds passed and nothing materialized, Kaz turned to Magius. "What was that? Are you familiar with the sound?"

The mage had regained his composure, as well as his arrogance. "A bird, perhaps. Possibly even a dragon. It would not surprise me to discover that the latter live here."

"Here?" Huma had sudden visions of great red dragons swooping down on the hapless group. Magius might be able to hold them off temporarily, but neither Kaz nor Huma would have much of a chance. A broadsword was of little use against the armored hide of a dragon.

The trail was a twisting series of slopes, ledges, and precarious turns. Buoron had said that dwarves, long since departed from this region, had created the path, the only one that granted travelers some hope of emerging on the opposite side. The knights traveled the mountains as little as possible, not because they were afraid but because they knew that even the few brigands of the region steered clear of the chain.

The wind whipped Huma's cloak wildly around, and he was forced at last to pin it around him. The chill wind created eerie sounds, like the calling of strange, unimaginable beasts.

Magius still had the lead, since he was the only one with any real idea where he was going. Huma was searching for a peak that matched the one on the tapestry, while Kaz was content merely to ride and let the others do the work. He cared little about what the magic-user was searching for. His own health, and Huma's, was all that truly mattered. The Red Robe could perish for all Kaz cared.

They rode around yet another turn and—came to a dead stop. Magius sputtered curses. Kaz laughed, despite the sinister look in the spellcaster's eyes.

The path lay buried beneath tons of rubble. Huma looked up and saw a new crevice in the side of one of the mountains. He tried to imagine the power required to create such a landslide.

"I'll not be cheated!" Magius stood in the saddle, crying out at the mountains. He whirled on the other two and said, "There were two diverging paths a short distance behind us. See if either curls back toward this one. I'll see if there is anything that can be done here."

The minotaur did not care to take orders from Magius, but Huma quieted him. It would not do for Kaz to cross the mage now.

While the spellcaster investigated the avalanche, Huma and Kaz rode back. The paths that Magius had spoken about seemed fairly unused, and one had even been obscured by the fragile shrubbery prevalent in the mountain chain. Huma chose the overgrown trail.

Kaz broke off to investigate the other path. Huma watched him disappear, then he climbed off his horse. The footing on the path was too tricky, and he had no desire to endanger himself and his horse. Better to leave the animal behind. If the path proved steadier ahead, he would return for the horse and investigate further.

It required the use of his broadsword to clear the path of foliage. Although the individual plants were weak, they grew in such profusion that it was like cutting into thick bales of hay. Huma was forced to chop continuously for several minutes before he made progress.

First glance indicated that the path continued a rocky, upward climb that made riding impossible and walking a slow, dragging tedium.

Suddenly, he stepped onto a gentle downward slope partly hidden by the vegetation. Huma smiled in relief. This path seemed to circle around to meet up with the original path beyond the avalanche. After a lengthy inspection, he finally concluded that the path was not only passable but that it would lead them more directly to the peaks Magius sought. It was also, he was pleased to note, a much less windblown path. The knight turned back, increasing his pace. By this time, he was sure that Kaz had completed his own search. He doubted also that Magius would have found a way around the avalanche in the meantime. Huma's path looked to be the best—and perhaps the only—choice.

He came to the meeting of the two slopes and stumbled back onto the rocky part of the trail. Huma turned a corner—and stopped dead before a great wall of rock. "What—?" he muttered, his brow raised in wonder. He looked up the length of the formation and laid a hand on its surface. It was all too real. He had to have taken a wrong turn, he realized.

Huma backtracked, and stood in puzzlement. Every indication was that he had followed the correct path the first time. Yet the rock formation looked as though it had been in place for years. Moss dotted its surface. The formation was quite weathered, almost round on top.

Finally, Huma gave up and returned to the other intersection he had discovered. Despite the feeling that this was the wrong route, he began to follow it. As he progressed, his confidence rose, for the trail seemed to lead back to where he wished to be. Then it abruptly curved toward the opposite direction. Soon, Huma was following a trail of twists and turns that kept his head spinning. The knight came to a halt. This path was leading him farther away. He grumbled to himself and then turned around to retrace his trail.

The path he had traveled, which he knew should have twisted to the right, now twisted to the left.

This was all wrong. Huma knew he could have made a mistake before, but not this time; he'd been especially cautious, painstakingly noting the way. Buoron and others had said many travelers never left these mountains; now he could see why. It was as if the mountains themselves moved against the unwary, although Huma knew it must really be the work of a mortal entity. His thoughts turned to Galan Dracos, but this did not seem to fit the renegade's style. He was being herded, he realized; Dracos would have captured him by now. No, this was magic with another purpose.

His sword unsheathed, Huma began following the only available path.

There was nothing out of the ordinary, just rocks, scraggly bushes, and a high-flying bird now and then.

The path suddenly split off into two directions. Huma paused, suspecting that he really had only one choice. But which?

He pondered for some time before he noticed the tap-tap beat coming from behind him. Huma whirled, his blade up and ready. He had been expecting an ogre or perhaps one of the Black Guard; instead, he found himself facing a hooded figure sitting on a large, flat rock.

The tap-tap came from a staff much like Magius's, and it was held by a gray, gloved hand partially covered by the sleeve of a cloak. The gray cloak, in turn, covered most of the form of a—Huma stepped closer to be sure—a gray-faced man.

The gray man stroked his long, gray beard and smiled almost imperceptively at the knight.

Huma lowered the blade—but not all the way. "Who are you?" he asked.

"Who are *you*?" the gray man rejoined.

The knight frowned but decided to play the game for now. "I am Huma, Knight of the Order of the Crown."

"A Knight of Solamnia." The dull-colored figure spoke as if he had known it all along. The staff went tap-tap.

"I've answered your question; now answer mine."

"I?" The gray man smiled, revealing gray teeth. "I am merely a fellow traveler."

Huma indicated the area around them. "This is not your doing?"

"The mountains? Oh, no. They've been here for a long time, I understand."

"I meant the paths that vanish." The other's eccentric attitude irritated Huma.

"I do not move mountains. It is quite possible that you are just not seeing well enough with your eyes." The figure on the rock blended perfectly into the background. Huma found that to look away even for a moment meant he had to look carefully to find the man again. No doubt, the gray man had been sitting on the rock when Huma came through moments earlier. The knight had never seen him.

"Are you a magic-user?" Huma queried.

The tap-tap of the staff ceased for the moment. "Now that *is* an interesting question."

The tapping resumed.

"Well?" Huma was fighting for control.

The gray man seemed to think for a moment. Then he pointed the staff toward the two paths behind Huma and asked, "Were you not choosing a path? You should get on with it, you know. You might be going somewhere important."

"Very well. Which one would you choose?" Huma held his breath, wondering if he was going to receive an answer that made some sense.

After further consultation with himself, the slate-colored man pointed the staff at the path to the left. "That one has been proved to be quite popular."

"Thank you." Huma stalked off toward the chosen path. He wanted nothing more to do with gray men and paths that came and went. The sooner he was away—

"Of course," the odd figure added, "Others have found the right path to be the *right* path."

Huma stopped. He turned and stared coldly at the gray man. "Which would you choose?"

"I'm not going anywhere."

The knight studied the two paths. From where he stood, they looked identical. He could not make a choice based on appearances. He would have to go with his instincts.

Purposefully, Huma stepped over to the trail on the right and began walking. He did not look back, even when the familiar tap-tap picked up again.

The parting comment, though, did cause him to pause momentarily.

"An interesting choice."

The tapping ceased. Huma, despite himself, turned around.

The path—and the gray man—had disappeared. In their place stood a tall, angling peak.

Huma trudged along the winding trail for hours. He noted that the sun was already low in the sky, which meant that he had been separated from the others a good part of the day. Calling out had proved futile.

The wind had picked up. Huma drew his cloak around him, daring to sheath his sword so he could pull the garment tighter. He wondered how cold it got in these mountains and then decided it would be best not to think about it.

Where were Magius and Kaz? He hoped the minotaur and the magic-user would not kill one another now that Huma was not there to keep both under rein.

His stomach stirred in hunger again, prompting a vague twinge of guilt. Fasting was a rite of purification for the knighthood. A few hours should not have affected him.

A few berries dotted the bushes he passed, but previous experiments had proved them to be inedible and possibly even poisonous. He had seen no sign of animal life and had heard none, save the occasional cry of whatever creature waited out there. A great bird, perhaps. What did it eat, then? Unwary and foolish travelers?

Evening finally fell, and Huma waited for a sign from Magius. Neither light nor sound came through the darkness, however. Huma was still on his own when night had grown to maturity.

The night was bright, for a change. Somehow, the stars always seemed to shine through the cloud cover where the sun could not. Perhaps most encouraging, Solinari was at last ascendant. The god of the White Robes now watched over the world, and although Magius wore the robes of crimson Huma hoped that Solinari would watch over his friend as well.

Huma finally paused for the night, tired and confused, determined to go on once morning came. He crawled under an overhang in a fairly level spot and wrapped his cloak around him; a fire was out of the question. Huma had survived worse, but hunger pangs continued to irritate him, even as he drifted away into sleep.

Huma stirred. A sound, like the flapping of mighty wings, had pulled him from his slumber. Peering from his shelter, he saw nothing but the night and decided it was only a rockfall or the wind. He was soon back to sleep.

From behind a far outcropping, two gleaming, blood-red eyes peered sightlessly at the unsuspecting figure. The dreadwolf was set to watch only, not to kill—not this time. Yet the slumbering human made a satisfactory target, and the abomination began to slink forward, yellowed teeth bared. It readied itself to leap—and a monstrous claw slashed out and crushed it beyond the undead thing's ability to regenerate. Not a sound broke the night stillness.

Huma stirred again but did not awaken.

The dawn brought with it the feeling that he was not alone.

Huma scanned the surrounding area. All remained as it had been the day before, save that the weather had grown a little warmer. Hunger still touched him, but he was beginning to gain control over it—or perhaps he had passed that point when it mattered.

He dared call out to his companions. The wind was weaker, and Huma thought that this time he might be heard. If that meant facing the creature that cried out yesterday, so be it.

There was no response to his shouts, either from the mage and minotaur or from the nameless creature. Huma gave up shouting and renewed his walk down the odd path. He no longer cared whether he could even retrace his steps.

To his surprise and pleasure, the trail became smoother and simpler to follow. And food was available—berries from a new type of bush. When they proved to be palatable, he began devouring all he could find. Of course, any poison might be slow in acting, but Huma recognized these plants. He decided that whatever had created the path wanted him alive for the time being.

At last, when he began to believe the path would go on forever, the trail stopped before a shining pool of water surrounded by fruit-bearing trees and a garden. Thirsty, he hurried to the edge of the pool. The water could not be poisonous if such life surrounded it, and Huma leaned down and scooped up a handful. The moisture trickled down his chin as he drank. Not satisfied with that, he knelt and bent forward to sip from the pool itself.

A dragon's face stared up from the water.

He jumped away from the water's edge and realized that the dragon's face had been a reflection. He looked up with rapidly widening eyes. Huma had reached his destination.

A great stone dragon, six times his size, flanked the pool, and Huma saw that it had once had a counterpart on the opposite end. Only the pedestal and part of the head remained of the second dragon. Both appeared to have been carved out of marble or some similar stone.

The one still standing appeared to be a silver dragon, while the fragmented one had been a gold dragon.

Huma drank his fill. When he had finished, he looked straight ahead and noticed a doorway hidden by the tangle of plant life and literally cut into the mountain itself. He moved closer and studied the doorway. Tiny figures had been carved in relief around the opening, most of them weathered away. Some, protected by the heavy covering of plant growth, perhaps, were still quite recognizable—at least as definite shapes. Huma wished desperately to know what the symbols might mean.

Pushing aside thick vines, he peered inside. It should have been dark inside, yet he could see a faint glow within. Almost as if someone had lit torches to guide his way, he thought uneasily.

Sighing in resignation, he stepped into the entrance of the mountain, expecting the cavelike entryway to be damp and moldy. Instead, it was as if he had stepped into the council chamber of Vingaard Keep. The entrance was warm and dry, and the walls and ceiling were smooth.

It took him some time to travel the length of the stark hallway, his attention concentrated on the flickering light ahead. He completed the final stretch of the corridor. Belatedly, he remembered his sword and removed the weapon from its sheath. The corridor opened into a great hall, once the court of some great king or emperor, Huma decided. It stretched high; it was a natural cavern carved to perfection. The light was indeed from torches, and Huma wondered who had lit them.

Metallic statues of armored knights lined each wall. They were lifeless—and very lifelike. They could almost be sentries commanded to sleep until needed—or the undead ordered to slay any who intruded.

Huma stepped into the center of the room and stared at the floor. Now he could see the pattern etched into the stone. It, above all else, gave him heart, for it was a huge representation of Paladine himself, the Platinum Dragon. The dragon curled from one end of the room to the other and, if the knight was any judge, the pattern was indeed made of platinum. Huma marveled over the intricate work.

His gaze roved to the single piece of furniture in this cavern—a high throne, carved from wood such as Huma had never seen, wood that seemed to glow with life. The edges of the throne were encrusted with jewels, and these, too, gleamed from the light of the torches.

Childlike wonder swept over him as he walked around the chamber. The armor, he noted, included many of the various types worn by the knighthood over the ages. He opened more than one visor and peered inside, finding nothing but dust.

At last, he simply stood and gave thanks to Paladine for allowing him to proceed this far. He also prayed that the Triumvirate would watch over his two companions, despite their differences. Then he knelt in reverence before the throne.

His vigil, though, was interrupted almost before it began. A pounding sound, as of metal upon metal, resounded from one of the darkened corridors. Huma came to his feet and peered around, trying to discern from which of the corridors the sound originated.

The pounding died even as he stood, and Huma was unable to fathom its direction.

Huma remembered where he had heard a sound like that before—back at Vingaard Keep.

It was the sound a heavy hammer made when beating hot metal into shape at a forge.

Chapter 16

A forge. Huma wondered what that might mean. He had expected any of a number of things here, but not an active smithy. For that matter, who held that hammer? Ghosts of ages past? Perhaps the dwarves had not left this place after all.

His eyes turned back toward the throne, and he discovered that he was no longer alone. Huma's first thought was that the gray man had returned, for the robe and hood, which covered all identity, were indeed dun-colored. But this new visitor was much more slight.

"You have come." Her voice was low and the cloak almost muffled it, but it was indeed a female voice. Small, feminine hands emerged from the billowing sleeves of the cloak, and the woman reached up to take hold of the hood. Slowly, she pulled it back, revealing long, thick, flowing hair and a face that both thrilled and shocked the knight, for he had known it and longed for it.

"Gwyneth."

She smiled. "I had thought perhaps you had forgotten me."

"Never."

The smile widened, then vanished abruptly. "I knew it would be you. When I first laid eyes on you in the—lying there, battling a mind-killing wound. Yes, your wound was far worse than you know. No bones had been broken, but your mind . . . Had not healers taken care of you as quickly as they did, you would have lost all senses permanently."

"Paladine," he breathed. To be struck deaf, dumb, and blind—or worse. "Gwyneth. What is this place?"

"Call it a gift of love. It was built by those with great love for Paladine and his house. They wanted nothing in return. It was magnificent in its day." She had a disconcerting way of talking as if she had actually been here in the past, Huma thought.

"Is this what Magius sought?"

"In a sense. Your friend is still a good man, Huma, despite his obsession. It may still consume him. Whether he believes it or not, the future he faced during his Test was nothing more than an intricate fabrication. The Tests are designed to highlight one's greatest weaknesses, and I fear that he did not pass as easily as the Conclave hoped."

"Then all of this has nothing to do with what he said."

Gwyneth looked surprised. "Oh, but it does! The idea of this place has been passed to man for centuries, ever since the first war with the Dragonqueen. It has not changed much. The Conclave knew the ego of their student, Magius. The greatest fault of your childhood companion is that, like the elves, he sees himself as the power to save the world. What better way of testing him than to make him fail at the greatest of all tasks."

Huma was silent as his mind digested this. Finally, he asked, "What of me? Magius seemed to think I am important to changing his future."

"You are important, but not in the way he thinks. What

has been sought so long is a single man or woman who embodies all that Paladine has attempted to teach this world. Some have come close, but all failed in the end." As his eyes widened, she nodded sadly. "You are not the first to come here, Huma. I pray—oh Paladine, I pray—that you are the one sought. Were it not Krynn itself that would suffer, I would tell you to turn from here now, before it is too late."

The knight stiffened. "Even if you told me to, I would not. I cannot. Not—and remain what I am."

"Is the knighthood so much to you?"

"Not the knighthood. What it teaches." He had never thought of it in those terms before.

Gwyneth looked pleased, but merely said, "If only there were others like you, even in the knighthood."

"Gwyneth, where are Kaz and Magius?"

"They will be watched. Have no fear, Huma." She paused. "It is time to start, I think."

"Start?" Huma looked around, half-expecting the room to fill with clerics and mages ready to perform some ceremony. Instead, Gwyneth stepped down from the throne and moved toward him. Although dressed simply and without expression on her face, she looked more beautiful than he had ever thought possible. Buoron's nymph paled in comparison.

She wavered only momentarily under his gaze. Huma tried fruitlessly to understand what was revealed in that lapse. When Gwyneth was no more than an arm's length from him, she pointed at the darkened corridors.

"You may choose whichever one you wish."

"What happens then?"

"You walk it. What happens next is up to you. I can only tell you that you must face three challenges. It is said that each member of the Triumvirate created part of the challenges, although no challenge represents one god, just as a man is the sum of his parts, not separate qualities that exist independent of one another."

Huma studied each of the corridors for a long time. If he was to proceed, he would have to trust in Paladine and hope to make the right choice.

He took a step toward his choice, but Gwyneth caught his arm. "Wait."

She kissed him lightly. "May Paladine watch over you. I do not want *you* to fail."

He could think of nothing adequate to say, so Huma quickly turned away and moved toward the corridor he had chosen. He knew that if he looked back and she was still there, he might be tempted to stay. He also knew that if he stayed, he would never be able to live with himself.

The corridor he picked was like a natural cave. In spots, the passage constricted, forcing him to duck or move sideways. It was also very, very long, and nearly plunged in blackness.

Soon the passage began to glow with a light of its own, a light that came from the very walls. Huma paused to study this phenomenon. He had heard tales of this sort of light.

The walls' glow gave Huma an idea. He knocked a piece of rock loose with the hilt of his sword and put it, still glowing, in his belt pouch.

An ear-splitting, earth-shaking cry tossed him to the ground. Rock fragments covered him.

It was the same cry Huma had heard in the pass. He now knew its source—straight ahead. And straight ahead was the only way left to Huma, for, as the trail had done, the corridor behind him revealed nothing but a stone wall.

Sword and shield ready, he crept down the tunnel toward the sound.

He stepped from that corridor—into yet another. This one broke off into three directions, any of which the thing might occupy. Huma straightened in nervous annoyance. The cry was echoing through the cavern system; the creature might be anywhere. It might be hours away in some deeper chamber. It might even be right behind him.

That thought on his mind, he shifted his feet—and did not meet solid ground. With a metal-rattling clang, Huma went down.

Huma cleared his head with a shake and looked at the thin pool of dark liquid that had made him slip. He put a finger in it and brought the sample close in order to study it better. For such a small puddle, it stank terribly. To his horror, Huma noticed the substance was eating into his metal glove. He wiped the foul stuff on the rock, which seemed much more resistant to the liquid.

"Heeeehhh."

It seemed like laughter, evil laughter, at first. Huma clambered to his feet, but he still could not tell from which of the three tunnels the noise had come. And as it repeated, he knew the sound was not laughter.

It was breathing.

Something incredibly large, unless the chambers amplified sound, lurked nearby.

While it might prove safer to remain anchored in this one location, Huma had no desire to do so. He chose the center corridor and hurried down it.

Physically, it was identical to the last one. Huma wondered how such an obviously large creature could make its way through some of these narrow confines. Even Huma had his difficulties.

This tunnel led him to another tunnel, which looked exactly like the two before it. The caverns made up a maze, with Huma as both contestant and prize in some subterranean game of peril.

As he walked, he noticed the dark liquid that flowed under his feet and the heat that emanated from several corridors. There was a sulfurous smell to the heat, which, Huma believed, pointed to a conduit to the mountain's fiery heart. Huma had heard of mountains such as this and prayed that this one would not erupt while he was within it.

"Hhhhheeeeehhhh."

Huma flattened himself around a corner. Echo or not, he knew now that he and the other were mere minutes apart. The other also apparently knew, for he chuckled madly— most definitely madly. When the laughter died, the other spoke in slow, deep tones.

"Manling. I smell you, manling. I smell the warmth of your body, the bitter chill of your metal armor. I smell your *fears.*"

Huma said nothing, but he fell back silently to the corridor from which he had entered. He did not want to face something as large as this tunnel-dweller unless he could find a place, where he could maneuver.

"Come to Wyrmfather, manling. Let me show you my strength."

Wyrmfather's hearing was obviously quite extraordinary, for the beast hissed loudly whenever Huma moved and the knight could hear the scraping of a large form against the sides of a tunnel.

Huma moved down an open corridor, circling Wyrmfather—he hoped. The hissing seemed to come from all around him. The corridors appeared endless.

The hissing abruptly halted, and Huma froze. There was silence for several minutes, save for the maddening beat of the knight's heart. Then the scraping sound echoed again as Wyrmfather seemed to move away from Huma.

He realized that the relative smoothness of the tunnel walls was the result of continual wearing away by the body of his pursuer.

The coarse, scraping sound died away while Huma pondered. Quietly, he made his way farther along the tunnel. If he could only find his way out of this maze—

Wild laughter—and the passageway exploded into flame!

Huma had no choice now but to run. Wyrmfather knew where he was. Huma abandoned stealth and simply fled in the direction of the nearest corridor.

Another burst of fire sent him scurrying out of that passage. How could Wyrmfather move so swiftly? What *was* Wyrmfather?

He would not count how many passageways he ran through or how many times the laughter of the tunnel dweller warned him just before more searing flame licked at his mustache.

Running frantically, Huma did not at first notice the wide opening to his left. It was not until he had passed it that the knight realized he had come across something other than a corridor. Huma came to an immediate halt and froze.

The malevolent hiss of Wyrmfather was far away for the moment, although Huma knew that could easily change at any second. Cautiously, the knight edged back to the side passage and then leaned forward enough so that he could peer into it.

It was a very short corridor, ending in what appeared to be more of a cavern. Huma stepped around into the new passageway and walked slowly down it.

The cavern loomed large. It appeared to have been honed the same way as the corridors—by the constant wear of some huge form against the rock itself.

But where was the leviathan itself? Where was Wyrmfather? Huma glanced around the cavern. Tunnel entrances dotted it on various levels. The knight's sharp gaze followed the contours of the floor. It was smooth enough to walk on, although the slopes became steep in a few places, especially where it suddenly rose—

Huma mentally cursed his predicament and stepped back into the corridor.

What he had seen, what he wished desperately to deny, was a massive serpentlike form that rose through the bottom of the cavern, like some cursed tree, and turned abruptly to the side, continuing on through one of the farther tunnels.

Here at last he beheld a portion of Wyrmfather.

The malevolent creature pulsated with life as it stretched from that gaping chasm in the center. All that was visible was a trunk whose reptilian diameter was twice Huma's height. Its otherwise dull-gray body was covered with splotches of green and blue, as if it were infected.

The trunk suddenly descended into the chasm. The terrible head of Wyrmfather emerged from the other passage, shocking Huma with a startling revelation.

Wyrmfather was a dragon.

The leviathan dwarfed all dragons that Huma had ever seen or heard of. Wyrmfather's maw could easily have snapped up a team of horses in two bites, a single man in much less. The long, wide teeth stretched nearly as high as Huma and the sinewy, forked tongue that flickered in and out of Wyrmfather's jaws could easily envelope him.

The smell of sulfur was everywhere, and Huma realized that the mountain peak did not have an active heart. The dragon caused the smell.

Huma froze as the ponderous head of the dragon turned his way. There was something odd about the head. It seemed larger in proportion to the thickness of the neck, which in turn was far too long for any dragon that Huma could recall.

Recognition made the knight gasp. Wyrmfather was the dragon after which the statuette in Magius's citadel had been patterned. Yet the statuette had to have been ancient even by elven standards. Could any dragon live that long?

Wyrmfather hissed. Its head was turned so that it could not possibly have missed the knight, yet the deadly beast continued to scan the cavern. It was only when Huma looked at the eyes that he knew why; a whitish film covered each. Wyrmfather was blind.

The creature was not deaf, though, and most certainly had a keen sense of smell. It had passed up the knight once; Huma doubted it would do so again. Even now, the lengthy snout seemed to be investigating some of the areas it had already passed. Unless Wyrmfather poked its head back into one of the corridors, the dragon would find Huma momentarily.

As if thinking the same thoughts, Wyrmfather spoke. The creature's words made the immense chamber tremble. "A tricky one. I am pleased. It has been so long since I had even the slightest challenge. The others were so easy."

The head swung near Huma. Gaping nostrils flared as the mighty dragon sniffed for the scent of the knight.

"I smell the taint of Paladine on you. Of Habbakuk. Of the most cursed of all the gods of light, my jailer, the damned Kiri-Jolith!"

Huma did not move, did not breath during this outburst. The leviathan had spoken of an encounter with at least one of the gods responsible for the creation of the knighthood. An encounter that had left the dragon quite the worse off, it seemed.

"Are you here for my treasure? It is the greatest horde that any dragon could ever gather. Even trapped as I am, I have ways of gathering it. Ah!" The massive jaws bent into a macabre, reptilian grin. "Perhaps it is the mirror you seek! Yes, the mirror would be worth all else I have!"

All the while it spoke, Wyrmfather sniffed around the cavernous chamber, seeking out Huma.

A sound of metal striking metal rang through the chamber. Huma reacted instinctively, covering his ears as the noise pounded at his mind. It was the forge again. The hammer at the forge.

If the hammering disturbed Huma, it enraged Wyrmfather to madness. The dragon added to the noise with shrieks of its own. Curses, crying, threats. All matter of words rushed from its mouth. Froth dripped from its maw.

"My queen! Why do you let them torment me? Have I not endured countless millenia gone to dust? Must I suffer yet more of the ceaseless hammering and hammering of that cursed smith! Have you forsaken me, great Takhisis?"

Across the chamber, a corridor glowed brighter than the others. Wyrmfather had spoken of its horde and how even here it had been able to seek out treasure. Might there not be something of use in such a horde? A weapon, perhaps, more deadly than Huma's own seemingly insignificant sword? It was, to be sure, a desperate measure. Even as the beast renewed its shouts, Huma was running.

The clatter of his boots on the rocky floor alerted Wyrmfather, but the hammering prevented the dragon from pinpointing the tiny human figure. In anger, the dragon roared and unleashed random bursts of searing flame.

Huma dove into the corridor. The dragon had mentioned a mirror of some great importance. Huma remembered the mirror of the nymph, the one she had used to gaze at the dreams of others. Might they be related? Hers, though, had only been a way of capturing others' dreams. This one had other properties, perhaps.

Still Wyrmfather ranted and raved at the sound of the hammer.

Huma made his way down the corridor, fearing that he had erred. All he might find were gold and jewels, useless at the moment. There might be nothing.

Huma fell, and his eyes caught a horrible, momentary glimpse of what he had tripped over. A battered skull grinned at him, while a disjointed arm pointed at him in mockery. The crumpled remains of armor wrapped much of the body's frame. Huma succeeded in rolling with the fall, though the collision unsettled him.

Huma stood and stared sadly at the partial skeleton. It was very old, and the armor was nearly all rust. There were some visible markings, though, and Huma, in horrid fascination, wiped dust from the breastplate and beheld the insignia of a Knight of the Rose.

A prayer instinctively jumped to his lips. Here was a knight who had made it this far, only to perish.

To perish.

As Huma might.

Even as the thought came unbidden, he realized the new danger. The hammering had stopped as abruptly as it had started. Huma took a few steps forward, almost without realizing it, and nearly stumbled onto an immense pile of valuables.

There were coins aplenty, gold and silver, more than Huma had ever seen. They glittered, almost entrancing him. Mixed in with them was a variety of rare items, many bejeweled, all of them fascinating. Necklaces of large, perfect pearls. Small figurines of some crystalline design, perhaps formed from emeralds or jade. Armor that might have been forged only yesterday, some so elaborate that it must have been created for mighty emperors, who could afford the craftsmanship and extravagant decorations. There were even weapons, although most were useless, having been designed more for style and expense than for use.

He quickly surveyed the room, his heart racing. All this before him, when he would have gladly traded it for a single weapon capable of defeating the huge cavern dweller.

"Where have you run, manling?"

Huma stiffened. Wyrmfather was very close by. Any second, the corridor might become filled with flame.

"The smith has abandoned you, Knight of Solamnia! Yes, I know you now. I can smell the taint of the Three in you, stronger than ever before. You are a Knight of Solamnia, a true believer, unlike those before. They thought they believed, but they only pretended. You, though, are different. I wonder what you will taste like?"

Rusted battle axes. Jeweled swords fit only for ceremony. This could not be the vast horde the dragon had spoken about—unless, in its madness, Wyrmfather had dreamed up its treasures.

The mirror, too?

"I have you now!"

Huma could hear the slithering and scraping as the massive head wormed its way into the corridor. He whirled and realized that the relatively meager horde of gold and jewels was only overflow from another chamber. He reached into the uppermost part of the mound of valuables and began digging. Sure enough, within a few seconds, the digging revealed an opening. It was only a small opening, so far, and it grew slowly as he continued to labor, each second expecting to feel the blistering heat of Wyrmfather's breath on his back. The effort was tiring. The continuous wedge of valuables made an effective blockade. Huma cursed silently as more coins and odd artifacts flowed to replace those he had removed. The knight took a deep breath. Digging was not good enough. As he cleared a tangle of jewels from the gap, he began crawling forward like a mole.

He had already burrowed deep into the pile when he felt the hot, fetid breath of the dragon. Wyrmfather could not use its flame here, lest it destroy its own treasure; thus the dragon was twisting its head and neck all the way to the entrance of the chamber of treasures.

The leviathan's head came around the corner—just in time to hear the knight vanish into the other chamber. Wyrmfather paused. After a moment, the huge reptilian lips curled into a malevolent smile and the great dragon began the process of removing itself from the chamber.

All was dark at first, strange after so many corridors filled with their own light. Huma wondered why this one was different.

Unable to see, he crawled awkwardly through the immense collection of treasures. Here must certainly be the main horde, but how was he to find anything in the dark? Was there anything to find? Somehow, he felt there must be. If this was a test, there must be some way of defeating the dragon.

His hand brushed against what felt like a sword hilt—and the room was suddenly lit by a dull, greenish glow. Huma jerked his hand away in surprise. He had hoped; he had prayed. Now, at last, he had found the very thing. Only . . . only he feared to touch it, for some reason. As if something instinctively warned him not to.

Grasp me. Wield me. Use me. I will be your will come to life.

The words rang clear in his mind, clear, sweet, seductive words.

They came from within the sword itself.

Chapter 17

Huma's hand hesitated mere inches from the sword. The glow persisted, but there was no repetition of the words.

The blade was impressive. The hilt was brilliantly bejeweled, including one massive green stone that seemed to be the source of the glow. A bell protected the user's hand. The blade itself was as sharp as if newly made. Huma's desire to touch it became almost undeniable. With the sword, he was sure that not even Wyrmfather could best him

Wyrmfather! The spell was broken as Huma remembered the dragon. With the sword—no! The knight recoiled from it. He could not say how he knew, but the sword was malevolent. It did not seek his companionship; it sought a slave to do its bidding.

As he turned away from the blade, the light reflected off a polished surface in one corner. Huma scampered over the jewels and coins to get a better look at the object.

It was as he hoped. An elaborate mirror, twice his size. The mirror of which Wyrmfather had spoken. Huma recalled the sightless eyes of the cavern dweller and wondered how a blind dragon used a mirror. It was evident that Wyrmfather had gathered his treasures over the centuries.

Mirrors. This was the third. One was owned by the nymph. Another hung in the citadel of Magius. All magical. Had they all been made by the same person? He doubted he would ever know.

"Manling, I would speak with you."

Huma started as the voice of Wyrmfather filled the room. The chamber suddenly was filled with brilliant light, and Huma cursed himself for not realizing his mistake. There were no other entrances to this chamber because the entrance was the ceiling! Even now, the ancient dragon was tugging away the huge slab of rock that served as the lid on his house-size treasure chest. Huma scanned the endless mounds of booty, seeking something and finding that his eyes always returned to the sinister emerald blade.

"Manling." Wyrmfather sniffed and a great smile lit its terrible face. "The smell of riches is intoxicating, is it not?"

Huma was positive he could cover the distance to the sword in ten seconds. Would he have that much time?

"It is futile to hide, manling. I can smell you out. I can lay waste to this chamber. Yet I do not have to kill you. There might be another way."

Huma edged toward the sword. Wyrmfather's massive head turned at the sound.

"A bargain, Knight of Solamnia? A task for me in exchange for one of my treasures? Surely, I have gathered a few things your brethren have lost over the years."

Huma remembered the ancient remains wearing the battered crest of a Knight of the Rose. Had Wyrmfather made the same offer to him? Had he been choosing his prize when the dragon overtook him?

Loose coins slid under Huma's foot, and the dragon's head suddenly blocked his path. Huma readied his sword, eyeing with regret the other one so near to him. So close!

Wyrmfather sniffed. "A Solamnic Knight, indeed! The game of hide-and-seek is at an end, manling! Do you accept my offer—" The massive jaws worked into a smile again. "—or shall we see what other arrangement can be made?'

"What do you want?"

The leviathan's ears perked up. "Ahhh! He does speak! It has been, by my estimate, nearly three hundred years since an intruder has dared to speak to me directly for reasons other than pleading! Even *your* voice pleases me after all this!"

"I'm glad," Huma said. He could not think of anything else to say.

The ensuing chuckle forced him to cover his ears. "A brave one, manling! I like you. What do you say to my offer?"

"I am willing to hear it."

"A *truly* brave one! Hear me, then, manling!" The great beast raised its head high. "I am Wyrmfather, first and greatest of my dread lady's children, first to rise at her call! I championed her cause against the hideous gods of light and their creeping toadies, and ever emerged triumphant! So great and fearful was my power that at last Kiri-Jolith himself was forced to fight me—and did so with dread, I tell you!

"We fought for over a year. Mountains were born, brought flat, and reborn. The land quaked with our struggle, the seas whipped high. At last, I erred and Kiri-Jolith defeated me. Victory was not enough, though! From the shattered earth he drew this mountain about me, enclosing me from the joyous sky! I would, he said, remain a part of this mountain. Even the slightest breeze would not reach me. Only, he mocked, only one of his own brethren would be able to release me! Only one such as he could set me free!"

The blind eyes stared meaningfully at Huma, who was beginning to understand what the dragon was leading to.

"For a long time, I believed he meant one of his fellow gods, and I raged and roared. Then I came to understand the trickery in his words. A god was *not* what he meant. A warrior, straight and true in the path, could do what I could not, and are not the Knights of Solamnia the sons of Paladine? Does that not make them brethren in spirit to Kiri-Jolith?"

Huma stared at the gleaming sword buried deep in the mound of jewels and coins. In him there was a yearning so strong that he nearly ran to it. But suddenly the terrible visage of Wyrmfather was again before him. The hot, sulfurous breath stung the knight's eyes.

"Free me, Knight of Solamnia, and anything here is yours! Even the mirror, which served me so well before the darkness came!"

The mirror. Huma looked at it. If he could learn its secrets . . . His own bluster amazed him. "How does it work? I might consider, then."

"You must think of a place you wish to go and then ask— No! Release me first!"

The very mountain trembled as Wyrmfather went into another berserk rage.

The hammering began anew—louder, if at all possible.

Wyrmfather raised its massive head and shrieked, "I will not be cheated again!"

Huma ran for the sword. The maddened dragon lashed out in anger. The massive jaws opened wide, and the long, draping, forked tongue whipped out. Wyrmfather meant to make a morsel out of the tiny human.

Huma's hand closed around the hilt of the sword. It burned in his grip, even through his gauntlets. Despite the pain, he pulled the sword free and held it high, moving through sheer reflex and skill.

Wyrmfather's jaws closed down on Huma, swallowing countless treasures in the process. For a moment, Huma vanished into the maw of the titan.

With a rock-shattering cry of pain, the ancient leviathan spasmed. Gold, silver, statuary, jewels, and a badly battered Huma fell from his jaws. The knight hit one of the piles below, sending shockwaves through his right arm.

Above, Wyrmfather shook its head back and forth, trying to dislodge the sword it had forced into its own head. It was a futile effort; the body was already reacting by reflex. The brain of the dragon was dead, the green blade having cut through all barriers protecting it. The dragon's actions only served to drive the blade deeper.

Huma rose to his feet just as the massive head began its final descent. Even in death, Wyrmfather could spell the end of Huma. The knight scrambled.

The massive skull struck the ground precipitously close to Huma. The knight—along with nearly a king's ransom in valuables—was flung forward, his last thoughts of Solamnia. His body struck the mirror—

—and landed in the muck and mire of a rain-soaked wasteland.

His first frantic thoughts were for the sword. It had remained jammed in the dying dragon's jaws. Huma had to retrieve it.

How? He surveyed his surroundings—and reeled in shock. This was Solamnia! Very near Vingaard Keep. Huma sat up and put his face in his hands. He had discovered the secret of the mirror. Now he was transported far from the mountains—and his companions!

His right arm was numb and nearly useless, but he felt no broken bones. The temporary paralysis would go away after a few hours. Both he and his armor were mud-covered. He felt quickly at his waist, then gave a small sigh of relief; he still had his own sword, puny as it seemed compared to the wonderful surge of power he had felt when holding the green blade. If only . . .

A thought came to him.

It was difficult to tell direction, but by the few still-recognizable landmarks, he was certain he was south of Vingaard Keep. Had it been a brightly lit day, he knew he could have glimpsed the mighty citadel.

Ineffectually wiping the mud from his face, Huma started north.

The habitations he passed would have provided little protection for a wild animal, much less a human. The wood frames were crumbling with rot. The thatched roofs could only barely be called that; there were too many holes and too little material to patch them with. The mud used to pack the stonework together had become so damp that in many places the walls had fallen completely away.

The haunted looks he saw in the faces of the emaciated survivors who peopled this poor excuse for a village sent chills through his body. What, he wondered, was the Keep doing about this situation? These people barely existed. Their homes were little more than lean-tos, and some people did not even have that. Instead, they sat in the mire and ravaged earth, and stared at the devastation around them.

He knew that the knighthood could not care for them all, but it still agonized him. Huma prayed that somehow he would gain new transportation so that he could return to the mountain and, if it was allowed, face the challenges once again. He also worried about his two companions. Were they looking for him?

Staring at the ruined land, Huma thought that the knighthood might have helped the people rebuild their villages, patrol their forests, and possibly gather or grow their own food. Instead, nothing.

Huma stopped walking for a moment, thinking about his nearly blasphemous ideas. What would Rennard have said if he had heard him? Huma smiled slightly. Probably very little, he decided.

Several villagers stepped out to gaze at Huma with a variety of expressions—fear, respect, anger, and disgust. Five men blocked his path. Huma blinked and waited. The five did not step aside.

Their apparent leader was a tall, wide man with a foul black beard, a receding hairline, a squashed nose, and more than two hundred pounds of what had once been pure muscle. He wore the typical mud-stained pants and much-repaired tunic of a farmer. The clothing was quite insufficient for the harsh weather. The man's beefy hand gripped a smith's hammer.

"Throw down your sword, little man, and we'll not hurt you. It's your stuff we want, not you."

A thin, pasty-faced lad giggled nervously, next to the big man. The boy was nearly bald, and he had all the signs of a plague survivor, including the touch of madness. The remaining three were rather nondescript remnants of men, faces and bodies that had wasted away long ago. None of the five were true bandits. Huma prayed silently that he would not be forced to raise a hand against them.

"Are you deaf?"

"I cannot surrender you my valuables or food, if that is what you desire. I have very little."

"You have no choice." The big man swung his hammer experimentally in Huma's direction with great precision. "I thinks you're missin' the point. We *take* what we get."

The hammer snapped up and into a striking position. Huma's blade was out, yet he was loath to use it, even on them. The choice was taken from him, though, for the brigand leader's hammer came screaming past Huma's face, narrowly missing.

Five forms converged on the single knight—or tried to. Suddenly, Huma's right foot caught an attacker in the stomach. His free hand stunned the giggling lad, who thought to slip under his guard with a rusty old shortsword. With the flat of his blade, Huma brought the lad to the ground, unconscious. With ease, he disarmed the watery-eyed old man. Weaponless, that one retreated quickly from the fight, leaving Huma free to take care of the two still standing, one of them the apparent leader.

Despair suffused Huma as he realized these last two were not about to yield. The one remaining swordsman fought from desperation, which added dangerous strength to his otherwise unremarkable form. The brigand leader smiled viciously as he advanced again and again.

With great sadness, Huma made his choice. Before the startled eyes of the other villagers, the Knight of the Crown broke through the swordsman's guard and thrust deep into the chest. The man gurgled something and collapsed. Even as his one opponent fell, Huma was beating back the leader with one stinging blow after another. The burly thug began swinging wildly at the knight, and Huma waited. When the opening came, as he knew it would, a single chop put an end to the last of the desperate band.

Huma, his breath ragged, looked up at the spectators. They showed no emotion. He could not guess whether they were pleased or angered.

He looked around for the three survivors. Two were

unconscious, and the third had run off. They would be no more trouble.

Disgusted, Huma wiped off his sword, sheathed it, and stalked north once more. He was not even out of the village before arguments flared as human vultures fought over the meager belongings of the dead thieves.

When he had first stood before Vingaard Keep, home of the knighthood since Vinas Solamnus had ordered its construction all those centuries ago, Huma had felt like a mote before the palace of the gods.

The feeling lessened only ever so slightly.

Vingaard Keep's walls rose to a great height. Only a few adversaries dared scale such walls. The walls surrounded the citadel and were punctuated by slits for archers. The only gap in the walls was where the massive iron gates stood guard. They were as thick as Huma's arm was long, and they could stand the full force of a dragon charge. Each of the gates was decorated with the three-part symbol of the knighthood—the majestic kingfisher, with wings half-extended, which grasped in its sharp claws a sword on which a rose was centered. Above its head was a crown.

After a long, wet wait, a sentry came in response to Huma's hoarse shouts. He peered down at the bedraggled figure clad in a mixture of Solamnic and Ergothian armor, and shouted, "Who goes there? State your name and mission!"

Huma removed his helmet. "I am Huma, Knight of the Order of the Crown, returned from lands far beyond. I must speak to Lord Oswal, or even the Grand Master himself! It is urgent!"

"The Grand Master?" Huma could not see the man's face well, but the surprise in his tone was obvious. "Wait!"

Huma wondered at the strange reaction.

At last, the gates began to swing slowly open.

The same sentry who had questioned him stood by the gate. At the guard's signal, Huma followed him into the Keep. Those knights who had opened the gate wore expressions matching that of Huma's guide. The mystery deepened.

The sentry, a young Knight of the Crown, pulled Huma over to a dark corner and out of the drizzle that had developed. "I know who you are, for Master Rennard speaks highly of you in training, so I have taken this chance to warn you before you make a slip."

"Warn me? About what?"

"Only this morning—" The other knight looked around. "—the Grand Master, Lord Trake, passed away, victim of some foul, wasting disease."

No! Huma nearly shouted. The Grand Master dead! Trake had never cared for Huma—in fact, despised him as did his son, Bennett—but Huma could not help feeling the grief, as would all his fellows at the death of the head of the knighthood.

"I did not know. The people in the village seemed uneasy, but they did not—"

"They do not know!" the other knight hissed. "Lord Oswal has decreed that no word shall pass from the Keep until a new Grand Master has been chosen! If word should leak out that we are in such disarray, our last defenses will crumble!"

Last defenses? "Tell me—"

"Garvin."

"Tell me, Garvin, what happened when the darkness overcame our lines? Where do we stand now?" Huma clutched at the arms of the other knight.

"Didn't you come through it?" Garvin eyed Huma curiously. "The front is no more than two days' ride either east or west. The warlord's Black Guard moves untouched through the south. Most of our outposts are cut off. *We* are cut off."

"Is there no hope?"

Garvin stiffened. "We are Knights of Solamnia, Huma."

Huma nodded, knowing they would fight to the end, regardless. His mind turned to the cavern, the challenges, and, mostly, to the sword. He yearned for it now. In his hand, it would cleave through the Queen's evil forces. Solamnia would be victorious. Huma might even carve for himself some tiny kingdom—

He shook his head violently, and Garvin frowned in puzzlement. Huma forced the ungodly thoughts from his mind. The sword was not Paladine's legacy to the knighthood. For all its majesty and power, something about it sickened Huma even as he yearned for it. Not that it mattered; he had lost everything when he had fallen through the mirror. It was hopeless.

No! He straightened and gave Garvin an apologetic smile for his odd actions. There was still time if he could make someone listen.

"Garvin, where might I find Lord Oswal?"

"Now?" The other knight stared at the darkened sky from the shelter. "It is past supper, I know that. He would be in his quarters. He is preparing for the Knightly Council tomorrow night."

"They are going to wait until *tomorrow night* before choosing a new Grand Master? The Queen's servants could be at our gates tonight! The dragons at the very least!"

Garvin nodded. "So Lord Oswal said, but the Council will be the Council."

"I must speak with him now, then."

Huma hurried out into the rain.

It had never really rained like this since the war's beginning, Lord Oswal decided. In the past, it had always been nothing more than a mist. Now, it was almost as if the rain could wash it all away.

The High Warrior started from his daydreaming. He was becoming senile, he decided, to be thinking of rain when the fate of the knighthood and of the world might rest on getting the dunderheads of the Council to speed up their decision on who would be Grand Master. He had ruined his own chances by admitting to his indecision at the rout. It had been only a momentary lapse, shock at the sudden turn in events and the realization that they could not fight this attack. The losses had been costly.

Oswal's nephew Bennett was maneuvering his own faction. He always remained within the bounds of the Oath and the Measure, but he was ambitious and would try to manipulate the decision. Logically, one of the three heads of the Orders should be the late Grand Master's successor. But

Bennett believed he should follow his father. Trake had always desired that. Only Oswal stood in his way, now.

"Lord Oswal?"

He looked up to see Rennard watching him intently. The pale knight stood next to the only other chair in Oswal's room.

Rennard. Despite his cold exterior, the High Warrior had almost as much regard for Rennard as he did for Huma. Only—Huma had been lost in the debacle. Huma apparently had stood fast in the end.

"What is it, Rennard?"

"You've still not formulated your plans. I think it might be wise—"

There was a commotion outside as the two guards stationed at his chamber doors argued with someone. The newcomer was insistent, and there was something familiar about his voice.

"Rennard, what—?"

The pale knight had opened the door and—the elder knight could scarcely believe it—now gaped open-mouthed at a bedraggled knight struggling with the two guards. It took only seconds for Lord Oswal to recognize the newcomer, and then he, too, was staring in surprise and delight.

"Huma!"

The sentries immediately stopped struggling as they noted the tone of their superior. Rennard recovered also and, typically, simply said, "Let him by."

Released, Huma burst into the room. "My Lord Oswal, Rennard—"

"At attention, Huma," the gaunt knight interrupted.

Huma immediately stiffened. Rennard turned to the High Warrior, who nodded. To the guards, Rennard said, "Resume your posts; that is the High Warrior's orders."

Once the door was closed, Lord Oswal stared at the trembling knight. Huma had something to say and wanted to say it before it burst from his head, it seemed.

"At ease, Huma. Come and sit down. Tell us about the miracle that allows you to return from the dead."

Huma knelt before the elder knight. Relieved at last, the story spilled from him in a torrent.

Lord Oswal and Rennard listened intently as each part of Huma's tale unfolded. The quest of Magius—the chase of the Black Guard—the ever-present dreadwolves—the mountains, the cavern, the dragon, the sword . . . Had it not been Huma who spoke, neither of the knights would have believed a word. As it was, they truly believed.

The great clang of metal upon metal, so much like the sounds of the Keep's own forge, interested Lord Oswal most. He asked Huma his opinion of the noise.

"A workplace of the gods. There is no other way to describe it. If it is not Reorx who shapes the metal somewhere within that mountain . . . I can add nothing more, save that I feel I must go back," Huma said, adding, "If Paladine wills it."

"Well." It was all the High Warrior could say at first. Rennard simply nodded.

Lord Oswal thought for a moment. "This sword sounds fascinating. Could it—?"

Huma interjected immediately. "I fear it is lost to us. Wyrmfather acts as its tomb."

His tone was cautious. He wanted them to forget the sword, not only because of his wariness of it, but because of the temptation Huma felt to grip the blade and wield it.

The High Warrior took his words at face value. "I'll trust to your judgment." He looked from Huma to Rennard and then back again. "It seems to me that we cannot let this matter sit for very long. Time is running out for all of us."

Nervous enthusiasm in control, Huma quickly spoke. "I need only transportation. A horse—are the dragons about? One of them, maybe?"

The High Warrior frowned. "There is nothing I can do for you anyway, Huma. Not at present. If I send you off on some wild quest, I lose the chance of keeping the knighthood from the hands of those more interested in power and esteem than the Oath and the Measure. You will have to wait until a new Grand Master is chosen."

Huma looked perplexed. "But, surely you—"

"I have been found wanting. It may be another."

"But—" Huma could not believe his mission was to be delayed—possibly denied—for such a petty reason.

"I believe I can win my case, Huma. I'm sorry, but you will have to wait. Rennard, he is one of yours. See to it that he is cleaned up, fed, and allowed to sleep. I'll want to see a clearer head on his shoulders come the morrow."

"Yes, milord." Rennard put a friendly but firm hand on Huma's shoulders. The younger knight stood up reluctantly.

They parted silently. Huma's depression deepened. Not only was his quest threatened, but so was the life of a man who had been the closest thing to a father he had ever had. No one but Lord Oswal could lead the knights in this time. Bennett, for all his prowess, lacked experience. Even Huma knew that. The Knights of Solamnia needed strong leadership, leadership that only Lord Oswal could provide, Huma believed. Without Oswal, the knighthood would splinter.

Without the High Warrior in command, Huma suddenly realized, he could never return to the mountain.

Chapter 18

The rain did not let up that night. Exhausted as he was, Huma could not sleep. Like Lord Oswal, he saw some significance in the sudden change from perpetual cloud cover to the incessant rain that so affected nerves as time passed.

He heard horses trotting past. Even in the dead of night, there was always activity. Some men slept, others worked. Vingaard Keep would never be caught off-guard.

A returning patrol, he decided. The sounds dwindled off in the direction of the stables. Huma wondered what news, if any, they would bring. Had the lines backed up even farther? Would the knights soon be able to view the front from the Keep itself? How long before the pincer finally closed upon the cradle of the knighthood?

Huma stood up slowly, so as not to disturb those around him in the common quarters shared by Knights of the Crown. The building was essentially one great room with row upon row of hard, flat beds and small storage areas for each occupant. As the knights slept in shifts, the room was never full. Also, many were away from the Keep for one reason or another. Only the higher-ranking knights had quarters of their own.

A breath of fresh air, he decided, would do him good. With careful steps, he maneuvered around his fellows and eventually made his way to the door.

The air was cool and the wind a little more brisk than he had imagined. He breathed in deeply, thankful for the moment when he could briefly relax from all the sorrows and confusion. Huma prayed that all would go well tomorrow.

He blinked. His eyes began to play tricks on him, and he was sure for a brief moment that a dark figure had moved near Lord Oswal's chambers, just behind the two guards. He considered alerting someone, but neither guard seemed disturbed, and when he looked again there was no sign of the supposed intruder. Huma had no desire to bring ridicule upon himself. Not now. He stared out into the night and, after a few minutes, retired. Sleep came more swiftly this time.

The next day passed far too quickly. It had been Huma's intention to steer clear of the other knights, at least until the question of leadership was resolved. Too much had happened to him, and he did not trust himself to remain neutral on the subject. What he said, he knew, would be a reflection on Lord Oswal, who had always stood by him. Even Rennard might be affected.

Yet Lord Oswal summoned Huma just two hours before the Knightly Council was to meet. The Knight of the Rose who brought the message eyed Huma with great curiosity, but, loyal as he was to the High Warrior, he asked no questions.

As Huma was crossing to Lord Oswal's quarters, he was confronted by the very figure he had intended to avoid.

"They told me you were alive. I had my doubts, though, until I saw you just now."

Bennett was clad in formal attire, including a purple cloak bearing the standard of both the knighthood and his family's personal holdings. A black sash ran diagonally across his breastplate. Even now, with the rain still lightly falling and the true night almost upon them, he seemed to gleam. Regardless of all else, Bennett was his father's son. The hawklike features were a copy of the elder knight.

"My apologies, Lord Bennett." The family holdings had been ruled equally by Oswal and Trake until the latter's rise to Grand Master. Now, as Trake's heir, Bennett held that title with his uncle. As Oswal had no heirs of his own, the holdings would someday be under the rule of only one man. "I had meant to offer my sympathies sooner—"

"Do not play me for a fool, goatherder," Bennett rejoined. "You have stayed away from me because we have ever been enemies. I still do not believe you belong among us, but my own good heart has made your ouster all but impossible now. Little did I know when I praised you—posthumously, I thought—that you would return."

Huma's entire body felt taut, but he would not allow himself to be provoked by Bennett. He was sure much of the anger in the son of the late Grand Master was due to his father's untimely death.

"I have never been your enemy, milord. Rather, I have always admired you, despite your protest over my selection." Bennett's face actually evidenced mild surprise as Huma spoke. "Your bearing, your skill, your ability to command under the most adverse conditions—you are what I strive to be, what I may never be. I only ask for the opportunity to do my duty."

Bennett's mouth clamped shut. He stared at Huma briefly, then muttered, "Perhaps."

"Perhaps?" Huma raised an eyebrow. "What do you mean?"

The newest Lord of Baxtrey, though, had already turned away. All Huma could do was watch him vanish into the midst of the Keep.

Huma proceeded to meet with Lord Oswal.

Rennard was there. Huma interrupted them as they inspected a map. Lord Oswal was pointing to a spot near the north. They looked up as Huma was admitted, and the High Warrior smiled thinly. Rennard merely nodded.

Lord Oswal rolled up the map. "Were you away from the Crown's general quarters?"

"No. I had the misfortune of confronting your nephew, milord."

The elder knight shook his head. He was looking much more drained than he had the night before. "Yes. Pay him no mind, Huma. He is unsettled by the fact that you've seemingly come back from the dead."

"He still hates what I am."

"Then he is a fool," Rennard suddenly interjected. "You have proved to be ten times the knight he is."

"I thank you, though I do not believe that."

"Then you are also a fool."

Lord Oswal interrupted. "The last thing we need is to fight among ourselves." The High Warrior put a hand to his forehead, nearly knocking over a lit candle in the process. Huma reached for him, but Oswal waved him away. "I'm fine. Didn't seem to get enough sleep last night, though. A bad night for insomnia, I should think."

"Will you be able to go through with the Council meeting?" asked Rennard.

"What choice have I? Perhaps it's only my personal opinion, but if my nephew—who I must point out thinks he is doing what is best—has any control over the next Grand Master, we will be plunged into disaster."

The intensity of the High Warrior's opinion of his nephew surprised Huma. He had known they did not get along, but this . . . "Why so?"

"Bennett, like many of us, is too caught up in the legends of the knighthood. He is the kind of leader who will have every able knight in Vingaard Keep attacking in one massive, heroic charge that will end in the death of all."

"Would he?" Huma's tone was doubtful. Even against the darkness, Bennett appeared calculating and in full command of his senses.

"He would. You never see Bennett in a command meeting;

he is the one for lighting strikes or waves of destruction, never solid, long-term strategies. Since Trake's death, I think he is even more determined to do something momentous—to honor his father's memory."

"Huma may have trouble believing that, but I have known Bennett longer. I would concur," added Rennard.

Lord Oswal looked up at Huma. "Another thing. He would never believe your story of enchanted swords, imprisoned dragons, and god-created challenges that hold the key to victory. I do. Call it faith in Paladine, but I do."

The elder knight leaned forward suddenly, holding a hand against his head.

"Rest. I need some rest," muttered Oswal.

"Help me with him, Huma."

Together, the two knights led the High Warrior to his bed. As they helped him lie down, Lord Oswal took hold of Rennard. "You must see to it that I am awake in time for the Council. Is that understood?"

The pale face turned toward Huma and then back to the High Warrior. With the same lack of emotion he always displayed, Rennard said, "Of course. You know I will."

"Good." Lord Oswal was asleep almost immediately after that. The two knights stepped away quietly. When they were backed up by the door, Rennard turned to Huma.

"He wants you at the Council meeting."

"What about him?" Huma feared for Oswal's health.

"He'll be there. I've promised to take care of him." Rennard actually smiled slightly. "I have everything in hand. You'll see."

Huma made sure that he was one of the first to arrive.

Not all Knightly Councils were open to the population of the Keep. Most consisted only of the ruling knights and any persons involved with some portion of the agenda. There was also a set pattern to events, steps that were followed under normal circumstances. It was the feeling of the ruling body, though, that selecting a replacement for the Grand Master was something all should be involved with and, while not everyone could fit into the chamber, the knighthood as a whole would be well represented.

The masters of the Orders of the Crown and the Sword were already seated. Arak Hawkeye tugged at his tiny goatee and stared rather arrogantly at his counterpart of the Sword. Huma did not recognize the man next to Lord Hawkeye. It was not the same knight who had commanded the Order of the Sword these past four years. The former commander had died in the war to the east, and his replacement had been chosen on the battlefield out of necessity. The knight's angular face reminded Huma of an idealized statue more than a man. His mustache was long and trimmed narrow, his eyes nearly invisible under a thick, shaggy brow. When Bennett entered, it was clear who was the true ruling power in the Order of the Sword, for the other stiffened.

Eventually, the chamber was filled and the waiting began. Only two people of consequence were missing, Rennard and Lord Oswal. The Knightly Council waited patiently, members constantly conferring with one another during that time. At last, Bennett stalked imperiously over to Lord Hawkeye and spoke sharply in an undertone. Hawkeye responded in kind, and the argument raged for several minutes. Regrettably, they were not speaking loud enough to be understood, and Huma could only guess at what might have passed between them.

Just then, Rennard rushed in, out of breath. There was intense strain on his face, and the image of the normally placid knight in such a high emotional state was enough to cause more than one person to rise in expectation of bad news.

Rennard whispered quickly to Lord Hawkeye. Bennett and the other Councilors listened in as best they could. Bennett's face turned white, and he gripped the nearest chair tightly. Arak Hawkeye stood up to face the suddenly anxious crowd.

"This meeting is postponed until further notice. I regret to inform those assembled that Lord Oswal of Baxtrey, High Warrior and master of the Order of the Rose, has been stricken ill—by the same disease that claimed the Grand Master."

"A quarantine has been imposed on the Keep. Lord

Oswal is not expected to live through the night."

Rennard was still shaking.

"I came to wake him as he requested and found him unconscious and shivering in his bed, despite being covered by two or three blankets. I administered what aid I knew and then fetched a cleric."

Huma had never seen him in such a state. It was almost as if the pale knight was reliving his own brush with the plague.

"What did the cleric do?"

"Little. The disease baffles him. Another gift from the Queen, I suppose, damn her existence."

"Is there nothing that can be done?" Huma suddenly felt weak. Lord Oswal was his mentor, his friend, the closest thing to his father. He must not die!

"We can only wait and pray." Was there a hint of bitter mockery in Rennard's voice? Huma could not really blame him. He himself felt so powerless. The Dragonqueen, Crynus, and the renegade mage Galan Dracos must be laughing at their fate, he supposed.

"Huma." Rennard laid a hand on his shoulder. The pale face was still strained. How much Rennard had cared for Oswal! "Get some sleep."

They were in the outer chamber of the Keep's Temple of Paladine, where the High Warrior had been carried in the hopes that the gods might influence Lord Oswal's recovery. At present, the clerics treating the elder knight were in a quandary. One moment they would believe they had beaten the disease, the next moment it would come back, stronger than before. Time was running out. Lord Oswal's body could not stand many more severe swings in health.

Rennard smiled faintly. "I promise you, I will alert you should there be any change."

Despite his good intentions, Huma suddenly felt sleepy, almost as if the mere mention of it had made him recognize that fact. He nodded to Rennard and stood up.

"You *will* wake me."

"I promised Lord Oswal that," Rennard replied bitterly.

As Huma departed, he could still hear Bennett's voice

coming from the side chamber where the clerics conferred.
Bennett seemed to care for his uncle almost as much as he
cared for his father. At news of the High Warrior's sickness,
it had been Bennett's voice that had prevented the panic and
organized the temporary quarantine and the shifting of the
ailing noble to the temple. Now, the Knight of the Sword
divided his time between praying for his uncle and arguing
with clerics, whom he thought were reacting too slowly to
the crisis.

What of the war? It was as if forgotten by those who clois-
tered themselves within the walls of the Keep. The thought
nagged Huma all the way to his cot.

He woke abruptly, his mind startlingly clear. Lord Oswal
was his first thought, and Huma immediately assumed the
worst. Others slept on, far more used to the daily loss of
precious life, it seemed to him.

Huma slipped out into the night and peered around. In
the dim torchlight, he could make out sentries keeping vigilant watch on the walls while others patrolled the courtyard. Guards still stood before the doorway leading to the
High Warrior's abode. That was a good sign.

Unable to sleep, Huma decided to return to the temple.
That Rennard had not come for him did not surprise him;
the pale knight evidently meant to keep vigil through the
entire crisis, if at all possible.

The rain had still not let up, and the courtyard was turning into a bowl of muck.

The temple of Paladine seemed oddly dark as he neared it.
No one stood guard, which did not surprise him. But as he
made his way up the steps and was about to knock upon the
temple doors, he noticed that one was slightly ajar. Pushing
it open, he discovered the main corridor also dark. That, he
knew, was not as it should be. Here there should have been
a sentry or at least a cleric.

Suddenly Huma found himself before one of the Knights
of the Rose whose duty it was to act as honor guard and—
for this crisis—guardian for the ill High Warrior. The knight
stood at the doorway, looking quite stern, and Huma
almost hailed him until he realized that the man would not

be standing in darkness unless there was a very good reason. Stepping cautiously, Huma made his way across the marble floor and did not stop until he was face-to-face with the guard.

The Knight of the Rose stared back, but did not see.

Huma held a hand before the other's face. He could feel and hear the man's breathing, but it was the breathing of one deep in sleep. Huma dared slap the knight lightly on the cheek. The guard did not stir.

Leaning closer, Huma inspected the open eyes. They were glazed. He had seen men like this before, men who had been drugged for one reason or another. Huma suspected the Knight of the Rose would remember nothing about his lapse of duty. He also suspected something similar had happened to the rest of the temple's inhabitants—including Rennard.

With a prayer to Paladine, Huma drew his sword. He followed the darkened halls until he came to the place where Rennard had sat, only to discover that the gaunt knight was gone. The doorway to the room where Lord Oswal lay resting also was partially open, and Huma discovered two more guards in the same comatose condition.

Huma feared the worst. Rennard and Lord Oswal had both been overwhelmed, he decided quickly.

With measured steps, Huma slowly opened the door to Lord Oswal's chamber. The darkness disoriented him for only a second, then his trained senses located the even darker blur—Lord Oswal standing by the makeshift bed.

Standing? Huma blinked and allowed his eyes to adjust. No, it was not the High Warrior. Oswal was, indeed, lying on the bed. What then? A shadow?

Huma stepped forward and the darkness seemed to shift. He blinked. The figure—or what he had thought was a figure—was no longer there. With some trepidation, Huma moved forward until he was standing next to the still form of Lord Oswal. He was relieved to hear the regular breathing of the High Warrior.

Huma's foot bumped against something. He peered down and found himself staring at the inert body of one of the clerics. The cleric slept as the guards had slept, his eyes glazed and wide. Huma shook him hard in an attempt to wake him, but the man did not even stir.

He felt, rather than heard, the darkness stir behind him. He hesitated and that hesitation might have nearly cost him his own life, for something metallic struck his breastplate and would have cut deep into his throat if he had moved any slower.

Cursing himself, Huma parried another vicious jab by a tiny, twisted blade. He had his first glance at his attacker, a figure in flowing darkness from which two red, glaring eyes peered. The figure threw the blade at his head, forcing Huma to duck. Even as Huma dodged the weapon, the specter brought forth a small pouch and raised it.

The knight scuttled back quickly. There was no denying what he faced now. The actions, the appearance—he was surprised he had not recognized the intruder immediately— were those of a cultist of Morgion, Lord of Disease and Decay. One of the vermin had made his way into Vingaard Keep—and had so far succeeded in killing one, and possibly two, of the most important figures in the knighthood.

The ragged figure hesitated before throwing the contents of the pouch.

Huma leaped forward, his broadsword up and before him. The flat of the blade slammed into the pouch, which burst, but not before the sword's momentum pushed much of it back at the hooded intruder. Huma stumbled back, avoiding the deadly shower that rained on the other.

The assassin coughed and hacked as dust flew into his face. He stumbled back, but Huma dared not step forward. The cultist fell toward a pew and then, slowly, pulled himself back up again.

"If you think—" the voice was rough and strained, but familiar "—to kill me with my own tools, know that Morgion protects his own. Besides, I only wished to put you to sleep. Now you leave me no choice."

It was all Huma could do to keep from dropping his sword as the hooded figure's throat cleared itself of dust and his identity was revealed. Huma took a desperate step back, even as the cultist pulled out a broadsword hidden in his robe.

"The knife point would have nicked you, and again you

would have slept. I fear, though, that this is all I have left now." The blade came up, its point directed at Huma's neck.

Huma could not bring himself to fight. It could not be happening like this. It could not be true. This was some terrible nightmare from which he would awaken!

The assassin laughed quietly. The sword lowered slightly. The laugh seemed to echo through Huma's mind, mocking everything he had ever believed in.

"I had tried to protect you from this. I *am* sorry, Huma."

And though Huma could not speak the words at first, they pounded in his head, cried in his heart.

Why, Rennard?

Chapter 19

"*Have you nothing to say?*" Rennard asked. "*We* have time. All sleep here. The walls are thick. They will not hear our swords. Yes. I think we have time."

"In Paladine's name, Rennard. *Why?*"

Huma could almost see the face, despite the hood and darkness. He could almost feel the bitterness as Rennard spoke.

"When I lay dying of plague all those years ago, I pleaded with Paladine, with Mishakal, with all the gods of that house for release. They did nothing. I lingered, wasting away. My visage shocks many now; it would have horrified them even more had they seen it then. I had contracted the Scarlet Plague, you see."

The Scarlet Plague. Of all the forms unleashed over the

years, the Scarlet Plague had been the worst. The knight-hood had been forced to burn whole villages when the greatest healers could not keep the disease under control. The victims wasted away, but each day was agony and many killed themselves long before the disease had the chance. The name came from the redness of the skin as the victim eventually burned up from the sickness. It was a frightening thing, still talked of in whispers.

"Then when I was sure the agony would finally kill me, I was visited—not by the gods I had pleaded to, but by the one god willing to take away my pain, for a price." The point of the blade rose again. "Morgion. Only he cared to answer my prayers, though I had never looked to him. He was willing to take my pain from me, make me whole if I would become his. It was no difficult decision, Huma. I accepted immediately and gladly."

Huma prayed for something—Lord Oswal stirring, knights coming to investigate the darkness, *something*—but all remained quiet. How long had Rennard planned? How long had he waited for this moment?

Huma heard more than saw the blade coming at him. That other knight moved confidently in the dark. Yet Huma managed again and again to counter each strike, though he knew that Rennard's skill in personal combat was consid-ered second to none. Especially now, when he faced a Huma who also fought within himself.

Then, as suddenly as he had attacked, Rennard ceased. He chuckled quietly. "Very good. Much like your father."

"My father?"

They had worked their way farther from the doors, toward where the clerics stood when they offered ceremo-nies. Rennard pulled back his hood, and even in the dark Huma could make out the pale, drawn skin. "Father. Oh yes. That was why I protected you, you know. The mark of Morgion, even on an unsuspecting person, is a sign that that one is not to be harmed by any who serve Morgion."

Huma remembered the words of the cultists in the ruins. They had seen the mark and had argued about it. Skularis had not known the reason for its existence.

"What a sentimental fool I am," Rennard continued, "for

wanting to save my kin."

Kin? Huma shook his head in growing horror.

"You are so very much like my brother was, Huma. Durac was his name—Durac, Lord of Eldor, a land overrun soon after he and I joined the knighthood. Nothing remains of Eldor today, save a few pitiful ruins. Just as well. Unlike the Baxtrey domains, where Oswal and Trake ruled jointly, I would have inherited nothing. As eldest son, your father inherited."

"Stop it!" Huma swung violently at the man who had betrayed all he believed in. A man who had once been a friend.

Rennard defended himself easily. After several moments, they parted again.

"I belonged to Morgion long before our father sent us as squires to Vingaard Keep. From the first, I tried to protect Durac. He was family, after all. The others who followed Morgion might not understand that, so I planted within him the same invisible mark that protected you from them. It proved to be a futile gesture. Your father died in battle only a year after becoming a knight. He stayed back with a handful of others to block a passage through the eastern mountains in Hylo—the only passage that would allow the Queen's forces to attack from the rear. The rest of us rode to warn the main army. There was nothing I could do. Ironic, is it not? I wanted to tell him the truth about me at that last moment, but of course I could not. Little did I know at that time that he had left a wife and son."

Huma quivered, part of him yearning to hear the story, part of him repulsed.

"You must ask Lord Oswal about Durac sometime—when you meet him on the other side!" Rennard charged Huma, catching the anguished knight off guard. They struggled together, and Huma found himself staring into a face half-twisted by madness. Gone was the emotionless facade that he had always wondered about, the mask behind which Rennard had hidden his treachery. Huma succeeded in pushing the other knight away.

"What was her name, nephew? Karina? I saw her only once, years later, when I finally located the village he had frequented before his death. She was a beautiful woman—wheat-colored hair, elfin face, slim—a woman full of life. I thought of wooing her, but then I saw you—Durac all over again, though only a lad—and knew that she would shun the horror that I was. I was a fool to think of anything other than my promise to my true lord." Rennard's sword cleaved the air as it came down at Huma. The younger knight rolled to the side and into a squatting position.

"You killed her, didn't you?" Huma's voice was cold and lifeless as he finally relived the days of his mother's fatal illness, which had seemed to come from nowhere.

"You should thank me. I thought of you. I wanted you to be the knight Durac should have been. I believed I could keep you unaware of the truth." Rennard smiled obscenely.

"The dream. I had a dream about your foul god."

"I thought I might draw you to my side, make you a comrade and spare us this."

"What by the platinum dragon goes on here?"

Both combatants froze as light streamed into the room. Bennett stood in the doorway, flanked by two of his fellows from the Order of the Sword. A quick glance showed Rennard's realization of his mistake; Bennett must have retired on his own or at least have departed, and Rennard had had no chance to treat him as he had treated all those unsuspecting others.

"Rennard? Huma?" Whatever his faults, the son of the late Grand Master was not slow. He took in the scene, saw the tattered cloak and hood that covered Rennard's armor, and knew what the knight represented.

Bennett pulled out his sword and pointed at the traitor. "I want him!"

"How quickly the veneer of dignity vanishes in the face of petty emotions," Rennard comment wryly. Without another word, he took a savage swing at Huma—who dodged—and then Rennard bolted over the pews.

"He has nowhere to go!" Bennett's resemblance to a bird of prey was even more obvious now. His eyes were wide and burned intensely, yet they caught every movement, studied all angles. His movements were fluid, calculated. Bennett was a hawk about to dive upon its prey. He stalked

Rennard now.

But Rennard stepped into the shadows of the wall—and slid through. Huma reached the walls before the others and felt the spot. He did not think that Rennard had used sorcery to get away, as Magius had done once. No, it might— yes! Huma's fingers found a slight indentation, and the wall suddenly gaped open to swallow him. Behind him, he could hear Bennett shouting for the other two to follow, then the wall closed once more. Huma had no time to wait for them.

Where did Rennard hope to go?

The elder knight's rapid footsteps were barely audible, moving upstairs. What did Rennard hope to find up there?

This was not an ancient, hidden stairway as Huma first suspected; he passed two windows on his way up to the next level.

The stairway ended at a trapdoor in the ceiling. Cautiously, he reached up and, with his blade ready in his other hand, pushed it open. Wind and rain rushed to meet him.

The attack he expected did not occur.

Footsteps behind him alerted him to the presence of Bennett and his two companions. Huma did not want them to be the ones to face Rennard. That was reserved for himself. Slowly, Huma stepped up and out, into the rain.

The roof was empty. There was no place to hide, no place to flee to. The knight walked to the nearest ledge and peered over. Knights were beginning to gather below; Bennett had sounded the alert.

The first of Bennett's two companions lifted himself out onto the roof. "Where is he? Did you catch him?"

Huma shook his head. Where *was* Rennard? The newcomers also combed the roof, but they could not discover a trace. Rennard had simply vanished.

Bennett refused to believe this. Knights searched all the nearby buildings and, when that failed to turn up anything, searched the rest of the Keep as well. Rennard's belongings were gathered and inspected, but they offered few clues.

The clerics had rushed to Lord Oswal's side the moment they learned of the attack. To their amazement, he appeared to be recovering. As one cleric explained to Huma, Bennett, and the others who had assembled, Lord Oswal's body was throwing off effects of the dose that Rennard had administered earlier—thus the assassin hoped to effect a second dose before the High Warrior had recovered.

As the knights dispersed, some to continue the search for the traitor, some to their various duties, Huma felt a hand on his shoulder. He started, his first thought that Rennard had come to finish him off. The figure behind him spoke.

"It's Bennett."

Huma turned slowly around, and the two faced one another. Oswal's nephew seemed to be fighting several emotions all at once, for his face registered traces of embarrassment, anger, and confusion. At last, he reached out a hand.

"My gratitude for all you've done."

Uncertain as to how to react, Huma simply took the hand in his own and shook it. "I failed to capture your father's killer."

Bennett forced his face into immobility. Huma knew that the other knight was very uncomfortable. "You unmasked him. You saved my uncle. Even—even fought that pale traitor to a standstill, something I never could have done."

The hawk-faced knight saluted briefly and departed. Huma watched him disappear, a brief smile playing on his lips before he, too, turned and left, hoping to find some trace of Rennard.

It came as no surprise, two days later, that Lord Oswal became the new Grand Master. He had remained isolated before that decision, with only the Council members speaking with him. All possible opposition by Bennett had vanished; in fact, the new Grand Master's nephew was petitioning to step up to the Order of the Rose. There was every likelihood that he would be recommended. It was also likely that he would be wearing the trappings of High Warrior himself before long.

Huma struggled to get through those two days. When he was at last granted an audience with Lord Oswal, Huma shook visibly. To him, the Grand Master was a figure almost as revered as Paladine, for he was, after all, the living symbol of the Triumvirate's desires.

As Huma knelt in supplication, an odd sound reached his

ears and he dared to look up. Flanked by an impressive honor guard consisting of veterans from all three Orders, the Grand Master was sitting on his throne and chuckling.

"Get up, Huma. You don't have to stand on ceremony with me. Not now."

Huma rose and came closer. "Grand Master—"

A sigh. "If you must be formal, make it Lord Oswal. I do not have the pretensions of my brother—not yet."

"Lord Oswal, before I start, tell me of Durac of Eldor."

"Durac? I've known two or three. Eldor . . . I'm not sure—"

"Please. You know which one. Rennard's brother. My—father."

The new Grand Master, stared open-mouthed. "Father? Durac? Then, Rennard—"

"My uncle." Huma forced the unsavory word from his mouth.

"Paladine!" Lord Oswal's voice was little more than a whisper. "Huma, I *am* sorry."

"Sir. My father?"

The Grand Master wiped something from his eye. "I'm sorry, Huma. I wish I could tell you everything, but I honestly don't remember much. Durac was a good knight, although a little overenthusiastic. He was a brilliant, almost natural fighter, picking up skills as easily as I might pick up a knife. I remember that he spent much of his time west, but I never knew it was because he had a family. I do remember, though," Oswal said, rubbing his chin, "him shouting to us as we left him and the others to hold the pass. Now I realize what he meant. When he said 'watch over them,' I thought he meant the men. What a fool! He meant his family, and only Rennard really knew."

There was little more the Grand Master could add, which disappointed Huma, though he did not show it. It was Oswal who broke the uneasy silence by saying, "You have my permission to start out for Ergoth and your mountains. How many knights will you need to accompany you?"

"None."

"None?" The Grand Master leaned forward, his hands gripping the throne tightly. "As you yourself mentioned, this is a matter of the utmost importance. I want to ensure your success. Paladine has seen fit to give us this chance, but I will not let you take unnecessary risks."

"What Paladine seeks must be from me alone," Huma replied. "I feel that now. I cannot explain how I know. It simply feels right."

Oswal sighed and leaned back. "You say that with great conviction. My head tells me that you are wrong, but my heart listens to you. I think, in this matter, I will go with my heart, for that is where belief begins."

"Thank you, milord."

Lord Oswal stood. Huma followed suit. The Grand Master clasped Huma on the shoulders. "Regardless of your birth and who your parents were, I shall always consider you *my* son."

They held one another briefly, then Oswal broke away. "Go on. Get out before I become even more a sentimental fool than I am."

Few knights were around the courtyard when Huma chose to leave. He had wanted it that way. It would make the departure easier, at least for him. A part of him felt as if he were running out, that he should remain in Vingaard Keep until Rennard was found and punished. Yet Huma no longer wanted any part in the other's capture. He had known the gaunt knight far too long to simply forget all those past times, when the two had been friends.

One figure he did note. Bennett, standing on the parapet and scanning the Keep. The Grand Master's nephew was still searching for his father's murderer. The search through Rennard's belongings had uncovered ancient plans for the Keep that had been thought lost forever. They included two passages within the temple that not even the clerics knew about.

The dour Bennett turned from gazing out at the lands surrounding Vingaard and noted Huma. He nodded slowly and then turned away. That was all.

Huma's path took him through another half-dead village. He had been riding for an hour. Twice, Huma had met patrolling knights, and each time he had brought them up to date on the futile search going on in Vingaard Keep for the traitorous Rennard.

The inhabitants of this particular village eyed the lone knight differently than those Huma had passed in other places. There was a tension in their very movements, a great sense of fear, as if they expected to see the Dragonqueen herself swoop out of the sky at any moment. Slowly, they began to mill around Huma and his horse.

The warhorse slowed nervously, its nostrils flaring as it stared at possible enemies. Huma pulled tight on the reins, re-exerting mastery over the beast. He did not want to have the lives of innocent commonfolk on his hands.

It soon proved impossible for the horse to proceed, so concentrated had the small crowd become. The villagers enveloped animal and rider in a wave of human fear. Huma began picking up muttered questions, dealing with the events in the Keep.

A grimy, bony claw touched his right leg. A rasping voice asked, "Is it true? Has the Grand Master been murdered? Are we no longer safe?"

"I heard that the Council wants to surrender!" cried out a voice that the knight could not locate.

That last statement increased the anxiety of the villagers. They crowded even closer, oblivious to the danger they faced from the hooves of the trained steed. Huma tried to wave them back.

"Stand aside! Let me through! If you don't, the horse might hurt you!"

"He's fleeing!" cried the same voice. "The knights are lost!"

"We're all lost!" shrilled an old woman. She fainted and was lost in the press of bodies.

"You can't leave us!"

"You're tryin' to save your own skin!"

"Get back!" Faces filled with anger and confusion moved through Huma's vision. Hands clawed at him. The horse, spooked, reared. Those closest to the animal's front came to their senses and turned to escape. But those who had been behind them continued to move forward.

An elderly man fell. The knight succeeded in calming his mount and then sought to clear a path so that he could help the old man.

"He's betrayed us all! He struck the elder down! Take him!"

Ragged, gaunt figures surged on Huma. He pulled out his sword and threatened them with it. The villagers backed away but were by no means ready to give up—not when they feared the Knights of Solamnia were abandoning them to the tenderness of the Dragonqueen.

This time, Huma spotted the instigator, a figure clad in the garments of a simple farmer, standing off to the side. The man made no move to run when he realized he had been seen. Instead, he drew a broadsword and revealed once more the face of evil.

Huma directed the horse through the crowd, forcing people back with his sword and thanking Paladine that no one had yet dared him to strike. He reined the steed to a stop less than six feet from the figure.

"Bennett still thinks you might be in the Keep."

Rennard smiled briefly. "I was until Lord Oswal's appointment became official. Then I came here to give them the news."

Huma leaped off his mount, never taking his eyes from his uncle nor sheathing the sword. "To put fear in their hearts, you mean. To break down trust, make us fight among ourselves."

"It is—my calling. But not just these. Villages all over this area. I've not slept since yesterday."

"They finally found your secret passages."

"I know. I left the maps on purpose. I had no more need of them."

"This is insane, uncle."

"Uncle. A word I never thought you would use. Yes, it is insane. The whole world is insane. I strive to make it less so." Rennard pointed at the villagers, speaking quietly enough that they would not hear him. "The fear will spread. They will march on the Keep in their desperation, and the knighthood will be forced to drive them away, with at least some loss of life, I believe. The great Knights of Solamnia

227

will suffer both the notoriety of their actions and a terrible blow to morale. I need not go on."

"This has all been planned."

"Of course. I could have killed the entire Council, but that only would have strengthened the knighthood's resolve. That is why I have traveled the near lands, in disguise, stirring the pot." Rennard straightened and the sword swung slowly back and forth. "My only remaining duty is you, Huma. I knew you would choose this route. I cannot allow you to return to this—cavern. It may be a madness on your part, but I think not. I cannot risk being wrong about something like that."

His sword came up swinging. Huma immediately blocked the thrust. The villagers stepped away as the two knights fought, but the people's horribly expectant looks showed Huma that they were waiting to see one of the knights die, so completely had they become Rennard's pawns.

The gaunt knight swung and gave Huma an opening. Rennard's skill allowed him to parry much of the blow, but Huma's blade still slipped under and struck a glancing blow on the other's right side. The blade clanged off a solid surface beneath Rennard's tunic, however, and a cunning smile flashed briefly across the pale knight's features. Beneath the cloth, he still wore his armor.

Their blades clashed time and time again as they struggled through the rain-soaked village. The human wall that surrounded them bent and twisted, but never revealed a gap. Huma wondered what would happen to him even if he defeated Rennard. The villagers might very well fall on him.

"Very good!" hissed Rennard. "I trained you well!"

"Well enough." Huma said no more. He knew he needed to save every ounce of strength, for Rennard was living off his madness and fighting with daunting power and ferocity.

Huma slipped in the mud just as Rennard's blade flashed past his throat. The traitor fell forward, and Huma caught him sharply in the leg. Rennard did not scream, though his leg was awash in blood almost immediately. He hobbled away from Huma.

They turned to face one another again. Huma was on the verge of exhaustion, while Rennard was becoming faint from the terrible wound across the front of his right leg. Huma's blade had just missed the muscles and tendons that would have cost Rennard the limb.

"Surrender, Rennard. You will be treated fairly; I swear it."

The pale knight looked more drawn than normal. "I think not. A traitor such as myself, who has killed one Grand Master and almost another, could hardly expect fair treatment from the knighthood."

Huma knew that his strength would return the longer they talked, while Rennard's would only continue to seep away. Even now, it was difficult for the other to stand.

"Come, nephew. Let us finish this." With amazing stamina, Rennard charged Huma, attacking with a variety of moves. Huma stood his ground and slowly began to move on the offensive. Rennard's face became blurred as all was reflex, and the lessons—ironically, Rennard's lessons— allowed Huma to counter each and every move.

A thrust broke through Rennard's defenses. It caught him in his sword arm and the traitor almost dropped his weapon as the injured limb jerked uncontrollably for a moment. He was left wide open, and Huma's blade came within an inch of his face.

They were both caked with mud now. Rennard had lost the madness that had possessed him, and he now seemed to realize that he had all but lost. Huma was better than he; his eyes knew it even if his face revealed no emotion. Now, it was all Rennard could do to prevent the killing blow.

Huma broke through his uncle's guard again, and Rennard suddenly wavered on two badly bleeding legs.

He collapsed to his knees.

That broke the spell. Huma blinked, looking down at Rennard, whose life fluids were mixing with the muck. A look of disgust spread across Huma's face.

"It's over, Rennard. I won't kill you. It would serve no purpose."

Rennard tried to stand. On one knee, he waited, his sword at shoulder level, ready to defend.

"I will not go back, Huma. I will not suffer the mockery of a trial."

Huma lowered his sword. "Let me help you. You *were* a good knight. One of the best."

The laugh that Rennard responded with became a hacking cough. The cultist barely kept from toppling over. "Do you not understand? I've never been a knight! Since that day, my life has been in the hands of another god, and I have failed even him. Look at me!" Rennard smiled feebly and Huma was shocked to see that his former companion's pallid skin was slowly turning scarlet. "My reward for failure. I never truly have been cured, I've merely lived day by day."

"Rennard. A patrol will be by. They can locate a cleric."

"No cleric will touch me."

Whatever spell or nightmare the former knight had cast upon the village was gone, for now the people were screaming and crying at the sight of this, one of the worst plagues. Within seconds, the two armored figures stood alone.

"Rennard—"

It had become a strain for the other knight even to speak. The plague was coursing through his body.

"Don't come near me, Huma. It spreads through touch." Rennard was smiling. "There'll be nothing left when it finishes. They'll be lucky if they find more than a shell."

Where was a patrol? Huma scanned the horizon in frustration.

"For whatever it is worth, nephew," sputtered the dying figure, "I hope you find what you are looking for. Perhaps there still is a chance."

There! Huma spotted distant figures on horseback. They were moving too slowly, though. Much too slowly.

"Huma . . ."

The young knight looked down. Rennard's face twisted with pain. "Pray to Paladine, Rennard! The patrol is nearing this village. When I explain—"

"There is nothing to explain, save that they must burn my body where I lie." Rennard straightened and gripped the hilt of his broadsword with both hands, to steady it.

With a speed that belied his sickness, Rennard ran the edge of his blade across his throat.

"No!" Only the realization that he would carry the plague prevented Huma from wrenching the sword from the ragged figure. It was too late already. No cleric could bind such a wound in time.

Rennard's limp hand released the sword, which fell and buried itself in the mud only a moment before Rennard's lifeless form did the same. Huma dropped his own weapon and fell to his knees.

"No." His voice was less than a whisper. Huma put his face in his hands and let his battered emotions run their course. Faintly, he heard the clattering sound of many horses, and then all was silent.

Chapter 20

Silence.

The intermingled cries of the oncoming horses and the terrified villagers who believed that the worst of plagues had been released in their midst, the tumult of hoofbeats—even the wind—all turned to silence.

The silence was interrupted by the distant beating of metal against metal.

Slowly, unbelievingly, Huma raised his head from his hands and stared wide-eyed at the world around him. The weary lands outside of Vingaard Keep, the entire outdoors, for that matter, were gone.

What stood before him now was the mirror—the same mirror that he had fallen through days ago. Now, all it revealed was the disheveled form of a worn knight who looked scarcely alive.

He was back in Wyrmfather's cavern.

Had it truly happened? It seemed unlikely at first. More conceivable that it had been an illusion. But Huma still felt the pains that had been inflicted on him in that so-called dream. A nightmare, then. One very real nightmare. For Rennard was indeed dead.

Huma leaned back and removed his gauntlets. He rubbed his eyes and stared at the cursed mirror.

He was both angered and relieved—angry at feeling like a puppet, relieved that he was going to be permitted to continue on his quest and perhaps reunite with Kaz and Magius.

Where had they been all this time?

Huma continued to stare at the mirror. The shock of Rennard's betrayal and death was still with him. Rennard was dead and Huma would pray for him, but the knighthood—no, all of Ansalon—still had a chance, if what Huma been told was truthful—that somewhere in these mountains was the key to victory.

His reflection stared back at him from the mirror, and Huma's mind finally registered what he was seeing.

He stumbled forward quickly. Huma had momentarily forgotten what had taken place in this chamber, what had happened to him. He had, as difficult it was to conceive, almost forgotten Wyrmfather.

If time passed here as it had at Vingaard Keep, the huge form should be ripe. Carrion-eaters of all shapes and sizes should have established their territories. But neither was true.

The gigantic head and neck lay exactly where they had fallen, true, but Wyrmfather's gigantic bulk had turned to metal, metal of the purest nature, more brilliant than silver. At the same time, it resembled that other metal more than any other. He ran his hands over it, feeling the smoothness and marveling at how great a quantity there must be. For lack of a better name, he called it dragonsilver.

He stumbled awkwardly around the great mass, his interest suddenly magnetized by the object that had destroyed Wyrmfather. Somewhere within its massive jaws, the huge corpse concealed the sword that had spoken to Huma. He was sure it had called to him, just as he was sure that he had to have it. If Huma gained nothing else from this experience, he wanted the sword.

The head of the dead titan was twisted upside down, and Huma discovered that the lower jaw rested firmly atop the upper. That meant that the sword was buried within a tremendous mass of pure metal, with no way to retrieve it. Angered, Huma banged his hand against the snout of the creature; the shock brought his senses back, and he briefly wondered at his obsession with the ancient blade. Best if he—

He kicked something with his foot. It made a metallic sound, and Huma looked down to see the very object he had been seeking. With a startled cry, he fell to his knees and practically cradled the weapon. It was to be his. This was a sign.

From the moment his hands touched it, the blade had begun to glow again. Huma basked happily in that glow, for it soothed him and made him forget the terrible events of the past few days. Reluctantly, he sheathed the sword and crawled on top of the great beast. Wyrmfather's sloping neck proved to be an excellent ramp from which Huma could climb to one of the upper tunnels that dotted the cavern and seek the mysterious smith. That was, he believed, his logical destination.

Neither the endless mounds of gold nor the gleaming caches of jewelry interested him, now that he had the sword. The mirror still intrigued him, but he could not carry it with him through the cavern. He consoled himself with the thought that he could return for it if he succeeded.

With a proper blade in his hands for once, Huma was soon feeling rested and confident as he strode up the amazingly long neck of Wyrmfather.

The tunnels immediately above were naturally lit, though not to the degree that the lower ones had been. Gazing down one, Huma could see no difference between it and the passages he had traversed originally. Dark shadows were everywhere. Emboldened, now that he held a weapon worthy of him, Huma stepped off the neck of the petrified Wyrmfather and entered the closest tunnel.

He became impatient as time dragged and he found only more corridors. Where were the challenges? Wyrmfather had been one, but Huma knew there must be two others. Still, he thought, they could not possibly compare to his brush with the huge beast. Perhaps having faced Wyrmfather was test enough.

One hand stroked the pommel of the sword. Maybe there was no actual need for whatever else lay within this mountain. The sword alone was worth an army, and Huma controlled the sword.

His impatience grew as he continued to follow what seemed like endless tunnels. All Huma wanted to do now was leave. Challenges no longer concerned him. The blade was all he needed. What could the cavern offer that would better a weapon of such power and perfection?

The thought of a flank under his command occurred suddenly to him. After all Huma had accomplished, Lord Oswal surely would reward him. Not only had he brought back a weapon of great value, but he had exposed Rennard and saved the elder knight's life.

A major command position had always been Huma's dream. From there, it could not be long before he would command an entire army.

A smile began to spread across his face.

"Step no further."

At first, Huma had not noticed the figure standing before him. Clad in a long, flowing cloak of gray, the figure blended in well with his surroundings, especially with the shadows now dominating. The figure's face was gray, as were his teeth and tongue. The only noticeable change from the previous encounter with the gray man was that he was not smiling in the least this time.

"You again!" Huma was happy to see the odd mage—if mage he was—because he now could boast to someone other than himself. "I have beaten your challenges, easily! I've come to claim my prize—not that it seems so important now."

"Certainly. Leave your sword where you are and walk forward."

"My sword?" The gray man might have asked for his arm.

"Your sword. I always assumed the acoustics in here were fairly good. Am I wrong, then?" At the moment, the mage's face was as unreadable as Rennard's had always been.

"Why?" Huma did not care for this suspicious move. The gray man was a servant of the Dragonqueen after all. It must be that the gods now feared Huma's power—and why not?

"That *thing* there is not allowed within these chambers. It should not be allowed anywhere."

"This?" The knight held aloft the magnificent sword, admiring the way it glowed so strongly. He had thought it well-made before, but the radiance of its fully awakened beauty was something to behold. Give it up? Huma would fight first!

"That 'wonderful' blade you bear is known as the Sword of Tears. It's a relic from the Age of Dreams. Through it, Takhisis seduced the ogre race, twisted them from beauty, until all but a handful strayed from the path. It is said to be the weapon with which the champion of darkness will challenge light on that final battle before the last day. It is pure evil, and should be banished. If there is any true choice."

"You're wrong. This is the key to our victory. Look at it!"

The gray man shaded his eyes. "I have. Many times. Its wicked travesty of illumination still irritates after all these centuries."

Huma lowered the blade, but only so he could point it toward the man barring his way. "Is it that? Or are you one who shuns the light in general? I think it is you who are the danger."

"If you could only see your face."

"My face?" Huma laughed arrogantly. "The Sword of Tears, you say. Could it actually be called that because of the tears that the Dragonqueen will shed when at last faced with a power stronger than she?"

The gray man's face screwed into an expression of disgust. "I see the horrid blade has not lost any of its charm."

Holding his sword possessively, Huma folded his arms. "I've listened to your little tirade long enough. Will you let me pass now?"

The guardian brought his staff up to eye level. "Not with

the sword."

Huma only smiled and thrust the sword into the rocky wall to his left. The blade sank in as if the tunnel were made of curdled milk rather than stone, and the weapon flared with emerald light. With similar ease, the knight drew it out. The blade looked unscratched, while that portion of the wall had lost its natural glow.

The gray man only curled his lip and said mockingly, "You had better strike it again. It may have some fight left in it."

Huma glared at him. "Your last chance. Will you yield?"

"Not unless the sword is forfeited."

"Then I shall slice a path through your body."

"If you can."

The knight raised the Sword of Tears, which seemed to glow more brilliantly—as if in anticipation—and stepped forward. The gray man stepped out of his defensive position and—threw his staff on the tunnel floor. Huma stood there, arm raised, momentarily stunned.

"Have you surrendered, then?"

The hooded figure shook his head. "If you would continue, you must strike me down."

Strike him down! a voice shouted in Huma's mind. The green glow of the Sword of Tears dominated the tunnel now. *Strike him down!* the voice repeated.

"This is—" Huma struggled to complete the thought. The voice became insistent. *Strike him down and gain your prize!*

"—wrong!"

"Give up the sword, Huma. Only then will you be free."

"No!" The word issued from the knight's mouth, but it was not he who had spoken. Instead, the source seemed to have been the blade itself, which now caused Huma's arm to rise as if he were intending to smote the gray mage.

"No!" This time, it was Huma who spoke. He collapsed against the side of the passageway and regarded with sudden disgust and horror the thing he held in his hand, despite the brilliance that caused even the gray man to turn away.

Take me! Wield me! I was meant to glory in blood! I was meant to rend the world for my mistress!

"No!" The denial came more firmly now as the shock in Huma's eyes gave way to anger. He had torn free from the malevolent artifact's spell. The blade had asked the impossible of him—to purposefully strike down one who neither deserved it nor sought to defend himself. Huma had not been able to do so with Rennard, and he could not do so now with the dun-colored guardian.

Power surged from the sword, and Huma screamed. The shockwaves threw the knight to the floor. It felt as if every fiber of his body were being torn apart. He could see only green, could feel only the pain, and could hear only the incessant command of the Sword of Tears as it sought to overcome his will.

"Huma!" Another voice, familiar, sought to assert its influence on him. He took the lifeline and concentrated.

"You must be willing to part from it—totally—or the demon sword will have your body and soul!"

Totally? Huma struggled against the pain. He saw now that the Sword of Tears worked only for its own wily purposes and would never truly be anyone's servant. That realization gave Huma the willpower he had lacked.

"I deny you!" He held the sword at arm's length, sickened by it. "I will have no part of you and, therefore, you have no power over me!"

The pain diminished and Huma pressed his advantage. Slowly, he forced the outside presence from his head, reviling it, confident now that it had no true power. The presence seemed to shrink back from his determination, and the emerald brilliance diminished dramatically.

Master, it called. *You are truly master.*

It cowed before his mind. Huma's confidence grew, until a thought flashed through his head. Now that he had defeated it, could he not use it safely?

No! Huma pushed the thought away. Sweat dripped from his forehead. His skin had gone white.

Huma threw the demonic blade wildly across the corridor. As he did, he thought he heard, or felt, a maddened cry. The sword clattered against the opposite wall and dropped to the ground. The glow had all but vanished.

"Never," Huma panted. He leaned against the wall, his

hands on his knees. "Not for all the power in the world."

Slow footsteps indicated the near presence of the gray man. A strong hand fell on Huma's shoulder. "There is no more reason to fear. The Sword of Tears is nothing. No more than smoke in the wind. See?"

Huma looked up. The demon sword was wavering and beginning to fade, to sink through the stone to nothingness. Within seconds, there was no trace of its physical form or the sinister presence within.

"Where is it?"

"Hopefully, back where it belongs. The thing has a mind of its own, but you know that. I think I've put it in a place where it will take some doing for it to break free."

The knight looked up. "You saved me—and my soul."

"I?" The gray man looked slightly amused. "I did nothing but make a few friendly suggestions. It was you who had to face the real battle. You persevered, though."

"What happens now?" Huma stood slowly. His body ached. His head ached. He did not think he was capable of anything just yet. Huma slumped against the wall.

"Now?" The gray man sounded amused. Huma could not see what was so funny. "Now . . . you step through and claim your prize. You have defeated all three challenges."

"Defeated—" The knight shook his head sadly. "You're mistaken. I barely escaped with my life, much less my soul."

"You live. Yes. That is the purpose of everything. To strive for life, for purpose."

"Wyrmfather. The Sword of Tears. That makes only two challenges. Unless—" The truth struck Huma forcefully.

The gray man smiled a sad, gray smile. "Your trip through the mirror was no accident. A dark stain had spread itself deep within the fabric of the knighthood, and who better to cleanse the knighthood of that foulness than one of its own? Most, I think, would have been pleased to slay Rennard without permitting him a chance to surrender. You wanted to save him, even then. That—the passion for life—is what the knighthood truly strives for, above all else."

Huma straightened, stared at the seemingly endless tunnel behind the gray man, and then turned back to the hooded figure.

"Are you Paladine?"

The gray mage smiled mischievously and tapped the side of his nose. "I could say I am, but I won't. Let us just say that the balance between good and evil must be maintained and I am one of those chosen to see to it—much like yourself, though I fear my part is small compared to your own." He gave Huma no opportunity to reply. "It is time you went through this last tunnel and claimed your reward. As I said before, you must go weaponless. Weaponless, save your faith."

As Huma stared, the gray man raised a hand, which held two daggers, gingerly, by the tips. Huma reached instinctively to his own belt, but his daggers were gone. They belonged to the gray man now, only the gray man was gone, too. Only the gaping tunnel stood before Huma.

He took a step toward the darkened passageway.

Huma said two prayers—one to Paladine and the second to Gilean, Lord of Neutrality—and walked into the darkness.

Huma could not judge time, but he was sure that he had been walking for a long period when the first echoes of the hammer reached him. They seemed neither far nor near, and the intensity never changed. It was not as it had been in the great chamber, where the towering, maddened leviathan had shrieked out at such torment. Rather, the familiar sounds of a smith at work put the knight at ease as he recalled a point in his training where he was taught the basics of the trade. All knights had some knowledge of the craft, for each might be called upon to mend armor or shoe a horse. A good smith, as the knighthood dictated, could do virtually anything with an anvil, a hammer, and fire-red metal.

Whoever worked at the anvil had to be a mighty man, Huma decided, for the fall of the hammer went on with such regular rhythm and for such a great length of time that most men would have fallen to their knees by now. At that, who said it must be a man? Might it not be Reorx himself? Here, he knew, was a place of gods and power. Anything might lie ahead.

Then, when he had not noticed it somehow, Huma found himself standing in the massive armory.

Countless implements of war and peace hung, stood or lay from wall to wall, as far as he could see in the dim light, and even from the ceiling high above. A sickle whose blade, if straightened, would be at least the length of Huma's body. Swords of all shapes and sizes, some curved, some straight, some thin, and some heavy. Jeweled and plain. One-handed and two-handed.

Here he saw even more suits of armor than in the chambers below. The suits ranged from the most primitive breastplates to the latest full armor as worn by the Ergothian emperor. Shields hung above the suits, representing every crest ever created, including that of the Knights of Solamnia.

There was so much more, and Huma longed to see all of it. He felt as if he had stepped into the lost tomb of some great warrior. Yet this was no lost resting place of the dead, for the weaponry and artifacts here were devoid of dust or any sign of age. Each piece he inspected might have been made only yesterday, so sharp were the edges and smooth were the sides. No rust infected the armor; the wooden handle of the sickle had not rotted. Huma knew, however, that these creations were even older than the chambers below, that before all else in this mountain maze, this set of chambers had been first. He could not say how he knew, just that he knew.

The fall of the hammer had become a pattern in his ears, and he did not notice at first when it stopped. When he did, he had already wandered midway through the armory, his gaze flickering back and forth. Huma paused then, momentarily unsure. It was at that moment that he saw the flicker of light from ahead and heard the unknown smith resume his work. Only two massive doors barred his way.

Huma reached forward to knock upon one of the doors, even as it swung open. The slight movement was accompanied by a tremendous squeak, and it amazed the knight that the hammer kept falling as if its wielder had heard nothing or did not care.

It was a smithy of godlike proportions. A huge tank of

water that could only be for cooling the product. A massive forge where—Huma had to squint—shadowy figures stoked the furnace with might and gusto.

The hammering ceased with finality. He wrenched his eyes from the sun-hot forge and turned.

The anvil stood as high as Huma's waist and would have weighed half a dozen times his weight in full armor. The soot-covered figure that stood beside it, a two-handed hammer held easily in one hand and raised high above his head, turned to study the newcomer. The figures at the forge ceased their activity, as did two others near the anvil. The smith lowered his arm and stepped forward. Huma's eyes did not go immediately to the face but were riveted instead by that arm. It was metal, a metal that gleamed like the material that Wyrmfather had become.

Then Huma looked into the face of the smith. Like the body, it was soot-covered, but Huma could see that the smith claimed no one race as his own, for the features were a blend of elf, human, dwarf, and something . . . unidentifiable.

The smith studied him from head to toe and, in a voice surprisingly quiet, asked, "Have you come at last for the Dragonlance?"

Chapter 21

Huma gave the towering smith a confused look and said, "The what?"

"The Dragonlance. Are you at last the one?" The dwarven features pinched together in outright anxiousness. The smith's eyes narrowed as he waited for a response and his thin, elven mouth was no more than a flat line across his mostly human face. That "other" gave him a frightening yet handsome appearance that was not common to any of the other three races.

"I have faced the challenges, or so I am told. That is what the gray man said."

"The gray man said it, did he? Even ancient Wyrmfather?" The hulking figure did not wait for a response. "Yes, I suppose you did, for he has been rather quiet of late.

It seems so strange not to hear his rantings and ravings any-more. I cannot recall a day when he was so quiet. I shall have to adjust, I suppose." He shrugged.

"Have I answered your question to your satisfaction?" Though Huma's confidence had not yet recovered, his dignity had. He did not want to appear overwhelmed.

"Indeed you have," the smith whispered, more to himself than to the knight. "Indeed you have."

The smith let out a strong, hearty laugh. "Great Reorx! Never did I think to see the day! At last, someone will be able to properly appreciate my handiwork. Do you know how long it has been since I've spoken to someone qualified?"

"What about them?" Huma pointed at the spectral figures behind the smith. They seemed unoffended.

"Them? They are my assistants. They *have* to like my work. They would not understand the true use of the Dragonlance as a knight would. Paladine, I've waited so long!" The huge man's voice echoed through the chambers.

"I forget myself." The smith's voice faded abruptly, and his face became dour. Huma noted that the other's mood changes were as abrupt as his features were unique. "I am Duncan Ironweaver, master smith, armorer, and student of Reorx himself. I have waited far longer than I wish to remember for your coming. For many a year, I worried that you might never set foot near here, but I should have known better." Duncan Ironweaver reached out a hand to Huma, who took it without thinking and found himself grasping warm metal.

The smith noticed him staring at the device and grinned. "Wyrmfather himself took my arm years ago, when I was a foolish young man. Though it pained me, I have never regretted its loss. This works so much better that I have often wondered what it might be to have an entire forged body." He seemed to consider this for several seconds before realizing he had drifted from his subject. "Of course, without the silver arm, I would lack the strength and resistance necessary to forge the great dragonsilver into a finely crafted Dragonlance."

Again, the Dragonlance. "What is the Dragonlance? If it

is what I have come for, can I see it?"

Ironweaver blinked. "I've not shown you?" He put a hand to his head, unheedful of the soot spread on both. "Of course not! My mind is addled. Come then. Follow me, and we shall gaze together on a wonder that encompasses more than my simple skills and your daring."

The smith turned and wound a path into the darkest depths of the chamber. The four shadowy assistants made way for their master and the knight. The helpers seemed to melt into the darkness itself by the time Huma was near enough, and the only things he could glimpse were four pairs of eyes that seemed to stare straight through him.

Several yards ahead of him, Ironweaver was whistling a tune that vaguely resembled a Solamnic marching song. That made Huma relax a little, though he did wonder just what connection the smith had with the Knights of Solamnia and how far back it went. By this point, the knight would not have been surprised if he had awakened back at Vingaard Keep and discovered that all of this was a dream.

They came to another door, and the huge smith stopped and turned to Huma. "Beyond that door, only you will go. I have much work to get back to. Another will lead you back to the outside world and your friends."

Friends? How did Duncan Ironweaver know about Kaz and Magius? "And the Dragonlance?"

"You will know it when you see it, my little friend."

"Where do—?" Huma started to ask something else but stopped abruptly when he found himself talking to air. He quickly turned back in the direction they had come, but the smithy itself was no longer visible. Only darkness. Huma took a few tentative steps in that direction and then retreated in disgust as his face came in contact with a spider's web of incredible size and thickness.

He spat the foul substance from his mouth and examined the web. It was old, the culmination of generations and generations. Dust lay thick on its surface. Here and there, it connected to rusting implements, swords, old metalworking equipment—things forgotten by their creators and users since long before Huma had been born.

But he had just come that way.

An uneasy thought intruded; what spider would need a web so great?

His eyes still on the web, Huma reached a hand out toward the door. The handle, a long, jagged one rusted with age, would cooperate only after a struggle. At last the door opened, unleashing a cloud of dust. Slowly, and with great reverence, Huma stepped into the room of the Dragonlance.

He saw a charging stallion, armored in purest platinum and snorting fire as it raced the winds. He saw the rider then, a knight bold and ready, the great lance poised to strike. The knight also was clad in platinum, and the crest on his helmet was that of a majestic dragon. On his chest he wore a breastplate with the symbol of the Triumvirate: the Crown, the Sword, and the Rose.

Within the visor that covered the face was light, brilliant and life-giving, and Huma knew that here was Paladine.

The great charger suddenly leaped into the air, and massive wings sprouted from its sides. Its head elongated, and its neck twisted and grew, but it lost none of its majesty or beauty. From a platinum-clad steed it became a platinum dragon, and together knight and companion drove the darkness before them with the aid of the lance . . . the Dragonlance. It shone with a life, a purpose of its own, and the darkness fell before it. Born of the world and the heavens, it was the true power, the true good.

The darkness destroyed, the dragon landed before Huma, who could only fall to his knees. The knight released the Dragonlance from its harness and held it toward the mortal figure below him. With some hesitation, Huma slowly rose and stepped forward. He reached out and took the lance by its shaft. Then the dragon and its rider were gone, leaving Huma alone with the wondrous gift.

He held it high and cried out in joy.

Sweat drenched him. Nearly all energy had been drained from his body, but Huma did not mind, for it was the exhaustion felt after the joyous exhilaration of achieving one's dreams. There would never be another rapture like it in his life, he knew.

He lay on the floor of the room, bathed in white, pure light. Rising to his knees, Huma gazed at the light and was awed.

Above him, life-size, stood the dragon. Its eyes gazed down upon the mortal, and it seemed to have just landed. It had been formed from pure platinum and sculpted by an artisan whose skills must have rivaled the gods. The wings were outspread, stretching far across the room, and Huma was amazed that the metal could stand the strain. Each scale of the dragon, from the largest to the smallest, had been finely wrought in detail. Had it breathed, Huma would not have been surprised, it was so lifelike.

The rider, too, might have been ready to leap off his companion of the skies, so real did he appear. Like the dragon, his gaze seemed to be on Huma, though it was difficult to tell; the visor was down. The armor was as accurate in every detail as the dragon's skin, and Huma could see every joint, every link, and even the detail of the scrollwork on the breastplate.

What had lit up the room was the Dragonlance.

Long, sleek, narrow, the lance would have stood almost three times the knight's height. The tip seemed to taper off to a point so sharp that nothing would bar its path. Behind the head, nearly two feet from the tip, sharp barbs arose on each side, assuring that any strike would be costly to the foe.

The back end of the lance ended with an elaborate shield guard formed into the fearsome visage of an attacking dragon with the shaft emerging like a river of flame from the leviathan's maw. Behind the guard, the platinum knight's arm steadied the lance for battle.

Huma felt unworthy to take the Dragonlance from the knight, so perfect was it. Nevertheless, he steeled himself and moved to it, climbing to undo it from the harness that held it in place on the saddle. The post of the harness pivoted, allowing Huma some flexibility, but he was unsure how to remove the metallic knight's hand from the weapon. As he touched the fingers, they seemed to loosen of their own regard and the lance nearly fell into Huma's waiting arms.

The Dragonlance was heavy, as was to be expected, but Huma did not care about that now. He was overwhelmed that this had come to him, the least of knights. That Paladine should so bless him was a miracle in itself and, when he had brought the lance to earth, he went to his knees and gave thanks. The Dragonlance seemed to glow even brighter.

When at last his initial awe had passed, he noted the other lances that decorated the walls around him. That he had somehow missed them perplexed him, but he gave thanks that again Paladine had foreseen things, for one lance certainly would not be enough. He counted twenty total, nineteen like his own and one smaller one that was no less brilliant and must, he decided, be for footsoldiers.

One by one, he removed the lances from their resting places, taking each into his hands with reverence. Here were tools with which Krynn could be rid of the Dragonqueen; there should be no end of volunteers.

Oddly, there seemed to be no other exit than the doorway he had come through earlier. Huma wondered how he was going to get the lances out of the mountain and back to Solamnia. Had he come this far to fail because of an obstruction so relatively minor?

Gazing around the chamber, his eyes fell upon the figure of the mounted knight. It was looking slightly off to the side and upward—as if it sought something near one of the far corners of the ceiling. So intense was the image that Huma could not help but turn and look the same direction.

He saw nothing at first. Then, Huma spied the nearly invisible outline of a trap door. Hurrying over to investigate, the knight discovered hand and footholds in the wall below the trap door. They were only indentations, impossible to make out unless one stood directly in front of them.

Huma turned and stared anxiously at the lances he had gathered together. He hated leaving them here, but he knew that he required assistance if he was to get even one of them out of this chamber. He needed Kaz and Magius.

Gingerly, he began his climb. It was not as difficult as he had expected and he was soon near the ceiling. Opening the door, however, proved to be difficult, for Huma was forced to lean back precariously in order to push properly. The muscles strained in the hand that held him back from a deadly plunge. Huma had been forced to remove his gauntlets for a better grip and now was paying for that as the skin slowly tore from his fingertips.

When the door was finally open, he let out a sigh of relief. Whoever had designed this had purposely made it difficult for reasons Huma doubted he could ever guess. Still, what mattered was that the way out was now open.

He reached up and felt a cool breeze dance through his fingers. Moving his hand around he discovered that something soft, perhaps snow, covered the ground. Gripping the sides of the hole, Huma pulled himself upward.

It was daylight. No rain. No cloud cover. The sun lit the mountainside, and Huma hung there, suspended halfway in the ground, as he drank in the view. How long had it been since he had really seen the sun? Huma could no longer remember. It was a magnificent sight and a sign, perhaps, that the tide had turned at last.

A thin layer of snow did indeed cover the ground. There were no tracks in the snow around him, so he was alone unless something flew above him. The skies were clear, though. Clear and blue. He had forgotten the heavens were blue.

Huma pulled himself from the unseen hole and then took care to study the site. The knight located a large rock nearby and placed it near the hole as a marker.

"I hoped you would succeed; I *prayed* you would succeed. Had you not, I don't know what I would have done."

"Gwyneth!" The name burst from his lips even as he whirled.

She was clad in a simple cloak of silver hue, her hair fluttering. The young woman who had seen to his recovery in the tent looked nothing like this stately—priestess? What was her part in all this?

"I have indeed succeeded, Gwyneth! Below our very feet lay the weapons that will rid this world of the Dragon-queen!"

She smiled at his enthusiasm and stepped forward. Her feet seemed to barely touch the snowy ground, and Huma noted then that she left no trace of any path.

"Tell me about it."

He tried to, how he tried to, but the words that tumbled from his mouth were too weak, too complicated, too simple for what he was trying to describe. It all sounded so improbable as he related his quest to Gwyneth. Had he really undergone all that? How had the ancient terror called Wyrmfather been turned into a gleaming metal artifact several times the size of the knight? Had the vision in the chamber of the Dragonlance been real or the product of his own delusion?

Gwyneth took it all in, her face impassive save for an unidentifiable look in her eyes as she observed Huma. When he was finished, she nodded sagely and said, "From the moment I first saw you, I saw greatness. I saw in you what so many others before you did not have. You truly care about the folk of Krynn. That is where the others have failed. They cared, but it was little compared to their personal ambitions."

Huma took her by the arms and held her. "Will you vanish now, like the gray man and the smith?"

"I will, for a time. You must locate your companions. When you return, another will be waiting for you. One whom you have met and who will be of aid in the coming days."

"And Kaz and Magius?"

"Near." She smiled. "I am surprised that they have tolerated one another this long."

"I must find them," Huma decided suddenly. There was so much to be done. He hated to leave Gwyneth, even though they would meet again. Wouldn't they?

An uneasy look came into her eyes, and she squirmed free from his grasp. The smile was still in place, but it grew weaker, more of a mask or defense. "Your friends are that way." She pointed to the east. "You had best go to them now. They are becoming anxious for you."

She turned from him and stepped quickly and lightly away. Huma almost followed, but he cared enough for her to respect her wishes in this matter. That he might never see her again tore at him, but he let her go and turned his back.

Eastward, Huma made his way through the soft snow. The cloud cover, he noticed, had not dispersed. It merely avoided this peak.

He had walked for no more than ten minutes when he heard the voice. There was no mistaking it. It was Kaz, angered. The knight's pace picked up. Only one person would anger the minotaur so.

"If only I had done what I had desired and ended your miserable existence there and then. You have no honor, no conscience." The minotaur stood tall. His fists emphasized each point as he battered the air as if it were the object of his reprimand.

Magius sat with odd quietude on a large rock, his head in his hands, unmoving, as the minotaur continued to berate him. Huma tensed as he stepped toward the pair.

It was Magius who sensed his approach. The mage's face was pale and drawn, his hair radiating wildly about his head. His eyes had sunken in. They widened as he raised his head, and his numbed mind finally recognized the figure of his only friend.

"Huma!"

"What?" Kaz jumped at the sudden shout. He saw the direction of the magic-user's gaze and turned. The blood-red look in his eyes vanished, and a toothy grin appeared on his bovine face. The anger of a moment before was temporarily forgotten. "Huma!"

As the minotaur stepped forward, Magius seemed to curl into himself. The mage stared pitifully in Huma's direction, but made no move to join Kaz in greeting their lost comrade.

The minotaur almost crushed Huma in a bear hug. Kaz looked down at him, smiling all the time, then suddenly lifted the hapless knight off the ground and spun him around. Huma felt like an infant in the hands of the huge man-beast.

"Where have you been? I sought you out, but could not find the path you had taken. I searched again and again calling to you, but only the wind and that infernal cry responded. Sarg—Gods! I finally thought you were dead." He put Huma down. Kaz turned on Magius, who stepped back as if struck. "When I told *that one* what had happened, he fairly shouted with glee at first."

"WHAT?" Huma gazed over at Magius. His childhood friend would not look at him.

Kaz thrust a finger at the knight. "Do you know why you were so important to him? It was not your friendship. It was not your skills. His mad vision had convinced him that there was indeed a gift from Paladine somewhere here but that he would die if he tried to claim it. So he intended to send you in his place. *You* would have taken the attack that would have killed him! Your life was expendable!" The angry warrior laughed coldly. "Can you believe it? He claimed a knight in sun-drenched armor and bearing a lance of incredible power would run him through; did you ever hear such nonsense?

"When he thought you were dead, he believed the vision had been altered forever. He was confident that he would almost immediately find this great secret and live to use it in your memory and his glory."

Kaz paused to catch his breath, and Huma chose that moment to step around the minotaur and confront Magius. The mage looked up at him, almost fearfully, and moved back a step. Huma reached out a hand, but Magius refused to take it.

The minotaur came up behind Huma. "When we found no path or cavern, he started to fall apart. I could have never believed this one could have a conscience. I suppose I helped, for I reminded him every hour of every day about what he had done. How you had talked of him as a good friend."

Huma leaned down. His voice was soft. "Magius. There is nothing to be fearful of. I do not hate you for what you did. That was not you; it was never you."

The shadow of the minotaur covered them both. Magius turned away.

"What are you saying, Huma?" the minotaur demanded. "This one betrayed you, had planned on betraying you since before you and I met. All for some utter, senseless madness!"

"You weren't there!" Huma snapped. "I've heard tales of how real the Tests are. Sometimes they exist only in the mind; sometimes they are completely and terribly existent. In either case, the magic-user who is being tested can die."

"Magius," Huma whispered to his conscience-stricken friend. The spellcaster seemed to be on the edge of collapse. It must have seemed that the knight's ghost had come back to haunt the one who had betrayed him. "Magius. Forget the vision. You were right about the mountain. I've found what we were searching for!"

The mage's eyes widened and narrowed, then he began to calm down. "You found it?"

"I did. I faced the challenges in the mountain and passed."

"What's that you're talking about?" roared Kaz. "What challenges?"

Huma briefly described what had taken place within the mountain. The story of Wyrmfather brought a strange light to the eyes of Magius, who, stuttering, confessed he had made a study of the design of the statuette years before, only to come up with nothing more than a few scraps of legend. The treachery of Rennard shook both listeners. Magius had grown up with Huma and often had wondered about the knight's father.

"By my ancestors twenty-five generations back! Would that I had been there when you fought the father of all dragons. Such a battle, and I missed it!" The minotaur shook his head.

The knight grimaced. "It was more a battle for survival than anything else. Luck had much to do with it."

"I think not. I do not see luck as a factor in these challenges. How many would have taken such action? How many would have run or stood trembling before the dragon? Many minotaurs would have thought it folly."

Magius tugged at Huma's arm, almost as a small child might do. "The Dragonlance? You have it with you? I have to see it!"

A solid, clawed fist materialized before the spellcaster's face. "You'll see nothing!"

Huma dared the minotaur's wrath by pushing the fist down. Kaz glared at Huma, then forced himself under control.

"That is what I need your help for now," Huma told them

both. "Another person may be waiting to aid us, but I'll need your help to pull the lances from the chamber. All but one are more than twice your height, Kaz. It will be difficult."

"We shall do it, though, and this vermin here will help."

Magius paled, but he stood his ground. "I will do every bit as much work as you—most likely more."

The wind whipped the minotaur's mane around his face, giving him a particularly wild look. "That remains to be seen, mage."

"Enough!" Huma shouted. He would drag the lances out himself if need be. "If you are coming, do so, or stay here and let the snows eventually cover you!"

He stalked away. A moment later, the other two followed quickly and without comment.

He had marked the spot as well as he could. The rock was where he had left it and he stepped over it and reached down. Kaz and Magius looked on in curiosity, especially when Huma's hand found only hard earth and not the hole that should have been there.

"What's the matter?" Kaz asked.

"I can't find it! I can't *find* it!"

The others fell to their knees and began searching the ground.

"There is no need to search further," a voice suddenly said. "The Dragonlances are safe and ready for their journey out into the world."

The voice came from above them. A great wind buffeted the trio, forcing them to step back. The voice apologized and the great wings slowed as the majestic dragon came to stop on a nearby outcropping.

"I heard the summons," said the same silver dragon who had given aid to Huma and Kaz, what seemed so long ago. "The lances are ready, awaiting us in a safe place." She gazed—fondly?—at the knight. "The next step in their journey, Huma, is up to you."

Chapter 22

"You? Gwyneth sent for you?"

The silver dragon's head bobbed in acknowledgment. "This was the area of my birth, long ago. I still come here; it is part of my duty, part of my destiny to stand watch here, waiting for the day the Dragonlances will be revealed to the world."

"How did you fare against the darkness?" Huma asked. He remembered the dragons as they waited for the magical blackness to envelop them. At that time, he had wondered whether they would live or die.

"We were vanquished." There was very human bitterness in her voice. "It was more than just the work of the renegades. We could feel the presence of the Black Robes, though they were reluctant to be involved, for some reason, and something else. Something so malevolent that two of our number died there and then, merely because of its presence. We suspected and by the time we had lost, we knew." She hesitated. "Takhisis has come to Krynn itself."

They were all stunned. The minotaur's mouth worked, but no sound emerged. Magius was shaking his head again and again, as if he could deny it. Huma just stood there, the stony look on his face masking well the fear and anguish he felt. The Dragonqueen on Krynn—hope, it would appear, was lost.

Or was it? Immediately, Huma remembered the vision of the platinum knight who had vanquished the darkness with the glory of the lance.

He cut off any comments by stating flatly, "This means nothing. We have the Dragonlances. Hope remains."

Kaz shook his head while Magius simply absorbed every word. The dragon looked on in satisfaction. She seemed quite pleased with Huma's reactions.

The wind was beginning to pick up, and neither Huma nor his companions had any intention of staying on the mountain any longer than necessary. They needed food and rest.

Huma asked the silver dragon, "Where are the lances?"

"They are far down below with your horses. I could carry them all, perhaps, but it would leave me barely able to maneuver, much less keep aloft. It would be best if I remain unhindered should we be attacked en route."

A thought occurred to Huma. The knight turned to his companions. "Kaz and Magius, you will take the horses. I would like to trust the two of you to work together. Is that possible?"

Kaz glowered at the mage, who, having been relieved of his guilt, was rapidly returning to his former arrogance and thus returned the glare with equal dislike. They would work together, though, because this goal far transcended their pettiness. Satisfied, Huma continued.

"There was a saddle on the dragon statue in the chamber of the lances," he told the dragon. "It enabled the rider to maintain control of his weapon. I would like to create a makeshift version of that saddle. Then, if you permit, I can ride upon your back, a Dragonlance ready should we be attacked."

She raised her head and seemed to consider. Finally, the silver dragon nodded. "An excellent thought. I must tell you that when I first arrived in the mountains, I ran across one of the dreadwolves of Galan Dracos and immediately slew it, but rest assured that Galan Dracos will send his lackey, the warlord Crynus, to deal with you." She extended her lengthy talons. "I would not dislike a second confrontation with that obscenity called Charr. Too many of my kind have fallen to that black dragon and his warlord companion."

That said, the silver dragon spread her wings, rose into the air as briefly and gently as possible, and then dropped to a point low enough so that she was almost eye level with the trio. "Climb aboard. I can take the three of you to the lances. Be prepared for many turns, however. The winds can be fierce in the mountains."

When they were securely upon her back, the leviathan spread her wings again and launched herself into the sky. At first, the trio saw the earth far below rushing up to meet them, then it seemed to be pulled back, as the silver dragon rose higher until she was able to maintain a proper balance.

Huma stared at the peak they were leaving. So much had happened there that he would never fully understand. He had not even climbed to the top, as he had first thought. At least a full quarter of the mighty giant still loomed above them.

Below lay the cloud-enshrouded world. As they entered the misty ceiling over Ansalon, Huma shuddered and prayed that, despite his victories in the mountain, he was up to the challenges ahead.

"There." The silver dragon indicated a spot on the southern base of the mountain. Huma looked down and saw the horses and a wagon. The silver dragon had planned well for the difficult journey.

Only when they were on the ground did Kaz argue. "You cannot expect horses such as these to pull a wagon! They have not been trained for such labor. They are beasts of war, not burden."

"They will do what they can," replied the majestic leviathan.

Huma, meanwhile, was fast at work on his own idea. He had removed the saddle from his mount. With the aid of a dagger borrowed from Kaz—his own still lay somewhere within the mountain—he cut the saddle on each side so that it would fit more comfortably on the dragon's back, which was much wider than that of any horse. As the straps would not reach around the midsection of a dragon, Huma was forced to employ rope. Fortunately, the skin of a dragon was much stronger and harder than that of a horse, so the coarse bonds would not irritate or hamper her.

There was little Huma could do about the post on which the lance should have pivoted. The most he could really do was carve away part of the pommel so that the lance could at least rest in something. Then, he strapped the Dragonlance securely to that side and tested it. Huma found he had some movement to his left, but his right had little. Satisfied that it would work, Huma removed the lance and presented the silver dragon with what he had created. She looked at it questioningly, then accepted its design.

"The saddle I saw," the knight explained, "was very much akin to a horse's saddle. It is a wider saddle since it must be worn by a dragon. Essentially, the true difference lies in the post on which the Dragonlance sits. The one on the dragon statue pivoted as I removed the lance. I cannot do that without more equipment and more time. Therefore, shaving the pommel to fit the handle of the Dragonlance was the only choice." Huma frowned at his handiwork. "I did very little actually."

"This will do," replied the winged creature.

While Huma was at work on the saddle, Magius investigated the wagon. He did not particularly care for the thought of dragging the lances by cart all the way back to Vingaard Keep—provided the Solamnic citadel was still standing—and he vocalized his doubts to those around him.

"There is no need for all this. I can transport the lances in virtually no time." The magic-user raised his hands and began to mutter.

Huma dropped the saddle as he realized what was happening. "Magius, no!"

It was too late. The mage completed his spell—and nothing happened, except that the Dragonlances seemed to gleam a little more brightly. Magius looked at the cart and then at his hands, as if the latter were somehow responsible for his failure.

Kaz let out a bellowing laugh.

"Don't ever do that again!" Huma practically shouted. "You are fortunate; the Dragonlances are impervious to your magic. There's no telling what might have happened if you had tried a more powerful spell."

The saddle was secured to the dragon shortly thereafter. It fit—barely. The cuts Huma had made into the sides of the saddle let it flatten out. The ropes were tight, but did not bind the dragon uncomfortably. When that was finished, the knight separated the original lance from the others and, with Kaz's help, tied it loosely to the left side of the saddle's pommel.

It was decided that Magius would drive the wagon and Kaz would ride along as escort on the remaining horse. Above them, Huma and the dragon would act as scout and protector.

Huma paused before mounting the dragon, and he stared at the peak. "Gwyneth? What of her?"

The silver dragon turned her head and peered at him with great interest. "You care for her?"

Though admittedly not the best judge of his own emotions, Huma finally nodded. "Though it's been a short time, I feel I have never known someone as well. Is she not coming with us?"

The dragon opened her massive jaws to speak, paused, and then visibly changed her mind about whatever she had planned to say. "There are things that she must do. It is possible you will see her again when you least expect it."

It was not what Huma had wanted to hear, but the knighthood needed these lances; there was no more time to waste.

"We may come across some of my kin on the way," the dragon commented. "If so, we could transport everything in the air and save much time."

Huma secured himself. He checked the Dragonlance. It felt right in his hand. "Let us be off."

A lone figure astride a massive warhorse awaited them when they departed the chain of mountains. From the distance, it was impossible to make out whether this was friend or foe, and so Huma, on the back of the silver dragon and high above his other companions, moved on ahead, low and swift, to investigate. Midway there, he saw the figure raise a hand and shout a greeting. Recognition came to Huma a moment later.

Buoron watched wide-eyed as the dragon landed before him. He saw the knight sitting high atop the back of the giant creature, the gleaming lance poised for use.

"Huma?"

"Buoron." Huma did not dismount. "Why are you still here? Has something happened to the outpost?"

The bearded knight shook his head. "No . . . I felt that someone should wait here, just in case."

The faith of the other knight touched Huma. "I appreciate your perseverance, my friend. We are on our way back to Solamnia. I fear we have little time to stop at the outpost, but we will have to do so in order to gather supplies."

"There is no need." Buoron indicated several large, heavy sacks attached to his saddle. "I have enough here for four for a week. The horses can graze; there is plenty of good land. Water is also no problem. I can show you a number of streams."

Huma squinted. "You speak as if you are going with us. I appreciate the thought, but we could not ask that of you."

Buoron smiled slightly. "I have received permission from Taggin to return with you to Solamnia. He feels that a report should be made of activities at the central command and to see if there is anything Grand Master Trake would have of us."

"Trake is dead. Oswal is now Grand Master."

"When did this happen?"

Huma opened his mouth to speak and then paused. He still had not quite convinced himself that it was all true. "I will explain later. If you are free to join us, I doubt if my comrades will have any complaint."

The other knight made a face. "The minotaur—and the mage?"

"Both are helping."

Kaz and Magius arrived at that point. Huma turned to them and broke the news that his fellow knight would be joining them. The minotaur greeted him as a fellow warrior while Magius seemed to regard him as a necessary adjunct.

They made little more distance that day. Though the war-horses performed excellently as substitute draft animals, they grew weary as the day lengthened. Eventually, Huma and the silver dragon landed ahead to supervise a camp for the group.

Later, as they settled down, Huma raised his head in alarm at a sound from the distance. It was faint, quite faint, but unmistakable. He caught hold of Buoron and asked, "Tell me, are there many wolves in this region?"

Buoron shrugged. "Enough. Other than ourselves, there really is not much in the way of civilization—at least as we know it. I daresay the elves would differ with me on that question. Why?"

Huma shook his head wearily. "No reason. Just nerves."

With Kaz and Buoron riding on each side of the wagon, the group started off again the next day. The silver dragon rose high in the air. For the time being, though, Buoron, more familiar with this territory, would guide them.

They reached the forested regions, and Huma tensed. From above, it was often impossible to see what lay beneath the treetops. Worse, because of the weapons, his companions below would have to stick to whatever trails existed in the woods.

So intent was Huma on maintaining visual contact with his companions that he neglected his own safety. The silver dragon, too, only barely saw the streak from above.

Huma clung to the saddle as foot-long claws barely missed pulling him from the back of his great companion.

A shriek, fierce, threatening, and deadly, rent the air. A large red dragon filled Huma's view momentarily before his own silver one dove even closer to the treetops. Huma glanced up quickly. There were two dragons, both crimson red.

The silver dragon did not hesitate when Huma shouted commands. She turned around and lifted herself as swiftly as possible toward the two attackers. Huma steadied the Dragonlance.

Both beasts had riders, and the knight's mind briefly registered that they wore the ebony of the Black Guard. Then the two red dragons were arcing toward them, and all thoughts of anything else vanished.

Huma tapped the left shoulder of the silver dragon and she immediately swerved to take on the red in the lead.

The thrust of the lance went through the terrible crimson beast so quickly, so suddenly, that the silver dragon was almost dragged to earth with it when she could not pull away fast enough. The rider of the dead leviathan was able to take one swing at Huma in that brief time, then struggled helplessly as the lance was extracted, and man and dragon plummeted toward the forest below.

The second dragon, above the brief battle, dove and attempted to wrench both rider and lance from the back of the silver dragon. The silver dragon, already backing up, increased her velocity. The red beast, instead of landing on its intended victim, came to a confused halt only a few lengths in front of its opponents.

The red's rider shouted something. The enemy dragon tried to continue its descent, but it hesitated a moment too long. Unfortunately, the lance succeeded only in penetrating the outer hide. The silver dragon, though, raked the left wing of her evil counterpart as she passed over.

The guardsman on the red dragon's back turned and swung at the silver dragon with a broadsword, striking a lucky blow across her snout. The sword had cut deeply. The Black Guard was not so defenseless as either Huma or his dragon had believed.

The red wobbled away, the damage to his wing severe. But it turned in a swift, jagged arc and came charging back.

At that moment, two more dragons broke through the cloud cover. One was red; the other was huge, bigger than the reds—and was coal black.

The black shrieked angrily—not at Huma and his companion, but at the wounded red dragon. The red ignored the call, so intent was it on avenging itself.

To the surprise of all, the black dragon—it was indeed Charr, Huma could finally see—unleashed a fearsome blast of liquid. The rider of the red turned just in time to see it coming.

The liquid engulfed both rider and dragon. They became one single burning mass, and Huma gasped. Acid. Charr's own desire for vengeance was so great that he destroyed the two. He wanted the silver dragon, and the knight who rode her, for the wounds they had inflicted on him and his master, Crynus. The remnants of the red dragon and rider plummeted earthward.

The sole red and its rider remained in the background as Charr and the tall figure astride him, the warlord Crynus, sought the two who had humiliated them earlier. This time, Huma knew, the battle would not end until one or the other was dead.

Huma chanced a look downward. As he feared, dark, armor-clad figures dotted some of the more open spaces in the woods. More of the Black Guard. He could see no sign of the wagon or his companions and prayed they could hold their own. Huma already had more than he could handle.

As if marking those thoughts, Charr dove at them.

"Be ready, Huma," the silver dragon called. "If I can, there are a couple of tricks that I can make use of, but the Dragonlance is our best hope of defeating this obscenity once and for all."

The two dragons battled for superiority. Higher and higher they rose, neither gaining an advantage. Huma felt the silver dragon shudder as she drew a deep breath. Was she tiring? he wondered. Charr, sensing this, seemed almost to smile in triumph.

Huma's companion suddenly unleashed a cone-shaped mist that enveloped the front portion of Charr. The black froze in mid-flight and began to fall earthward.

"Huma!" the silver dragon cried hoarsely. "I did not strike him directly, and he is terribly strong-willed. We must attack before he recovers from the paralysis."

Even as she spoke, she slowed to dive. Huma gripped the

saddle with one hand, the Dragonlance with the other, and the neck of his companion with both legs. Had he not ridden before and faced so many trials since then, he was certain that he would have blacked out long before now.

As they dove, Huma watched the black slowly return to life. Charr was already slowing his descent. Astride him, Crynus ranted and waved his battle ax and pointed at the knight and silver dragon above them. Charr's head turned slowly upward. This time the two dragons came together and fought to the maximum.

The Dragonlance pinned the sinister dragon by its shoulder. Blood dripped freely from that wound.

As the two massive heads thrust at one another, time and time again, the riders drew near enough to strike. Huma, hampered by the weight of the lance, could not draw his sword. Crynus swung his two-headed battle ax, barely missing the top of Huma's helmet.

Both dragons had become splashed with blood, and it was difficult to decide who had suffered more. The necks of both bore dozens of cuts, bites, and gashes. The black dragon had been raked in the front but had managed to slice apart some of the lower membrane on the silver one's right wing.

The shoulder wound and the earlier wound to his wing were beginning to tell on Charr. He sank a little, and the silver dragon succeeded in giving the side of his neck a nasty set of gashes. Once more the Dragonlance dug into Charr's shoulder.

In desperation, the black inhaled sharply, and Huma, afraid that his companion did not notice it, kicked her sharply in the sides. Whether because of his warning or not, her snout came down hard on Charr's own, clamping the dark dragon's mouth shut. The acidic blast that Charr had been ready to exhale found itself stopped and reversed. The black shivered and shook, suffocating and burning at the same time.

The frenzy of his wounding sent his claws jabbing deep into the torso of the silver dragon. Charr stopped flying, as his entire system reeled from the acid and the loss of oxygen. All four combatants found themselves falling.

"My wings will slow us, but we still will strike with great severity!" the silver dragon shouted. "If I can, I will shift so as to act as a cushion for you."

Crynus, meanwhile, seemed unconcerned with the fall. Even now, he struggled to reach Huma or the silver dragon. The wind prevented him from doing too much, and in anger or madness, the warlord unhooked himself from the safety of the saddle—and promptly was sucked away from the rest of the group.

He did not even scream.

Huma stared at the vanishing figure, unable to believe the insanity of the black-armored warlord.

The trees rushed up toward them. Charr's grip suddenly became limp, and the silver dragon at last was able to release herself.

By then, it was too late. They dropped into the treetops with a tremendous crash.

Chapter 23

WHEN HUMA AWOKE, HE FELT BRUISED OVER EVERY INCH
of his body, but otherwise he seemed unharmed.

He stood up and gazed at the wholesale destruction. The
force of two such tremendous masses as the dragons had
been enough to level much of the timber in the immediate
area.

Charr's inert form lay to one side, its neck snapped. The
hideous face still had a toothy, upside-down smile. The
deadly claws pointed uselessly into the air.

There was no sign of the silver dragon, even though at
least some of the blood came from her. She must have
moved under her own power, but to where?

Where, also, were his companions? Huma could hear no
sounds and was disoriented as to what direction they must

be in.

The Dragonlance and saddle lay nearby, where he supposed the silver dragon had fallen. The Dragonlance still gleamed brightly, and Huma felt a little better just to see it. At least one enemy rider and one red dragon remained—but where were they?

He could not very well carry the lance on his shoulders; it was more than twice his height. His only real option was to drag it. He looped some rope around the shield, tied it together, and then pulled it over his head and one arm. In his free arm, he held his sword, which had managed to survive the fall.

Dragging proved awkward, and Huma was barely away from the scene of destruction before he caught the lance on an upturned tree root. The knight put down his sword and began to work the very lengthy weapon around. It came loose suddenly, and Huma fell against a tree trunk. Every bruise in his body screamed, and more than a minute elapsed before he was able to sit up and coordinate his thoughts. The first thing he did was to reach for his blade. It proved to be an excellent decision.

The heavy ax struck the tree exactly at the level where his neck had been.

Huma tumbled forward as he grabbed his sword and attempted to untangle himself. To his surprise, no other attack was forthcoming. Instead, his attacker boomed forth with laughter.

"You can have all the time you need, Knight of Solamnia! It won't do you a bit of good."

Huma threw the rope down. He tightened his grip on the sword. He looked up to study his adversary—and shook his head, not believing what he saw. It had to be a trick!

Warlord Crynus was casually removing his battle ax from the tree trunk he had nearly severed. His plain ebony armor was dented and dirty in many places, but the warlord seemed in perfect health otherwise. His face remained hidden behind his visor, but his eyes glowed frost blue.

The tall, ominous figure should have been dead.

Crynus took a step forward. His deep voice hissed. "I am so pleased you survived, Huma of the Order of the Crown.

You were lucky that day when we first met in the sky over that no-man's land. By rights, I would've cleaved your head from your body. That *accidental* victory of yours never should have happened, and I have remembered ever since."

One of the warlord's heavy boots came down on the limb of a fallen tree and snapped it neatly. "I am the greatest of her infernal majesty's commanders. She would have lost the war long ago if it had not been for me."

"I have heard different," Huma dared to say. "Some say the greatest is Galan Dracos."

Crynus gave the double-bladed ax a practice swing. "He has his uses, but I distrust his loyalty." The warlord paused and went on in a different tack. "Your thrust in that first, short encounter was a lucky one. As I said, that never should have happened."

"Why not?"

"See for yourself, if you are fortunate enough." The warlord charged Huma.

Huma ducked the first swing, and the ax bit into yet another tree. With incredible strength, the warlord turned the pull into a second attack, forcing the knight back as the ax suddenly came singing back over his head.

This time, Huma found an opening and thrust, but his aim was off, and the weapon deflected off the commander's breastplate. Crynus laughed and renewed his vicious assault. Huma stumbled back and back as he sought to escape the continuing onslaught.

The ax missed Huma again by only inches. This time, though, the warlord had miscalculated, and the shaft of the ax struck hard against the side of a tree, bouncing out of Crynus's hands. Daring everything, Huma lunged. This time, there was no mistaking the accuracy of his thrust. The sword came up and caught Crynus in the unprotected portion of his neck. Huma's blade did not stop until it reached the back of the warlord's helmet.

The black-clad figure stumbled away, attempting to wrest the sword from his opponent as he did so. The warlord stumbled, dropped his ax, and tripped. On his hands and knees, he gave a death rattle.

Then, the warlord's maddening sound reverted to something more familiar—and chilling. While Huma watched, spellbound, Crynus slowly lifted himself to his feet, turned toward Huma, and smiled.

The mortal wound across the warlord's neck was little more than a scar. He seemed—proud.

"I cannot die, Knight of Solamnia. I will heal instantly. I am, as I said, the greatest commander my lady has. My death would be a terrible blow to her. Thus I demanded of Galan Dracos this protection. At first, his attempt was only partially successful—almost to my eternal regret. Thus our foreshortened battle. My men would have taken you, but I wanted you for myself and they would not dare go against my wishes. I wanted you for what you had almost done."

The battle ax came at Huma again. The knight was fully on the defensive now, for how does one slay an opponent who heals instantly? Crynus had the strength of many and stamina to match.

The warlord laughed at Huma's efforts to dodge him and stay alive. Crynus was being openly careless, allowing his swings to go wild, taunting the knight with his immortality.

"I had expected more of a fight from you, young knight. You disappoint me."

Huma backed into a tree. Crynus screamed as he swung the ax. The deadly blade narrowly missed Huma as the knight dove at the warlord. Behind him, the ax cut deep into the tree. The two collapsed into a heap and struggled. It was evident to Huma that he did not have the strength to match the warlord. Crynus pushed the knight away and tried to strangle him, but Huma kicked with his knee and threw his adversary off-balance. Both scrambled to their feet and faced one another. Huma still had his sword. The warlord was weaponless.

"What are you waiting for?" the ebony-armored commander gloated. "Run me through. I will still kill you with my hands."

Huma tried to stall while his mind raced for ideas. "How is it your army functions without you? Aren't you afraid they will blunder?"

Crynus laughed shortly. "Dracos is a competent commander. Besides, the time has come when my leadership can be spared. It is simply a matter of mopping up those who remain around Vingaard Keep. I leave such minor details to my staff."

The battle ax lay only a short distance away. Huma took a step toward the weapon. If only he could get the ax.

Crynus screamed and threw himself on Huma's blade. The knight released his hold and leaped for the battle ax. The warlord's movements slowed as he attempted to pull the sword from his body. Huma picked up the battle ax and turned back to his opponent. Seemingly in no pain, the warlord began extricating the blade from his body.

Huma raised the ax. Crynus turned toward him.

The cut was clean and the helmeted head of the warlord went flying. The warlord's body slumped to its knees. Huma threw down the battle ax with distaste. This was not his way.

The headless corpse rose to its feet again. All color drained from Huma's face.

With definite precision, the hands of the decapitated creature removed the broadsword and tossed it away. Huma could see the wound healing itself. Even the armor, like a second skin, sealed itself. Huma waited for the thing to turn to him, but it was as if he had never existed, for the headless body began to walk off, toward where the warlord's head had flown.

Huma could run, he knew, but the warlord would follow, never tiring.

"SARGAS!"

The cry came from the direction of the undead Crynus. Huma scooped up his sword. He knew of only one who would give such an oath.

If Kaz were around, the others were likely to be nearby. And the Dragonlance—

Of course!

Huma broke through the foliage. There was Kaz astride his horse, the minotaur's mouth agape. The others were nowhere to be seen. The minotaur's eyes stretched wide as the body of Crynus neared the disembodied head, which wobbled and tipped as if it still functioned.

"Kaz! It must not reach the head!"

The minotaur urged his horse forward—at the abomination that called itself Crynus.

The warhorse charged forward until it was within six feet of the headless Crynus, then abruptly came to a halt, shrieking. Kaz wasted no time. He jumped off the panicked steed and raced the body for the head.

Huma, meanwhile, had returned to the Dragonlance. The knight picked up the shaft.

"Huuummmmaaa!"

Kaz burst through the foliage, nearly impaling himself on the Dragonlance. In his right hand he held a grisly prize, which still vibrated with ghastly life. Behind the minotaur came the sounds of something thrashing toward them with great purpose.

"Drop it!" Huma indicated the head. "Over there! Quickly!"

The minotaur tossed the head in front of the tip of the Dragonlance just as a gauntleted hand came into sight.

The headless body froze and then dove to the side before they could impale it.

"It knows!" said the minotaur with a snort.

Worse yet, as the body rose, it held out one hand, clutching the fallen and forgotten battle ax.

"This is madness," Kaz muttered.

"WHAT is going on here?" cried a new voice.

Both Huma and Kaz looked up as the silver dragon hovered above them. She appeared drawn, and one of her forelegs hung limply, but much power still resided within her.

She turned her gaze from the two and stared at the horrible creature. "Is that—?"

The body reached for its head.

"Paladine!" the silver dragon uttered in shock. She inhaled sharply even as Crynus put down the battle ax and picked up his head. The arms of the monstrosity were raising the head high even as she unleashed a torrent of flame.

Dragonflame engulfed the warlord. The body wobbled, sank to its knees, and both head and trunk vanished in the purifying flame. Within seconds, no sign of the unliving Crynus could be seen within the miniature inferno.

The silver dragon landed in the clearing and readied herself for a second strike. "That should be the end of that thing," she said.

"Wait!" Kaz cried. He rushed to the fire and picked up the battle ax, which had escaped the blast. He tossed the ax into the fire—then raced away as the weapon exploded. Bits of metal and wood scattered through the forest. Kaz cursed as a tiny piece of metal struck him on the shoulder.

"Sar—Gods! I cannot leave you alone at any time, Huma!" The two rose and dusted themselves off. The silver dragon, meanwhile, blew out the fire with a cold blast that left ice clinging to the nearest trees.

"I didn't know you could do that," Huma said to her.

Her shoulders slumped from exhaustion. "The chill and the paralysis are among our normal abilities. The flame—the flame is possible for any dragon save the cowardly, ice-dwelling white, but it requires much of us—and I am afraid I overexerted myself. I must rest."

Huma nodded understanding, then glanced around. "Kaz! Where are Buoron and Magius? Where are the Dragonlances?"

"Where I left them, I suppose. When we saw the dragons fall in the distance, I volunteered to go ahead and see if you were still alive."

"Then you didn't SEE them?"

"Who?"

"We must get to them, fast!" Huma turned to the silver dragon, but the great beast was slumped on the ground. Between the multiple wounds received from Charr, the fall from which she had cushioned Huma, and the tremendous final effort she had expended on the rampaging Crynus, she had reached her limit.

"Can we leave you here?" he asked.

Shining eyes opened and regarded him. "I will be all right. I'm sorry I can be of no assistance."

Kaz retrieved his horse, the largest of their mounts. Once Huma was secure, Kaz urged the animal onward.

They could hear the clash of arms well before they neared the spot where Kaz had left the others. Huma had assumed that what he had seen from above was an out-and-out attack. In this, he was wrong. The Black Guard came upon Magius and Buoron from an ambush.

A bright light flashed before them, and Huma saw an ebony-armored figure go flying against a tree. It was not too late. Both Magius and Buoron still lived, still fought.

Huma did not wait for the horse to slow, but rather slid off and rolled to a crouch. Kaz removed his own battle ax and, with a cry, charged into the fray.

Magius crouched on the wagon, keeping most of the attackers at bay with short-lived spells. Buoron stood on the ground behind the wagon, fighting off those guardsmen who had encircled the mage. The enemy was drawing tighter.

Huma picked off his first opponent and charged into the next. As their blades clashed, Huma heard the howl. It was very near, and there was no mistaking it this time. A dreadwolf.

It leaped up onto the back of the wagon. Buoron saw it first, but that brave knight could only shout; he was already engaged with two other foes. Magius, pale and drawn, turned to face the creature. The mage shouted and unleashed a spell, but it sputtered and evanesced before it reached its target. Magius had reached his limit.

This time, the dreadwolf—or rather Galan Dracos, since his was the mind that controlled the unliving creatures—did laugh. Huma succeeded in disposing of his guardsman adversary and tried to reach the wagon. He was cut off by two more ebony-armored guardsmen and could only glance helplessly as the burning eyes of the creature brightened and the renegade unleashed a spell of his own. Huma did not see what happened next, but when the wagon came into his view again, Magius was standing unharmed. The Dragonlances had in some way protected him from Dracos's foul power. The dreadwolf cringed back. Dracos had not expected this setback.

Then Huma was pressed back and Kaz was pulled from his horse. There was a flash of light and a tall, circular opening materialized in the air itself. It was a portal, the knight realized, a gate large enough to drive a wagon through. Huma struggled against the two warriors who blocked his path, and they gave quarter.

A guardsman leaped up behind Magius, and the spellcaster turned just in time. The hapless attacker crashed to the ground. The dreadwolf was nowhere to be seen.

One of Huma's opponents made a fatal mistake and paid for it. The other fought with desperation. More guardsmen were swarming around the wagon. Buoron seemed to have vanished.

Two more black figures jumped on the wagon and this time Magius was not quick enough. One caught his arms and held him back while the other sought the reins. Other warriors began retreating through the portal, their destination most likely Galan Dracos's citadel.

Another guardsman joined the other two on the wagon. Huma finally slew his last adversary and charged toward the wagon. A white abomination blocked his path briefly, but it appeared more intent on retreating through the portal than anything else. It did not even glance in the knight's direction.

Though the wagon was only yards from the portal, the driver hesitated as the portal seemed to blink in and out of existence. The horses fought him for control. One guardsman leaped off the cart as Huma reached it. At the same time, Magius succeeded in breaking the hold of his captor and pushed his hand in the man's visored face. A small burst threw the guardsman back, but it was only enough to stun him. Magius half-collapsed, the final effort exhausting him. He had no more power and little strength. He crawled forward and tried to wrap his arm around the driver's neck. He succeeded in halting the progress of the wagon, but both men fell from the vehicle.

One of the few remaining guardsmen shouted something, and then they were all retreating toward the gate.

The horses, unsettled by all the commotion, again began to move. Huma grabbed the reins. The horses protested, but Huma began to shout commands to them. Kaz, daring everything, stood before the steeds and took hold of the bridles. With strength no human could match, he held the horses firm. They struggled a little more, then finally gave in to his control. Huma slumped down on the driver's seat and nodded thankfully at the minotaur.

The portal vanished.

A groan came from behind the wagon. Huma jumped up, sword ready, only to feel a sting of pain from his left leg. He looked down to see a long gash that a broadsword must have opened during the fighting.

Kaz reached the groaning figure first. It was Buoron, lying half-underneath the wagon. His left arm was covered with blood, and there was a gash across his face. The blood from the facial wound had momentarily blinded him.

"Are you hurt severely?" asked Huma.

"My eyes sting and I fear no one will ever use me as a sculptor's model, but the only true pain is in my arm. I am thankful it was not my sword arm. I fear it will be useless for some time." Even as Buoron spoke, Kaz was already at work on the knight's wounds. The minotaur himself was covered with countless minor wounds, but he seemed unconcerned with his own welfare.

Huma nodded and limped slowly to the front of the wagon. He peered over the far side and then froze.

Magius! Where was the spellcaster? Ignoring his pain, Huma leaped out of the wagon and searched the dead. All wore the black of Takhisis and her commanders. The few who had suffered at the power of the mage were easy to identify. Of Magius himself there was no sign.

Near the woods, Huma spotted a small rod lying among the scattered remains of the attackers. He walked over and picked it up.

The rod quivered, and Huma almost dropped it out of surprise. The surprise turned to fascination as the rod expanded, growing and growing until it was taller than Huma. It was the staff of Magius. The spellcaster was never without the staff.

It had been lying directly beneath where the portal had been.

Magius was in the hands of Galan Dracos.

Chapter 24

"We do not know if he has indeed been taken, Huma," and even if he is a prisoner of Galan Dracos, it would be impossible for us to rescue him. They must have him in the citadel of the renegade, himself," Kaz pointed out for the hundredth time.

"Our best hope is to deliver the Dragonlances to Vingaard Keep and the Grand Master, Huma," Buoron added.

Huma nodded. They were both correct, he knew, but his inability to protect Magius, whom he had known nearly all his life, gnawed at him.

Buoron, the wounded arm in a sling, drove the wagon now. Huma sat with the lances, watching the trio's backside. The silver dragon had volunteered to seek out the assistance of her kin, and Huma had approved the idea.

With Crynus destroyed and his guardsmen in disarray, the trio should be safe for the time being. In actuality, a part of Huma almost desired a second accounting.

The next few days passed without incident as the companions traveled toward Solamnia and Vingaard Keep. There were times when Huma would wake to what he was sure were the cries of the dreadwolves, but nothing came of these.

In all this time, the silver dragon did not return. No one cared to conjecture on this, although all three assumed it had something to do with the steadily advancing hordes of the Dragonqueen. Huma recalled the words of Crynus— that the Knights of Solamnia had been virtually defeated and that Vingaard soon would fall. As much as he wished to believe otherwise, Huma tasted too much truth in those statements.

By this time, they were far to the northwest of Caergoth. Huma recalled Lord Guy Avondale and prayed they would pass this region without confronting the Ergothian commander. After Huma's abrupt departure, he was not sure how Avondale would welcome him. Nor was Huma confident as to what the Ergothians would do once they saw the Dragonlances. They might very well confiscate them.

The trio was making good time, all things considered, but it was still not fast enough for Huma. The evil of Takhisis was enveloping everything, and Huma felt impotent.

They crossed plains now. That would continue for much of the journey. While it made their going easier, it also provided them with little cover.

At midday, only two days from the border, they sighted a huge patrol, too far away to be identified. But it was plain the patrol had seen the trio as well, for the soldiers shifted in their direction and their pace quickened.

Kaz removed his battle ax. Huma leaped from the back of the wagon and unsheathed his blade. Buoron remained with the wagon, but he pulled out his sword and waited for the approach of the patrol.

The bearded knight was the first to identify them. Turning to Huma, he said, "Ergothians. Part of their northern army,

I would say."

There was no way to outrun them. How would Ergothians act when confronted with an ax-wielding minotaur and two knights from an order responsible in great part for the decay of the once-mighty Ergothian Empire?

The commander of the patrol raised his hand as the group neared the trio. A broad, almost fat man with a small beard and thin gray hair, he studied each of them in turn, his gaze lingering on Kaz, who, despite his nature, tried his best to look unthreatening. In Huma's opinion, the minotaur failed completely.

First, the Ergothian addressed Buoron. "You are from one of the outposts in the south, are you not?"

"I am." Both knights stiffened. This commander was a keen observer.

"Your companion knight is not?"

Huma answered. "Lord, I am Knight Huma of the Order of the Crown."

"I see," said the Ergothian with about as much interest as if he had been told that there was grass growing on the plains. He pointed at Kaz. "And that? Where did that come from? I've heard rumors . . ."

"I," the minotaur announced proudly, "am Kaz. I have rebelled from my former masters and am now companion to Huma, most noble and brave of knights."

That might have brought a few smiles to the faces of the Ergothians if they had not seen the dark look on the face of Kaz and knew he meant every word of it.

"I am also a minotaur, not a 'that.'"

"I see." The commander shifted his girth in the saddle and turned to Huma. "I am Faran and though we have never met, I and my men are presently attached to an acquaintance of yours, Lord Guy Avondale."

Huma could not help but flinch.

"I see you remember him. I have been asked to escort you to him, and I will not take 'no' for an answer."

Huma looked at his two companions. The patrol outnumbered them and included more than a few archers. To resist would be foolish. As long as they lived, there was hope. "We will gladly accept your escort."

Faran smirked. "I thought you might." He waved his hand and the patrol split, one half flanking each side of the wagon. There would be no escape. "We have a day's journey ahead of us, so I recommend we waste no more valuable time."

"I must admit to being greatly surprised at your sudden absence that night, Huma," Lord Guy Avondale was saying the next day.

The three of them sat, alone, before the chief commander in his tent.

"I have explained those circumstances."

"Yes, you have." Lord Avondale put down his goblet. The trio had been offered wine as well, but none of them had accepted. "I should have known better, I grant that, but when we discovered that nest of pestilence, I was more than happy to accept the mage's assistance."

Kaz, his patience wearing thin, stood up fiercely. "We have been sitting here for the past three hours, two of which were wasted waiting for you, commander. For the past hour, you have spoken of nothing but false pleasantries and news so old—how much longer are we to put up with this? Are you going to let us pass into Solamnia with the lances?"

Two guards came rushing in, but the commander waved them off. They did not leave the tent, Huma noticed.

The Ergothian put down his goblet. "For the past three hours, and all of last night, I have been debating in my mind as to what to do about you and those weapons. In answer to your last question, yes, you may pass through with the lances. For what reason would I turn them over to the emperor? He would merely mount them on some palace wall as the latest of his trophies, despite what they could do for *all* of Ansalon."

Huma and Avondale locked gazes. "Other than a few diehards, most of us are realistic enough to admit the truth. It is no longer the emperor we truly fight for, although perhaps that once might have been the case. We are fighting for Ergoth, our homeland, and our families. That is what matters in the long run. Emperors come and go, but it is the people who sustain. We lost sight of that at some point, and a good portion of the empire decided they could do better without us—but you know that, of course."

"Then," Huma said calmly, "if what you say is true, why are we being held here?"

"You are not. We are waiting."

"Waiting for what?"

A horn signaled the approach of someone or something. Guy Avondale rose and smiled knowingly. "I think that is them now. Come with me, please."

They stood and followed the Ergothian commander. They were trailed by the two guards.

When they had entered the camp, the first thing Huma had noticed was the vast, open plain situated before the tent of the commander. He had wondered at its purpose then, even as he had wondered until now how Avondale had known where they were and that they were coming at all. Now the knight understood.

The first to land was the silver dragon herself. She seemed fully healed and, in fact, greeted Huma with such enthusiasm that he was overwhelmed.

"I apologize for the delay, Huma, but it proved more difficult than I thought to locate assistance. But I have found them!"

Two more silver dragons landed, one female and one male. They were introduced as the silver dragon's siblings, and both greeted and gazed at Huma with such seriousness it was as if they were inspecting him. Huma returned their greeting with some unease.

The final newcomer was a bronze-colored dragon, slightly smaller than all the rest. What he lacked in size, though, he more than made up for in muscle and speed. He had, from humans, acquired the nickname of Bolt, which he wore proudly. Here at last, Huma decided, was a kindred spirit for Kaz.

"Four or five lances between us will be no difficulty," Huma's silver dragon explained.

"The saddle—" Huma began.

"I have had someone working on that," interjected Avondale. "We have four saddles, which should suffice. I assure you that they will be more than capable of withstanding the rigors ahead."

"They had better be," Kaz muttered.

"You said four," Huma said. "We have only three, without Magius. "Unless you think—"

"I do not!" The Ergothian commander looked Huma straight in the eye. "In the name of Paladine and all of Ansalon, I forbid you from going and throwing yourself at the renegade in a futile attempt to rescue the mage! You yourself have spoken of how much the Dragonlances mean to the future of all of us. If you throw your life away, you are condemning us to the Dragonqueen's dark dreams!"

Inwardly, Huma felt shame at the relief that flowed through him upon hearing Avondale's words. Part of him desperately wanted to rescue his companion, while another part of him yearned for his own safety. Huma was torn.

"Who is to be our fourth member, then?"

"I am."

"You?" Kaz snorted in derision. "Have all the world's commanders gone mad?"

Lord Avondale replied coldly. "Faran is more than capable of stepping into my role. Despite his dislike of Solamnia, he is a practical man. He will not do anything to upset the situation. I would trust no one more."

"What would your emperor say?" asked Buoron, silent until now.

"What the emperor would say, he may tell me if I survive. As I told you, I am fighting for Ergoth. I would never forgive myself if I placed another's life in such danger, though I am sure many would volunteer. Someone must go with you, to represent Ergoth to your Grand Master, and it may as well be me."

Huma agreed, albeit with great reluctance. They were in Avondale's hands at present; there really was no choice— and he would be a good man to have on one's side, Huma decided.

It was agreed that Huma would again ride the silver dragon, while Buoron and Avondale would take the younger male and female, respectively. This left Kaz with the volatile Bolt. As Huma had suspected, the minotaur and the bronze dragon took to one another like two old soldiers. His only fear was that the two might take it on themselves to charge on ahead, and he voiced this opinion to the silver dragon.

She chuckled. "Bolt and Kaz do indeed make a troublesome pair, but the dragon at least knows better—I think. I shall warn him once we are in the air."

"Make sure it's understood that the warning is for both of them."

"There will be no doubts."

They had wanted to leave without fanfare, but Faran would not hear of it. The second-in-command had an honor guard waiting to see them off.

Bolt, especially, was intrigued by the Dragonlance. Already a terror in the skies—according to himself—he claimed he now had the perfect edge with the lance and Kaz in the saddle. The silver dragons all looked on in poorly masked amusement, although Huma's did admit shortly thereafter that the bronze dragon's words were not bluster. He was indeed a formidable opponent.

The dragons rose into the sky one at a time, with Huma and his mount the first, Kaz and Bolt last. The sun was already well into the sky, but with the dragons bearing them, they would cover a vast distance that day in any case.

By the time night had triumphed, they had long passed the border into Solamnia. One thing they had not thought of slowed them, though. The drizzle that had started in Ergoth was a downpour at this point, and all four riders were soaked. The dragons seemed unaffected, especially the bronze, who seemed to enjoy the shafts of lightning that almost skewered them twice. At Huma's urging, they finally landed for the night in the hope that the morning would bring better conditions. The dragons formed a protective square around them and the four set up the two tents Avondale had thought to bring along. The tents kept the rain from them and Huma's only regret was that the true smell of a wet minotaur became very obvious as the night aged.

In the morning, Kaz had the same comment about him.

The rain did not cease, but it did lighten. The riders covered themselves with their cloaks or in the few blankets they had brought. Thanks to the dragons, they would be within the vicinity of Vingaard Keep in two days. Had they not been burdened by the extra lances, it would have taken even less time.

Still, their journey was by no means over, for now they were to face the Dragonqueen's forces. Dracos had a stranglehold on the heart of Solamnia, for he had finally cut off northern and southern routes into and out of Vingaard, effectively creating a wall that encircled the Keep. Supplies were becoming scarce. Control of the sky was still a question, but morale was having its effect even on the dragons of light. The only thing that had kept them going, the silver dragon revealed, was the rumor of the Dragonlance.

The male silver was in the lead when they felt the first probe in their direction. A presence was nearby, reaching out with magic to detect outsiders. The probe was no more than a momentary contact with their minds, but it was enough to send the entire group into an abrupt halt.

"Back!" cried the male.

The four leviathans whirled and retreated some distance back along their route. They conferred as they flew.

"What was it we felt?" Huma's female asked.

"A mind—not a dragon's mind, but a powerful human mind. Undisciplined, too. This one was never a student of the Orders of Magic."

"Not a cleric?"

The male shook his massive head. "No, definitely a mage. A renegade."

Huma looked around nervously. "Surely, he is not a threat to you!"

"Physically, no, Huma." It was his own silver dragon who replied. "But he would have no trouble warning others of our presence—if he hasn't already—and those others may be a threat. His sole purpose is to watch the skies."

"Let me take him!" Bolt shouted.

"What would you do," the young female silver asked, "that could possibly prevent him from sending out a message before you strike?"

The bronze dragon clamped his mouth shut.

"I think," the silver male commented, "that an opening has been left for us. He is, after all, only human. I will fly to a level much higher than we normally fly. Once there, it is possible that I can discover whether his range of power can extend that high. I must risk our discovery to be sure." He added, "If my companion has no objections . . ."

Buoron shook his head, although he gripped the saddle pommel tightly.

"What of the rest of you?"

There was no argument from the others. Taking that as a positive response, the male spiraled once and then turned skyward. As Buoron held on, the silver male began to soar higher and higher and higher until he was lost in the cloud cover. Several minutes passed while the others waited anxiously. Then Huma spotted a form breaking through the clouds.

Buoron was rather pale, but otherwise seemed none the worse. His dragon seemed elated. "I was correct. So typical of many earthbound minds; his search extends only to the cloud cover. As far as he is concerned, anything above that does not exist."

"I could've thought of that!" complained Bolt.

"You did not, and neither did I," commented Huma's dragon. "Now that I hear it, it amazes me. I had forgotten how closed-minded some humans are. Still, he may yet come to that realization by accident, so we had better move quickly."

The others followed Huma and his companion skyward, soaring up until they burst into the cloud cover, the mists, and then broke through to the other side. From there, they estimated their present position from Vingaard Keep and continued their journey.

The dragons flew on through the night while their riders slept. Huma awoke to the sound of Kaz arguing with the great reptilian creatures about the need for them to land before every muscle in his body stiffened, war or no war. The dragons themselves were visibly tired and ready to land in order to get a new fix on their positions.

First Bolt, then the others spiraled swiftly downward.

The bronze dragon disappeared into the silky, white sea, followed quickly by the other silver female. Huma and the silver dragon followed next.

The cool mist surrounded him, and he could not even see the dragon's head. A harsh, grating crashing came from below them and Huma's first thoughts were that they were entering into a tremendous storm. Then, suddenly, they were out of the cloudcover—

—and into chaos.

They had assumed, incorrectly, that they had crossed beyond the enemy forces. Huma's mind spun with horrible nightmares as he realized how tightly the Keep was surrounded. Fighting raged everywhere.

Men and ogres were clashing furiously with one another. In Huma's eyes, it seemed as if the land below was swarming with the dead and dying. Both sides were advancing and retreating at the same time, depending upon where he looked. It was chaos. Dragons of Takhisis continually dove down, assaulting both the ravaged lines of the knights and any of their ogre allies who were unfortunate enough to be too near. There were dragons of gold, silver, bronze, and copper, but they always seemed outnumbered. Worse yet, there prevailed a sense of malevolent power all about that the courage of the good dragons could not seem to counter. Even up here, away from the battle, Huma could feel discouragement and surrender building up within his soul.

"Takhisis is here," Huma's companion muttered to him. "She is here on Krynn, feeding our cousins with her power, chilling the minds of her enemies. I did not think she could retain so much of her power on the mortal plain. It is as if she were before us herself."

It was true. The Dragonqueen's presence was overwhelming. Huma shivered from a cold that threatened to numb his mind more than his body. How did one fight a goddess?

"Up ahead, Huma. Can you see it?"

His gaze followed the direction her head pointed and, after wiping his eyes more than once, he identified the tiny object on the horizon.

"Vingaard Keep!" Kaz shouted from ahead of them. By now, they all could see it—and the battle that seemed to cover every inch of ground all the way to its walls.

Lord Avondale cried out and pointed to their right. A gold dragon battled two reds. The combat was fierce, and all three bore wounds. When it became obvious that the gold dragon was beginning to lose, Bolt waited no longer. With Kaz readying his Dragonlance, the two charged into the fray.

Suddenly, there were dragons everywhere, most of them foes. All thoughts of food and rest vanished. There were only the claws and the teeth, the cries and the screams, the blood and the pain.

And the Dragonlances.

The dark dragons here knew nothing of the lances, perhaps because Dracos had not wanted them to fear. They soon learned that fear, however, as one after another perished on the points of lances which, when pulled free, were unstained and unscratched, and glowed with a brilliance all their own.

The children of Takhisis soon began to turn and flee from that brilliance, for they marked it easily as the sign of Paladine and they had no power against him. Others, farther off, noted the frenzy with which their brethren fled the battle and assumed then that the day was lost. The fleeing of the first dragons soon became a wave of confusion in the sky as more and more retreated in uncomprehending panic.

Freed from battling their counterparts, the dragons of Paladine added to the strength of the knighthood, and the tide on the ground began to turn as well. First the west, then the eastern lines of the Dragonqueen's forces began to bend, give, and then at last crumble. Without the aid of their dragon allies, the ogres and humans who fought for the darkness lost courage, and many simply threw down their weapons and fled.

Eventually, the fighting died. That the skies rumbled ominously and lightning blasted the mountains to the west disturbed only a few. A victory of some kind had been desperately needed, and it had been produced. No one at the time knew how, but they gave thanks to Paladine and his house for the miracle and then grimly waited to see what would happen next.

Well past midday, four exhausted dragons landed in the courtyard of Vingaard Keep. On their backs they each bore a rider, all of whom also were pale and exhausted. A silvery glow encompassed the newcomers and eventually someone realized it was the great lances that glowed so godlike, and not the dragons and riders themselves.

By that time, though, the stories were already spreading.

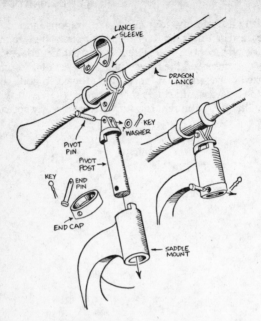

Chapter 25

"They told me it was you, but I could not believe it! Not after the tales that have circulated."

"Tales?" Huma and his companions had climbed down from the dragons—where they would have been swarmed by knights and commonfolk alike if not for the quick thinking of Lord Grendal, who controlled the Keep's defenses. Several of the well-trained veterans who made up Grendal's force were out and around the newcomers within the first minute after the landing.

Lord Oswal, Grand Master, indicated Huma himself. "You know what I speak of. The stories of your battle with the demon who seeded plague and dissension throughout the land."

"Rennard?"

"Rennard. Amazing how faulty their memories can be. When he was revealed for what he was and you defeated him there, they quickly forgot how much they wanted to believe the rumors he spread. They blamed him as an evil demon or cleric—I forget what exactly. Then, to top it all off, you supposedly vanish into thin air like Paladine himself."

Huma's face turned dark crimson. "The part about my vanishing is true, but I assure my lord that it was not by my own power."

"Indeed." Lord Oswal's eyes strayed to the Dragonlances and his body seemed to shake momentarily. "Are those, then, what you have been seeking? What we have so desperately needed?"

"Yes, milord. The Dragonlances. We would have been here sooner, but we became caught up in the battle."

"I daresay. I've had men and dragons alike speak of how the eight of you came from nowhere, dealing fear and death to the Dragonqueen's lackeys. Perhaps they are right; perhaps you *are* Paladine in mortal guise come to Krynn."

"Lord Oswal!"

The Grand Master chuckled. "I have not come around to that way of thinking, Huma. Not yet." Despite his evident desire to inspect the lances, Oswal turned to the rest of Huma's band. "I know you, minotaur, and glad I am that I had faith in you. You live up to all the good I have heard of your kind. I thank you for your assistance."

Kaz was oddly quiet. "I did what I was required to do. I have sworn an oath to Huma."

"Is that all it was?" The Grand Master smiled and turned to the others, starting with Lord Avondale. There was just the hint of coolness in the Grand Master's tone. "I welcome you, Ergothian commander, as a fellow knight. I do not suppose you have brought your army with you?"

"When we met that one time, Grand Master, I knew you would someday hold your present position, but I hoped it would mellow you before we had to face each other again."

Oswal accepted the veiled reprimand with a more genuine smile. "Forgive me if I sometimes forget I am also in the presence of a cleric of Paladine."

Huma, Kaz, and Buoron looked at one another. While they respected Lord Avondale, they would have never taken him for a cleric of Paladine. Then again, who was to say what a cleric *had* to look like so long as his belief and his ways did not contradict the teachings?

"You've let out my secret, but it's just as well. Perhaps Huma now will understand why I wanted him to accompany me to Caergoth. When I noted the sign of Morgion on such an obviously loyal knight, I worried that he might be marked for some foul deed." Avondale turned back to Huma and smiled.

The Grand Master turned from Avondale and regarded Buoron with some amusement. With his great beard, the knight from the southwest stood out. Buoron was shaking in the presence of the Grand Master.

"You are . . ."

The knight blinked several times before blurting out his name. "Buoron, milord!"

"From one of our remote Ergothian outposts, I imagine."

"Yes, milord." Buoron was white.

"Good man." Lord Oswal patted him on the shoulder and turned away. Buoron breathed a sigh of relief and gave a sickly smile.

"Now, then, Huma." The Grand Master was all seriousness. "If you would be so kind, I would like you and your companions to join me in my quarters. I want to hear everything."

"Yes, milord, but the Dragonlances—"

"Will be handled with care and placed in a safe location until we decide what can be done with them. Now come; I suspect you all could do with something to drink. I know after today's near-catastrophe, I could."

Huma's report was punctuated every now and then by the thunder and lightning playing havoc in the mountains to the west. Takhisis letting loose her rage on those who had failed her, Kaz suggested, or perhaps Galan Dracos furious over his followers' failed attempts to seize the Dragonlances.

Lord Oswal tapped the table as he absorbed all Huma had related. "Paladine! I never would have believed it if it had not been you—and to actually see them! You make an old man proud, Huma. Durac would have been proud, I know that."

"Thank you, milord." That compliment meant more to him than all others.

"Made from dragonsilver by a smith with one silver arm, and bearing a god-forged hammer, as well."

Huma looked perplexed. "I made no mention of that."

The Grand Master smiled knowingly. "I am a student of old lore, Huma, which is one reason I believed in you all along. If this smith is as you described him, he must be bearing a hammer that was forged by Reorx himself. I am thankful that our ancient records are true after all and you have lived to bring the weapon to us."

Something had been building up inside Huma and he finally stood. "Milord, I beg of you. I appreciate all you have been saying and I know there was much you had to hear, but we now have the Dragonlances and I must ask of you a favor. There are twenty lances that may be utilized in the heavens. Give me but one lance and let me fly to the domain of Galan Dracos and his dark mistress. I *must* free Magius!"

"Knight Huma." The Grand Master's voice was toneless, frighteningly akin to Rennard's. Lord Oswal stared at him until Huma sat. "One man or woman, be they companion, lover, or blood kin, is not worth the lives of hundreds—and I say that even if I were that one. You may disagree with me, and that is your prerogative—in private. We are fighting for the existence of all Solamnia, of all Ansalon if not Krynn itself. I cannot condone your idea."

"He was taken *defending* the lances." Huma's bitterness began to show.

"I understand that, Knight Huma, as I understand the dangers to you that I think you do not. My answer remains the same. Understood?"

Huma said nothing.

"Now, then, you have twenty-one lances, one of which is designed for a footsoldier, you said."

"Yes."

"Twenty lances are hardly sufficient. We were fortunate

this time, in that the dragons did not expect you, and your sudden appearance threw them into confusion."

"They fled with their tails between their legs," remarked Kaz smugly.

"*This* time. When next they come—and do not believe they will not—they will act with more cunning and more confidence, and four lances, let alone twenty, will not prevail."

"You are claiming the fight is lost already. This is not what I expected to hear from the Grand Master of the Knights of Solamnia," Lord Avondale commented.

The Grand Master ignored the look of disdain on the Ergothian's face and kept his gaze fixed on Huma. "While some may see this as accepting defeat, it is only because they have not bothered to wait and hear. What we need to do is clear the smithy of all else and create, as accurately as possible, lances as near in quality to the originals as we can."

Guy Avondale's eyes narrowed, and a thin smile played across his lips. Kaz and Buoron exchanged looks of puzzlement. Huma hesitated, then saw where the elder knight was leading.

"A ploy! We're going to ensnare them with a great bluff!"

Lord Oswal smiled, an edge in his gaze. "A bluff. Exactly. We already have the setup for creating ordinary lances. Now we shall make as many faithful forgeries of the Dragonlances as possible."

"How long will all this take?" asked Avondale. "As you yourself have indicated, it will not be long before they return."

"Metalworking in most of its forms is an art with us, commander. It is part of the secret of our success. Shoddy weaponry and protection make for shoddy armies—a paraphrasing of something in the Measure. Given two days, we will have more than a hundred lances. They will be, as I said, copies, forgeries of the true Dragonlances. The word has no doubt spread as to the cause of the rout. When next we face them, I hope to have at least a hundred lances ready. When the Dragons of Takhisis come, they will find themselves facing a veritable cavalry charge. The element of surprise will be ours. I am hoping that a hundred lances, supposedly actual Dragonlances, will cause a new panic. With the dragons at bay, our own forces will advance and meet the ogres."

"This is more than a bluff. You intend to win, Dragonlances or not. It is an interesting plan. You have faith in it? Truly?"

"As a cleric of Paladine, you should know. Besides, it is not so much the plan I have faith in as it is in my men. We are, after all, Knights of Solamnia."

"Huma."

He had been walking alone, trying to sort out all that was happening. Magius, the Dragonlances, Galan Dracos, Gwyneth—

"Huma?"

He whirled. She was there in the shadows of the stable. She was clad in a flowing robe of silver-blue, her slim form partially revealed as she walked toward him. Huma could only gape.

"Gwyneth?"

She smiled. "You expect someone else?"

"No!"

"I wanted to come to you earlier, but it wasn't possible. There are—some things—I must sort out. I hope you don't mind if I walk with you, though."

"No. Not at all."

Gwyneth took his arm, and the two walked slowly around the courtyard. It was the first nearly clear night that Huma could recall. There were even patches of actual sky, as if the cloud cover at last were breaking up. Huma knew better than to hope it would vanish. Only one thing would bring that about: total defeat of the Dragonqueen.

It took him some time to build up the nerve, but at last Huma asked, "How did you get here?"

She turned her face from him. "Please don't ask that now. I promise I'll tell you soon."

"Very well. I'm just glad to see you."

That made her turn back. "I'm glad of that. It makes everything worthwhile." Gwyneth's expression suddenly darkened again. "I heard something about you wanting to go after Magius by yourself."

"The Grand Master forbids it."

"What will you do?"

"I obey the Grand Master. It's my duty."

They were silent after that. Gwyneth had rested one hand on Huma's arm and, as they walked, he was astonished at the strength in that hand. There was so much he did not know about her, including her connection with the Dragonlance. She must be a cleric, he decided, but of which god he was not sure.

Gwyneth suddenly stared ahead and stiffened. Huma followed her gaze and caught sight of an unfamiliar male of approximately his own age. The man was dressed like a villager—they had come straggling in to Vingaard Keep just before the war reached their homes—but his stance was not like one of them. The face was fairly well hidden by shadow, but Huma could have sworn that the eyes blazed. After glancing at both of them, the stranger disappeared around a corner.

"Who is that?" Huma's hand fell to the hilt of his sword. If someone stalked Gwyneth . . .

"No one," she replied, much too quickly. Gwyneth disengaged herself from Huma's arm. "I have to leave now. I'll see you again later, I promise."

She turned the way they had come, and hurried away. Huma thought to follow her, but she was out of sight almost instantly. The knight blinked; he could not recall when or where she had turned.

Reaction to the Dragonlances was not what Huma and the others had expected.

He had offered to demonstrate the methods and uses of the Dragonlance. To his amazement, only a handful of knights came to see him. One of them revealed the reason for the astonishing apathy among his brethren. Huma, stunned, told the others what the knight had said and how widespread those feelings were among the knighthood.

"The time for miracles is past. They will not accept the magic of the lances, and who can blame them? We are asking them to risk their lives uselessly as far as they are concerned. Those who ride with the true Dragonlances will bear the brunt of the assault and then attempt to break through and strike at the heart of evil, Galan Dracos and his infernal mistress. But suicide is against the Oath and Measure. And few have the true faith in Paladine where this is concerned. I was told a few believe I created the lances myself. They want to know why they should risk their lives so needlessly when they could be here, with their comrades, fighting a definite foe on more equal terms. Fighting dragons is one thing; facing the Dragonqueen herself is folly. That message was relayed to me more than once."

Lord Oswal rose at that point. "They'll risk it, curse them! They're knights, not skulking thieves! I'll order them to take the lances and use them!"

"And they'll die," Avondale threw in.

"What's that?" The two commanders locked eyes.

"They'll die, Grand Master. With little or no faith, they'll simply die. It's not a matter of whether the power of Paladine flows within the Dragonlances. The hand that guides the weapon also must believe or else reactions will be a little too slow, a little off the mark. They must have faith, as we do, or they will lose because they will see these lances as they have seen all lances—objects that will bend, break, or shatter on the hides of the dark dragons."

"But a Dragonlance—"

The Ergothian cleric held up a hand for silence. "We have twenty Dragonlances, correct?"

"Plus the footman's lance," Huma quickly added.

"Twenty lances. All we need are twenty men. I think Paladine is watching over us. If there are only twenty Dragonlances, then there is a reason. If we are to obtain more, Paladine will see that we do. If our faith is strong, twenty lances or a thousand, we will triumph."

Lord Oswal looked at Huma. "He's right."

Huma studied those assembled in the room. Kaz, Buoron, and Avondale would follow him on this. He needed only sixteen other men. "Let there just be the twenty, then."

More than one eyebrow was raised at that. Huma did not wait for questions, instead plunging immediately into his thoughts.

"Buoron, Kaz, milord Avondale. I know that you three will join with me. You know the Dragonlance; you know what it can do. If twenty lances are all that stand between us and defeat by the Dark Queen, then we should thank Paladine we have even those and use them to the utmost."

"You should have been a cleric, Huma, for your faith is stronger than any I have ever known." There was no mockery in Lord Guy's tone.

There was a knock on the Grand Master's chamber door, and one of the Knights of the Rose who made up the ruling knight's guard entered. "Grand Master, Knight Bennett wishes to speak with you."

"I summoned him from the Keep walls some time ago. Where has he been?"

"He did not say, milord."

Lord Oswal glanced at Huma and then nodded slowly. "Allow him to enter."

"Milord." The guard spoke to someone in the hall and then stood at attention. Bennett, looking more like his father than Huma had ever seen him, stalked imperiously into the room. He saluted his uncle deferentially and acknowledged the presence of the others politely, though he stared long and hard at the Ergothian commander.

"What is it, Bennett?"

"Unc—Grand Master, I have been studying the Dragonlances."

The elder knight's expression darkened. "Who gave you permission?"

Some of the imperiousness vanished. "I did it of my own accord. I could not help it, after you spoke to me of it following Huma's—his disappearance."

Bennett looked at Huma as he talked, but the latter could read nothing in the stiff, hawklike features.

"And?"

His nephew's eyes widened, the mask fell away, and both Huma and Lord Oswal were astonished at the wonder that spread over Bennett's face as he spoke. "They were smooth to the touch—so smooth they must cut the air effortlessly. I've never seen a point so sharp, nor a metal so bright—so alive. I've heard that many doubt the authenticity of the lances, but I cannot believe but these were sent to us by Paladine, through his chosen champion."

For the first time ever, Huma felt a deep respect emanating from the Grand Master's nephew, and directed at Huma himself.

Lord Oswal was no less surprised. Kaz snorted quietly in derision, but the look Bennett threw him caused him to stop immediately.

"I want to be one of them, Grand Master. I counted but twenty and I know not if we will have any more, but I want to be one of them. It is what I have trained for—to give myself in service to the Triumvirate and to Paladine. I will face any test if needed to prove I am worthy." Bennett exhaled and his shoulders slumped. He had bared himself to all present and now awaited judgment.

The Grand Master looked from Huma to Avondale and then back to his nephew.

"Knight Bennett, you are, I see, the son of my brother—my brother before the strain of leadership tore us apart. If you can but remain as you are now, I see in you what many have always believed—that you will be among the first and best in our ranks." Bennett's shoulders stiffened in unconcealed pride. Oswal continued, "If you would truly be what we all strive to be, then I ask that you make your example this knight here—" he pointed at a stunned Huma—"for he is the embodiment of our teachings, whether or not he believes it so himself."

"Am I then—"

"You are, and I charge you with a special task. Find others like yourself, from all three Orders and numbering fifteen total, who are willing to believe in the strength and will of Paladine and who will ride the skies with the Dragonlance before them."

Bennett nearly stumbled toward the door, then turned to his uncle. Lord Oswal waved him off. The Knight of the Rose departed with haste.

Bennett did exactly as he was told. He sought volunteers from all three Orders and chose them based on merit and belief, not whether they were loyal to him, as he would have done prior to his father's death. Among the volunteers were veterans and near-novices. Included by Bennett, surprisingly enough, were three knights who lacked limbs or were permanently disabled, all from the war. Had this been peacetime, Lord Oswal would have given these men work in the Keep, something to keep them active but away from awkward situations. Now, though, every man who could fight was needed. Men who had lost a leg could still ride and swing a sword. One useless arm still meant that the knight could use his other. A Knight of Solamnia did not quit until he was either triumphant or slain. Had they eliminated such men from the ranks, the available forces in the Keep would have been cut by nearly a quarter.

With the retreat of the Dragonqueen's forces from the vicinity of the Keep, lines of supply reopened, albeit sporadically. Awaiting their first opportunity, knights in the southern reaches shipped food and raw materials. It was dangerous going, for the ogres and dragons still harried the routes, and some wagons never completed their journey.

The mountains to the west were ominously quiet, and Huma found himself staring at them, on and off. Magius was still out there, and Huma still felt the desire to attempt some sort of rescue. Waiting in the Keep for whatever Galan Dracos and his mistress plotted next irked him.

It might have been easier if Gwyneth had been with him, but she had not returned since that one night. Huma had taken to conversing with the silver dragon. They spoke only when alone together, for the presence of the other dragons guarding the Keep—and especially the silver dragon's two siblings, who watched Huma intently each time he came around—embarrassed him.

She listened to his every word and answered his questions with such intensity that it was often easy to forget he was speaking with a creature vastly larger and more ancient than he. At the same time, she seemed filled with a sadness that Huma was never able to identify. He pressed her only once on it. When Huma had probed too far, the great dragon had turned and moved away without another word.

Huma could not explain the reasoning behind the feeling that had surged through him then, but he somehow knew that the sadness which had become so much a part of the leviathan was due to him.

He was careful never to bring up the point again, for fear of what truth he might discover.

Three days passed, and then it was as if the heavens themselves had erupted. Knights in the Keep pointed skyward, and the murmuring began. Though they would deny fear, many turned pale as they remembered the last time the sky had looked like this.

Huma rushed to the battlements, Kaz and Buoron close behind him. Both Huma and the minotaur stared through narrow eyes at the horror before them. Buoron, having come from the southwest outpost, had not been present at that time, but he studied the scene and then turned to his companions, seeing for the first time the looks on their faces.

Turning pale himself, he asked, "What does it mean? Why is it so black?"

The rolling darkness, which had nearly lost the war for the knighthood in that earlier battle, spread slowly toward the outermost lines of defense. The winds around the Keep were building to a pitch.

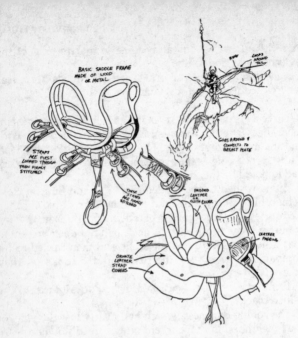

Chapter 26

"The Dragonlances! We must fly now!"

The others were gathering even as Huma and his companions entered the courtyard. Bennett looked to him as an aide might look to his commander. Here, Huma was in charge.

The dragons were there, also. They had had trouble in choosing who would join with the knights. Unlike the humans, all the dragons volunteered. It was the silver dragon who finally chose, she being most closely associated with the lances. Her choices were not questioned, for each of the volunteers was picked on the basis of past performance and physical endurance. There were silver ones, bronze ones—Bolt being the most vocal of these—and even a gold dragon.

More than enough saddles had been made and the well-trained knights were already finishing with that part of the preparations. Someone also had thought to secure the footman's lance to the silver dragon Huma would be riding.

When all was ready, Huma turned to see everyone waiting. Then he grimaced, realizing that they were awaiting his orders. Even Lord Avondale, who Huma felt was certainly a more qualified flight leader, was deferring to him. Turning forward and assuring himself that all was secure, Huma kicked the silver dragon lightly and gave the signal to depart.

What an impressive sight, he thought, as he momentarily turned back to look. The twenty dragons made an arrowhead formation with Huma at the point; Kaz and Bolt were to his left, a little farther back, and Buoron was to his right. He could not see Lord Avondale, who was flying to the rear.

His thought were broken by the visage of the silver dragon as she turned to speak to him. "Huma, I . . ." He looked ahead, expecting to see the Dragonqueen's children breaking through the darkness. "Nothing. I—I merely wished to say you may count on me in all things."

"I will always be thankful," he shouted, for the wind was now so great that it roared in his ears, and he could not be sure how well she heard him. She had already turned away.

It became a battle merely to enter the curtain of blackness that had been raised by the followers of Galan Dracos. The winds were fierce. The riders were strapped down and the Dragonlances were hooked to their mounts for safety. Huma and the silver dragon were the first to enter and it was as if there were no Krynn. Sky and earth were gone. There was only the knight, his dragon, and his lance. No, Huma realized. There was more. Behind him, he could see the glow of the other Dragonlances. At first, Huma worried that they would shine like beacons to the forces of Takhisis. Then he saw how the lances ate away at the darkness, destroying the spell. It did not matter then whether they were seen or not. The darkness ceased to be a threat.

"We're through!" the silver dragon shouted.

The world snapped back into existence. When Huma had wandered on foot, it seemed such an incredible distance, an endless darkness in which things not of this plane chittered and slunk toward their unseeing prey. Now, it seemed like nothing.

The enemy dragons were upon them.

The first came at Huma and the silver dragon as they emerged again into the light. One lone rider and dragon must have seemed easy prey for the red dragons, and the two of them turned from their brethren to deal with Huma. The other dragonriders began to emerge behind Huma, though, and the easy prey became the deadly hunter. The two overconfident reds fell swiftly, unable to break away in time. The others, blue, black, and red, came more hesitantly. It seemed to Huma that they attacked only for fear of their own mistress, a fear greater than that of the Dragonlances.

One of the twenty, Hallerin, a newly appointed but skilled Knight of the Crown, went down, burning from the acidic blast of his foe. The other knights had accounted for four of the enemy and the rest of the dark dragons turned in retreat, deciding to risk the wrath of their mistress.

Some knights wanted to chase after them, but Huma signaled against that idea by remaining on his present course. Huma's target was the source of the shifting darkness.

Several times, they faced onslaughts of creatures of the air. There were dragons of nearly every color. At one point, they clashed with large, birdlike creatures with leonine jaws and three pairs of claws. Another dragonrider was lost to horrors that only could have been the mad creations of Dracos himself. Huma was particularly saddened by this loss, a scarred veteran of the Rose, named Marik Ogrebane. He had been one of the disabled knights and was the first to volunteer. Now only eighteen remained. As they flew, Huma memorized the place and circumstances of each death, hoping to mark the bravery of these men in some way, later on, in song or verse.

They were close, Huma knew, close to the source of the spell. He could feel it.

"I spy something, Huma," said the silver dragon.

"Where?"

"Down there to the right."

He followed her gaze. There was nothing but a hill, barren but for a few bent and decaying trees, arranged almost in a pattern. It was certainly not what he was anticipating, and he told the silver dragon so.

She smiled knowingly. "Look not with your eyes, Huma. Look with the wisdom of Paladine. Have you ever seen trees growing in the form of a pentagram?"

The knight looked again—and realized how precise the pattern was. As he observed, the trees began to waver, as if they were not real. They did not fade, but twisted into brown-robed forms, like the mage who had attacked Huma in the woods in what seemed such a long time ago.

Now he saw them more precisely. Nearly a dozen figures squatted in the dirt, their heads down, their arms outstretched toward the center of the pentagram, where one of their number stood with arms raised high.

"Shall we take them? They seem unaware," Kaz shouted from the side. Bolt eagerly expressed similar sentiments.

"I want to take them alive if possible."

Kaz snorted. "If possible?"

Bolt plunged ahead—and barely missed being grievously wounded as something rose and shattered the air currents, as if lightning had emanated from the earth. Kaz and Bolt circled for another try and this time, when the attack came, Bolt easily dodged it. A crack of lightning split the heavens and struck the hill. When the smoke cleared, a small crater marked where the figures had been.

Huma turned at the sound of laughter coming from the silver dragon. "Thus his nickname, Bolt. All bronze dragons are capable of that trick, but only a few have such precision as he has shown, and none are his equal."

Their defenses shattered, the renegade mages were suddenly active. They rose as one and turned toward the newcomers. Though Huma could not be sure from this distance, he thought their faces remarkably similar. They all might have been siblings. Then Huma realized what was so similar about each figure. They acted as if under a spell or with such concentration that it had become etched in their faces and movements. They were, in a sense, one being and they were pointing their hands toward Huma and the silver dragon.

"Dive!" he cried, but she was already doing that. The renegades tried to follow their progress, but the silver dragon wove a complex tapestry of turns and dives. While the mages concentrated on her, the other dragonriders moved closer.

How long could the renegades keep up this defense and still maintain the darkness? Huma wondered.

"Huma, beyond!"

Just over the hill, and marching steadily along, was the ogre army. The land was literally crawling with ogres, their human allies, goblins, and a few unidentifiables—experiments of the mages, no doubt. Things with too many arms, too many legs—even too many heads and trunks.

The very air ripped apart as he watched, and Huma had a glimpse of a place known to him only in nightmares and prayer. It was only a glimpse, but of a blackness so overwhelming, so ready to devour him, that he knew it could only be the Abyss.

They had that much strength. They had opened a rift in the mortal plane—and it would swallow him! Huma shook uncontrollably, and even the silver dragon wavered at that sight. The rip seemed to widen, giving them no place to run or hide. It came closer—then the power keeping the rift open crumbled as the renegades fell to the oncoming dragons of light. The mages had reached their limits in concentration; too many things were happening of too great importance. As the dragons attacked, first one, then another, then another, a few of the renegades stood to fight and died on the spot; the rest scattered, the link between them destroyed.

Behind them, the darkness dissipated. Things screeched in horror at the light. They had been bred in the darkness, perhaps even in the Abyss. Light to them was death. Their forms could not exist without the darkness; they faded away like dew, leaving no trace of their coming or going.

That would not, however, deter the massive force that marched even now toward the hill where the mages had scattered. The Dragonqueen's commanders, lacking the imagination and daring of Crynus, were throwing all they had into the first battle.

The silver dragon turned to Huma again. "They are

frightened, Huma. Not of us, but of Galan Dracos and the Dragonqueen, I think."

"What can we do?"

"YOU CAN DIE."

Behind him, Huma heard shouts and cries from the others. Before him, a figure hovered in mid-air with arms folded, smiling smugly from beneath a brown hood. He was tall, perhaps even taller than Huma, and slim, more like a well-trained knight than the mage he obviously was. Other than his reptilian smile, the floating spellcaster's face was little more than a shadow.

"Galan Dracos." Huma whispered the name to himself, but it was apparent the mage understood, for he cocked his head in acknowledgment of his identity.

"You are Huma. You look quite different when seen through human eyes. The one failing of the dreadwolves. One sees as they see."

Huma could barely restrain himself from ordering the silver dragon to charge the floating figure. Here was the living embodiment of all that was evil.

Galan Dracos was smiling broadly. "You are wasting your time, good knight. True, those lances are an advantage over the dragons, but you have—pardon, had—only twenty, and there are far too many dragons. See for yourself." The mage indicated the horizon behind him.

Huma squinted. A dark mass was coming up over the horizon. At first he thought it to be another spell of darkness. Then he saw that the mass was not one thing, but many large, flying creatures.

Dragons. The children of Takhisis. Hundreds of them.

Galan Dracos was still smiling when Huma turned to him. "With my dark lady's aid, I have summoned them from all over Krynn. Every last one. Black, red, white, green—all the different dragons. They have been flying for days to come here, and they have almost arrived."

Twenty lances—eighteen now. Eighteen against hundreds and hundreds of dragons. If only they had more lances . . .

"If you surrender now, there might still be a place for you. My mistress has been quite impressed with your ability to survive. If you would be willing to turn your talents to her, she would prove most—grateful." The renegade smiled. "You've really seen only her warrior persona. She has other—talents—of equal wonder."

Below him, the silver dragon gave an uncharacteristic hiss of fury, and Huma suddenly found himself closing in on the mage. Oddly, Dracos only laughed as the great leviathan leapt at him, jaws wide, claws foremost.

The jaws clamped harmlessly together.

"Illusion," Huma muttered.

A mocking laugh seemed to hang in the air. The group hovered uncertainly, awaiting instructions from Huma. He continued to stare at the spot where the illusion of Galan Dracos had floated.

Unable to stand the waiting anymore, an unidentified knight behind Huma cried, "We've lost!"

"We have not lost until the last knight is dead, Derrick," Bennett shouted at the man. He whispered to the gold dragon, who promptly moved him close enough so that he could speak to Huma without being overheard by the other riders. "What do we do now?"

Bennett asking him for guidance? If the whole situation had not been so tragic, Huma might have laughed. "Pull back. We must warn the Keep. With so few lances, we ought to circle Vingaard. Make the taking of it as costly a task as possible."

"You're giving up?"

"Not at all. For now, the defense of the Keep remains our best option." Huma turned to the others. "Back to Vingaard!"

Huma tried to hide his own disappointment as they turned to flee the coming horde. The situation seemed hopeless.

Something bright glittered in his eyes then, and at first Huma thought it was the reflection of the sun. Only, he suddenly realized, there was no sun. What glittered in his eyes was a light with no visible source.

As Huma's eyes focused on the tiny flickering light, it seemed to beckon. It was not exactly light, more a greenish glow. It reminded Huma of the glow emanating from the Sword of Tears.

The glow seemed to flutter earthward, and Huma hesitated. Huma drew the silver dragon's attention to the glittering object.

"What do you make of it?"

"A messenger of some sort, but I suspect its maker wears black. Ignore it and a let us return before things worsen. I—I do not like it here." She was acting strangely, Huma realized. She had been quiet and almost sullen since her attack on Dracos had failed. It had been Dracos's comment on his mistress's charms that had set her off, Huma realized. But why? Had the silver dragon been afraid that he would fall prey to such a false dream?

Huma took a deep breath—and shook his head. "Follow the light down."

"Huma—"

"DO IT." He had never spoken to her like that, but he did not think he could trust her reactions at this moment. The decision would be his.

"Huma!" Kaz called from ahead of them. Huma shook his head and pointed back toward the Keep, his face expressionless. The minotaur muttered something to Bolt, then turned to the others, to see what was happening. Kaz shouted something. Regardless, the massive easterner would wait with his dragon while the knight investigated whatever held his fascination.

With reluctance, the silver dragon began following the greenish glow downward. When they had reached the base of a particular hill, the greenish glow twinkled abruptly out of existence. The silver dragon landed, and Huma looked around expectantly.

"I come in peace, Knight of Solamnia." The voice was low and grated on the ears. Its owner was the image of a short, wiry man with an oversized head and narrow, weasel-like features. Not a stitch of hair grew on his head.

He wore a black robe.

"A trick! I told you!" The silver dragon reared up, ready to defend Huma. The Black Robe cowered, though there was no fear in his eyes. Huma shouted until his companion quieted. He was becoming disturbed with her new restiveness.

"Hear me out," grated the dark mage.

307

Huma stared sullenly at the Black Robe. "What do you have to say? I've already spoken with your master."

The magic-user made a face. "There you touch on the point of this meeting. The renegade who has styled himself our master. That carrion!"

"You both serve the same mistress do you not?"

"Listen carefully, Knight of Solamnia, for I've no way of knowing when the cur will notice my absence. We need your agreement."

"Mine?" Huma blinked. A Black Robe seeking aid from him?

"We know of you—through one who has worn many robes in his life and who even now wears another, in spirit if not in body."

"Magius!" The knight leaped on the vague description. "Where?"

The spellcaster raised a hand to silence him. "No time for that. Listen. We know now that if the Dragonqueen is victorious, we will be no more to her than you are. Dracos has already become her mortal voice, and his world will seem one born from the Abyss itself. You have seen his abominations. Would you like to see them made permanent? We wish to join with you. Better to die fighting than to be forever at her mercy—and she will have a special place for both our orders, mark me."

An offer of alliance . . . from a Black Robe? "How can I possibly believe you, one of her creatures?"

The mage straightened. "My first and foremost loyalty is to Nuitari, Dark Lord of Magic. We erred in believing we served him when we chose to serve—I will not call her his mother—let us say she who had given birth to him. Nuitari, though, cares for this world. That is why he, Lunitari, and—" The spellcaster hesitated at saying the name. "—even Solinari of the Light abandoned the struggle for Krynn and created the Orders of Sorcery as a separate entity, one that should work for the betterment of magic in the world. If Takhisis is victorious, Krynn will become little more than a cold rock among the stars. Our lord's dream will perish. We cannot have that."

"What do you want?"

"It is not so much what we want as what we can give."

"Give?" The silver dragon, silent through much of this exchange, narrowed her eyes and laughed sarcastically. "A Black Robe gives nothing but misery and death."

"An unjust falsehood. However, in this case, any misery and death we deal shall be aimed toward Dracos and his rag-tag band—but we need an opening."

"An opening? What do you mean?"

"I offer you this." The mage held out a bony hand. In his palm rested a tiny green sphere. "Unless you can get close enough, you will never see the castle of Galan Dracos; it lies on the edge between our plane and the Abyss. With this, you will be able to locate it."

The silver dragon scoffed. "Is there not the matter of your former mistress, the Dragonqueen? Is she to step idly aside while we charge the domain of her most trusted servant?"

The spellcaster indicated the Dragonlance. "I'm told that she has doubts about these. That she remains within the confines of the castle, near the path to the Abyss, because she fears the power of the Dragonlances."

"Preposterous! Huma, I won't let you . . ." The silver dragon turned as she spoke and froze at the look on his face. "Huma . . . you cannot believe this."

The knight ignored her. "What will you do when we strike, assuming we do?"

"Within the castle, the remainder of the Black Guard and those renegades who willingly follow Dracos will be your greatest threat. We shall deal with them. If possible, we shall strive to turn away the dragons as well."

"Madness!"

A shadow loomed above. All three looked up to see Kaz and Bolt hovering. The minotaur was shouting.

"Be quick! I see dragons scouting ahead."

The mage quickly turned back to Huma. "By Nuitari, I swear that my name is Gunther and that you may trust me. Take it!"

The Black Robe had sworn by his lord. For the followers of Nuitari, the penalties for breaking oaths were ofttimes fatal. Huma reached down and accepted the small green sphere.

"We are with you." The mage vanished abruptly. Huma kicked his mount gently. She spread her wings and began rising, relief evident on her features.

Kaz saw Huma's closed fist and blinked. "What is it?"

Huma stared at the approaching sea of destruction and thought how simple the spell of darkness seemed now. He glanced down at the hand that held the small sphere. "A desperate hope, at best, I think."

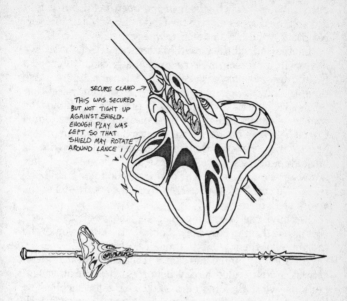

SECURE CLAMP

THIS WAS SECURED
BUT NOT TIGHT UP
AGAINST SHIELD.
ENOUGH PLAY WAS
LEFT SO THAT
SHIELD MAY ROTATE
AROUND LANCE !

Chapter 27

*"By the Triumvirate! How much more can they possi-*bly throw against us?"

Guy Avondale shook his head. "Evil always grows abundant when given the chance to take root. Melodramatic statement by my predecessor, but all too true."

They stood in the courtyard where the dragons and their riders had landed. The loss of two of their elite number disturbed the Grand Master, as did news of yet another wave of evil rising toward them.

"What of this deal with the followers of Nuitari, Huma?" asked Bennett. "Can they be trusted, in your opinion?"

After deep thought, Huma finally answered. "I believe so." He held up the tiny, emerald globe. It pulsated. "They gave this. Granted, it might be a means for them to draw us out so that we fall to them in the open field, but it was accompanied by an oath to the God of Dark Magic himself. No Black Robe with a desire to live will cross Nuitari."

"I agree," added the Grand Master. He sighed. "Well, we have quite a problem. We cannot possibly defend Vingaard for too long against a siege of this intensity. At the same time, it would be simple madness to go out and meet that horde." He hesitated, then added, "I offered the dragons the chance to depart if they felt the cause was lost here." Lord Oswal held up a hand to silence his anxious companions. "I had to ask. I believe, though, that they will stay with us until the end. We shall see. Where was I? Ah. We still do not know all about the east. The ogres are said to be stabilizing there. We can look for no help from the south—blast the elves! The north—water."

"We have the fake Dragonlances," interrupted Bennett. "Let us use them in one final assault. In the confusion of the foe, a few of them will buy time, if nothing else."

Lord Oswal grunted and stared at the lances of the riders. "I think insanity rules the day, but unless there are other suggestions, we shall combine the epic charge my nephew so desperately craves with a coordinated search for and attack on the castle of Galan Dracos." He looked around. No one, not even Lord Avondale, cleric and veteran soldier, could oppose the suicidal strategy.

Oswal shook his head. "If I am remembered at all, it will probably be as the Grand Master cursed for sending his men to the slaughter."

A horn sounded.

"They've spotted the first wave," someone said anxiously. Knights suddenly were moving all about. Horses were being readied and lined up. Row upon row of knights formed. Pikemen, lancers, bowmen, each and every type moved to assure that there was no disorder in this hour of peril.

"Break out the footmen's lances!" shouted the Grand Master to one of his aides. The man saluted hastily and went to inform the squires, whose job it would be.

Huma wanted to order the remaining Dragonlancers into battle formation, but Lord Oswal prevented him. "No. If you hope to break through and make your way to the mountains, you'll have to go when the dragons are engaged."

"But the ground forces—"

"Will receive as much protection as they can get from the dragons. I—"

The horn sounded again, a different note this time.

"What in the name of Kiri-Jolith is that?" The Grand Master and the others hurried toward the front, where Lord Hawkeye was in direct command.

"Lord Hawkeye." The ruling Knight of the Order of the Crown whirled.

"Grand Master, they've come to a halt, just in sight. Even the dragons have stopped. It's as if they're waiting for something. I've put everybody on standby."

"Very good." Huma held his breath until the Grand Master relaxed the evident strain on his face. "They are going to play with our minds. They want us to come charging out to meet them. The abysmal fools. We can't be tricked into such an easy death!

"Let *them* sweat a little. Let *them* wait. When Galan Dracos or his mistress runs out of patience, then we will make our move."

A gold dragon fluttered from a spire down to the courtyard. He was old, even for a dragon, for his hide was cracked and covered with ancient battle scars. There was no weakness in his form, though.

"I conveyed to the others your earlier offer." The voice was deep and rumbling, a bit like the earth elemental that had served Magius.

The knights became silent.

Lord Oswal had hesitated, but now he asked, "And what was their response?"

The dragon gave him a look that could only be described as I-told-you-so. "We will not abandon you. Without Vingaard Keep, the outposts will not stand. This is the place of decision. Vingaard falls, then Ergoth falls, then the elfin lands and dwarven lands fall. The Queen rules all."

"I only sought to keep the cause of Paladine alive if we failed here."

"The cause for good will always live. Even Takhisis must

know that."

Despite the activity around them, it was as if all sound had ceased for the group. Huma understood that the dragons had committed themselves to a battle to the death. For the sake of their human allies. For the sake of their belief in the teachings of Paladine.

The Grand Master did something unprecedented then. He went down on one knee and paid homage, not to that particular dragon, but to all of its kind. With the way to freedom open, they were remaining.

"Thank you. I hoped—but one never knows."

The gold dragon gave a majestic nod, spread his lengthy wings, and departed skyward. The Grand Master watched quietly, then turned at a new sound. Squires bearing the simulated Dragonlances for footmen rushed toward the assembled knights. Huma stared at the lances that were removed from the boxes. How they glowed! It was as if . . .

"Milord!" Huma surprised himself as he interrupted the Grand Master.

"Yes, Huma?"

"If you'll excuse me, there are some things I must prepare."

"Then go."

"Kaz." Huma pulled the minotaur aside. "Retrieve one of the lances the squires are passing out and compare it to one of the real Dragonlances."

"What—" The minotaur got no further.

"I'll explain when I return." Huma rushed away, leaving the minotaur to puzzle over his comrade's request.

The smithy itself was only a short distance away, just out of sight of the Grand Master and the others.

Even as Huma approached it, the massive wooden doors swung forward and Huma stepped back quickly, coming face-to-face with a stranger.

"It would be best to avoid standing near doors if you do not wish to injure yourself." The newcomer had silver-black hair and a narrow, long head. His eyes seemed to burn for a moment, and Huma was reminded of the figure who had stared at Gwyneth the one night when they had walked the courtyard. She had been afraid of that man. This could not be the same person, though. This one was taller and thinner. But the eyes . . .

"You are Huma of the Lance," the stranger decided. His eyes were piercing.

"I am Huma." The knight was no bard's hero that he should carry a title such as that.

"The master smith has been busy, but I think he can spare a bit of time for you." The smile was odd, so alien that Huma shivered. What was he reminded of?

Voices carried from inside. Both were familiar, but one especially so.

"—Can you give me no advice?"

"—I have been away from the world of men much too long—and my time on Krynn is almost done. Best you should seek one of your own."

"—None of them understand! How am I to tell him that I am not what he thinks I am? That I have flown with him nearly every day without him realizing it? Do you think he could love me if he knew I—we—"

There was little light, save around the forge, and that only served to silhouette the two figures standing there.

"Gwyneth?"

The one figure, female, turned at his voice, uttered a gasp, and fled through the rear doorway. Huma made to follow, but the remaining figure blocked his way and greeted him heartily.

"Huma! How good it is to see you one last time!" Duncan Ironweaver lifted him high, shook him like a babe, and set him down again. Huma glanced behind the towering smith, but there was no sign of where Gwyneth had gone.

"You actually thought I'd leave you with only twenty lances? Lad, you surprise me!"

"Then they are real! It isn't my imagination!"

"Not hardly! I had many, many more than twenty, but not situated near. Besides, you would never have been able to bring them all back. Too many of her spies about. Besides," he smiled, "I needed the trip."

"And the smithy . . ."

Duncan Ironweaver indicated the work area. "They were

in need of a master armorer and weaponry expert. I bent the truth a little and said you had summoned me from the south—which, in a sense, you did. They were understandably impressed with my work and let me take over. Soon it was just me and my assistants."

"It's—it's incredible!" All this time, real Dragonlances were being created in the smithy.

The huge smith tapped his chest. "You've proved to them that the Dragonlances work, Huma. I don't think even your illustrious Grand Master realizes just how many of those men believe in the lances."

Huma's mind began to spin. "Saddles! We'll need more saddles."

"Khildith!"

For the first time, Huma noticed the smith's assistants. An elf, a human, and the dwarf who was evidently Khildith, as it was he who stepped forward.

"Master Ironweaver?"

"Are the saddles ready?"

The dwarf broke into a grin much like the smith's. The dwarf was well-whiskered and, though he appeared quite ancient, moved with the speed and grace of one in his prime. "More than enough to go around."

"Fine, fine." Duncan Ironweaver walked over to Huma and put a hand on his shoulder. The knight felt himself politely but forcibly being steered away.

"Master Ironweaver. One question. Gwyneth—"

"That's between you and her." The change in expression on the smith's face was enough to quiet Huma. "Remember, you have the lances now. Make use of them."

Huma was out the door before he could say goodbye. The one-armed smith flexed his mechanical limb. "Paladine be with you, lad. Even the lances cannot help you if you truly lose faith."

The horn sounded a new warning. Huma bolted. All other questions receded in the face of battle. The Dragonlances were real!

Kaz met him, carrying a footman's lance in each hand. "Is this some trick, Huma? I'd swear—"

"They're real! They're all real! Where's Lord Oswal?"

The minotaur used one of the lances as a pointer. "On the wall. He insisted on seeing it for himself."

Huma turned and caught sight of Bennett organizing the riders. Huma hailed him. Bennett barked out one last order and then joined him.

"What is it?" Every muscle in the face of the Grand Master's nephew was alive. Bennett was in his element and unconsciously reveling in it.

"The Dragonlances—they're all real!"

The other knight looked at him quizzically. "Of course they're real."

Huma hesitated. Bennett had never been told the original plan. No one at that time had known that Duncan Ironweaver was going to appear.

Bennett waited silently until Huma at last let the tale come tumbling out. The Knight of the Sword's visage slowly froze into an unreadable mask. When Huma finally finished, the two stared at one another.

The predatory eyes of Bennett flickered to where the rank and file of the knighthood had gathered to await commands. His eyes quickly returned to Huma. "Was there anything else? I have much more to do."

The flat, toneless words shocked Huma. He had expected anger and surprise, but nothing? "Bennett—"

His sentence was cut off by an unblinking look from the other. Bennett indicated the knights around them. "Does what you say make any real difference, Huma? Whether the Dragonlances existed or not, these men would still be readying for battle—despite the probable outcome. I would be first among them, as I think you would be, too. Any damage we create, any strength we cost them, even in defeat, is a victory of sorts." He took a breath and some of the fanaticism faded from his eyes. "It does please me to have it reaffirmed that we will not go naked into the maw, but that is all. Tell them that the Dragonlances are of no use; they will still march out and give the enemy their all. Would you yourself act any different?"

The faith Bennett had always displayed in the past took on new meaning to Huma now. He knew that the other knight was correct in his assumptions, especially where

Huma himself was concerned. No matter how terrible the odds, one of the first knights at the forefront would have been Huma.

"Now, if you will excuse me, there is much that still needs to be done. You should find my uncle up there." Bennett indicated a portion of the front wall to their right. "I think he'll be happy to hear your news."

Bennett walked off, shouting orders as he went and acting as if the conversation had never happened. Huma stirred and hurried off toward the walls.

At the top of the wall, the Grand Master was standing on an observation ledge.

Lord Oswal heard him approach and glanced his way. When he saw it was Huma, he said, "There's movement over here. Something is forming in the sky."

It was only a small blot in an overcast sky, far beyond the oncoming army, but once sighted, it held the viewer's attention as nothing else in the heavens could. Huma felt as if a part of him were being wrenched toward that blot, as if his soul itself was being drawn to it. He caught his breath and tore his eyes away.

"What is it?"

The Grand Master shook his head. "I don't know, but it drives the dragons and ogres toward us, I think."

Huma recalled his reason for coming here and quickly informed Oswal of what he had discovered.

The elder knight acted even before Huma had finished. To his aides he shouted, "Alert all commanders! The dragons! Someone must alert the dragons! Have the ranks ready themselves!"

Turning back toward the oncoming horde, Lord Oswal shook his head. Even as they watched, the dragons of darkness were beginning to pull ahead of the ground forces. They would be here much too soon.

"Milord," Huma said urgently, "let me take the original riders. We will delay the enemy while the others prepare. Send them up in groups of twenty, but have them wait above the Keep until their numbers are great. Then send them out, followed by the footmen. If we gain control of the air, the ground will also be ours."

"You'll be dead!"

The younger knight hesitated—only for a second. "Then I will have given my life over to Paladine, as any knight should do."

Oswal nodded wearily. Huma hurried back down, wondering just how long it would take to gather the others. To his surprise, however, he found them all waiting, riders seated and lances at the ready. In the short time they had been together, the group had become one entity. The silver dragon was there, too, waiting for Huma's orders.

In the deadly calm that can occur before battle, Huma stood before his assembled band and explained the danger of their mission and the likely outcome. He expected opposition, voices of dry logic that would tear down his plan. Instead, he was stunned to discover that they believed in what he proposed, though their lives might be forfeit. Bennett nodded in approval and even some of the dragons indicated their agreement. Oddly, only his own mount gave no response. She appeared withdrawn, though she also made no protest when he climbed onto her back. When he gave the signal to depart, she obeyed with speed and coordination, if not enthusiasm.

Once in the air, Kaz and Bolt edged closer. "We shall make them remember us well, before we perish. Mark me on that, Huma."

"We must seek out Dracos," Huma replied. "He is the key to everything."

"He and his dark mistress."

Huma nodded.

When they were high up, Lord Avondale, who was peering to the southwest, suddenly pointed. "Look there!" he shouted. "Do you see anything?"

Bolt was the first to reply. "It is another army. The enemy grow even stronger!"

Avondale laughed at that. "It is we," he shouted, "who grow even stronger!"

It was the northern Ergothian army. Knowing that only defeat and slavery awaited them if the knighthood fell, they were risking all in the hope of making a lightning strike at the foe from the rear. That they had not been noticed thus far by the servants of Takhisis was good fortune, indeed.

"How long before the others will be aloft?" shouted Avondale.

"Not long." It was Bennett who shouted the response, for which Huma was grateful. He would not have wanted to guarantee anything at this point.

Even as they spoke, the group was moving closer to intercept the first of the dragon scouts. They kept in tight formation, knowing too well that individually they would be cut down.

It seemed that the dark dragons realized their intentions, for some moved accordingly. Others, however, were obviously of different opinions as to what the knights were capable of and broke away from the rest, speeding toward their enemies. Huma could not help smiling briefly. As the evil dragons bared teeth and claw and challenged the newcomers, he realized that they did not believe in the strength of the Dragonlances.

All but a few of the attackers perished in minutes; most of them skewered themselves on the lances of Huma and his companions. Two more died before Huma signaled for his band to allow the survivors to escape. They would bring their terror to the other dragons who had waited.

Huma glanced briefly at his comrades. Kaz was flushed and full of life; Bolt could barely restrain himself from chasing the survivors. Lord Avondale stared toward his army. Buoron was quiet and almost expressionless. His arm had healed, and he was keeping the Dragonlance as steady as he could.

Scores of manned dragons came to meet them. Red, black, green, and blue. White dragons also charged, but they were without riders and Huma suspected they were to be fodder, for they worked more by animal cunning than intelligence, and this environment was not suited for them at all. Though smaller than the other dragons, they could be deadly, and their presence would buy an advantage for the Dragonqueen.

Below, the course of the two armies had altered. The Ergothians were forming a long, wide line, and the southern portion of the ogre forces was turning to meet this new threat. The northern half, having yet to learn of the attack, began to pull away, leaving the middle to scatter about as warriors sought proper orders. Confusion seemed to be spreading.

Now! Huma shrieked in his head. We should be attacking now! Of course, the knights in the Keep could not see the Ergothian army. But they most certainly saw the splintering of the ogres and realized that something to their benefit was occurring. How long before they reacted?

Then, the tiny group of lancers met the first of the seemingly endless waves of foes and there was no time to think of anything but survival.

At first, dragons seemed to appear and disappear each time Huma blinked. There were screams all about him. It became as black as the Abyss and as bright as the sun, for the dragons unleashed their various magics, and riders, some of whom were clerics or sorcerers, added their own powers to the battle.

As the silver dragon dodged a blow from an attacker, Huma saw one of the lancers and his mount fall prey to a band of at least six dragons. Rider and mount vanished beneath the terrible power of the creatures, and it was all Huma could do not to scream at the brave deaths. In the chaos, he could not identify who had perished.

They were becoming separated. Kaz and Bolt still remained with Huma and the silver dragon. At one point, the knight heard the powerful voice of Guy Avondale as he shouted something.

A fearsome black bearing one of the Black Guard came diving from above. Huma shouted at the silver dragon, but she was hopelessly engaged with a red dragon who was pushing the Dragonlance deeper and deeper into his own shoulder, too furious to even realize it. The knight pulled out his sword, useless against such a dragon, and prepared himself for the impact.

Suddenly there was a silver streak, and a sleek dragon intercepted the black. There was a rider on the silver dragon's back, and Huma realized it was Buoron. The other knight already had been struck more than once; blood stained his armor and his mount.

Pain! Huma fell back as something sent shockwaves through his left leg. He stared down at blood flowing from a deep wound. The leg twitched and the shockwaves continued to assault his mind. Through tear-covered eyes, he caught sight of an ogre straddling a dragon. With strength beyond that of a human, the ogre had attacked with an ax and his blow had been lucky.

Huma deflected another blow from the ogre, but felt himself unable to concentrate. The pain demanded too much.

To his relief, the silver dragon was at last able to push away her own adversary. The red, weakened by the loss of so much blood from so many wounds, fluttered helplessly toward the ground, taking his hapless rider with him.

"Huma!"

It took him a few moments to realize the silver dragon was calling to him. She looked at him with eyes filled with terrible fear—and not for herself. He had seen eyes like that before, but—

His thoughts were interrupted by a renewal of cries from all around. His first thought was that this was the end, that more dragons were coming to join the ones already attacking the small band.

He was wrong. The dragons he saw as he looked up and around were gold, silver—all the bright metallic colors of the dragons of Paladine. There were more than one hundred, and each had a rider and a knight, armed with a lance that gleamed brightly and aimed true. Dragonlances.

There was mass confusion among the dark dragons. If they had been told anything, they had been told that there were but a handful of Dragonlances. The nearest of the dragons perished without raising claws in defense, so disbelieving were they.

Huma put a hand to his brow and came away with blood—his own. He wondered when that had happened and how.

Thinking of injuries, he again looked down at his leg. The blood was flowing freely still, and he knew he would pass out soon if he didn't do something to stop it. The silver dragon began to pull away from the fighting.

More and more dragons were coming from the Keep. How many Dragonlances had the smith made?

The silver dragon flew as if pursued by the Dark Queen herself. She would glance back in his direction every now and then, that same fearful look in her eyes. He frowned and clamped his hands against the leg wound in order to stanch the flow.

At last, they flew over the Keep walls, narrowly avoiding another set of lancers rising, and she brought him to where other survivors of his band were being treated.

"Take him from me!" The dragon's voice was so commanding, so harsh, that no one dallied. Huma lost sight of her and the world as a whole.

When he awoke, Gwyneth was over him, cleaning the wound, touching it with her hands in a way that deadened the pain. He could almost feel power flowing from her fingertips. Her face was pale and covered partially by her hair as she leaned over the leg.

Huma's eyes wandered. They were on a hill, away from the fighting, but not so far that they could no longer hear the sounds of battle. Avondale was there, his left side a bloody mess. Kaz was nowhere to be seen. Of the original band, only nine remained. Bennett, uninjured but looking as if he and his armor had been dragged across the plains, was staring at Gwyneth with an emotion somewhere between revulsion and fascination. His eyes briefly met Huma's, then turned swiftly away.

"Buoron is dead, Huma," Oswal's nephew finally said, his gaze still on Gwyneth. "The last I saw, he and his dragon took on that black one to save you. They perished."

This last shook not only Huma, but Gwyneth as well. She removed her hands from the wound and cried in them. Huma reached out and touched her arm.

"It's not Buoron she weeps for—" Bennett was having trouble finding the right words.

"Let it be, Bennett." Guy Avondale tried to rise.

"Huma!" Bolt flew into sight, with Kaz waving his battle ax in greeting. Both dragon and minotaur were covered with scratches and minor wounds, but neither seemed to be weakened by them. Huma glanced at them only momentarily, then his eyes returned to Gwyneth. She looked away. He continued to stare at her, even when he finally responded to Bennett's statement.

"What do you mean, Bennett? What are you trying to say?"

The hawklike features of Bennett swerved toward the Ergothian cleric/commander. "Everyone else saw it. Why hide it? If she cannot tell him, someone surely will. He needs to know. I know how he feels about her."

"It is between them!" Avondale was furious.

"Stop it."

The words were from Gwyneth. She rose, all the while staring at Huma. Her arms hung limply by her side.

Avondale slumped back suddenly. He glanced at Bennett and Kaz. "You two, help me up. A chill is coming over me. I need to move somewhere less open."

Reluctantly, Kaz and Bennett helped him rise, and the three moved off.

Gwyneth finally spoke. "I weep for Buoron. I weep for any who fall fighting the Dragonqueen."

"As have I."

She tried to smile. "I weep especially for the dragon Buoron rode, the large silver one."

Brother to his own, Huma recalled. Why would Gwyneth cry so for this one dragon?

She stared moodily around. The area had been emptied. As Huma looked puzzled, her features softened. "Before I tell you this, know that I love you, Huma. I would never do anything to harm you."

"I love you too." The words seemed to flow so easily all of a sudden.

"I think you may change your mind," she said enigmatically.

Huma did not have time to ask what she meant, for Gwyneth was suddenly aglow—almost like the Dragonlances. As he watched in horrid fascination, her face elongated and her nose and mouth grew into a toothy snout. Huma thought of witchery and rose to help her, but his leg was not well yet and the head wound had not been salved. He slumped to the ground.

Her long, slim arms grew even longer—and more muscular. The small hands twisted and turned, becoming terrible claws. She fell onto all fours and seemed to grow and grow and grow. Something wiggled and moved on her back. She was no longer remotely human, and what she did resemble caused the knight to shake his head again and again and again.

Her garments vanished—to Paladine knows where—but she had no more need of them in her present form. The odd wiggling and moving on her backside came from two great humps that burst open, revealing batlike wings. They spread wide, and in moments the transformation was complete. The thing that had been Gwyneth stepped forward, tall, straight—and frightened.

It was a dragon—a silver dragon.

His own.

Chapter 28

The silver dragon's eyes were downcast. "Huma, in Paladine's name, please say something!"

The voice was unmistakably Gwyneth's. He looked up into that reptilian face and saw the fear in it—fear that he would reject her. Huma could not say what was truly going through his own mind. Everything seemed to be tumbling down around him. This could not be Gwyneth. Could it?

"You saw my brother that night—as you saw the other who served Duncan Ironweaver—dragons both, but in human form. We admire you so, Huma, you and your kind. In your short lives, you accomplish so much."

Huma said nothing. Involuntarily, he pulled himself slightly farther from her. It was not out of fear, but out of confusion.

She did not interpret it that way, and her words spilled out faster. Even as she spoke, her form reverted. The wings shriveled. Her four limbs smoothed and twisted until they were once more human and she was able to stand. Her body shrank rapidly, as if the huge form were melting before his horrified eyes. The face grew smaller and rounder and the great maw of the dragon dwindled down to the full, perfect lips. Hair of shimmering silver came sprouting from the dragon's head, cascading down the back. Huma nearly fled. The metamorphosis he had witnessed could not be real.

"My brother told me what I did not see at first, that I had fallen prey to what has happened to only a few others in the past. I had lived among you for so long that I had come to love as you do."

"Why?"

She frowned, unsure exactly what he was asking, and then replied, "You embody the very beliefs of Paladine. You are brave, kind, never hateful. I came to love you for you, nothing else."

"Ah, the happy lovers."

The cold, triumphant voice woke Huma from his stupor. It could not be, not here . . .

Galan Dracos, looking much as he had earlier, materialized before the knight and the dragon maiden and smiled. "I would have made my presence known sooner, but I did not care to interrupt such a beautiful scene."

Gwyneth gave a cry that no human could have been capable of and would have struck him, but Huma was already moving and barred her way. The knight succeeded in taking only a few steps before his leg gave out and he fell to the ground. Only then did he remember that the figure before him was an illusion. He silently cursed his own stupidity.

The renegade laughed. "I've come to add to your miseries, Huma. I've come to repay you for the loss of Crynus. I must admit, his insanity grew unpredictable in the end. But he was my best commander and I shall miss him. Pity."

Kaz and Bennett, alerted by the voice of one they knew all too well, came racing around the corner. The illusory Dracos raised a hand and they halted, as if striking a wall.

"An eye for an eye, you pathetic mortal." Dracos raised his hands, and something began to materialize before them. It was not until it was nearly fully formed that Huma recognized it.

"Magius!"

They had tortured him. His face was a bloody pulp, and one eye was swollen shut. His robes were in tatters, and Huma was surprised to see that they were white, not red. One arm was bent at an impossible angle, and neither leg seemed in the least functional. Magius forced himself up with his good arm.

"Hu—Huma." Several of his teeth were missing. "I was right—in the end."

Dracos smiled indulgently. "He babbles like that occasionally."

With great effort, Magius turned around and spat on the garments of the renegade. Galan Dracos became furious and stretched an open palm toward his captive. Magius screamed as his body rippled from the renegade's torture.

Gwyneth moved forward. "Test your spells against me, Galan Dracos."

The phantasm smiled nastily. "I have more power than you could believe, but I do not choose to use it now. I have merely come to show Huma the foolishness of his dreams of victory."

Huma rolled forward, desperately trying to reach his tortured friend.

Magius shook his battered head. "Don't, Huma. There's no reason anymore. Defeat Dracos. That's all I ask."

Dracos raised both hands toward Magius. "Your time is up, my friend."

With a gesture, the renegade sent shafts of green light at his captive. The shafts seemed to pass through Magius, and he screamed as if each were a steel lance. He wavered just a moment, then toppled forward to lie in a heap, very real, at Huma's feet. His death was no illusion. Huma shouted and struggled to move. The others stepped forward, but Dracos was already fading out of existence.

"The price of defiance, Knight of Solamnia. The price you all will be paying before long unless you embrace my mistress."

"No, renegade," the knight said, raising himself high. "If anyone pays a price, it will be you."

He could not tell if Dracos heard him, for the last was said to empty air.

Bennett and Kaz stumbled forward. The minotaur was the first to speak. "Huma! Are you all right?"

Without answering, Huma looked intensely at the crumpled form of Magius.

"If you seek vengeance, Huma, I will gladly stand at your side." Kaz had never cared for the magic-user, but he had, in the end, gained respect for him.

Huma shook his head. "Vengeance is not the way." He raised an arm. "Help me over to him."

They did. It was odd, but now Magius looked at peace. He certainly had never looked this calm in life.

Putting the mage's head down softly, Huma gritted his teeth and rose by his own power. Bennett and Kaz waited to assist him, but he waved them off. When he finally stood, Huma turned to face the three.

"I need your help—all three of you. It is time that the balance be restored. It is time that Galan Dracos and his dark lady learn that where there is evil, there must also be a balance with good. Magius was living proof of that. In his time, he wore the robes of all three Orders, ending with the white of Solinari. From evil to good, the pendulum swings both ways. It is time it swung to our side."

"You intend to seek out the castle?" asked Bennett.

"I do. I ask your help and that of any surviving from our band. If you hesitate, I will understand, for it is surely suicide."

Kaz seemed ready to burst with indignation. "If you expect me to turn from any battle, especially this one, you know nothing of my people. I may not be a Knight of Solamnia—" he ignored the sharp look from Bennett "—but I know when I must fight. I will join you."

Bennett nodded. "I will come. I am sure those who can still ride will say the same."

"Give me a few minutes alone, then. Bennett, please tell the Grand Master what has occurred here. I would like him to give Magius a proper funeral no matter what occurs."

"As you wish."

Both the minotaur and the knight departed. Huma stared at the body of Magius, remembering simpler times. He was interrupted by a female voice.

"What of me, Huma? We were interrupted by this tragedy. I do not ask for a response to my feelings; I do not even hope that you can return my love. I will say this: In the matter of Galan Dracos and Krynn, I am still your partner. When you fly into the maw of the Dragonqueen, it will be I who will carry you." She waited for a response. Huma could say nothing. "I will be waiting, ready when you are."

He heard footsteps then. They faded until he could hear nothing more. Huma did not move from the spot until clerics from the temple came to carry Magius to a place where his body could rest.

Huma limped toward the group. All of the original members who could still ride were ready. There were eight men in all, and eight dragon steeds. Lord Avondale could not accompany them because of his wounds, but he was there to see them go.

Huma spoke first to Avondale. "Any word on your men?"

"Bogged down, but still very much alive. Your Grand Master has released the ground forces. They are advancing. The ogres have ground to a halt."

Huma nodded numbly. He heard only part of what the Ergothian was saying. The renegade's killing of Magius had been a desperate act, an attempt to break Huma's spirit. Indeed, he felt broken and confused as he entered into this, his important and shining hour.

"Wish us luck, cleric."

"I'll do better than that." Avondale reached up to his own neck and tugged on a chain. As he pulled it over his head, a medallion, buried under his armor and clothing, came into view. "Lean forward."

Huma did. Avondale placed the medallion around his neck. "You are more deserving of this than I."

The knight took the medallion in one hand and gazed at

it. A representation of Paladine stared back at him. The medallion seemed comfortably warm in his hand. "My— gratitude."

"Do not thank me. Find Dracos!"

Huma nodded and rose. The others were all mounted. Huma walked over to the silver dragon. He started to say something to her, thought better of it, and mounted. Someone handed him his lance. He noted that the footman's lance was again strapped onto the silver dragon.

On his signal, they rose into the air, determined to make their way past the enemy and seek out the stronghold of the mage. Huma held up the small, greenish sphere and concentrated. He willed it to lead them to the citadel.

The sphere glowed brightly, rose from his hand, and began to fly toward the mountains in the west.

The eight pairs followed.

The battle was turning into a slaughter. The dragons, spurred by their fear of their mistress, charged again and again at the lancers. They were repulsed each time with heavy losses.

More than a fifth of the lancers and their mounts had perished in the meantime, overwhelmed by sheer numbers. The ground forces also had suffered, especially at first. Once they learned of the effectiveness of their lances, however, casualties dwindled. Soon, no dragon dared come near. Their magic and breath weapons still rained chaos on the knights, but there was a limit to those powers, and many of the Dark Queen's children became easy prey for flying lancers, so greatly had they exhausted themselves.

Despite their intentions, Huma and his band could not avoid the battle completely; it was too widespread by now. More than once, they swooped down to help a remnant that was in danger of being overrun. The children of Takhisis were in no way defeated, though. They had formed into groups and were charging whatever point seemed weakest. Already, many had broken through and were heading toward the Keep. They would be in for a surprise, Huma knew. The Grand Master was no novice. More than fifty knights and dragons were ready to fly at a moment's notice.

Below them, the ogres and their allies were a mass of confusion. They were now being forced to fight a war on two fronts, for the Ergothians had found good ground and were harrying the southern flank with great success.

The sky suddenly became dark all around them, and Huma and his companions were filled with a sense of terrible, oncoming evil.

Lightning bolts moved with terrifying accuracy, striking dragons and riders and leaving few remains. The advancing Dragonlancers faltered, were pushed back. The children of the Dark Queen began to fight with new energy.

Huma slammed a fist against the lance shield. How did one fight a storm? No mage had created this. He put a hand over his eyes. If he had a physical target, then he might be able to do something, but what could even the Dragonlance do against the elements?

His question was answered even as he entered the heart of the storm. The presence of evil was so great that Huma could almost picture the Dragonqueen before him, hurling the rain and lightning toward him. A flash of lightning struck close behind him, and Huma heard a scream. By now, he could not tell whether it was rain or tears that dripped down his face.

The Dragonlance suddenly burst into such brilliance that he was forced to close his eyes momentarily. From the shouts around him, he gathered that the same thing was occurring to his companions. When his eyes had recovered, Huma dared open them—and continued opening them until they were wide with disbelief.

The storm clouds were dispersing. Rapidly. To his shock, Huma found the sun shining bright upon his armor. Was that right? By all calculations, it would be late day. The sun should be setting, yet here it was, high in the sky.

No one on either side needed a more dramatic sign of which way the battle was going. The dragons of darkness lost their momentum, backtracked, and began to retreat from the fight in ones and twos. Even the powerful fear of their mistress was not sufficient to deter them. Paladine was proving to be the greater of gods.

The ogres, though, fought with near-berserk fury. The

dragons might flee to fight another day, but not the ogres and their human allies. There was nowhere they could hide that the knights could not hunt them down. For them, it was victory or nothing.

Kaz and Bennett rode to each side and a little back of Huma. Huma fingered the medallion given to him by Lord Avondale. The warmth remained strong and, on impulse he leaned forward and touched it to the Dragonlance.

A surge of strength channeled through him.

The mountains were directly ahead. Somehow, the green sphere had stayed with them all that time, unaffected by the storm or the Dragonqueen's fury. Huma became alert for any sign of a castle. There was no telling how near they might be, and the castle certainly would not be undefended.

Suddenly, a burst of energy shot from one of the smaller peaks to the southwest. Huma turned to face it, hoping the lance would break its power, when the burst was met by another. The two canceled one another out. Huma's gaze shot to the source of the second burst. Even as he watched, the groups on the two peaks began to battle in earnest. After a few seconds of watching, Huma understood. He smiled grimly and turned to Kaz.

"The Black Robes are making their move! They've turned on Galan Dracos and his band!" He repeated the message to Bennett, who passed it on to the stalwarts behind them.

A dozen red dragons, each bearing a rider, rose suddenly from within the mountains. The riders were all clad in black and—to the horror of Huma and his companions—each had a Dragonlance.

They had, no doubt, lifted them from the dead. He should have recognized the danger, Huma decided. A lance was just as deadly no matter whose hand controlled its path.

They outnumbered Huma's band two-to-one.

Bennett and the others came up alongside Huma. The apparent commander of the guardsmen, cloaked and wearing a visored helmet topped with two wicked horns, signaled to the others. In alternating order, the red dragons rose or fell, creating two levels. Their strategy was immediately apparent. Whatever group Huma's men chose to attack, they would be left open to a second attack from the others.

When the red dragons neared, Huma lifted both arms wide and then brought his hands together as if he were clapping.

The knights split into two groups, one to the left, one to the right.

The maneuver spread confusion through their opponents. The evil dragons hesitated, then their order began to crumble as each moved to protect its own flank from the deadly lances. Clustered together as they were, this proved more detrimental. Two red dragons collided with one another. Huma skewered one hapless creature. The others moved in. Speed was of the essence in this strike.

The knights wasted no time or opportunity. Ducking a blast of flame from one ferocious red, the silver dragon brought Huma and the lance directly toward its underbelly. The Dragonlance sank in without resistance, and the red dragon quivered. The rider, realizing his lance was useless at this angle, frantically pulled at a bow on his back. He did not have time. His dragon convulsed and, to Huma's surprise, burst into flames, turning both man and leviathan into ash.

Huma had a brief glimpse of the commanding guardsman as the ebony-armored figure caught an unsuspecting gold dragon in the neck with one of the plundered lances. The dragon shook violently, pulling himself free from the Dragonlance. The wound was deep. The gold dragon thrashed around, throwing his rider free. The wound seemed to erupt. There was nothing Huma could do for the helpless rider, for now the guardsman was turning his dragon toward him.

The blood of the gold dragon dripped from the point of the lance, and Huma briefly noted that the weapon was stained, something that had never occurred before. Then both dragons were roaring, claws bared and jaws wide open in a terrifying display.

Silver dragon met red dragon. Both lances were in perfect position to strike, and Huma saw no way to prevent the death of Gwyneth—as he was finally able to think of her. As the lances thrust forward, he uttered a single-word prayer to

Paladine.

The point of the stolen Dragonlance touched the right side of the silver dragon's unprotected chest—then slid off the side and shot past her, puncturing the lower membrane of her wing.

Huma's lance continued through, piercing so deeply that it came out the back of the red dragon. Because of that, Gwyneth was forced to grapple with the dying creature so that they could free themselves. Her damaged wing made the task all the more difficult.

The black-suited rider was no stranger to opportunity, and he unstrapped himself from the dying red dragon and crawled quickly forward. The silver dragon, busy with her counterpart, did not notice him until he had jumped onto her and behind Huma. By then, there was nothing she could do that would not imperil Huma.

The attacker gripped her shoulder tightly and reached back to a sheath behind him. The sword he pulled from there was a massive, wicked weapon with tiny barbs all along the edges.

Huma's own blade seemed woefully inadequate, but, lacking anything else, he turned and met the guardsman head on. The two weapons struck together, and the knight's was almost pulled from his grip as it caught on the barbs.

With a tremendous effort, the silver dragon at last freed herself from the massive corpse. Even as it spiraled toward the ground, she sought a way to buck the ebony-armored attacker without losing Huma as well.

Meanwhile, neither fighter had gained any advantage. Secure in the saddle, Huma was on a more stable base, but he could not turn easily. The guardsman, straddling the lower half of the dragon, was forced to stay his ground or risk losing his grip. He had no way to secure himself.

The knight tugged violently at the bonds securing him to his saddle and crawled forward to give himself some breathing room while he turned around. The other chopped with his jagged blade, but missed. Huma, now facing his opponent, reached across the saddle and struck a blow at the guardsman's side. His adversary parried the attack and caught Huma's blade in the barbs. They struggled, each attempting to wrest the other's sword away.

This new struggle proved to be a fatal error for the guardsman. Huma's position allowed him to use both hands; the other could not. The dark knight reached up with his other hand in order to save his grip on his sword—and lost his balance, slipping from the silver dragon's back. He tried making a grab for her wings, but they moved out of reach, and the Black Guard commander could only clutch wildly at the air before plummeting out of sight, screaming.

Huma looked upward. Kaz and Bolt were looking down at the scene with mutual expressions of triumph.

Surprisingly, the Dragonlancers had lost only the one man in the battle. Huma gave thanks that no more than that had perished, but wondered what else lay ahead.

Then, the air began to shimmer all about them and Huma, strapping himself back in the saddle, thought for a moment that they were again under attack. The shimmering was disorienting, and a great chill accompanied it. The entire mountain range looked distorted, as if they were flying in several directions at once. There was nothing Huma could do but hold on tight and pray that it would end soon.

Perhaps Paladine had heard him or perhaps they had finally reached the other side of whatever spell Dracos had cast, for the strange disturbance suddenly ceased and when Huma opened his eyes again, the mountains were as they had been.

Save for one additional feature—a tall, massive black castle perched on the side of a jagged peak.

The citadel of Galan Dracos, renegade and servant of Takhisis, the Dragonqueen.

The place of final victory—or everlasting defeat.

Chapter 29

The castle stood like a neglected sore upon the northernmost side of the ravaged peak. Blacker than the night, blacker than the ebony armor of the guardsmen, it could only truly be compared to the Abyss of Huma's dreams, so foul was it. Huma wondered if perhaps he should have waited until he could have gathered more lancers. Yet there was no turning back. The Dragonqueen had to be confronted.

"What now, Huma?" The silver dragon looked up at him. There was death in her eyes—not for him, but rather for herself. He could see that she had given up all hope of becoming his. The knight wanted to say something, anything, but he could not. Not to that reptilian visage, so alien. He felt ashamed.

"We find a way in. We find Galan Dracos."

Seen closely, the castle was even more obscene. It looked to be rotting before their very eyes. Small chunks of mortar fell from time to time, but no substance seemed to be lost. Withered vines wrapped around its outer walls and, even while Huma pondered how vines such as these could exist at so cold a level, he noted that they appeared to have been dying for some time.

Gruesome gargoyles stood watch on the battlements. Close examination proved them to be not demonic creatures, but the works of some mad sculptor.

Two towers rose above all else in this edifice. One appeared to be a watchtower, for it had been placed on the far edge, away from the mountain, giving those at the top a fantastic view of both the mountain range and the lands to the east.

The other tower seemed completely out of place. It was broad, taking up nearly a quarter of the inner grounds. Where the rest of the castle seemed decrepit with age, the tower seemed new and nearly spotless. Huma had no doubt that this was where to find the renegade.

"There are no defenders!" Bennett shouted.

Not one sentry walked the walls. There was no one in the watch tower, nor were there any guardsmen in the courtyard. The entire structure looked as if it were abandoned, though Huma knew Galan Dracos awaited them.

Huma turned to the others. "Disperse! I'm going in alone."

Below him, the silver dragon quivered but kept her eyes straight ahead. Kaz was not so silent.

"Disperse? Are you mad? Do you think we'd leave you?"

"Dracos wants me. That shall be the way it is."

Bennett had his dragon shift closer. "I will not permit you to do this."

"It is madness, indeed, Huma," remarked the gold dragon serving Bennett.

With a suddenness that made Huma grab for the pommel of the saddle, the silver dragon swooped down toward the castle, leaving the others open-mouthed. She had taken the decision out of their hands. They might follow, but they would not be able to catch up.

The courtyard lay directly below. Huma wondered at the size of the castle. Galan Dracos could not be so powerful as to keep his citadel perpetually standing on the side of a peak and hidden from the sight of men and still have the strength for all he had done.

He was still pondering when something of tremendous power struck him and Gwyneth. What seemed to be a giant hand plucked him from the saddle.

The world vanished.

He awoke in a narrow hall. Only one torch lit a dim corridor. The walls were cold stone, and the place had a dank smell. It nauseated Huma.

Why was he here? If it was a trap created and sprung by Dracos, why was the knight not locked in a dungeon cell, his weapons and armor stripped?

Weapons. He reached down by his side and felt the hilt of his sword. After a quick inspection, he determined that he still had his knives as well. What sort of trick was this?

The clank of metal alerted him to the presence of armored figures just down a side corridor. Huma drew his sword carefully. He did not trust these corridors enough to go racing down them blindly. They reminded him too much of the cavern tunnels in which he had been hounded by Wyrmfather.

Sword raised, he stood on the right side of the corridor intersection and held his breath. By his reckoning, there were at least two. He could hope to get the first one and possibly the second, but not three without a general alarm being raised.

A dark boot came into sight. The familiar ebony armor swerved to the left. A second guardsman followed the first. Huma held his breath.

A gauntleted hand shot toward the long, wicked blade Huma had seen earlier in the hands of the dragonrider commander. The first guardsman turned around at the noise and went for his. Though the second had noticed Huma, he was unable to draw his sword quickly enough. Huma ran him through the neck before the jagged blade was even halfway out of its scabbard.

The walls rang as Huma ducked a swing by the other attacker. The guardsman's blade cut deep into the stone and yet slid out easily. Huma parried a second attack and then took the lead.

His opponent was good, but not as good as a well-trained Knight of Solamnia. Defenses became more and more sloppy as the jet-black figure realized he lacked the skill to overcome the trespasser. Huma forced the other's sword high, and kicked. Quarters were too close for the guardsman to dodge. As his opponent fell back and tried to recover, the knight ran him through.

The noise would surely bring someone.

Huma stared down both the corridor the guards had come from and the one they had chosen at the intersection. Both seemed to go on and on.

As quietly as possible, he began to make his way down the corridor in the opposite direction. It was virtually dark and Huma had to feel along the walls to make sure he was not missing any side corridors or intersections.

Where was the silver dragon? he wondered. Where was Gwyneth? the knight corrected himself. Whatever shape or form she wore, she was Gwyneth; he understood that much even if he really did not understand his own feelings. She had to be here somewhere, Huma reasoned. Perhaps, like himself, she was wandering aimlessly in some darkened part of the citadel in a fruitless search for him.

On impulse, he withdrew the medallion from his chest and held it close. Its warmth filled him, and the medallion began to glow with an intensity akin to the Dragonlances. Just then, a voice echoed down the hallway.

Two voices spoke in hisses. Not members of the warlord's Black Guard, for they rarely spoke, Huma had noticed. Mages—but were they renegades or those who had sworn to aid the knighthood?

He held his blade ready, silently cursing the lack of true light. Darkness was a magic-user's friend, for, like an assassin, magic-users were notorious for sleight-of-hand skills. Huma hoped he could take both of them quickly.

"He must be here!"

"Why did you do it?"

"The renegade had them both. He—aaaugh!"

The first of the two spellcasters suddenly found himself standing with a sword point beneath his chin. His companion made no move to attack Huma.

"No false moves," the knight whispered.

"It *is* him!" the other mage hissed at his comrade.

"I can see that!" the spellcaster said, then added to Huma, "We are allies! Did not Gunther tell you?" The spellcaster's face was difficult to read in the dark, but Huma thought his eyes were wide with fear.

"Gunther?"

"Slight, with animal features. Bald."

A simple description, but fairly accurate. That did not mean these two were friends, however.

"He gave you a tiny, emerald sphere."

"All right." It was risky, but Huma decided to lower the sword. The mages sighed audibly. Both were of average height and one was on the heavy side, but Huma could only guess at details.

"Another time and we might have taught you what it is to threaten one of the Order of Nuitari," the heavier one grumbled. "But now circumstances force us to aid you."

"I care for it as little as you."

"Dracos knew you would take the empty courtyard as an invitation to land, but he planned a surprise for you. We did not have the time to seize both of you, so we settled on you as most important. In order to prevent one of the renegades from tracing you, we were forced to fling you to a random location in the castle and hope for the best."

"I had a very good idea where you would land; there was no reason to worry." The narrower of the two mages gave an audible sniff of contempt.

"Some of us are purely lucky at times." The words of the stocky mage were aimed at his companion, and Huma got the vague notion that they were brothers of the flesh as well as of the cloth. "Be that as it may, we want you—"

"You want?" Huma's grip on his sword tightened, and he waved it at the level of the two spellcasters' throats. "I do not take orders from Black Robes. We work together, yes, but as equals."

Twin sighs. Allies such as these Huma could have done without, yet they had saved his life once already.

"What happened to the dragon I was riding?"

"That thing?" asked the first mage. "It's frozen. In stasis. Galan Dracos wastes no raw material."

"What does that mean?" The thought that something terrible might be happening to Gwyneth even now nearly put Huma into a panic. The mages mistook that panic for murderous anger and quickly did their best to placate him.

"Nothing! He's much too busy at the moment! He has some grand spell which he claims is going to change Krynn forever. He has no time for the dragon."

Huma took a deep breath and calmed. "You've been of invaluable assistance up to now, but I think you have compromised yourselves. Surely he suspects all Black Robes by this time?"

The thin mage sniffed again. "He does not know how great the revolt has become. He suspects it is only a few disgruntled members of our Order. He does not suspect that it is a mass conversion. We will not bow down as slaves to the cur and his mistress."

"Be silent," hissed the first. "You'll draw her attention, and that is the one thing we cannot face!"

"Cannot?" Huma looked at both of them in disgust and wished they could truly see his expression. "So. You still intend for me to do all the work for you. Fine. Which way lies Galan Dracos?"

"You cannot be that mad!" It was difficult to tell which of the two had spoken.

"Which way?"

"We brought him here," said the first to the second. "We may as well get it over with."

"This is not the way we planned."

"Has anything we planned from the beginning gone as we thought? Sagathanus died the first time he spoke up against the renegades—and he was the one who recruited them, promised them that we would agree to coexistence with them! That they would no longer be hunted down and destroyed if they refused to join the Three Orders and obey the guiding laws set down by the Conclave!"

"That was our mistake! We promised them freedom to continue their abominable experiments—experiments that go beyond even our tolerant limits."

Huma prevented the present argument from going any further by thrusting the tip of his blade between the faces of the two bickering spellcasters. They became stone-silent instantly.

"Galan Dracos? *Last time.* Where?"

The stocky mage listed a sequence of turns and distances, repeated it again, and then asked Huma if he had it memorized. Huma did.

"We shall endeavor to free the dragon if we can. If not . . ." The mage shrugged.

"What about my other companions?"

"They departed when the trap was sprung. I cannot say whether they will return. Perhaps they have scurried back to Vingaard."

Huma ignored the jibe. He was sure the others were nearby and were planning. It would be best if he continued his present course of action.

Footsteps echoed in the hall. The two magic-users literally jumped.

"Go," whispered the narrow one.

With quick steps, Huma moved away from the Black Robes. He faintly heard the sounds of voices and realized that the two were stalling for him as long as they could.

Ahead he saw the shadows of armored men. Huma ducked back into another corridor and waited.

Six guards walked by silently, their attention fixed on whatever duties they had been given.

The Black Robes were in more danger than they knew. If Huma read the situation correctly, the guardsmen were beginning the process of rounding them up—if they did not intend to kill them immediately. That would leave Huma alone to deal with Galan Dracos and his goddess of pure evil.

Huma paused at the next turn, for he was suddenly confronted by three brightly lit passages.

Voices. Huma crept closer—then froze as he recognized one.

"You know what to do with the gem, Gharis?"

"A place has been chosen, Master Galan. We will wait for your signal there."

"It's merely a safeguard, Gharis. She demanded it—but it is my signal that you will obey when the time comes. Understand?"

The one called Gharis answered with a slurring voice. Huma suspected Dracos had need to reinforce his commands with something akin to mesmerism.

Apparently satisfied that he would be obeyed, Galan Dracos ordered the other to depart immediately. Huma stumbled back, but Gharis—seemingly a renegade like his master, for he wore a plain, brown cloak and not one of black—did not depart through that entrance. Instead, his footsteps dwindled away in another direction.

There was more than one entrance to the chamber. Apprehensively, Huma set off toward the chamber down another corridor. Slowly, as he edged closer, he peeked into the room.

If anything, the chamber was more a design in madness than the rest of the castle was. Huge, demonic figures lined the walls, each appearing ready to pounce upon any unsuspecting intruder. The thought made Huma shiver. Chief among the artifacts in the room was a platform seemingly made of black crystal. It rose in four tiers, upon the last of which stood a gleaming emerald sphere.

The knight pulled back quickly. Dracos was indeed there and standing before the sphere, his back turned toward Huma. The presence of the mage had been expected, but sitting calmly behind the sphere, three times the size of a man and watching intently, was a green dragon.

Huma had never seen such a dragon, and that was what disturbed him.

"You see now why I have always held the upper hand, do you not, my little friend?"

"Great is Master Galan," the young dragon hissed. It had a cruel, sly voice even for one of its kind. What little Huma knew of the green dragons revealed them to be the most sinister, for they worked most often through trickery and deceit. Open combat was not their way, but they were just as respected for their physical abilities as their minds—their convoluted, treacherous minds.

"Cyan Bloodbane learns much watching Master Galan."

The renegade's laugh was just as cold and cruel as the young dragon's voice. "Cyan Bloodbane will never grow to his full potential if he thinks to ever *master* me. You are an experiment, Cyan. Through me, you have come to understand the minds of humans, elves, dwarves, and all the other races as none of your kind has. When you are fully grown, your name will strike terror even in their dreams—but not if you cross *me*."

Something began to choke uncontrollably, and Huma wondered if perhaps the dragon had decided to end the mage's arrogant speech. A moment later, he heard Cyan Bloodbane apologizing frantically.

"Master Galan is all-powerful! No more! Please!"

"This room grows too foul from your chlorine-infested breath. Depart! I will summon you when I wish your presence again."

"Master!" Wings flapped, and Huma realized that this chamber must have an outside entrance on a higher level.

The sound of footsteps alerted him that Dracos was moving away. Huma dared peer around again and caught sight of the mage's back before the latter disappeared through another archway. The chamber torches seemed to dim as he departed.

Huma took a step into the chamber. He half expected some sorcerous trap, but nothing so much as flickered.

With carefully measured steps, he made his way to the black, crystalline platform and stared at the large sphere. Perhaps, he thought, this was what his tiny guide had been drawn to. Perhaps this was how Dracos kept the existence of the castle from the outside world—or it might be—

He was struck by a wave of revulsion that made him stagger and nearly caused him to drop his sword. It was coming, he realized dimly, from the globe itself. Huma closed his eyes briefly and concentrated. The hatred vanished, to be replaced with contempt and humor as someone mocked him—mocked his very existence. Huma forced his eyes open, knowing what he would see and refusing to let it daunt him.

She was there, staring at him from somewhere, staring at him through the sphere.

Takhisis.

Oddly, Huma's first thought was whether Galan Dracos knew that she could reach into this chamber. Did she suspect—as Huma was just beginning to—that, based on his commands to the mesmerized servant, Dracos plotted something against her? Surely she suspected that one as ambitious as the renegade would never be satisfied unless he controlled all. Was that perhaps why she smiled?

Smiled? There had been no true face there at first. Now, though, the Dark Queen permitted herself eyes, a nose, and a mouth. It was a feminine face, though she might very well have appeared as an armored warrior or even a tree if it suited her fancy.

In truth, the more he stared, the more Huma knew that he had never seen such a beautiful face. These were the sculpted features of a queen among queens, truly an immortal. A man could easily become lost in that beauty—for eternity. For such a small price. What had the knighthood given him but misery? Because of it, he had lost his parents, Rennard, and countless comrades, including Buoron. Even his love had been taken away from him—

Lies! The fog lifted from his mind and he saw the lies behind the so-called truths. Rennard had been lost long before the knighthood; he had been responsible for the death of Huma's mother. Huma's father, Durac, had died fighting for something he believed in desperately, something he found worth dying for. As for Gwyneth—the thought remained unfinished.

Rather than strike him down, the Dark Queen merely smiled.

The face vanished. Only a touch of the evil that was the Dragonqueen remained behind to remind him what he had just experienced.

"I think it is time to end this game," said Galan Dracos suddenly.

Chapter 30

Galan Dracos folded his arms and stared at the knight. His thin lips were curled in a smile like a scavenger.

The renegade mage reached up and pulled back the hood of his cloak so that his face was fully visible. His hair, thin and straggly, was plastered to his skull and formed a widow's peak on his forehead. The head itself was elongated, almost inhuman. The mage reached out and patted the bone-white head of one of a pair of dreadwolfs that flanked him; the motion revealed long, bony fingers ending in talons.

"And so, we come to the end. I would have wanted it no other way. You had to be here to see my triumph . . . the ultimate triumph."

"You knew I was here?"

"The followers of Nuitari do him no credit. They are so caught up in their self-importance that they do not realize what one can do when unconstrained by the laws set by those fools running the Conclave of the Three Orders. I wouldn't look for support from them."

As Dracos spoke, Huma was gauging his options—and there were not many. A plan born of desperation filtered through his mind. Huma took a step back and held his free hand over the great sphere in which the knight, only moments before, had faced the vision of the Dragonqueen. "One motion and I shatter this. Where will your dreams be then?

"They would literally fall to pieces—if you could indeed break the globe. I offer you the opportunity to try."

Huma struck the top of the emerald sphere as hard as he could. His gauntleted hand bounced off. There was not even a single scratch on the globe.

"You see?"

Huma nodded and allowed his free hand to fall casually to his belt.

"I think—" was all Galan Dracos managed to say before Huma pulled out a sharp blade and threw it directly at the mage.

The dagger flew with accuracy. Yet, the renegade merely raised a finger and the blade slowed, arched—and blew back toward Huma. The knight dove forward and tumbled down the steps of the crystalline platform. The knife bounced off the huge green sphere and fell with a clatter to the floor.

"Pathetic. I had expected more of you after all this." Before Huma could steady himself, Dracos snapped his fingers. The knight suddenly was gripped from behind by massive hands seemingly made of stone. He struggled, trying to pry apart the thick, monstrous fingers. The unseen menace did not waver, and Huma's armor began to dig into his flesh.

"Against that wall." Dracos pointed.

Huma was whirled around and lifted up. Something cold and rocky caught hold of each wrist and then his ankles. The knight was trapped.

The rapid, precise movements had given Huma no opportunity to glimpse the mage's servant. Suddenly, Huma could see with dismay that his captor had actually been one of the gargoyles lining the room. As Huma watched, the gargoyle slowly returned to its niche. Over his shoulder, Huma could see that another gargoyle, little more than arms, held him tight against the wall.

"I see you admire my handiwork." Dracos stepped closer, and the captive knight saw that a thin layer of scales covered much of his face. The renegade was almost reptilian in appearance, and Huma found himself wondering just how much of his humanity the mage surrendered for his power.

"To be fair, I underestimated you in the beginning. I thought you only a pawn of Magius, a former friend he once more found useful. Imagine my surprise to discover that not only weren't you a pawn, but our mutual friend actually trusted you."

Talk of Magius made Huma struggle, but the paws of the gargoyle permitted him no slack. He glared helplessly at the renegade, who only beamed in greater satisfaction.

"He renounced everything he had done, you know. I doubt there was a whiter robe in all of Krynn in those last few days. Pity. You should have heard the screams. My—assistants—can be imaginative. I had to punish one for overenthusiasm. He would have killed our friend." The renegade chuckled. "I do so hate to discourage imagination, though. Not that it mattered by then. I fear that Magius was not really with us after that. He began to talk to himself—childhood things, I gather. It annoyed my servants to no end. He paid no attention to their fine work. In fact, he didn't speak again until you and I met. You must have meant a great deal to him for him to come back from whatever safe haven he had thrust his mind into." Dracos shrugged. "Enough talk of the past. Let us deal now with the future—for those of us who still have one."

Huma smiled back at the mage, though his mind raced with worry. "The dragons are defeated; your renegades are defeated; Crynus and most of his Black Guard are dead. Before the day is through, the ogres will be retreating. You've lost. Within a few weeks, the war will be only a memory."

The eyes of Dracos flared, and Huma saw he had struck a nerve. When the spellcaster spoke again, his voice was rough, angry.

"Correct on all counts save one. The ogres will retreat; they are bullies at heart, and bullies are cowards. They are fodder, nothing more, and they would be quite surprised to know what little importance they would have in my world."

"Your world?"

"My world—as voice of my mistress, Takhisis, of course." Dracos executed a flawless, courtly bow.

"You have no army."

"That was the trouble with Crynus. He saw everything as a battle. Even when he conceded the benefits of my powers, he saw them only as the means to his own ends."

Galan Dracos had crossed over to the dark crystalline platform and was now at the top, practically caressing the sphere. The emerald glow from it lit his face, making him look like a long-dead corpse. Huma shuddered involuntarily.

"The intensity of my power comes from my followers, both willing and unwilling. When the Black Robe, Sagathanus, found me, this was what interested him at first. I was a fool at that time, keeping no more than a few of the locals under my control—I actually had some sentiment for the foul place because it had been my place of birth." He looked up at Huma. "Have you ever heard of Culthairai? No? I am not surprised. It's a tiny farm province in the midst of Istar. Other than oats, the only thing of value they can sell are a few strong backs for mercenary troops. Imagine! The greatest mage who will ever exist—born in a worthless province!"

"It must have been terrible for you." Huma surprised himself with the comment.

The reptilian features twisted into a harsh smile. "How true. No one else has been able to appreciate that. I imagine it is because you found yourself growing up under similar circumstances."

Dracos, it seemed, had learned much about him.

It was left for you. The sudden clarity of that thought overwhelmed Huma. It was not his own. Rather, it almost sounded like Magius . . . What had been left for him?

Sensing something, one of the dreadwolves trotted over to him and sniffed. Its smell of decay sickened Huma.

For his part, Dracos stared at something within the sphere, something that perhaps only he could see.

The sound of long, leathery wings caused both to look up. Cyan Bloodbane had returned without his master's permission. The look in the young green dragon's eyes spoke of fear.

"Master Galan! The ogres begin to break! My brethren flee in panic—the cowards! What shall we do?"

Dracos was actually jubilant. "The time has come. The level of chaos is at a peak unprecendented since before the Age of Dreams." To the anxious dragon he replied, "Leave us! I will not have your stench fouling this room at such a time!"

The young dragon departed in haste. Dracos summoned the two dreadwolves, who began to shiver uncontrollably.

Huma watched with disgust and amazement. He could actually see the life essence—if that was what one called it—depart from the two ghoulish abominations. They did not even struggle. Galan Dracos removed his hands from the two gaunt, motionless forms. The dreadwolves crumbled to ash.

"Fear is Chaos. War is Chaos. Chaos is unlimited power. It is a power that even the gods respect. Do you understand?"

Huma blinked. In his morbid fascination over the destruction of the two dreadwolves, he had not been listening. "What are you going to do?"

"This." The mage stroked the globe. "This is the key to creating a conduit between our plane and the Abyss. A portal or gateway to the Dragonqueen's domain beyond. Understand this: When gods come to the mortal plane—I mean truly come to the mortal plane—they are but shadows of their true selves. Which is not to say that they are weak. Far from it. However, their counterparts have them at a disadvantage."

The knight's eyes brightened with understanding. "Which is why the Dragonqueen has never been far from the gateway she has created. She fears that Paladine will strike at her during some moment of crisis. Now, though, you have created a way that she can draw upon her full strength even while on our world."

Galan Dracos tensed, then smiled coldly. A tremor seemed to shake the citadel, but the mage paid it no mind. "You are more astute than I thought. Still, the small matter of your interference will be history before long."

Almost! A vague image flickered into and out of Huma's memory.

"Consider yourself honored. You are about to witness an event that will change *all* of Krynn!"

With that remark, the great emerald sphere flared with stronger intensity. Galan Dracos pulled his hood forward again and summoned a pale, bone-colored staff from thin air.

Huma's eyes focused completely on the renegade's staff. That was the key! The staff of Magius. Dropped by his companion after his capture by the Black Guard. Dropped? Left behind by its owner, more likely. Magius easily could have summoned it at any time just the way Galan Dracos had summoned his own.

What was he supposed to do though? Where was it now?

The torches flickered as the renegade raised high his own staff. He seemed to be drawing the flames to him. The chamber grew darker.

"Takhisis, great queen, mistress of the dark, the time has come to fully open the portal! The time has come to let your full power flow from your domain into this one!'

The staff of Magius was temporarily forgotten. Huma watched in horror as the wall behind the sphere began to warp and twist, as some mad dreamscape. Then, slowly, that part of the building seemed to completely fall away.

It was not the mountains, though, that stood revealed by the spell. Rather, it was a dark and chaotic landscape that seemed to spill into a gaping, endless pit from which no light could escape.

Even as Huma watched, the landscape changed again. It was wooded now, but the trees were either dead or dying, and they were as black as night.

Next, it became a burning desert from which the bones of forgotten travelers protruded. Within moments, it was a veritable sea of bones.

"What is it?" Huma thought he knew, but he hoped that the mage would deny it.

Galan Dracos turned from the maddening scene and stared through narrowed eyes at the knight. "That is the domain of my mistress—that is the Abyss."

"It keeps changing."

"It is your mind that is perceiving changes. The Abyss is based on one's experiences. In this case, yours. I have learned to control such unconscious thoughts."

Galan Dracos stepped down from the platform and approached Huma, who struggled vainly. The citadel shook again, but Dracos seemed still unaware of it. He reached up a taloned hand to the knight's forehead.

"You needn't worry." The renegade's tone was patronizing. "I have neither the time nor the power to spend on you. I'm simply going to block your thoughts from the Abyss. Like putting up a wall."

Huma's head was knocked back by a percussive force. For a brief moment, all thought vanished. Soon, Dracos was atop the platform again. He tapped his ivory staff twice and began muttering in some magical tongue. The emerald sphere gleamed like a miniature sun. The castle shook again.

"The bond with the Abyss is secure!" the renegade shouted out triumphantly. Something glimmered within the globe. Dracos caused his staff to vanish and put both hands on the glowing artifact. He stared into it, oblivious to the near-blinding light. The muttering renewed.

Huma summoned the staff by thought.

He could not say whether the thought was his own or, as he half-believed, that of the vengeful spirit of Magius. He only knew that he had to concentrate on calling the staff of the dead mage, and he had to do it now.

So simple—now that he knew. One minute his hands were empty, the next his left held the compacted version of the staff. His eyes suddenly widened as he felt a quiver in the palm that clutched the magic item. As if moving with a life of its own, it turned in his hand and tapped the stone claw that held his wrist.

The gargoyle released his wrist.

Galan Dracos was still facing the sphere. His hands were outstretched as if imploring some private god.

Huma freed his right wrist.

Dracos shouted incomprehensibly. The glow from the globe had spread to encompass the mage. He was taller now. Huma stared at the sphere. Energy seemed to swirl chaotically within it. The citadel shook violently this time.

"No!" This time, Dracos seemed to be talking to someone else. "The flow is too great! I need to draw more power or the energy will overwhelm me!"

Huma did not understand the words, but he knew he had to break the link between the planes. If Takhisis was drawing on that power—

This time, the tremor was so violent that several gargoyles tipped forward and smashed on the floor. Galan Dracos's expression did not change when he saw that Huma was free; he only muttered something under his breath and then immediately returned his attention to his spell.

The moment Huma was free, the staff, as if alive, began to stretch and widen. It was growing as it had before.

Gargoyles were suddenly stepping from their niches, creating a hodgepodge collection of monstrosities that all had one thing in mind—the death of Huma.

Having been trained in the quarterstaff, Huma found the mage's staff effective as such a weapon. Each touch sent sparks flying, and the gargoyles might as well have been made of butter for the way it cut through them. Still, a severed limb or decapitation was not sufficient to stop even one of the creatures. They came at him from all directions, and Huma knew the renegade would never run out of unliving servants. Nevertheless, he fought with all his determination and faith in Paladine.

Huma knew he needed only one good swing at Dracos, but the gargoyles were pressing him in from all sides and the staff was virtually useless at such close quarters. Unless something happened, he had only seconds left before the crush of stone creatures brought him down.

"Huuuuummaaa!"

The voice came from above, shouting down even the reverberations of the citadel. What was Dracos doing? Did he need to bring down the mountains themselves?

"Huuuummaaa!"

Huma could see her now.

"Gwyneth!"

She spied him and spiraled down even as a gargoyle knocked the staff from Huma's hand. The silver dragon roared and struck out at the nearest of the stone creatures. They shattered into sand. She flew up, around, and then back down to attack once more. Several of the gargoyles were turning away from Huma to attack this new foe. Gwyneth found herself being dragged down by the combined weight of four of the animals who had attached themselves to her underside. Roaring more from annoyance than pain, she whirled as best she could in the wide chamber in an attempt to throw the gargoyles from her. They clung tight, though, and she was forced to fly upward and out of the room in order to shake them off.

Even so, the silver dragon had bought Huma time. He grabbed the staff of Magius and whirled again, eliminating the nearest attacker with his first swing. The others attempted to close once more.

Several figures came rushing toward the room. Black Guard. The ebony-armored figures paused in the archway and gaped at what they saw.

Huma glimpsed the mad gaze of Dracos as he briefly turned toward his soldiers. A light much like the glow of the emerald sphere glittered in his eyes. He spoke a single word, the strain of even that causing him to flinch.

A thin, deadly bolt of green energy originating from the globe whipped toward the unsuspecting warriors with frightening speed. It split into two and then into four separate bolts before it was halfway to them. Belatedly, the guardsmen realized their plight and turned to run. Four did not even have time to move. They were harpooned like fish by the bolts of energy and dragged into the chamber. Huma shivered. The spell seemed to be as much in control of Galan Dracos as he was of the spell. The knight doubted the renegade really even knew what he had done. All that mattered to Dracos now was the power.

The other guardsmen fled. From his vantage, Huma watched helplessly as another bolt issued forth, this time at him.

It slammed into his chest, the very force of it spilling over to strike a host of the gargoyles. At first, Huma felt his energy literally being drained from him. Then something repelled the parasitic bolt and sent it writhing back into the emerald globe. Huma felt his chest and discovered the medallion given to him by Avondale. A medallion for a cleric of Paladine.

"Huma! The castle is breaking up!"

A gargoyle fell to its knees. Another simply collapsed. Huma turned to find himself facing Galan Dracos. The renegade had a crazed look on his already inhuman face.

"I—I will bend—bend it to my will! I am Dracos, greatest mage ever to live!"

The mage revealed his staff again and tapped it on the platform three times. "Shurak! Gestay Shurak Kaok!"

The gargoyles had lost all semblance of life. As they collapsed around Huma, the silver dragon materialized again and flew to him. Dracos made no move toward them, did not even see them. Instead, he was grinning at the heavens. His form coursed with energy.

"I have done it, mistress! The power is mine!"

So caught up in his apparent triumph, the renegade did not see the image that formed in the emerald sphere. A mocking face, an inhuman face. Even as Huma watched, the face within the globe split and became two. Then three. The faces twisted, became reptilian. Dragons. Five heads at least. All mocking.

"Huma, we must leave!"

"I cannot!" Huma stared at the Dragonlances that Gwyneth carried. They were too awkward for his purposes. Even the footman's lance was unwieldy. Then his eyes came to rest on the staff of Magius. An impulse came to him.

He hefted the staff. Words he could not understand flowed from his mouth, and the staff was suddenly luminous. He threw it with all his might.

The staff missed Galan Dracos, but neither was he the target. Instead, the staff, so much like a spear, flew with perfect accuracy at the very center of the glowing sphere. It seemed to hesitate when the tip made contact with the artifact, but then it continued through, shattering all resistance.

"Don't look!" Huma cried to Gwyneth.

The emerald sphere exploded with a roar.

The citadel shook—and the chamber tipped—as the castle felt the impact of the artifact's destruction.

"Huma!" The silver dragon nudged him. "We must flee! Hurry!"

He regained his footing, partially clutching one of her wings. A quick glance showed him that the platform was being engulfed in a greenish inferno that seemed to cover the entire wall.

From without, something roared.

"Paladine!" he whispered. It could not be! Huma could imagine only one creature that could emit such a deafening, earth-shaking cry. A dragon. A giant dragon. A titan with five heads, he suspected. Takhisis.

"Yyyyooooouuu!"

Huma forgot the roar and whirled back to the blaze where this new cry had originated.

Something slowly emerged from the emerald fire. It blazed but did not burn. It walked on two legs but was no longer human in any way. It raised a taloned claw that had once been a hand. A demonic face with twisted features, like some distorted serpent, was evident under the torn and tattered remains of a hood.

"Hhhuuuuummmaaaaa!"

Galan Dracos stumbled forward.

"I will see you dead!"

Something with tendrils shot out toward him—and was daunted by what momentarily seemed a silver shield. Galan Dracos took a step back.

"You have your—your patron as well! Pity it is too late for Krynn!" The face twisted.

Huma took a step forward. Gwyneth began to protest, but the knight stared her into silence. Then he slowly began to walk toward the mad mage.

"Too many people have perished because of you, Galan Dracos. As Paladine as my witness, I cannot allow you to remain free. It must end here."

When Dracos finally spoke, his voice was under control. He stared off into the distance.

"Yes. It will end here. With the victorious—with my treachery unmasked. I have gambled and I have lost." Dracos turned back to Huma and then seemed to shrug.

The renegade stumbled back to the edge of the inferno. His legs could barely walk anymore. He relied more and more on his staff.

Huma came purposefully toward him. "I cannot let you go."

The deformed mage laughed, a laugh that seemed to go on much too long. The eyes of Galan Dracos were narrow slits that gleamed. "I'll not wait for the Queen's justice. I prefer oblivion to that. She shall not have my damned spirit to toy with for eternity."

Galan Dracos, master mage, renegade, spoke a single word.

The emerald flames engulfed him. Whatever immunity he had was discarded. Huma covered his eyes as the fire flickered more brightly. When he looked again, there was nothing remaining of the mage.

"He burned himself."

"No." The silver dragon shook her head. "He's ceased to exist. It was that last spell he unleashed. It's as if he never was. Before long, those who ever knew him will never remember—save his former mistress, I think." She frowned. "He's actually escaped from the Dragonqueen. Amazing."

The citadel began to shift downward again.

"Huma!" Her momentary fascination faded immediately as Gwyneth realized the danger.

"Yes!" He began to climb atop her, then stopped. "No! The staff of Magius! I have to see—"

"Is that the small rod on your belt?"

He looked down. On his right side, stuck securely through his pouch belt, was a familiar, foot-long stick. "How—"

Gwyneth finally grew exasperated. "I will explain to you

about magic some other day! Huma, as Paladine is *my* witness, I love you! I will not see you die here if I can help it!"

At those words, he scrambled clumsily aboard. Each moment she stayed risked her own existence—and for what? His hesitations, his fears.

Yet she loved him.

The silver dragon rose swiftly into the air.

"Lie flat against me—and hold the Dragonlance straight!" she cried.

The citadel continued to shift as it slid downward. The gargoyles were tossed like rags. Parts of the chamber began to break off. A portion of the upper passage collapsed. Now the silver dragon would not be able to escape through its narrow funnel.

Huma heard her shout something in one of the magical tongues. He heard masonry shatter, and then bits of rock flew by his head.

"Steady! This is it!'

He felt the Dragonlance as it cut into the thick, stone wall, enlarging the gap. Gwyneth's wings folded back, and she glided up like an arrow shot from a bow. Huma knew she was shielding him with her own body as much as possible.

Then they were out. Huma realized he had been holding his breath, and exhaled. The silver dragon spiraled upward. From above, they could see that a green blaze now engulfed much of the castle.

What remained standing of the mage's tower stood perched momentarily over the precipice. It weaved there, then slowly began to tip over. First the tower went, a great shaft that tipped forward and then plummeted over.

Huma turned his eyes up to the heavens. "Paladine!"

A new and greater darkness had come suddenly.

"Huma . . ." The silver dragon's voice was unsteady.

He followed her gaze to the very top of the same peak that the citadel of Galan Dracos had fallen from. Something huge, multi-headed, and radiating evil gazed their direction.

Huma—Champion of Paladine. Come to me. Come to my embrace.

Takhisis.

Chapter 31

The near-hypnotic quality of the Dragonqueen's call was broken by a familiar voice.

"Huma! Thank the gods! We were afraid you had fallen with the citadel!"

He turned in the saddle. Bennett and Kaz rode near him. Kaz quickly explained, "We sent the others to seek aid. Only, Sargas!—what is that?"

Bennett's voice was drained of emotion. "It is the Dragon-queen, is it not?"

Huma only nodded. He stared up at the shadowy monstrosity above them. The portal through which the Dark Queen had come was expanding, and she seemed to be growing more solid, more real.

A thought struck the knight. He reached down to his side

for the compacted staff of Magius and handed it to Bennett. "Take this back to Vingaard Keep. It must be turned over to the Conclave. As ruling mages, they'll know what to do with it. It belonged to Magius, and I fear that it won't be of much use to me anymore."

Kaz and Bennett looked at one another.

Huma fixed each of them with a gaze. "It must be told that Dracos is no more. I also need you to organize the lancers. Bennett, you are the son of one Grand Master and the nephew of another. You were born to lead.

"I will draw the Dark Queen's ire for as long as I can, but a mass attack remains our only true chance. There must be at least a hundred lances left. Then, Paladine willing, we will be able to count for something."

Bennett shook his head. "Huma, this is a goddess! We are less than a single breath to her!"

"But we are Knights of Solamnia," Huma responded, "a knighthood forged by the holy Triumvirate of which Paladine is senior. Our mission has been to keep the justice and see that evil never holds sway over Krynn. *This* is our ultimate test. *This* is where we truly test ourselves against the Oath and the Measure."

The other knight could think of no response. Bennett's face had reddened slightly.

"I have no time to argue. Return, Bennett. Kaz, go with him," Huma said.

The minotaur looked down at his mount, then back at Huma. "I agree that one of us should return, and it is right that it be Bennett. But I will stay. I swore an oath, too, and I have not yet proved myself. And Bolt thinks as I do."

Huma sighed. "Kaz, I cannot stop you. Bennett, do your duty."

Bennett gritted his teeth, but nodded. At a signal, his silver dragon turned—but not before meeting the gaze of Gwyneth. Some message passed between them, and Huma remembered that here was kin of his own dragon. Parting was no easier for them.

When Bennett was gone, Huma turned to the minotaur. "Now."

The two dragons rose higher and higher. Above them,

Takhisis's five-headed dragon form seemed to waver. The entire mountain, and even the heavens above, were being warped by a vast hole in the fabric of the sky itself. The gateway from which the Dragonqueen had materialized in this world. The portal through which she had drawn her absolute power with the help of the unlamented Galan Dracos. Her full power was cut off from her because Huma had shattered the emerald sphere, but the gateway remained. And Takhisis already had the power she had drawn earlier. Never in her invasions of the mortal plane had she ever been so strong.

Enchanting. Even more interesting than your constant need to argue with one another over hopeless causes.

The cold, cruel thoughts buffeted Huma's mind.

I will have to gather a few such as you and study this amusing, transitory thing called love. It seems so . . . wasteful.

At least Huma had some satisfaction in that he knew Takhisis could never experience any of the emotions he felt. They would ever be a mystery to one such as her. In that, she was less than any mortal.

Teach me, then.

Though he knew her dragon form still perched atop the mountain, he also saw the graceful, enticing figure of a raven-haired enchantress, clad in the thinnest of dark silks. When she smiled, it was as if for the first time anyone had truly done so.

I could be whatever you desire me to be. You could show me this love you think so much of. I would be a very willing student.

In his mind, the seductive form turned to the side slightly, revealing new and provocative poses. Huma found it impossible to concentrate. She *was* beautiful beyond compare, and she was willing to learn what it meant to love, to be a mortal. If he could show her what it meant, then Krynn might never again have to know evil or suffering.

There was added—and it weighed heavily—the interesting aspects that would surely be involved in teaching her.

She smiled and seemed to hold out a slim, perfectly sculpted hand.

Huma felt a warmth on his chest. Involuntarily, he clutched at it. A familiar object seemed to fall into his hand.

"No!" he shouted on impulse. "I will not fall to your dark charms! You cannot ever know love or life and I want no part of you. My love is for another!"

He felt a jolt beneath him, as if Gwyneth had caught herself. He had no more time to think of her, because the Dragonqueen once again clutched his thoughts.

You might have known joy such as no man has ever known. You might have commanded my armies, for no warrior has proved more resourceful, more adaptable, and more determined than you. You could have been second only to me, and I would have rewarded you beyond your expectations.

A horrible wind rose up. The silver dragon was nearly swept against the mountainside, and Bolt and Kaz fell behind. Huma gripped the Dragonlance with one hand and fingered the medallion of Paladine with the other. With both of them, he was able to maintain hope.

Very well! You have rejected me. You have opened the doorway to your own destruction—and that of the one you love.

Unable to know love, the Dark Queen was all too familiar with hate.

"Huuummmaaa!"

The knight turned back briefly and saw Bolt being forced to land on a rocky ledge. Kaz was clutching the saddle, desperately.

This is between us now, oh, so mortal Knight of Solamnia! You will beg for forgiveness for all you have done! You will plead with me for an end to the agony, but it will not be until the end of eternity that I may even consider granting it.

Huma recalled the choice made by Galan Dracos: oblivion of body and soul rather than the tender "justice" of the Queen of Darkness. This from one who had no compassion, who had cruelly tortured Magius, and who had sent thousands to their needless deaths. In the end, there had been only fear for Dracos, fear at the thought of being at the mercy of his mistress.

First will I batter your physical form to jelly—but you

will not die. Then I will take your mind and reveal to it the full dark beauty of my domain. Madness will not save you. I will not allow it. Then I will take your love and treat her to only the finest of my—entertainments—while you help-lessly watch.

Huma had seen wonders and terrors that few men had faced, and only his belief in Paladine and the justice and good the god represented had saved him. Each time, that belief had strengthened him. Huma had come to love Krynn as much as Paladine, and he was willing to sacrifice all for the sake of the world if it meant the defeat of darkness.

Rather than urge Gwyneth back, Huma pressed her on.

The silver dragon obeyed. She would not abandon him.

You are fools. Bigger fools than Dracos, who believed he could become a god. His escape to oblivion saved him from my tender mercy. What will save you?

It was as if a curtain had suddenly been drawn away. The Dragonqueen stood watching, her beauty breathtaking and terrible at the same time.

Each head of the gigantic dragon mocked him. Five in all, and each one representing one of her children. Cunning and cruel green. Tenacious white. Powerfully destructive red. Unpredictable black. Dominating blue.

They swerved sinuously back and forth, as if weaving a hypnotic spell. Never did their eyes leave Huma. Never did a single head pause in its movements.

The Dark Queen was well over sixty feet of pure power. Each movement was grace and strength incarnate. In each movement, no matter how subtle, she revealed the foolish-ness of daring to forestall her will.

Now you see. Now you know.

The quick, tinier white dragon suddenly exhaled in his direction. Huma barely saw the cone of intense frost pro-jected at him, but Gwyneth swerved easily and flew out of range.

The Dragon of Many Colors and of None—the ancient name came back to Huma—laughed scathingly. The attack had been no more than play to the goddess, as a cat plays with a mouse before eating it whole.

Wind continued to whip around, and the silver dragon

veered perilously close to the side of the mountain. The heads of the Dragonqueen laughed in amusement.

There was a slight hesitation in the actions of the godly leviathan as Huma's mind shifted. She also was mocking him no longer. The focus of each pair of eyes was more intense, as if she studied him anew. The massive wings spread in what Huma might have termed the anxiousness of a normal dragon.

Huma signaled to Gwyneth. She turned, gave herself plenty of space from the terrible form of the Dragonqueen, and turned to face the goddess. Huma's hand steadied the Dragonlance. The five heads froze in position.

The knight signaled again.

The tempest unleashed by the Dragonqueen increased tenfold, forcing both Kaz and Bolt to seek safety at the innermost part of the ledge. They had only a brief glimpse as the silver dragon defied the ripping winds and the sudden torrential downpour, and continued forward with ever-increasing speed. Then knight and dragon vanished as they neared the top of the peak.

Kaz muttered a prayer to every god of Paladine's house that his hazy memory could recall. He saved his last and longest for the Platinum Dragon—the god known to humans as Paladine.

Chilling frost. Quick, deadly lightning. A hissing stream of poisonous gas. Bright flame. Sputtering and splattering acid.

Each head unleashed its power against the two. Gwyneth turned and dodged, dodged and turned, then spiraled as she sought to escape one hideous attack after another. Sometimes even her skill was not enough. Acid burned a multitude of tiny holes in her wings. Flames singed her back. Huma maintained his grip on the Dragonlance despite all.

As yet, they had made no strike against the Dragonqueen. That she had not struck them down with all her powers was of vital interest. It meant that the Queen of Darkness had but a fragile hold on her increased strength. She was seeking to do much, spreading her power too thin, extending too many disparate spells.

Gwyneth unleashed a cone of frost at the green head of the goddess, who shook it off as one might shake a leaf.

Jaws snapped dangerously close. Huma glimpsed the head of a red dragon as Gwyneth flew out of reach.

When she turned toward the Dragonqueen one more time, Huma saw that the great creature was at last rising from the peak. No longer did the Dark Lady believe her victory assured. She was taking the battle to Huma, determined to prolong this fight no more than necessary.

Seen in the air, the Dragonqueen was at least ten times larger than the silver dragon. Her wingspan covered the sky. Each of her foreclaws could have taken the head of Huma's companion and crushed it easily.

I am bored with games. You flutter like a butterfly.

The silver dragon started, and Huma realized that this was the fist time Takhisis had spoken to Gwyneth.

The black head of Takhisis shouted something in a magical tongue. Knight and dragon were suddenly plunged into darkness.

A roar.

Claws raked the air above Huma. The silver dragon dropped at the last instant. The Dragonlance still glowed, the only illumination in the sky.

Light? You cannot have light!

Even Huma had not noticed it at first, but it was true. The darkness became shadow, and the shadow became light again. Takhisis hovered, infuriated by the power of the Dragonlance.

Paladine cannot protect you forever!

"Huma" the silver dragon called to him, her breath painfully short, "I cannot evade her much longer."

Huma touched the medallion hanging on the center of his chest. He nodded. "It is time we met her."

Come to me, then. Meet my embrace.

"I offer you the same chance I gave to Galan Dracos, Dark Queen. I offer you the chance to surrender."

You jest in the time of your destruction, mortal Huma. I find your humor interesting. I shall have an eternity to amuse myself.

Huma steadied the Dragonlance so that it pointed directly toward the center of the Dragonqueen's great form.

"See if I am jesting. This is the power of Paladine. No mortal weapon can strike you down—but the Dragonlance is no mortal weapon."

You are mortal, though, Knight of Solamnia.

Huma dipped his head in acknowledgment.

"I am a Knight of Solamnia. I am the hand of Paladine, of Kiri-Jolith, and of Habbakuk on this world. You are on Krynn. You are mine, Queen of Darkness."

He kicked Gwyneth in the sides, and she burst forward with new energy. The Dragonlance shone brightly.

A strange thing happened.

It seemed to Huma that the armor he wore became brighter, felt different. To the look and touch it appeared as platinum. Gone were the dents and tears he had accumulated. His gauntleted hand seemed to glow with the same brilliance as the lance. He recalled then the vision he had had and the sculpture from which he had taken the first of the lances.

Below him, Gwyneth was also transformed. She was longer, sleeker, and far more beautiful. She was a gleaming white charger, a platinum dragon, a majestic kingfisher.

All he saw might have been illusion—but did the Dragonqueen see the same thing?

He could not be sure. Huma only knew that the huge chromatic beast hesitated again. This time, dragon met dragon. Claws and teeth struck out. The Dragonlance was only momentarily impeded. Huma braced himself for contact.

The Dragonqueen had not counted on her own momentum to such an extreme. Her body tipped forward and the Dragonlance suddenly found the unprotected neck of the centermost head.

Ichor splattered Huma. Some of it burned his injured leg, momentarily startling him from his almost trancelike state. Huma forced the thought of pain from his mind.

Takhisis shuddered uncontrollably as pain coursed through her.

Her scream literally shook the mountains and was heard

over miles. Four heads turned blindly to the source of that pain. The fifth, the blue one, dangled awkwardly, useless now. Takhisis clawed wildly. In vain, she tried to pry the Dragonlance from its bind, but the silver dragon would not back off. The four remaining heads snapped at the silver dragon, at Gwyneth.

The Queen of Darkness had never felt pain before, Huma realized.

Takhisis clawed and bit at them in her agony. Huma signaled Gwyneth to retreat. To his horror, he discovered that the lance would not come loose. The silver dragon was beginning to bleed heavily, and Huma saw that she was covered with a vast number of ragged, dripping cuts. Her tattered wings flapped slowly and her breathing became more shallow.

The Dragonqueen continued screaming and her wings thrashed back and forth. The mounting for the Dragonlance bent considerably. Huma tried in vain to steady the lance. The back end of the weapon suddenly shot upward, striking him soundly in the side of the head. Huma fell back, dazed and bleeding.

He heard something snap.

With gargantuan effort, he pulled himself forward—and found only splinters remained of the mounting. Takhisis had stripped him of the lance.

Where was she?

"Hu—uma."

"Gwyneth!" He leaned forward. She was breathing irregularly and each movement of her mouth dripped with blood.

"She—I—down there. I—cannot—"

Her wings froze in midmotion.

They began plummeting toward the mountainside. He screamed her name once before they hit. Then he felt his body thrown from the saddle, and all was night.

When he awoke, the world was red. Blood. Blood and pain. For hours, it seemed, he just lay there. His eyes were stinging red and his vision was bleary. All he could really see were shapes. The winds still howled.

There was nothing he could do about the pain. It coursed through his body. His wounded leg was numb.

With great effort, Huma raised himself to a sitting position.

Huma attempted to rise then, but he only fell over, face first, into the cool earth of the mountainside. His mind again blazed with pain.

He crawled now. He saw no sign of Gwyneth or the Dragonqueen. The knight managed to pull himself along, inch by inch.

As he struggled, something near the top of the mountain caught his attention.

A hand. A human hand.

He was not quite sure where the reserves of energy came from, but Huma succeeded in pulling himself up toward the figure lying near an outcropping.

"Gwyneth."

She had shifted to her human form. The wounds that covered her natural form were no less terrible. One arm lay twisted beneath her. Her face was now as pale as her silvery hair. Her breath came in short, rasping shudders. Time and again, she twitched uncontrollably and small sounds of pain, akin to what an animal might make, escaped her cracked and bleeding lips. There were bleeding cuts and dark bruises all over her body. It was a marvel that she lived.

His mouth open in a soundless cry, Huma dragged himself to her side, ignoring his raw, bloody hands and the agony that jolted him continuously from within.

When he reached her, he finally noticed that, with her good arm, she clutched the footman's Dragonlance as if it were life itself. Even as torn and battered as she was, Gwyneth had saved the smaller Dragonlance, knowing that it was the only weapon that could save them if the Dragonqueen returned.

He repeated Gwyneth's name.

Something roared. Gwyneth's eyes opened wide and she stared straight up.

"Huma?"

"Rest. Kaz or someone will come."

"No!" Her eyes teared. "Takhisis! You mustn't let her go free!"

The knight looked up. Something thrashed beyond the rise. Something huge and in terrible pain. The roar came again.

"She—" Gwyneth coughed up blood. "Sooner or later, she will overcome the Dragonlance. You have to do—do something before she does."

"What can I do?" Huma could barely prop himself up.

"Take this." She indicated the smaller Dragonlance. "I—I managed to save it." Gwyneth suddenly clutched at him. "Are you hurt badly? Let me help you!"

"Forget me. Forget the Dragonqueen. What is happening to you? Why are you human? Are you healing yourself?"

"It—it doesn't matter. The fall only—hastened the damage. I only thank Paladine that y—you are still alive."

"Don't talk anymore."

She couldn't be dying, Huma thought in horror.

I—I can save her, mortal!

The wind suddenly seemed frigid. Huma stood silently as the words sank in. How? he thought.

Sh—sh—the pain! She is not beyond me yet! Release me fro—from this agony and I will gladly restore you both! I swear it by—by the beyond! I swear it, highgod!

Huma looked down to see Gwyneth looking up at him intently. Her breathing was faint.

"What is it?"

"She offers us—you—life."

"In return for what?"

He hesitated. "Her release."

"Hu—" Gwyneth coughed uncontrollably. She closed her eyes. For a moment, the knight was afraid she was gone. She opened her eyes again, though, and fixed her gaze on him. "You cannot kill her—that is not possible. But you cannot release her, either. All Krynn will suffer for her torment. My life is not—not worth that." She paused. The strain of speaking was using up what little strength she had left.

Huma draped her with his body so that the harsh wind did not strike her full force. "I won't let you die."

"You don't have any choice." She smiled faintly.

"You can't," Huma stammered, then finally spoke the words he had long ago admitted to himself. "I love you. I am ashamed I could not say it before. I will not lose you."

Her face became radiant despite the fearsome wounds.

"I want—want—you to remember me as I am now—now, for this is truly me. I first truly lived as a human." She took a deep breath. "I loved as a human."

Her hand slipped from him. "I will die as a human—knowing at last that you—" Gwyneth closed her eyes as pain wracked her. Huma held her as she quivered. "—you—"

The shaking subsided. The knight loosened his hold. Gwyneth's eyes were closed and in her deathly visage there was now an odd serenity.

"Gwyneth?"

Moortaal! It isss not too late!

Huma lowered her head.

A tail flickered briefly in sight and then vanished again behind the rise. The sky was dark once more. The portal, Takhisis's gateway to and from the Abyss, had dwindled to a mere shadow of its former sinister majesty—yet it was still there.

Seizing hold of the Dragonlance, Huma began to drag himself toward the rise. His actions were involuntary; his mind contained only vague thoughts about what might have been. He no longer existed in the present. He was not even aware that he had reached the rise until he found himself looking at the Dragonqueen.

She lay some distance below in a crater shaped by her fall.

Huma lay there for a long time. Breath came hard to him now, and he realized that his ribs must be broken. The scene faded in and out, again and again.

Somehow, he managed to pull the Dragonlance up to the top of the ridge and force it over, point first. The chill wind no longer bothered him. It only served to clear his mind for the purpose at hand.

What—are you doing?

The Dragonqueen's thoughts suddenly flickered into his head. He was so startled, he nearly dropped the lance over the side. Pulling it back, he used it to bring himself to a wobbly standing position.

The Dragonlance readied like a spear, Huma stared down at the thrashing goddess.

She lay on her back, her wings folded awkwardly behind her. The four remaining heads snapped wildly at the severed Dragonlance still embedded in her form. The weapon sparked each time the heads came near, and again and again they pulled away in pain.

"Hear me," said Huma.

At first, there was only the thrashing and the horrible cries of pain and fury.

"Hear me," he repeated.

Mortal . . . what is it you want?

The huge dragon attempted to rise. And failed.

"You are beaten, Takhisis, Dragonqueen."

I am not! I cannot be!

"Your armies are being routed. Your renegades are dead or scattered. The Conclave will hunt them down. Such will be watched more closely in the future. There will never again be another Galan Dracos."

More time passed. The Dragonqueen was visibly struggling for control.

What do you want, mortal?

"The balance must be maintained. Without good, evil cannot grow. Without evil, good stagnates. I know I cannot kill you."

Release me, then!

Huma stumbled back at the intensity of the moment. The Dragonlance almost slipped from his grasp.

"First, you must surrender."

The wind had ceased. The sky was strangely clear. Sunlight warmed Huma's body.

The portal was nearly nonexistent.

The form of the Dragonqueen had become very still. She almost seemed—dead. Huma pulled the lance away from the edge and leaned over.

A dragon's head, emerald green, shot up. Huma pulled back too late.

A thick, hissing stream of noxious, green gas shot forth, enveloping him before he could even think. He fell forward and this time his grip on the lance loosened completely. It clattered down the ridge. The hapless knight also fell, toward the Dragonqueen.

He screamed with each bounce against the rock-strewn side of the crater.

If he had been in pain before, now he learned the meaning of agony. He screamed and screamed, but he did not die.

You still live! What does it take to kill you? You are only mortal!

Despite the pain, then, he laughed.

"I belong to Paladine. I belong to Gwyneth. Neither will ever let you have me."

Huma pulled himself upward. He coughed and his hands shook. He had inhaled too much of the gas. The fall had wracked his body and it was all Huma could do to keep himself sitting up, so violently did his head swim. He knew that despite his words, he did not have much time left.

"They are coming, Takhisis."

Who?

"The other Dragonlances. More than a hundred. A hundred times the pain and agony. I offered you a chance. They will not be so willing. You know that."

They cannot kill me!

"They can give you eternal suffering."

They cannot! The balance! You spoke of it!

"What do they care about the balance? So much better to have peace; that is what they will say."

A long pause. Huma started to close his eyes, then fought to open them yet one more time.

"You will never free yourself before they arrive. Even if I die, they will still have you. A goddess at the mercy of mortals."

What do you want?

It was evidently a strain for her to continue. Only one head still stared in Huma's direction. The other three wavered uncontrollably.

"Withdraw from Krynn."

I—

"Withdraw now!"

Very well.

"Withdraw your dragons as well. Never again must they

come to Krynn. Take them with you."

A long pause.

"Swear to it," he added.

She hesitated.

I do.

"I want to hear you swear by that you hold most holy."

Both witnessed the single dragon flying overhead and heard the call of its rider, a voice familiar to Huma.

Kaz. His voice was shaky and the dragon was visibly weary, but they circled above, ready to close.

"Your time is short, Queen."

*I swear that I shall withdr—withdraw—*she writhed in pain and for one moment Huma thought he might be crushed beneath her form—*withdraw from Krynn along with my children for so long as the world is whole. So do I swear by—*

She said it. *By the beyond. By the highgod.*

Bolt had landed nearby, vigilant. Kaz, disregarding the looming presence of the foul Dragonqueen, raced to Huma's side.

"You've won! You've defeated her!" Kaz stopped abruptly, and his expression became serious. "As I am your witness, Huma. I—I will remember as I remember my ancestors."

Huma silenced him with a look. "Kaz, you must pull the Dragonlance from her body."

"What?" Kaz rose and stared at Huma as if the knight was bereft of his senses. "Release her? She will wreak havoc all over! We will die—if we are lucky!"

Huma shook his head. "No. She. Swore. I can—promise you that she will—" He wanted to shut his eyes. "—she will depart."

"I cannot!"

"Kaz." Huma grimaced. "I promised her. It—it is a question of my honor. You understand honor. We say—say 'Est Sularis Oth Mithas' in the old tongue. 'My Honor is My Life.' "

The minotaur looked from the knight to the goddess, silent now, shuddering with pain.

"Hurry. The lance. My honor. The others—they won't let you."

Reluctantly, the minotaur moved. "My honor—" he said, half to himself, his eyes riveted on the task. "—is my life."

The heads of the Dragonqueen swerved his way, but only one, treacherous green, remained fixed on Kaz. The others merely weaved back and forth, as if all control had been lost.

The lance was lodged deeply at the base of the neck of the blue head. With great distaste and more than a little trepidation, Kaz climbed atop Takhisis, the Dark Queen.

The green dragon head eyed him intently.

In an act of mad bravado, the huge warrior snorted with disdain. He flinched when it looked as if the head were about to strike, but then the head turned to gaze grimly at the source of the Queen's agony.

"Gods," muttered Kaz, then clamped his mouth shut when he thought about the oath. He had reached the Dragonlance. Getting a solid grip on it, the minotaur heaved.

The Dragonlance slid free without the slightest resistance. Kaz lost his footing and went tumbling off the gargantuan form, the lance still in his hands.

A horrible, mind-numbing laugh filled the air.

Kaz came to a stop, turned over, and stared—up.

She was there in all her infernal glory. Wings spread, enveloping the sky. All five heads looked up to the heavens and laughed. The pain, the wounds—it was as if they had never been.

Five terrible dragon heads looked down at the helpless and battered knight, then at the minotaur who had freed her. Each draconian visage wore a malevolent smile.

The sky burst into flames and Kaz was forced to cover his eyes.

When he opened them again, the sky was clear of clouds, and the sun—the long forgotten sun—was shining majestically—triumphantly.

The sun gleamed brightly now. Huma no longer felt cold, though he did not really feel warm, either. Sleepy. That was how he felt.

He discovered the medallion from Lord Avondale in his

open hand. Paladine's face shone brilliantly in the sunlight. The glare was too much. Huma closed his eyes. He could not close his grip on the talisman. That was all right. When the sun began to shift, he would like to look at it again.

His thoughts turned to Gwyneth and what they would do, now that the war was over at last.

Chapter 32

*"A temple. They're building you a kender-cursed tem-*ple when all you wanted was a place to rest."

Kaz turned his horse away from the magnificent tomb. Lord Oswal shared the minotaur's distaste for the elaborate trappings Huma had never cared for in life, but there had been other things to consider.

"The people need a hero," the Grand Master had explained with a somewhat dubious expression on his aged face, "and the knighthood needs a standard to grow by. Huma has provided both."

Kaz wondered then how long it would take the people to forget Huma, or to think of him as they did other legends— as just one more story. Humans, dwarves, kender, and elves—they all had a tendency to forget or gloss over truth as time went on. Even minotaurs were guilty of that.

He studied the path ahead. Bennett said he believed the plains could be back to pre-war conditions within five or six years. Kaz estimated nine or ten. Still, the road was serviceable and that was what counted. He wanted to be far away before the knights discovered him missing. There was so much that one of his kind had never seen before. Qualinesti sounded interesting. The elves might offer an experience.

The day was bright and warm, something Kaz was unaccustomed to. He was thankful he had packed plenty of waterskins. Until he was more familiar with the land, he would have to be careful to conserve.

The massive warhorse Lord Oswal had given him moved swiftly along the trail. There were many dips in the ravaged path and much of his equipment was jostled around. The belt pouch slapping against his right side became such a nuisance that he finally pulled it off. Metal clanked against metal from within.

Kaz pulled his steed to a halt and reached into the pouch. He pulled out two objects. The first was a seal bearing the sign of the knighthood on one side. The reverse side had the minotaur's name chiseled in it, as well as the fact that he was indeed a minotaur. A mark above his name indicated he was under the protection of the Knights of Solamnia. Kaz had scoffed at first, but the Grand Master was quick to point out that few people had anything good to say about minotaurs. The tales of Huma that had already circulated made no mention of Kaz. Many of the knights still could not reconcile the legendary knight's friendship with a being that most people considered a beast.

Kaz carefully replaced the seal in the pouch and eyed the second item. It was the medallion of Paladine that the knight's lifeless hand had released when Kaz had lifted him up to Bolt's back. The minotaur had stuffed it into the pouch for safekeeping and until now he had forgotten it.

Sunlight gleamed off the medallion and Kaz looked up at the sky again. Things were changing. The dark dragons were gone, but so were the metallic ones. Bolt had departed without comment after they had brought back the bodies. No one had seen a dragon since.

He kicked the warhorse lightly in the sides. As Kaz rode, he continued to finger the medallion. It had occurred to him to keep it, so that he would always have a token of his encounter with Huma. But now he was not so sure that it was, by rights, his.

The medallion was halfway back into the pouch when he came upon the lone tree on the right side of his path. The others near it either lay uprooted or were dead. Only this one held any life—a few branches sprouting new green.

On impulse, Kaz reached over and, when he was even with the tree, hung the talisman by its chain on a branch that overlooked a part of the trail.

"*Est Sularis Oth Mithas*," the minotaur muttered.

Turning his gaze back to the trail before him, Kaz suddenly urged his mount to great speed. He would not slow the horse until the tree and the tomb were long out of view.

Explore the FORGOTTEN REALMS™ Fantasy Campaign Setting!

From the fog-enshrouded moors of Moonshae to the pristine peaks overlooking Bloodstone Pass; from Waterdeep, City of Splendors to Thay; from the Pirates of the Inner Sea to the kingdoms of Calimshan in the South—these are the lands of the Forgotten Realms.

The FORGOTTEN REALMS Fantasy Campaign Setting is the most elaborate and detailed presented by TSR to date. An entire new line of novels, AD&D® adventure modules and sourcebooks, and other exciting accessories have been created for gamers adventurous enough to explore the ultimate adventure game setting.

The FORGOTTEN REALMS Boxed Campaign Setting
Ed Greenwood and Jeff Grubb

The cornerstone for AD&D® adventures set in the Forgotten Realms, and the basis for all novels and sourcebooks in the series, this set includes four-color maps of the world and almost 200 pages of vital information, both on the Forgotten Realms themselves and on setting up AD&D campaigns in this fabulous land.

AD&D® Sourcebooks:

WATERDEEP AND THE NORTH
Ed Greenwood

Waterdeep, the largest city of the northern realms, home to half a million humans, dwarves, elves, and halflings, is a city of power and evil, intrigue and wealth, ruled by unseen and mysterious lords. FORGOTTEN REALMS creator Ed Greenwood takes you on a grand tour of this, the mightiest city of the Realms.

MOONSHAE
Doug Niles

Exploring in depth the islands off the Sword Coast, home to *Darkwalker on Moonshae*, this sourcebook provides further detailed information on the Realms and adapts adventures found within this novel to an AD&D® game campaign.

EMPIRES OF THE SANDS
Scott Haring

The arid, inhospitable countries on the southeastern corner of the continent of Faerun are the subject of *Empires of the Sands*, a 64-page sourcebook. Players wanting to explore this section of the FORGOTTEN REALMS™ campaign setting can decide whether they prefer to seek their fortunes in the mercenary, Machiavellian country of Amn; the merchant state of Calimshan; or the anarchic land of Tethyr.

THE MAGISTER
Ed Greenwood and Steve Perrin

The Magister is the first word on magic in the FORGOTTEN REALMS campaign setting. It provides thorough coverage of new spells and magical items and instructions for generating new magical items.

AD&D Adventure Modules:

UNDER ILLEFARN
Steve Perrin

An introductory campaign base for new players of the AD&D game or for experienced players starting a new campaign in the Forgotten Realms. An earthquake rattles the small town of Daggerford, south of Waterdeep. Can your characters handle what the earth brings forth?

DESERT OF DESOLATION
Tracy and Laura Hickman,
Phil Meyers, Peter Rice, and John Wheeler

This epic trilogy outlining the power and mystery of tremendous magical forces is set in the great dust desert of Raurin. For characters of intermediate level.

THE BLOODSTONE PASS SERIES
Michael Dobson and Doug Niles

Only the powerful need apply. A great danger is growing in the North, in the ice-blasted desolation that is Vaasa, and threatening to engulf the shattered nation of Damara. Can your characters stem the tide in this epic four-volume series?

SWORDS OF THE IRON LEGION

An evil power is training armies in a lonely stretch of the Forgotten Realms, and a band of tough-guy player characters—namely the Iron Legion—is the only thing that can keep the power from taking over. *Swords of the Iron Legion* is a series of short adventurers, each by a different author, and each incorporating BATTLESYSTEM™ rules.

Moonshaes in Danger Again!

BLACK WIZARDS
Doug Niles

The Black Wizards have usurped the will of the High King, and an army of orgres and zombies, guided by Bhaal, god of death, is terrorizing the gentle Ffolk of Moonshae, the Celtic isles of the Forgotten Realms.

Black Wizards is Douglas Niles' sequel to his best-selling FORGOTTEN REALMS™ novel, *Darkwalker on Moonshae.* It takes up the story of Tristan, the king's son who earned his birthright defending the land against amazing creatures, and Robyn, the druid sorceress who added her powers to Tristan's in the fight against evil. Once again, they must defend their land, but this time, the enemy knows of their power and plans to kill them. . . .

Doug Niles is one of TSR's top designers. In addition to *Darkwalker on Moonshae*, his credits include the award-winning BATTLESYSTEM™ rules, the best-selling *Dungeoneer's Survival Guide*, numerous AD&D® modules and gamebooks, and the TOP SECRET/S.I.™ role-playing game.